*And After the Fire*

ALSO BY LAUREN BELFER

*A Fierce Radiance*

*City of Light*

# And After the Fire

A NOVEL

## Lauren Belfer

HARPER  PERENNIAL

NEW YORK • LONDON • TORONTO • SYDNEY • NEW DELHI • AUCKLAND

A hardcover edition of this book was published in 2016 by HarperCollins Publishers.

FIRST HARPER PERENNIAL EDITION PUBLISHED 2017.

*Designed by Jessica Shatan Heslin/Studio Shatan, Inc.*

Library of Congress has catalogued the hardcover edition as follows:

Names: Belfer, Lauren, author.
Title: And after the fire : a novel / Lauren Belfer.
Description: First edition. | New York : Harper, 2016.
Identifiers: LCCN 2015038472| ISBN 9780062428516 (hardcover : acid-free paper) | ISBN 9780062428523 (softcover) | ISBN 9780062428547 (ebook)
Subjects: LCSH: Family secrets—Fiction. | Americans—Germany—Fiction. | Germany—History—Fiction. | BISAC: FICTION / Historical. | FICTION / Biographical. | FICTION / Literary. | GSAFD: Historical fiction.
Classification: LCC PS3552.E467 A85 2016 | DDC 813/.54—dc23 LC record available at http://lccn.loc.gov/2015038472

17 18 19 20 21  OV/LSC  10 9 8 7 6 5 4 3 2

*For Michael*

To hear footsteps in the evening—and see no one.

*—from "Unwritten Elegy for Krakow's Jews"*
*by Adam Zagajewski (translated from the Polish by*
*Clare Cavanagh)*

*And After the Fire*

# *Prologue*

He never meant to kill her.

The afternoon had started out nice enough, for war-ravaged Germany right after the surrender. As Corporal Henry Sachs reclined on the parapet of a ruined castle and enjoyed a smoke in the sunshine, he reflected that life was going fine. A cooling breeze whipped around him. The view across the valley spread for miles. Hawks soared. Church steeples marked the towns. A half-dozen castles perched on the distant hills.

The war was over. He was alive. You couldn't ask for more than that, and he didn't. He was twenty-one years old and full of beans, if he did say so himself. At five feet nine (okay, in his boots), with dark hair, brown eyes, and a suave, devil-may-care edge, he reminded himself of Humphrey Bogart. He'd signed up in '42, the day after he graduated from high school, and he prided himself on making the military work for him instead of the other way around.

Like today. Soon the Third Army would be pulling out and the Soviets would take over this part of Germany. Before the Americans said *auf Wiedersehen*, Henry had a hankering to do some sightseeing. He'd recruited his best buddy, Pete Galinsky—right now pacing around to take in the view—to join him. They'd borrowed, so to speak, a military jeep, and they'd gone on a drive. They'd visited medieval towns and toured old churches. In exchange for chocolate and cigarettes, the currency of the day, they'd bought lunch at a prosperous-looking farmhouse where they teased the kids and Henry noticed that there wasn't a man in sight.

He checked his watch. The time was going on 16:00 hours, 4:00 p.m. "Let's start heading back," Henry said. *Back* meant Weimar, the city where they were based.

"Sounds good," Pete said.

Henry tossed his cigarette butt over the parapet. They returned to the jeep, and Henry took the wheel. Pete navigated, examining the map and checking the compass balanced on his knee. Pete was twenty going on fifty, and his long, thin face matched his long, thin body. He was from Buffalo, New York, where he'd progressed from high school into working at his family's clothing store. The army in its wisdom had decided he should be a mechanic and trained him to repair trucks.

Soon they were on the main road. They curved around a hillside, and the landscape opened onto a wide vista, meadows stretching into an endless distance. Henry pressed down hard on the gas pedal, and he was free. The wind hitting his face smelled rich and fertile. He inhaled, filling his lungs. The war in Europe was over. The good guys won. He felt elated. Triumphant. Invincible.

"It's a straight shot from here," Pete said. "We'll have time to visit Tiefurt Palace along the way."

Visiting hours at the palace (if there were any) didn't apply to them, not with Henry speaking German like a native and carrying an ample supply of chocolate and cigarettes in his rucksack to smooth over any hard feelings. Henry had been born in Brooklyn, where his family owned a shoe store, but his father was from East Prussia and his mother was from the Sudetenland. They spoke German at home, and Henry had learned the niceties of German grammar in high school. He'd spent the war translating for an intelligence unit.

"'The chateau and park of Tiefurt, once the summer residence of Duchess Anna Amalia . . . ,'" Pete read aloud from the Baedeker guide, a gift from Henry's father on the day he shipped out.

When she came to America, Henry's mother had left a big family behind in the Sudetenland, in the town of Eger. She exchanged letters and photographs with them frequently. Henry had never met any of these relatives, but he knew them from their photos: gorgeous cousin Shoshanna, with her hair pulled back; Aunt Chana, with her round face and a body to match, wearing fur in winter and in summer, at least for photographs; Uncle Max, who stood proudly in front of the family's dry goods shop; cousin Jakob, Henry's age, wearing thick glasses and reading a book; youngest cousin Franz, with his bright blond hair and Tyrolean jacket. Franz gripped old Grandpa Abraham's hand and seemed afraid of the camera. Abraham smiled down at the boy with a mixture of love and indulgence that almost made Henry jealous. Abraham was Henry's grandpa, too.

After the war started, Henry's mother didn't receive any more letters or photographs from the family.

Henry glanced at Pete. Did Pete have family living in Europe when the war broke out? He couldn't ask. Sure, he and Pete joked about their hometowns and their baseball teams (Henry, the Brooklyn Dodgers; Pete, the New York Yankees, because Pete's hometown didn't have a major league team).

But prying into stuff that actually mattered? No.

Henry and Pete took some ribbing from the other guys about being Jewish, but no more than, say, the Irish guys took for being Irish.

Anti-Irish, anti-Italian, anti-Catholic, anti-Jew, anti-Negro, that was America for you, and nobody, usually, was getting murdered over it, at least if your skin was white. Before he signed up, Henry had heard taunts on the street about Jew draft dodgers, but once Henry wore the uniform, he'd put a stop to that. The high-class officers Henry translated for made cracks about dirty Jews, cheap Jews, President Rosenfeld and his Jew Deal, the usual garbage. Henry kept his rage to himself, because being a translator on the back lines was a whole lot better than being cannon fodder on the front lines.

"The road to Tiefurt Palace is going to be on the left when we get near town," Pete was saying.

When Henry first signed up, things were tough, sure. During basic, a bunch of guys showed up from a small town (was there any other kind?) in Arkansas. They'd never seen a Jew and asked Henry if he had horns and a tail, the age-old slur. *Why, you boys want to see?* Henry had replied in his best Brooklyn street-fighter tone. Surprise, surprise: they didn't.

"The turnoff should be coming up," Pete said.

They'd reached the outskirts of Weimar, and everything was starting to look confused. This must have been an industrial area before the Allied bombing and the battle for the town. Potholes the size of tanks pocked the roads. Downed electrical wires crossed ponds of muck. The tower of Schloss Weimar, the town's palace, rose in the distance, but getting there would be tricky.

"Let's call it a day," Henry said.

"Don't worry," Pete said. "It's not far. Tiefurt Palace—when will we ever be here again?"

They were approaching the town center. Municipal buildings were on their right, a steep hill on their left.

And then a road, leading up the hill. Henry made the turn, just like that, because Pete was right: When would they ever be here again? He shifted into first to get the jeep up the incline. At the top of the hill, a church loomed before him. He made a sharp left, the only option.

"Holy shit," Pete said.

Henry seconded that remark.

A peaceful residential neighborhood opened before them, a broad street of stone houses, green lawns, and tall trees. The houses were four stories tall, with columns, carved doorways, and wrought-iron gates. They were mansions.

Henry drove slowly along the street. For all their size, the houses sat on small lots. One mansion after another, like stone giants squeezed close. Henry felt a strange unease. The neighborhood hadn't been bombed, but the houses looked deserted. The shutters were closed, and the windows that didn't have shutters were sealed with wooden boards nailed from the inside. The lawns were uncut, the gardens overgrown. Henry had spent enough time in this misbegotten country to know that Germans liked to keep their lawns trimmed and their gardens pruned.

"You see how the houses don't have much land?" Pete said. "That shows how valuable the property is, when you build one mansion right next to another."

"How come you know a thing like that?"

"Some guy came into the store, wanted to buy a tuxedo. Worked in real estate. Thought he was a big shot. He talked, I listened."

Was this Pete's future, selling clothes in Buffalo, making his customers happy because he was willing to listen while they talked? Henry wanted more out of life than this, although he didn't know what.

"Street looks evacuated," Pete said. "The rich people getting out before the Russians arrive. Or maybe the Nazi bigwigs lived here, and they're hiding in the attics."

"Sounds about right." Henry parked at the side of the road, as if they were stopping to visit friends. "Let's take a look around." He got out of the jeep and picked up his rucksack.

"The jeep's not safe," Pete said.

"Come on, Grandma. It's safe enough," Henry said, even though he knew it wasn't, especially not the spare tire and the jerry cans of gasoline. "We'll be gone for five minutes at most."

Pete shrugged, but he followed along. With helmets on and rifles at the ready, they made their way down the deserted street. Peering between the mansions, Henry saw that the houses on the left were built along a ridge with a view of a green valley. On the other side of the valley, the land rose steeply, dense with trees. The entire scene was basking in the orange light of late afternoon.

When they came to a house without a fence, Henry crossed the lawn to take a better look at the view. The brilliant, raking light, combined with huge gray clouds against a pure blue sky, gave off an *and-then-God-created-the-universe* feel. Henry wasn't religious, and his parents weren't religious, but he had made his bar mitzvah when he was thirteen *just in case*, as his mother had put it. Seeing the light fill the valley, Henry felt a spiritual pull that he'd never before experienced.

Henry wondered: Was the Buchenwald concentration camp over there, somewhere on the opposite ridge? Buchenwald meant "beech forest," but it wasn't a place you'd want to go for a hike in the woods. The camp was built on a hilltop clearing four miles outside of Weimar. Because Henry spoke German and worked in intelligence, he'd been assigned to lead the defeated locals on tours of the camp and eavesdrop on their conversations. For these visits, the good citizens of Weimar dressed in their Sunday best. The ladies wore sturdy high heels and felt hats, and gripped their leather handbags. The men (all past military age) wore suits and ties, or tweed jackets with sweater vests and ties, and they wore hats, too. In the trucks going to the camp, most of the people joked and laughed, as if they were on a festive holiday outing.

When they arrived at the camp, they were greeted by the vacant stares of the survivors, skeletons that inched along. They saw the stacks of bodies, arms and legs sticking out at broken angles. Looking at the piles of naked dead men, the teenage girls hid anxious giggles behind their hands. The women covered their mouths and noses with handkerchiefs to keep away the stench. Henry wanted to pull the handkerchiefs away and push those fat faces into the rotting corpses.

The stench of the camp—it assaulted him all over again, making him queasy.

Henry must have played Buchenwald tour guide for five hundred people. Sometimes understanding German was a curse. To hell with the lie the Germans told the GIs, that they didn't know about the camp. Some of them were employed at the camp, for God's sake. Local grocers supplied food to the administrators and their families, and to the guards. The residents of Weimar shared their suburban rail line with prisoners going to the camp. Henry's tourists even talked among themselves about the wind of ashes that blew upon the city, leaving a grayish white dusting upon their windowsills and front steps. The citizens knew very well where the ashes came from: the Buchenwald crematorium.

Henry's concentration-camp tourists probably thought his German wasn't good enough to understand what they were saying. But Henry understood. Every word. He learned that Weimar's Hauptbahnhof, the main train station, was a transit point for civilian captives going east. When you went to the station, you saw old women, little kids, mothers and fathers from across Europe changing trains. Thousands upon thousands of civilians, pushed onto cattle cars and heading east, where things were really bad. Or so the rumors said. Henry happened to know that the rumors were true. Buchenwald was mainly a slave-labor camp, not a murder factory like places he'd learned about in the east. In the east, people were exterminated by poison gas and then cremated. Buchenwald didn't have gas chambers for killing people. Even so, when you were working people to death, not giving them enough food, basically doing nothing to heal the sick, and hanging and shooting men for offenses real and imagined, you ended up with a lot of dead bodies, more than the ovens of the camp's crematorium could deal with.

As Henry stood at the ridge and gazed out at the view, a question kept pushing into his mind: If God created the entire universe, as Henry had been taught, did that mean God had created Buchenwald, too?

No. *No.* Forget all that, he ordered himself. The war was over. He'd made it through alive. Today he was sightseeing, like a normal guy visiting a foreign country. With luck, he'd be going home soon. He imagined a day at Coney Island, the sand beneath his feet, the salty tang of the ocean in the air. He'd run into the water and let the awful memories wash off him.

He saw himself sitting at the dinner table with his parents and his little sister, Evelyn. She was seven now and reading nonstop, according to a letter from Henry's mother. Cute, too. He kept a photo of her in his wallet. Once he was settled, he'd call up a few girls he'd known in high school. Find out how the years had treated them. He'd be a veteran, with his college paid for by the GI bill and a great future ahead of him. The girls would be all over him.

He saw himself signing up at Brooklyn College. To study what? He had no idea. Inside him, a knot was tightening at the prospect of returning to civilian life.

"Come on," Pete said, "let's get moving."

"Good idea." Henry turned away from the valley and faced the back of the house. This side wasn't boarded up. A terrace led to wide doors which were open to the afternoon breezes. Wrought-iron chairs and a glass-and-wrought-iron table were positioned on the terrace to take advantage of the view. Henry imagined SS officers relaxing after work, enjoying drinks and a smoke before dinner.

He walked closer. A cup and saucer were on the table, and a book.

He had a feeling that a second ago somebody had gotten up and gone into the house for a sweater. That person would return in a moment.

Henry walked up the steps onto the terrace. Behind him, Pete was cautioning, but Henry ignored him. He went through the open door. Pete followed.

They entered a room that was oval-shaped and bright. Henry looked up. A domed skylight. Delicate furniture filled the room, the kind Henry recognized as antiques . . . wooden chairs with spindly legs that would collapse under his weight; a small round table that looked like it was standing on tiptoe. The fireplace's marble mantelpiece was carved into intricate feather shapes. One wall had a picture painted right onto it: the view across the valley. A grand piano filled the other side of the room. Its lid was down, its keyboard closed.

"Look," Pete said. "A cooking pot. Hanging in the fireplace."

The electricity was off. Probably the gas, too. Somebody was making do, trying to survive.

"They're burning books for fuel," Pete said.

Sure enough, books were piled on one side. Taking a closer look at the debris in the fireplace, Henry saw the remains of printed pages, curled and blackened.

Pete was examining the stack of books. "Get a load of this: gold lettering on the front." He held up a book for Henry to see, then leafed through it. "Published in 1811." Pete picked up another. "This one says 1793. Look at this leather binding."

Some of the books were fancy, Henry could see that.

"I'm going to take a few of these books as souvenirs," Pete said. "They'll be burnt up tonight anyway, so what the hell."

Taking souvenirs was against the rules, but everybody was doing it. Henry had buddies who'd sent home packages stuffed with German swords, cameras, silver, china, paintings.

Henry hadn't taken any souvenirs yet. Nothing had turned up that really grabbed him.

"Who knows, an old book could be worth a lot of money," Pete said.

Henry went to the piano bench and opened it. Sheet music was layered into the bench every which way. Some was printed, some handwritten. Some old, some new.

When Henry was a boy, his mother had forced him to take piano lessons with Mrs. Kaminsky, who lived on the second floor of their apartment building. After her husband died, she supported herself by teaching piano to kids. She wasn't about to accept charity, Henry's mother had told him with approval. So every week for four years, until Mrs. Kaminsky's son took her to live with his family in Cincinnati, Henry went downstairs for a lesson on Mrs. Kaminsky's battered upright and passed her a few coins. Not having a piano in his own apartment, he couldn't practice, but he learned a few things. In fact, he learned a lot. He developed a passion for classical music, and he listened to concerts on WQXR. He would never admit such a passion to his Army buddies, but because of it, he felt curious about this sheet music.

He pulled out a folder that looked old. The music inside, pages and pages of it, was handwritten in a rush, judging from the cross-outs and overwriting. The ink had bled through the paper. He stuck the folder with its sheet music into his rucksack. There was space for more. Why the hell not? He reached out—

*"Was machen Sie?"* A female voice, behind him. *What are you doing?*

He swung around. A woman was aiming a pistol at him. She held it with both hands, trying to keep it steady. The gun was a heavy, military-issue German pistol. The woman was so thin her arms looked as if they were going to break from the weight of it. Except she wasn't a woman, Henry realized with a shock. She was a girl, fifteen, sixteen. Her dress gaped in front. Her skin was sallow. Her hair lay in clumps.

*"Was machen Sie hier?"* She managed to keep the pistol aimed at his chest. *What are you doing here?*

*"Ruhig,"* Henry said. *Easy now.* *"Seien Sie ruhig."* *Easy does it.*

"Oh, fuck," Pete said.

"It's okay," Henry said in English to Pete. Then in German: *"We've got cigarettes. And chocolate. Put down the pistol and we'll share."*

The girl's smell was reaching him. She hadn't bathed anytime recently. She had the war smell, different from the rot of the dead. The sickly, repulsive rot of the living. She seemed to be concentrating all her strength on keeping the pistol upright. On keeping it aimed at him.

*"Come on now, Fräulein, we're not going to hurt you."*

"Make her put down the gun," Pete said.

"I'm working on it," Henry said. *"Fräulein, the war is over."*

"Why doesn't she put down the gun?" Pete said.

*"You think I don't know Jews when I see them? You speak German like a Jew,"* she said.

The retching reek of Buchenwald swept over him.

"What did she say?" Pete gripped his rifle.

*"This house belonged to Jews. Nice Jews—not like you."*

"Tell me what she's saying."

"Nothing," Henry said. "She's saying nothing." To the girl: *"Who were they, the Jews who owned this house?"* He had to ask, he had to know. He wanted to understand this godforsaken country. *"What happened to them?"*

*"The Jews? They left."*

They didn't leave, Henry realized. They'd been rounded up. *"Were they friends of yours?"* Her accent was different from what he'd heard at home and in school. Lower class, maybe. *"Did you work here?"*

*"You Jews aren't going to take your revenge on me."*

Revenge? He didn't like Germans, but he wasn't about to kill a German civilian. In fact, Henry would prove himself better than the Germans. He would help her.

*"You shouldn't be here. The Americans are pulling out. The Russians are*

*coming in. We've been hearing bad things about what happens when the Russians get ahold of German women."*

Intelligence reports said that Russian soldiers were raping their way across Germany. Women, girls, grandmothers, cripples even, the Russians didn't care.

*"You should move west. We can help you. Put down the pistol and we'll help you."*

*"You two thieves will help* me?" Her arms and hands became absolutely still. She aimed the gun at Henry's chest and pulled the trigger.

The bullet missed, hitting the wall behind him. Pete fired his rifle at her feet, to scare her. Neither of them had ever shot at a woman. The truth was, neither of them had ever fired upon anyone. They were in the backup—the translator, the mechanic—not at the front lines. The girl shot again, at Pete. She hit his arm. She turned, aiming at Henry.

Finally snapping into his military training, Henry pivoted his rifle into position and shot her. She fell backward, onto the floor in a heap. Her body heaved. Blood began to seep around her. Time, which had been moving fast, slowed and then stopped. Henry couldn't move. He couldn't grasp what he'd done.

"Shit, I'm wounded," Pete said. "The fucking bitch shot me."

Henry undid his belt and wrapped it around the top of Pete's arm to staunch the wound. "Hold your arm up, hold it up."

The bleeding slowed. It wasn't much of a wound. It was nothing, in fact, compared to the ever-widening and thickening puddle around the girl at their feet. Her open, unblinking eyes stared at the skylight.

"Oh, Christ," Pete said. "Let's get out of here." He moved toward the door. "Coming in here was the most fucked-up idea you ever had. Let's hope the jeep is still there."

Henry said nothing. He couldn't catch up with himself.

"Let's go!"

Pete was right, they had to get away. As they left the house, Henry closed the door behind them. He didn't want animals going in, drawn by the smell of blood. What else could he do? Call an ambulance? Europe was littered with dead bodies. Ambulances enough didn't exist, to pick up all the bodies.

Miraculously, the jeep was fine. Spare tire in place, jerry cans under the tarp. Neither Henry nor Pete mentioned Tiefurt Palace. They drove back in silence.

A deranged Gauleiter. That's how they filed the report, because Pete had to see the medic to get patched up. They couldn't pretend the whole thing had never happened. A deranged Gauleiter, and they shot him.

Enough said. The war was over. Nobody cared about details, especially German details. The medic dressed Pete's arm, and in a few months, Pete had nothing but a scar to show for it.

The girl had been weak. She could barely hold up the pistol. But she shot first. So Henry's killing her was self-defense. Right?

In the years that followed, Henry went through this again and again, trying to convince himself.

A half-crazed girl, lying dead on floorboards covered with blood. How many days or months until her body was found? Until she was buried?

For the next sixty-five years, Henry Sachs never stopped wondering.

# Chapter 1

## NEW YORK CITY

*June 2010*

Susanna Kessler spent her days giving away money. Not her own money. She was the executive director of the Barstow Family Foundation, based in the family offices on the twenty-seventh floor of a skyscraper overlooking West Fifty-seventh Street. She coordinated grants of ten million dollars a year aimed at helping children in New York City.

As she prepared for her usual Monday morning meeting with her boss, she took stock: thirty-four years old, dark hair curling around her shoulders, makeup understated. On this summery day, she wore a sleeveless dress with a fitted jacket. Her shoes were the extra-high-heeled black patent pumps that she kept in her desk drawer for meetings. Recently Susanna had been having a tough time in her personal life, but at work, she was able to keep herself moving forward. Her clothes made her appear to be a woman in charge of herself, who could do what was expected of her and do it well, all day, every day. At least from Monday to Friday.

Reports in hand, she walked down the hallway, greeting colleagues as she passed. The office suite housed experts who advised the family on accounting, tax law, investment management, and trusts and estates. (The foundation's financial and tax advisers were independent, however, and headquartered elsewhere.) Her boss's office was in the far corner. The décor was modern, but the lines of authority were strictly traditional.

"Susanna, good morning." Robertson Barstow, head of the foundation board, rose from behind his desk and motioned to a chair. "Have a seat."

"Thank you."

"What's on your agenda this week?" Rob was a striking man in his early seventies. His manner combined courtesy with playfulness, and he addressed most topics with dramatic flair. He performed with an amateur Gilbert and Sullivan troupe and enjoyed some renown, within a limited arena, for such roles as the Major General in *The Pirates of Penzance* and Captain Corcoran in *H.M.S. Pinafore*. He was also an astute businessman, which Susanna kept in mind during their conversations.

"I'm going uptown to evaluate progress on the library renovation at P.S. 629. I'll confirm that they're on schedule to reopen in September, with new books on the shelves."

Unlike Robertson Barstow, Susanna had attended public schools until college. Her elementary school had boasted a terrific library where she'd learned to love reading. Susanna wanted the same for public-school kids in New York City, and the foundation was working in conjunction with the Fund for Public Schools to make this happen.

When Susanna discussed her job with her friends—a twenty-thousand-dollar grant here, thirty or forty thousand there, a million or more for a capital project—she tried not to sound naïvely idealistic. Nevertheless, she *was* making a difference, and this fact gave her a reason, beyond the necessity of her salary, to go to work in the morning.

"Tomorrow I have a meeting at the Greenwich Music School to discuss expanding their after-school programs in the autumn."

Item by item, she went through her list. The foundation supported dozens of projects across the city: shelters for homeless families, store-front health clinics for kids, remedial tutoring, ballet scholarships. Susanna's job involved initiating and evaluating grant proposals and making recommendations to the board. If it approved the grants, she followed up to determine how the funding was actually used and whether the children involved had benefitted from the programs.

"Next: I've been approached by the city parks department about increasing our funding for their free learn-to-swim programs at city pools this coming summer. The demand for this is tremendous. The swim programs already have long waiting lists."

Rob said, "According to the department's own statistics, not every child learns to swim in their programs. Are the programs as effective as they could be or should be?"

"This is a gray area. Overcoming panic in the water is itself a positive step for kids. Not panicking can prevent drowning. Knowing how to float can prevent drowning. I don't think we should hold the programs to the standard of a Red Cross swimming test."

"Meet with the parks department, collect the most recent statis-tics, and we'll discuss this again next week. Investigate whether other swimming programs have better results."

"Will do. The final item on my list is your anniversary gift for Cornelia."

Rob and Cornelia had been married for forty-five years and shared a mutual sympathy that Susanna hoped to find for herself someday. The money for their anniversary gifts came out of their personal funds, not the foundation; Susanna kept these lines clear.

"I believe I've found the ideal choice," she said.

The official portion of their meeting complete, Rob leaned forward with boyish eagerness. "Yes?"

"In a word, rats."

"Rats?"

"Giant rats with a mission."

"I do like the sound of that. What's the mission of these giant rats?"

"They have two missions: to sniff out land mines, and to identify tuberculosis infections."

"I must say, that's perfect."

"I know." Cornelia Barstow had interests in both medical care and the clearance of land mines. "Giving credit where credit is due, I first read about the rats in *The New York Times*."

"Tell me more."

"The rats are a type called the African giant pouched rat. They're calm and cooperative. Easy to train. Most important, they have an amazing sense of smell. They have a terrific record sniffing out land mines in Mozambique. They're beginning land-mine work in Thailand, along the Thai-Cambodia border. In Tanzania they've been picking up the scent of tuberculosis on people and thus identifying infections that established methods miss."

Susanna gave him a folder with the charity's annual report, a collection of photographs, and her own summary and opinion sheet. He studied the materials.

Glancing out the window as she waited, Susanna saw Central Park, Fifth Avenue . . . the city and its infinite possibilities laid out in silent magnificence. From a certain perspective, say the perspective of a young woman like herself who'd only recently finished paying back her college and business-school loans, the job of advising a wealthy family on how to give away its money was a little daunting. After Susanna's father died when she was young, her mother had worked as a legal secretary. Susanna's family had never been poor, but the cost of things had been a constant question for them.

Not so for Rob and his family. Back in the 1870s, Rob's great-grandfather Joshua Barstow had patented the Barstow process for refining oil, still used around the world. Rob had worked in the oil refinery business for more than forty years, and when he retired, he set up this office to manage financial affairs for himself and his extended family. He expanded their charitable foundation and hired Susanna to run it.

"I must admit, I've never seen anything quite like this," Rob said. "Although from the photos I don't think the rats are truly 'giants.' They aren't as big as, for example, Hoover."

Hoover was Rob and Cornelia's overweight cat.

"Hoover is large for a domestic cat," Susanna said.

"Only too true, alas."

"And even if these rats aren't as big as Hoover, you wouldn't want to meet one in a dark alley."

"Indeed. I see that when they're working, they eat bananas. They consider bananas a treat. *I* consider bananas a treat."

"So you already have something in common. Cornelia is sure to appreciate that."

Rob gave her a wry smile. He enjoyed being teased. "I also see that you can sign up to receive letters from your rat. Cornelia would delight in snail mail from a rat."

"I know I'd delight in it."

"Let's sponsor forty-five rats in Cornelia's honor," Rob said, closing the folder. "That's a lot of rats, but after forty-five years of marriage, it's a meet and fitting number."

"I agree."

"You wouldn't happen to know what she's giving me?"

"Yes, I do know." In view of his love of honey, Rob was receiving from Cornelia a donation of forty-five beehives to farmers in Albania. "I'm not at liberty to say, however."

"That's very unfair."

"Totally unfair," Susanna agreed.

She stood. Rob stood. He was forever a gentleman.

"After our anniversary, let's put up a large-format photo of the rats in here. An inspiration to one and all."

"Excellent idea."

"And Susanna," he said, his mood shifting, "I want you to know that Cornelia and I are keeping you in our hearts. You're on our prayer list."

Rob attended St. James' Church. Although Susanna was not a believer, and her family background was Jewish, his oblique allusion to her difficult divorce touched her.

"Thank you, Rob. I appreciate it."

He looked away. "Just what we do."

Returning to her office, Susanna stood at her desk and scrolled through the two dozen e-mails she'd received during the meeting. No emergencies. Outside her office window, a geometric panoply of towers glinted in the sunlight, a sliver of the Hudson River visible among them.

She checked the voice-mail messages on her cell. Lisa O'Shea, a close friend since high school, had called to confirm their plan for a girls' night out this evening.

The tailor reported that the two dresses she'd brought him for alteration were ready to be picked up.

Third message: "Susanna," a woman said. "It's Aurelia."

Susanna felt taken aback. Aurelia was her uncle Henry's home health aide.

"Susanna," Aurelia repeated, as if she could overpower the voice-mail recorder and reach Susanna immediately, wherever she was. "Mr. Henry . . ."

## Chapter 2

Susanna leaned against the front-porch balustrade of the two-family home in Buffalo where she'd grown up. The overhang of the second-story porch sheltered her. After Susanna's father died, she and her mother had lived upstairs from Uncle Henry and Aunt Greta, in the rental unit.

Reluctant to return inside, she studied the street. The longest day of the year was approaching, and the lingering sunlight felt consoling. Lynfield between Bird and Forest Avenues was a block of two-family houses on narrow lots. During her childhood, the street had been treeless and bare. Today it was a luxuriant garden, part of the city's yearly garden festival. Lilies, hydrangeas, and peonies covered the front lawns. The young trees, replacing those killed by Dutch elm disease, reached only the second story of the houses, but their foliage was thick. In front of Susanna's family home, ornamental grasses concealed the broken pegs of the porch's balustrade. Susanna ran her hand across the tops of the grasses. Still warm from the day's sun, they were a velvety caress upon her skin.

She was alone now, waiting for her mother and stepfather, Evelyn and Jack, to arrive from Tampa, where they'd retired. This afternoon, after the brief flight from New York to Buffalo, Susanna had spoken to the police, identified Henry's body, arranged to receive the death certificate, contacted an attorney.

And she'd searched Uncle Henry's desk and his bedroom for a suicide note. She didn't find one.

Everything she'd needed to do had stopped her from confronting what Henry had done. She faced it now.

He'd covered his chest with the fentanyl patches his doctor prescribed for chronic back pain. He must have been saving up unused patches for weeks. An empty bottle of vodka was on the bedside table. Henry didn't drink, except for a beer or two at dinner. Boxes of fentanyl carried warnings against drinking alcohol when using the patches.

The last time Susanna had spoken to him, several days before, he'd sounded fine, keeping up with politics and the news, making plans for his usual Friday night fish fry with the neighbors. He was eighty-six. He had the right to end his life whenever and however he wished, no explanations necessary. Or so Susanna tried to convince herself. Her thoughts circled . . . she should have visited more often on the weekends. She should have phoned him every day.

The wind came up, cold against her bare arms. Susanna turned and went inside. She paused at the entry to the living room to give her eyes a moment to adjust to the shadows.

Photographs filled the room. It was like a shrine, and because Susanna was the object of the shrine, it embarrassed her. Not the photos themselves, but what they represented: the hopes of the entire family, placed upon her. She was an only child, born when her mother was close to forty and had suffered several miscarriages. Henry and Greta had no children, and Henry had taken on the role of Susanna's father. *You're our miracle baby*, Evelyn had told her.

On the credenza, she was an infant, toddler, and schoolgirl. On top of the upright piano, she performed at her first ballet recital and at her first piano recital. No matter how tight money was, Evelyn always found enough for her ballet and piano lessons. On the television stand, she posed with her high school swimming team, medals around their necks. On the mantel, she graduated high school, college, and business school. On the coffee table, she was in Paris, the Eiffel Tower behind her. This photo represented the honeymoon she'd taken with Alan, her soon-to-be-former husband. The pictures that included him had been put away. She and Alan had been married for six years. They'd separated just when they were trying to have a baby, before she was too old.

She felt too old already. Too old to find someone else. Too old to begin again.

---

It was 1:03 a.m., according to the hotel's bedside clock. Susanna lay in bed, gazing at the glow of downtown Buffalo through the gauzy curtains. She didn't want to close her eyes. When she did, the images started up in her mind like a movie she couldn't walk out of. She glanced at the digital clock again: 1:05 a.m.

Dinner with Jack and Evelyn had been silent, and the excellent food—they went to the much-praised Bacchus on Chippewa Street, near their hotel—had been wasted on them. They were simply marking time at the restaurant, doing something appropriate to fill the evening.

When finally Susanna was alone in her hotel room and checked her phone, she saw a voice mail from Alan. Before dinner, she'd texted several friends, and Alan must have heard about Henry's death from one of them. Alan tried to be kind. She knew what he'd say about their marriage if they spoke, because he'd repeated the cliché a dozen times already: *It wasn't you, it was me.* He'd beg her to forgive him, not so they could get back together, but so that he could get on with his life without feeling guilty. As far as Susanna was concerned, he could get on with his life *with* feeling guilty. She suspected he had a girl-friend, and some scruple stopped him from moving forward with this new woman until he had Susanna's forgiveness. Although she considered herself understanding and forgiving, she'd never understand or forgive *him*. She deleted his message without listening to it.

Now 1:09 a.m. She wondered whether to admit defeat, turn on the bedside lamp, and read. She didn't want to resume taking antianxiety medications or antidepressants or sleeping pills. She'd tried them, and they made her feel worse. More precisely, they made her feel groggy, sometimes so dull-witted that she could barely keep her head up at her desk or stay focused during meetings with Rob. She couldn't risk losing her job on top of everything else.

For the past several months, she'd been fine without the medica-tions. When she closed her eyes, the images didn't prey upon her, and she was able to fall asleep.

The shock of Henry's death had brought the images back.

The movie began running in her mind. This was the short version. *The trailer*, as she ruefully called it: There she was, Susanna Kessler, a happily married woman with a great job who was trying to become pregnant. One August evening, Susanna was returning home from work and had reached her own street, West Seventy-first between Central Park West and Columbus. Out of nowhere, a man pulled her down to the lower entryway of a brownstone. In the concealing shad-ows beneath the building's high front stoop, he raped her.

The next shot in the movie trailer showed her five months later, when her husband left her.

The trailer faded. It didn't even begin to capture the reality. Now the full movie version started, from the beginning, the narrative moving in slow motion, a compulsion within her. She searched and questioned. Why did the stranger choose her? What was it about *her* that made him act? On each replaying of the film, she searched for a frame that would cause everything to turn out differently. If only there'd been a shorter line at the wine store. Or was it a longer line that would have made her safe? If only she'd remembered that she needed to stop at the shoemaker. If only she'd worn a different dress, or carried a different handbag.

From her office on West Fifty-seventh Street, Susanna usually walked home through the park or along Central Park West. On that particular day, however, she'd needed to pick up groceries, so she took the subway to the Sixty-sixth Street and Broadway stop. At Gourmet Garage, she bought several items for dinner and headed home. She wore a belted, pleated dress. The sweater she needed for her overly air-conditioned office was stashed in her tote bag. Because of the heat, she'd pulled back her hair and clipped it loosely with a barrette. She wore high-heeled sandals, and she swayed with each step. Alan loved the way the sandals looked, and he especially loved the way she walked when she wore them, although more than once he'd asked, "Are you *sure* those are comfortable?" Surprisingly, they were. Really.

As she headed to the wine store, the bearded guy who sold hats from a sidewalk stand on Columbus Avenue looked her over. "Hi, beautiful," he said as she walked past him, and she had to admit, this made her feel good.

Life was going well for Susanna that summer. She and Alan were in a good place, as the saying went. With their baby in mind, they were having a wonderful time together, as if they'd just met all over again, only better, because they knew each other well and loved each other deeply. In June, they'd traveled to London for a week of museums and theater. They were planning a trip to the Caribbean over New Year's (although they'd adjust this plan depending on their hoped-for baby). Their apartment had a second bedroom which they used as a study but which, she felt confident, would soon become a nursery. Already she knew where she would put the crib and the changing table. More than once, she'd slipped into Upper East Side boutiques to look at layettes.

Alan worked in finance. His clients were individual investors, and his business was thriving. Several of his college friends had already made fortunes, and these friends trusted Alan because he had a conservative bent. No shouting, bad language, drunken evenings, and no investments in risky or incomprehensible assets. Alan's parents were high school teachers, and they'd never earned enough to be extravagant. Alan shared their caution. Your widowed mother, your disabled brother . . . their futures are protected. Whatever happens, your kids will go to college. You'll keep your house. You'll be safe. With me.

At the wine shop, Susanna bought a Malbec recommended by the staff, although she drank little these days, no more than a sip or two, because of the possible pregnancy. She left the wine store, heading north on Columbus, passing the small shops and cafés, the grocery, the pizza place, as well as the upscale clothing and cosmetic stores. Across the street was a branch of Magnolia Bakery. People stood in line outside, tourists who wanted to experience the West Village bakery made famous in *Sex and the City*, even though this was only the uptown branch. Susanna and Alan had gone to Magnolia once and been appalled by the too-sweet cupcakes. They always told their out-of-town visitors that the cupcakes weren't worth the calories, but their visitors ignored the advice and joined the line.

Susanna turned onto West Seventy-first Street.

As she walked down the street, she carried the bag with the wine in her right hand and the grocery bag in her left. It was a perfect evening, with low humidity and cooling temperatures. Perhaps tonight she and Alan could turn off the air conditioner and sleep with the windows open to the night breezes. The town houses and small apartment buildings glowed in the orange light of the lowering sun.

Susanna and Alan loved walking in the city, looking at the architecture, the shops, the people. Often on the weekends, they took the subway to neighborhoods they'd never visited and simply walked, to see what they might discover. Once they'd ended up watching birds at the Jamaica Bay nature preserve near JFK Airport—who could have imagined such a wilderness in New York City? Another afternoon they stumbled upon the historic Trinity Cemetery, a sylvan retreat in gritty Washington Heights. Alan had grown up in a small town in New Hampshire, and he'd embraced New York City life as fully as she did. They were both Jewish, but secular, and their family backgrounds were similar. They'd met in business school.

This evening, walking down West Seventy-first Street, her street, with Central Park at the end of the block, and a breeze against her cheeks, Susanna felt as if she lived in a dream come true.

A hand—big, sweaty, oily—was over her mouth and nose. An arm around her waist. She was pulled backward down four steps. She dropped the bags. She heard the wine bottle hit the cement, and even as her eyes saw sky instead of street, she wondered if the wine bottle had broken. She was dragged into a concealed area where garbage cans were stored. She smelled orange peels, sour milk, cat litter. She didn't understand. What was happening?

Then she realized, and she fought back, biting and thrashing against him. He kept his hand on her face. Gasping for air, she twisted beneath him, scratching at his face, biting his hand. She tasted blood. He was too big and too strong for her. He was alert, and she was dazed. He pushed her head against the concrete. She wouldn't allow herself to die from him bashing her head against the ground. She tried to hold up her head. She didn't want to look at him, but she knew she had to, to impress his features on her mind, so she could tell the police. If she got away. If he didn't smash her skull. If he didn't choke her to death. His skin was white. His eyes were blue. His hair was reddish and thinning, his scaly scalp showing through. His cheeks looked pudgy with baby fat, although the wrinkles around his eyes proved that he was far from infancy. His jaw was too big for his face. He wore a black polo shirt. His chest was broad and fleshy, trapping her. He put one hand on her neck and pressed down in the middle of her throat. She couldn't scream and could barely breathe.

With the hand that wasn't on her throat, he pushed up her dress. She wasn't wearing stockings. The concrete flagstones were tiny knives beneath her. He pulled at her underwear. She twisted her legs, struggling to keep him away. Then he was inside her. She felt him swelling. She recoiled at the horrifying realization of the two of them linked as one.

After an instant, he groaned. Susanna felt a second of stillness, before he withdrew. He kneeled, pulling at his sweatpants. Gray sweatpants, Susanna willed herself to remember. He was gone. She was alone amid the garbage cans.

With effort, she took stock of herself. She turned her head, to make certain she could. She moved her legs a quarter inch, to test them. A warm liquid, smelling foul, seeped between them.

Rage filled her. Sitting up, she found her purse and fumbled inside for her cell phone. She called 911. She wouldn't let him escape. His blood was on her face, on her hands, his semen was pouring out of her.

After three rings, the 911 operator answered, but Susanna had trouble understanding what the operator said.

"Hello?" Susanna didn't recognize her own voice. She sounded hoarse. "Are you there?"

"I'm here."

"I was attacked." Her throat hurt. She forced herself to swallow. "Can you hear me?"

"I can hear you. What's your location?" The 911 operator's tone was flat. Unemotional. Information, that's what Susanna had to focus on.

"Seventy-first between Columbus and Central Park West." She looked around. "Closer to Columbus. South side of the street. A man attacked me. I was *raped*." She began to panic. "You have to get here. *Right now*."

He'd left her alive, with her cell phone. Once he realized . . . she crouched, trying to make herself smaller. Trying to hide.

"Hold on," the telephone voice said.

"Okay," she whispered.

"Stay with me." The more upset Susanna became, the more calm the telephone voice sounded.

"Okay."

"I'm notifying the police."

"What if he comes back?" He might even be listening to her talking on the phone.

"I'm going off the line for a second." The line clicked. Susanna was alone again. She couldn't keep hiding. She had to move into the open, where people could see her and protect her. At this hour, the sidewalks were crowded with people returning home from work or heading out for dinner. She crawled into the open.

*"Help!"* Susanna realized she was screaming.

The phone line clicked. "The police are on their way," the 911 operator said.

*"Help!"*

A young couple was with her, coming down the steps, finding her. Susanna dropped her phone and reached for the young woman's hands. Susanna was panting, unable to catch her breath.

"Be careful," the man said. "The blood. That's evidence, isn't it?"

The woman pulled away.

"Don't worry," the man said to Susanna, even as he denied her the comfort of another's hand. "Everything's going to be okay."

The woman was searching in her own bag, retrieving her own phone, calling 911, explaining, listening. "The police are already on their way," she said, ending the call.

"Stay with me. Don't leave me."

"Don't worry," the man said. "We're staying right here."

The man and woman were college age. They both wore black T-shirts and black jeans. The man had a nose ring. The woman wore black nail polish. Her black hair was parted in the middle and hung down flat. One lock was bleached white. They were Goth, or whatever it was called nowadays.

Others began to stop, men, women, making certain she was okay. In New York City you were both anonymous and never alone. People noticed and responded when you needed help.

"What did he look like?" a male voice said.

"Gray sweatpants," Susanna said. "Black polo shirt."

"What direction did he go?"

"I don't know." How could this happen, that she didn't know? This must be the most important fact to know. *"I don't know."*

"It's okay," the Goth woman said.

A man came up with a dog, a chocolate lab. "Breathe deep and slow," the dog owner said. The dog stared at her. "She's hyperventilating. From panic," the dog owner said to the Goth couple, as if Susanna were their responsibility.

"Breathe slow," the woman instructed Susanna. "Slow and deep. Like this." The woman demonstrated, and Susanna tried to imitate her, tried to bring her breathing under control. The woman reached toward Susanna's shoulder.

"*No*, don't touch her," the Goth man said.

Evidence. Susanna needed to protect the evidence. *She* was the evidence. Her body was the evidence.

"Do you want us to phone someone for you?" the woman asked.

Susanna wondered what the woman meant by this, then realized. "Yes, yes, my husband. I can call him."

She found her phone on the concrete. It was sticky with blood. Alan answered.

"Alan," Susanna moaned or cried, she wasn't sure which. She couldn't say anything more.

With a tissue, the woman took Susanna's phone and brought it to her own face, holding it at a distance. Speaking loudly. She explained to Alan what had happened. He was two blocks away, also on his way home from work. He'd be there soon, he told the woman. He would run.

The police arrived, the marvelous police, two police cars, four middle-aged men taking charge as if she were their daughter. Soon an ambulance and paramedics joined them. The Goth couple was gone. Susanna didn't have a chance to thank them or say goodbye. Then Alan was with her, and she didn't need to worry about anything anymore. Now she could cry.

Alan sat beside her in the ambulance on the way to the hospital. He reached for her hands, but since blood was on them and the blood had to be tested, he held back. Nonetheless his presence made her feel safe. She was with the man she loved and who loved her. He put his arm around her. She leaned against his shoulder. He caressed her hair.

"Don't worry," he said. His hand was trembling. "Everything's fine now." He sounded choked up. He squeezed her shoulder. "You're going to be okay."

She felt her pulse slow and her breathing return to normal, although she still felt disconnected from herself. Her task right now, she realized, was to stay alert and steady and to remember every detail of the man's face and body to tell the police. Gray sweatpants. Black polo shirt. Reddish hair, thinning on top. Baby fat.

At the hospital, everything was done correctly. The rape kit, everything. By the book, as Detective Loretta Lazetera, suddenly at Susanna's bedside, assured her. The detective was broad-shouldered and tough-talking. Susanna trusted her instinctively. The next day, Susanna went downtown to police headquarters with Detective

Lazetera to work with an artist to create a composite sketch. This was easy, because Susanna saw the man in her mind whenever she closed her eyes. In fact, with each day that passed she saw the man more clearly. Caucasian. Big, but with delicate, boyish features, except for his jaw, which was too large for the rest of his face. Pale blue eyes, the kind that look almost white. Freckles on his nose. A month later, they caught him. He'd been responsible for a string of attacks on the Upper West Side, always the same MO, as Detective Lazetera described it, with DNA evidence splashed across skin, clothing, and concrete. Susanna was among three women willing to testify at the trial. He was given a long prison sentence.

What an irony: they caught the perp, as the police called him, but Alan would get away.

Susanna and Alan began counseling sessions, in a group, as a couple, as individuals. The therapists told them that recovery would take a long time. Gradually Susanna understood what they meant. She experienced panic attacks on the streets of her beloved neighborhood while she was doing everyday chores, like stopping for shampoo at the drugstore or picking up a quart of milk at the deli. Anxieties beset her, fears so irrational she was afraid to tell Alan or Dr. Cindy, as Susanna called her counselor, because they might think she was going crazy. She took a leave from her volunteer job at the Metropolitan Museum, because the tourists began to frighten her with their ever-eager stares. When she went to the health club to swim, she had visions of the fourth-floor pool collapsing through the building to the ground. She couldn't bear to go to a movie, because of the strangers surrounding her on all sides. She thought she saw the man who attacked her buying coffee at Starbucks, or standing in line outside the Magnolia Bakery, even after he was in jail. Sometimes he looked at her and grinned.

She remembered the sort of person she used to be . . . confident, forthright, carefree, meeting friends for shopping sprees downtown, hurrying to restaurants, riding the subways at all hours, at ease with herself and the city. Where had her real self gone? When would that woman come back?

Dr. Cindy said her reactions were normal, which was a comfort even though hearing it didn't cure her anxieties or her panic attacks. Susanna had tests for AIDS and other STDs, and her doctor repeated these three times. She took a round of anti-HIV medications, routine in cases of rape, a fact that Susanna hadn't known. She had two pregnancy tests. The perp hadn't used "protection," as the euphemism went. The professionals advised that she and Alan "refrain from intimacies," another euphemism, or "use protection carefully, every time, for all intimate contact," until the medical results were verified and complete.

In Susanna's group therapy sessions with other women who'd been sexually assaulted, several confessed that they found themselves recoiling from intimacy with their partners. Likewise their partners hesitated to touch them, for fear of provoking this reaction.

Susanna and Alan were experiencing this, too. They could still be affectionate with each other, sitting close together on the sofa while watching movies on TV, cuddling in bed as they fell asleep. But moving beyond simple affection felt impossible. Luckily they were able to talk about this issue. Susanna believed they were moving forward. Her life with Alan seemed stable and secure. She tried to think of the rape as a glitch, something that could be dealt with and put behind her.

The economy collapsed in the autumn, but Susanna and Alan held on to their jobs. By January, Susanna woke up to the realization that for weeks, Alan had been slipping into himself. He'd become uncharacteristically quiet. Susanna assumed he had professional worries because of the economic situation and that he was reluctant to share these concerns with her. From the earliest days of their marriage, he'd never wanted to bring his work problems home. She didn't press him.

Maybe if she'd pressed him, things would have turned out differently.

"I'm sorry, Susanna."

They were in the bedroom, getting ready for bed. Today, Susanna had received a clean bill of health. Physical health, at least. The pregnancy tests were negative, the thrice-repeated AIDS tests were negative, the other STD tests were negative. They no longer needed to protect themselves from each other. They could resume where they'd left off. Susanna felt ready to think about their baby again.

Alan sat down on the side of the bed. He was still dressed in his oxford shirt and suit trousers. He hadn't changed out of his work clothes. She wore her robe. She'd taken a bath. Her skin radiated heat. She went to embrace him, to stand between his legs the way they often held each other. This time, instead of parting his legs, bringing her close, and wrapping his arms around her, he took her hands, which had the effect of keeping her away.

"I'm not ready," he said.

His cheekbones were sharply defined. He'd lost weight.

"I can't."

With his dark eyes and chiseled features, his thick curling hair, and tall, lanky frame, she'd always found him attractive and stirring. Now his handsomeness had become a mask, concealing his thoughts and feelings.

"I might never be ready."

"Never?" What did he mean, *never*?

"It's tearing me apart."

"What is?"

"I don't want to hurt you."

"Hurt me? How?"

"It's the violation. It's—I can't explain."

And then he didn't need to explain. She understood. The sense of contamination. Of a filth that could never be cleansed. She'd heard this from others, in her therapy sessions.

"I just—"

She put her hand over his mouth, so she wouldn't have to hear him describe his feelings about the prospect of resuming their lives, of creating their baby.

When she took her hand away, he said, "I'm sorry." He began to cry.

Like the good wife she was, she held him close to comfort him. She didn't cry. She was stunned. As she caressed his hair, she stared out the window. Their bedroom faced south, overlooking the rooftops of the brownstones. The skyscrapers glittered in the distance. Each night before they turned off the lights, Susanna opened the curtains so that she could fall asleep to this view, becoming part of the luminous city around her.

"I'm sorry," he repeated.

Their marriage, their future, the focus of her life. Finished. Ended in a few minutes on a concrete slab next to three green plastic garbage cans. Plus the sky-blue can for recyclables.

## Chapter 3

On a Saturday afternoon in late summer, in Uncle Henry's living room, Susanna sat down to rest for a moment. The windows were open, and the breeze carried the scent of freshly cut grass. She heard snatches of the neighbors' conversations as they worked in their gardens. On the piano was a vase of white snapdragons, a gift from the upstairs renters, Diane and Jenna.

She'd begun the job of clearing out Henry's home. A specialized firm would handle the bulk of the organizing and removal, but she was going through everything beforehand, to find what she and her mother might want to keep. This morning, she'd packed the photographs to send to Evelyn in Florida. Without pictures of herself everywhere she turned, she felt more relaxed. She'd already reviewed the books and CDs, making a stack of items she wanted. Progress was slow, but her attention to the task was a way of honoring her uncle, or so she told herself as she once again sneezed from the dust.

The piano bench caught her eye, and she got up and opened it. Her childhood music books were piled inside: *Teaching Little Fingers to Play*; *Scales and Chords Are Fun*. She remembered herself at seven and eight, making her way through these collections. She'd hated taking piano lessons, but Evelyn had insisted on it. When she was a teenager, Henry had dragged her to concerts by the Buffalo Philharmonic.

*Pieces Are Fun*, Books One, Two, and Three. From the progression of the books, she recalled that even though she'd hated the lessons, she'd gradually advanced. In *My Favorite Solo Album*, she'd dog-eared the page for Carl Philipp Emanuel Bach's "Solfeggietto." In *My Favorite Program Album*, the page for Mozart's "Rondo alla Turca" was paper-clipped, the music marked with her teacher's notations. She'd performed this piece in a year-end recital, and she remembered her happiness that she'd gotten through it with only a few mistakes. Here were Johann Sebastian Bach's *Fifteen Two-Part Inventions*, also marked by her teacher, high-flown pieces indeed for someone who professed to hate her music lessons.

She came upon a manila envelope about the size of a large-format magazine. A letter-sized envelope was taped to it, and *For Susanna* was written on this smaller envelope in Henry's scrawl.

She returned to the chair and sat down. She detached the letter and opened it. Henry had used the thick stationery that Aunt Greta reserved for special correspondence.

It was dated the same day he pressed fentanyl patches onto his chest, drank a bottle of vodka, and went to bed.

*Dear Susanna,*

*I knew that sooner or later you'd find this note.*

He was teasing her? He thought hiding a suicide note was a joke?

*The truth is, I've had enough. That's all I can say.*

Her anger flared, mixed with anguish. His suicide felt like an attack against her, an act of hostility and rejection.

*I took this from Germany at the end of the war. I found it in Weimar, which*

*became part of East Germany. It was in a piano bench stuffed with music, in a
house that belonged to murdered Jews. In those days I saw and did things that
have stayed with me forever. I was at Buchenwald after the liberation. I killed a
girl when I didn't mean to.*

*I've always protected you from that. I'm telling you a little now only so that
you'll understand.*

She would have understood better if he'd told her when he was
alive, when they could have talked about it. Susanna knew Henry
was brilliant, with wide-ranging interests and a gift for languages.
He always kept a stack of books, mostly history, beside his reading chair, the faux-leather recliner positioned on the opposite side
of the room. And yet Henry had settled for what seemed, to Susanna, like so little. He'd never gone to college. He'd moved to
Buffalo when his army buddy, Pete Galinsky, offered him a job at
his family's clothing store, and he worked there for forty-five years.
To Susanna, he'd seemed somehow haunted. Preoccupied. He was
always kind to her, but he lashed out at Greta and at Evelyn un-
predictably.

She cautioned herself against judging him. She had no idea what
the war, or any other experiences, had done to him, because he never
talked about himself. At least not to her.

*After I figured out what this is, and what it says, I was angry, but I couldn't
destroy it, not the work of the great master, not even after what the Germans did
to our family. I still think about the cousins you should have grown up knowing.*

From whispered conversations among Henry, Evelyn, and Greta,
conversations that Susanna had overheard and pieced together by
standing outside doorways after she was supposed to be asleep, she
knew she'd had many relatives in Europe before the war. *Susanna looks
like her*, Greta said. *Little Franz, just a child*, said Evelyn. *Jakob was my
age*, Henry said.

Once Susanna had interrupted, demanding to know who they
were talking about. *We aren't talking about anyone. Go back to bed.* Their

brutal reactions taught Susanna that such questions from her were forbidden.

These unknown relatives would have been the companions of Susanna's life. Their photographs would have filled the living room shrine, too.

*I leave it to you, Susanna, to decide what to do with this. If you discover it's a forgery, that would make me happy even though I'll never know.*

The last phrase, the bleak joke, sounded so much like Henry, he might have been in the room with her.

*After the Iron Curtain fell, I wondered about going back to see if by some miracle the owner's family survived. I even made a map, so I'd know where to go. Then I realized I never wanted to set foot in that country again. I've enclosed the map, though, because I know how curious you are about everything. There were no road signs then, so it's a little confused, and so many years ago, too, but I think my memory's pretty good.*

The second page of the letter was a roughly drawn map of roads in and around the town of Weimar, Germany, with arrows and descriptions to explain the route.

*You're a smart girl, and you'll figure out what's right.*

*Love, Uncle Henry.*

Susanna felt tears smarting in her eyes. *You're a smart girl, and you'll figure out what's right.* Henry had told her this throughout her childhood. Despite his desire to protect her from the past, he'd always supported her future. He'd told her that she could, and would, accomplish whatever she set out to do.

Susanna put the letter aside. She stared at the manila envelope. She felt reluctant to open it. She pushed herself forward and unsealed it. Inside she found a folder made of—it wasn't any type of paper she recognized. It was thick, and the surface was scratchy against her fingertips. *Vellum* might be the word for it. Its color was brownish beige, and the corners were stained black.

A few lines of German were written across the folder in a showy style. This looked like a title, although she didn't know German and she wasn't even able to identify many of the letters. A listing of musical instruments appeared under the title, and these she could mostly make out.

Two sentences followed the listing. These were also in German, each sentence written by a different hand, using a different ink. This much was evident to her. The most she could read, however, was a place and year, *Berlin . . . 1783.*

She opened the folder. It contained five folded sheets nested into one another. Musical notation covered both sides of every sheet, creating twenty pages of music. The sheets were the same brownish beige as the outer folder. The ink was brown and had bled through to the opposite side, so that each sheet showed both what was written on it and a faint image of the notation on the other side. The edges of the paper were soft, nothing like the sharp-edged paper she was accustomed to.

Susanna leafed through the sheets. Cross-outs and smudges covered parts of some pages. The ink went from gloppy to thin, gloppy to thin—a quill pen, dipped and used until it ran out of ink, dipped and used again. At the end of the lines, the notes were cramped together, as if the composer realized he or she was running out of space at the end of a measure and tried to fit everything in. Between some of the lines of music, words had been written, hastily. Susanna couldn't decipher them. On the sixth page, the paper had been scraped to make a correction, and the scrape had created a small hole.

Despite the smudges and cross-outs, the notes seemed to flow easily from the hand. Susanna sensed that the person writing the music had been pressured to finish, with no time for the niceties of proper spacing and perfect presentation. The impression of forward momentum brought an immediacy to the work, a tactile feeling of creativity that glided across the pages.

This was nothing like the collections of printed sheet music she'd used during her years of piano lessons, nothing like *Teaching Little Fingers to Play* or *My Favorite Program Album*. Nor was it a neat, final, handwritten copy created for the publisher after everything was in place. This must be an original composing manuscript. As she turned the pages, she experienced an eerie sense of the composer's presence.

She returned to the first page of music. Studying the writing at the top, she was able to decipher some of the words. The calligraphy was graceful, with well-practiced curves that added a hint of playfulness.

On the upper left, a lithe hand had written *J.J.* She didn't know what that meant. Two words of Latin followed: *Dominica Exaudi*. And then, *Concerto*, followed by words in German that she couldn't make out. On the upper right was a name she recognized among the flourishes: *J. S. Bach*.

## Chapter 4

*October 1776*

Today, for the first time in his life, he felt like an old man. Yes, he—Wilhelm Friedemann Bach, eldest son of the mostly forgotten master Johann Sebastian Bach—felt like an old man. Leaning upon his walking stick amid the Aubusson carpets and the French bric-a-brac that were *de rigueur* in palaces these days, he stared at the vivacious girl playing the harpsichord before him.

"I finished the first section without a mistake, Monsieur Bach," Sara called to him, tossing her head in pleasure. Such high spirits, she had. She spoke French, *mais oui*, also *de rigueur* in palaces. The wealthy followed the example of King Frederick (he who was commonly called *the Great*), and the king worshipped French language and literature.

"Kindly concentrate on playing the piece through, Mademoiselle." He hated to curb her high spirits, but he must. He was her teacher. By definition, teachers curbed high spirits. "We will discuss your supposed perfection when you've reached the end."

Sara frowned. Her dark, thick eyebrows gave her an exotic look. *Exotic* was, he knew, a standard description for Jewish females, yet it suited her. He admired her full, brown, wavy hair, so different from that of the ubiquitous blondes he saw on the streets of Berlin. He felt within himself a cutting regret that he would never be more than an honorary uncle or father figure to her. She was fifteen. He was sixty-five.

"*Brava* for the *Passagen*," he said.

"*Merci.*" Sara bit her lower lip, and he knew she was girding herself for the fugal section ahead, the most challenging part. So typical of her, so poignant, that bite of the lower lip when she prepared for a section of special difficulty.

He had composed the piece to highlight her talents. And to bring out the qualities of this instrument. She played a six-octave harpsichord, with F as the lowest note. Designed and built by Johann Adolph Hass in Hamburg, its sound was powerful and clear. Physically it was an instrument of beauty, too. Carnations, tulips, and periwinkles had been painted upon the board, with birds frolicking among them. It was the best harpsichord he'd ever come across.

As he watched Sara play, he felt a protective delicacy toward her. The fact that she lived in a palace contributed to his sense of restraint, he had to admit. The expansive music room, with its two harpsichords and a fortepiano, was on the second floor of the house and faced the river Spree. At this hour of the day, sunlight poured at an oblique angle through the long, open windows. He heard the sound of water tumbling through the fountains in the gardens below. Paintings of voluptuous women decorated the walls. He recognized the styles of Rubens and Poussin, although he would never be so ill-bred as to ask if he was correct in these identifications.

Sara's father, the owner of this palace, was Daniel Itzig, "the King's Jew," as he was called. He had served as the king's banker and Master of the Mint. He had investments in silver, ironworks, and God alone knew what else. Considering that Sara's grandfather had been a lowly horse trader, her father was, above all, a financial genius. Rumor held that the Palais Itzig included a synagogue, although Friedemann had never seen it. Also rumored was a room with a detachable roof for use in some type of primitive holiday celebration.

"And no mistakes in the second part, either!" she said, as if daring him to contradict her.

He did not respond to this outburst. He kept his face impassive, like the proper pedagogue he was.

Today Sara wore a satin gown covered with intricate embroidery. Her leather shoes shone with their softness and polish. He'd never seen clothes like hers. These were not the type of clothes worn by his sisters, or by his wife. His sisters, of course, were the children of Kantor Johann Sebastian Bach, a Lutheran minister of music, somber and serious. And Friedemann's wife was, well, she was his wife. Friedemann dressed in his very best on the days he came to the palace. He made certain that his clothes were clean and that he didn't give off a foul odor. The Palais Itzig was said to harbor that absolute height of luxury: a bath. No one, neither family nor servant, gave off a foul odor here.

He stared at the finely wrought lace that covered Sara's bodice, and he sensed, with a tingling on his fingertips, her developing figure. He sighed. As usual, Madame Goldberg, Sara's prunelike governess, sat in the corner next to the window, clutching her needlework while she glared at him.

Friedemann hadn't known what to expect when he was first invited to the Palais Itzig to hear Sara play. He'd never visited a Jewish home. From their initial meeting two years before, he'd recognized Sara's talent. In Berlin, he taught no students but her. No one else was worthy of him, not even Sara's sisters, too numerous to recall, all of them playing musical instruments and engaging in family recitals for their private amusement. The two mornings he spent with Sara each week were the organizer of all his doings. He wished she had more time for him, but he knew her extensive study schedule. Tutors educated her in history, the sciences, and languages. He gathered she was the tenth among fifteen surviving children. He assumed there were others who had not survived. He himself was one of twenty children, of whom only ten had survived, so he understood her bustling family life with its undercurrent of loss. He was able to imagine how she filled her days when he wasn't with her.

At the conclusion of each of their lessons, a footman arrived with coffee and cake. Sara, Friedemann, and the governess would sit together at the small round table with dainty legs that perched itself near the windows. Sara would pour the coffee. Speaking French, they'd discuss Sara's studies. Her French was exquisite, fully equal to his. Friedemann had been to university, so he was able to ask questions appropriate to their conversation. He took pride in Sara's erudition, which made her especially worthy of his musical pedagogy.

"The fugue is difficult," she admitted.

"You're playing it well. Don't stop."

"*Never stop,*" she said, mimicking one of his performance rules.

Soon after he undertook the instruction of the Itzig girl, his friends at the tavern had asked him what Jews were like. Surprisingly, he could truthfully respond that Jews were much like everyone else. He'd seen Sara's father many times during the past two years, and Friedemann reported to his incredulous friends that if you happened to chance upon Daniel Itzig on the street, you'd believe him to be any other man of wealth and position. No beard, no head-covering, no special clothes. Blue eyes, even. No tail or horns, so far as Friedemann could ascertain. You'd never suspect Daniel Itzig of being what he was.

"Steady," Friedemann cautioned Sara. "Don't pick up speed simply because you want to get through it."

She nodded. She approached the coda. He'd embedded a little trick at the end. Would she notice it?

At the moment of the *stretto* and inversion, she gave him a split-second grin. Yes, she'd caught it. Naturally. She was his darling.

"You tried to trick me, Monsieur Bach. But you didn't succeed."

"No talking!"

She laughed at his order. The truth was he adored Sara's disobedience. His own daughter, Friederica, the only one of his children to survive, was disobedient, too. She was several years older than this angel. But Friederica's disobedience was mean-spirited and immoral.

*No.* He must put Friederica out of his mind. When he was at the Palais Itzig, he must never let his thoughts drift to the difficulties he confronted at home. At the Palais, he entered a better, more elevated way of life.

She completed the final cadence. She let the last chord resonate in the air, as he'd taught her. She turned to him with a blissful smile. "How was that? Have I made you happy?"

"Indeed, you have."

Pride came into her expression, her chin rising. He adored her pride, too, even as he tempered it: "Nonetheless, the fugue was a bit muddy at the C-minor entry."

Outrage ensued. "Muddy? In what way muddy? Show me."

He exchanged a glance with the ever-glaring Madame Goldberg. He pulled a chair over to the harpsichord, placing it close to Sara's chair but not so close that his leg would touch her flowing gown. Forever considerate, she leaned away from him, alas, to give him more room.

"You played it this way." He exaggerated her faults. "It should be played this way. Exploit the virtues of the instrument." He played it twice, once for her to hear and understand, and once for himself, to indulge himself in the astonishing textural clarity of this harpsichord.

Sara responded not with words but by playing the relevant measures over and over. He didn't need to instruct her to do so. She knew to do it. Repetition was the only way to achieve an effortless flow. Those particular measures, until . . .

"There." She lifted her hands from the keyboard. "It's perfect now, isn't it?"

"It's better. Let us not put more faith in ourselves than may be warranted. You are good, for a fifteen-year-old. Talented, even. For a fifteen-year-old. How you play at eighteen will be our goal. Perform the piece again, from the beginning, with my corrections in mind." He stood and returned to his place some five feet away, to listen and observe.

She began at a proper tempo and fitting affect, playing with a combination of fluidity and sprightliness. She played as if her outstanding technical gifts were an aside. Her love of the music glowed upon her face.

As Sara brought the piece to life, he experienced a quivering sense that his own life had in fact been worthwhile. This notion went against the general opinion outside the palace gates. He knew that his peers viewed him as a wastrel. Years ago he'd been called the greatest organist in Germany. In all of Europe. He'd been a composer of renown. His skills at improvisation had once been considered miraculous.

*Had once been. Years ago.* The litany of his life. His real trouble was that he didn't have a gift for pretending that idiots were smart. He didn't defer to his intellectual inferiors, no matter what their place in society. Because of this, he'd been forced to move from position to position until finally he could obtain no position at all. He enjoyed teaching, but he could bring himself to teach only those who were worthy of his gifts, like Sara, so his students had been few.

He'd lived to see his sanctimonious prig of a younger brother, Carl Philipp Emanuel, surpass him and be praised for compositions that were—Friedemann regretted to say it—trivial. Emanuel's compositions were *Berliner blue*: they faded. Naturally Emanuel now held the prestigious position of director of music for the city of Hamburg. Meanwhile Friedemann's music was criticized for being old-fashioned, more in his father's tradition of counterpoint and fugue than in the modern *galant* style. Friedemann refused to create frivolous work, and if as a result his work was dismissed by frivolous men, so be it.

How did he support himself? A host of ways. Upon his father's death twenty-six years before, Friedemann had inherited many of his father's musical manuscripts. He'd sold them one by one when he needed funds. Some he'd sold to Daniel Itzig. The Itzig family showed proper appreciation for the compositions of Johann Sebastian Bach.

Friedemann knew he was criticized by many among the local *Besserwisser*, know-it-alls that they indeed were, for his lax methods of preserving the manuscripts he still retained. Did they think he was a librarian? He wasn't a librarian.

His Sara. What would become of her, and of her talents, when she grew up? Fifteen was old enough for marriage, but thank God, he'd heard no talk of that for her. Not yet, at least. He hoped she wouldn't be buried away in an arranged marriage followed by pregnancy after pregnancy. He prayed she wouldn't suffer an early death in childbirth. She was skilled enough even now to perform in public. He wished for her this opportunity, scandalous as it was considered for a woman, especially of her high social position.

These Jews, however . . . one never knew what they'd accomplish, or what rules they'd break. Perhaps Sara would manage somehow to devote her life to music.

At this thought, he experienced an unfamiliar emotion: happiness. Whatever he'd done and not done with his many wasted years, through the jobs his father secured for him and which he could not keep, through his days and nights at the tavern—all this was redeemed, because it had led him here, to this music room, in a palace overlooking the Spree, where this lovely girl embodied the music that he himself had written for her.

He felt tears in his eyes. Tears gliding down his old, wrinkled skin.

She finished the piece flawlessly. She turned toward him. "Monsieur Bach?"

He didn't respond. He couldn't.

"Are you sad?" Concern filled her face. Concern for him. He couldn't remember when last he'd seen concern for him on the face of anyone.

"Yes," he managed. *"No,"* he corrected himself. He wouldn't admit to her the reason for his tears. He begged himself to stop these tears, but he could not. They were as disobedient as she. "Not sad. Merely overwhelmed by the beauty you have created."

Hearing this, Sara treated him to a long smile filled with mischief, innocence, and grace. "It's because of *you*, Monsieur Bach, that I am able to create it."

How he loved her.

## Chapter 5

On a Sunday afternoon, in the midst of a cold September rain, Susanna stood under her umbrella on Central Park West and read a sign posted outside the Church of the Holy Shepherd.

BACH VESPERS! TODAY AT 5 P.M.

CANTATA 100, "WAS GOTT TUT, DAS IST WOHLGETAN"
("WHAT GOD DOES IS DONE WELL"), BY JOHANN SEBASTIAN BACH.

PRE-SERVICE LECTURE BY PROFESSOR DANIEL ERHARDT
OF GRANVILLE COLLEGE, 4 P.M.

Hanging above the sign, stretched between the arches of the church's entryway, was a banner proclaiming BACH! The top of the banner curled over from the weight of the rain.

The time was 4:15. Susanna was on her way to the subway station at Columbus Circle. She'd spent the afternoon at a celebration for a colleague who'd recently become engaged.

She glanced at Central Park across the street. The leaves were deep green, without a hint of the autumn to come. The heavy rain made the air smell fertile. When she and Alan lived in this neighborhood, only several blocks away, sometimes on Sundays they'd take a morning run in the park. They'd stop for coffee at the model boat pond, where they'd watch the children (and many adults) sailing miniature radio-controlled boats. Afterward, they'd—enough. All that was over and done with.

Susanna turned and walked up the church steps, closing her umbrella and shaking off the rain. She opened the heavy door and stepped into the shadows of the Church of the Holy Shepherd.

An usher whispered a welcome and gave her a program. The center pews were full, so she found a place to sit on the side aisle. Among her New York friends, she didn't know anyone who went to church or synagogue, except after they had children and even then, mostly on holidays, or if their children were preparing for a special ceremony. She had been raised as an atheist, and what went on in churches and synagogues was mostly a mystery to her.

The Church of the Holy Shepherd was old-fashioned and lovely, with traditional Gothic arches and a vaulted ceiling. On this rainy day, the stained-glass windows were dark.

Professor Daniel Erhardt stood in front of the pews, but not at the altar. Tall, with blond hair, he wore black jeans and a blue button-down shirt, sleeves rolled up, without a tie.

"In the years before writing this cantata," Professor Erhardt was saying, "Bach, like many German composers, caught what scholarly types now call 'Vivaldi Fever.' It's comparable to Disco Fever, or so I'm told by those who suffered from that disease in the 1970s."

Some of the parishioners laughed.

"Vivaldi's musical style revolutionized Bach's work. Vivaldi alternated rhythmically driven *ritornellos*, performed by the entire ensemble, with so-called *episodes*, performed by a soloist or a subset of the group."

He spoke without notes, pacing from one side of the pews to the other.

"Bach uses this form in Cantata 100—and not surprisingly, Bach being Bach, he does something unusual with it, thwarting our expectations when he reaches the moment at bar seventeen . . ."

Susanna lost the thread of Professor Erhardt's argument.

"Let's turn to how the chorale plays out in Lutheran theology. Luther, as you all know, constantly rails against *works righteousness* . . ."

Susanna stopped even trying to follow what he was saying. When he finished his presentation, the audience applauded, and he walked to the back of the church.

After a short break, the Vespers service began. A young man wearing a flowing white robe lit candles along the aisles and upon the altar. The candlelight created a soft glow in the sanctuary and illuminated the altar's Art Nouveau–style mosaics of angels and apostles. The golden mosaics shimmered in the flickering candlelight. The minister and his assistants, also dressed in white robes, chanted as they walked down the center aisle.

The service consisted of prayers and hymn singing, followed by more prayers. To avoid giving offense, Susanna paid attention to what the others were doing. She stood when everyone else stood, sat down when they did, and opened her hymnbook when necessary, following along. The minister was a big man with white hair and a heavily lined face. He looked sad and burdened, charged with duties that he was forever unable to fulfill.

He took the podium and turned on the reading light. "Today, let us reflect upon Luke 10:27, *Thou shalt love the Lord thy God with all thy heart, and with all thy soul, and with all thy strength, and with all thy mind, and thy neighbor as thyself.*"

Susanna wondered, did people really believe that, as more than a theory or an ideal? Believe it enough to obey it? History revealed plenty of *not* loving one's neighbor by God's people. This was a Lutheran church, and Germany was primarily a Lutheran country. Because she didn't practice a religion, Susanna perhaps naïvely assumed that people who did so were committed to obeying its tenets. But she'd never heard about German pastors instructing their parishioners to love their German Jewish neighbors as themselves and save them from the Nazis.

"Let us ponder the crucial phrase, *love the Lord thy God with all thy heart*. How do we go about doing this, in our daily lives?" the minister asked.

To Susanna, the most important phrase surely had to be the injunction to love your neighbor as yourself.

She looked around. Some parishioners gave the minister their full attention. Several kept their eyes closed and moved their lips in silent prayer. A few older men were slouched over. Some younger people checked their phones and sent text messages. Susanna's wet feet began to feel cold. Her clothes had become damp through her trench coat, adding to the chill creeping over her.

With nothing else to do, she read the program notes, which included a biography of the lecturer, Daniel Erhardt. He'd attended Wisconsin Lutheran College and had a PhD from Yale. He'd taught at the Yale Institute of Sacred Music, and for the past ten years he'd been a professor at Granville College. He was the author of three books, published by university presses, on various aspects of Bach studies. He'd been a visiting professor at the University of Chicago and at Vanderbilt. He did consulting work for universities and music groups.

Perfect. A few weeks ago, when she brought Uncle Henry's music manuscript back to New York, she'd taken it to her local Chase branch and rented a safe deposit box for it. In order to figure out what to do, she needed to learn more. She wondered whether, after so much time had passed, she could be accused of harboring stolen property. She'd reviewed websites that listed art and other objects lost or stolen during the war, but she'd found nothing like the music manuscript. She'd also searched the websites of Columbia and NYU, looking for scholars she might talk to, but no clear path had presented itself. Until now.

When the minister concluded his sermon, singers and instrumentalists gathered in front of the pews. The players tuned their instruments. When they finished setting up, the conductor walked down the central aisle of the church. He tapped his baton against his music stand and raised his hands. The music began.

And everything changed. The horn flourishes wove in and around the other instruments, in and around the voices, riveting her attention. No longer was she sitting with cold, wet feet and a soggy coat in a shadowed church. She felt an absolute alertness, as if this were the first time she'd been truly awake all day. She didn't need to know what the cantata was about, to feel its transcendence. The music was both ethereal and breathtaking. Even though she wasn't a believer, the music touched her spirit in a way that felt like an epiphany; at least that was the word that came into her mind to define it. It was like a spiritual wave passing over her.

When the cantata ended, no one applauded. The musicians and singers dispersed. The strangers around her in the pews behaved as if nothing special had occurred. The gray-haired woman diagonally in front of Susanna checked her program. The red-cheeked man on her left drifted into sleep. Susanna felt energy cascading through her, as if she were seeing everything around her with a newfound clarity. What could she do with this awareness?

Nothing, apparently. The service plodded on. The minister recited more prayers, a hymn was sung, the parishioners stood up and sat down, and Susanna followed along. The organ began to play what the program called a postlude, by Buxtehude. When this was over, the parishioners filed out.

The program notes concluded, *You are invited to join us in the community center downstairs for coffee and cake after the service!!* The two exclamation points evoked a determined optimism that Susanna couldn't share, but a reception was convenient from her perspective. She'd introduce herself to Daniel Erhardt and inquire about a private consultation.

She followed the others downstairs. The community room was dingy, with a scuffed linoleum floor, musty odor, and peeling paint. Several tubes of the fluorescent lights flickered. In the corner, a roasting pan collected rainwater that dripped from the ceiling. Daniel Erhardt was surrounded by parishioners eager to talk to him.

"Is this your first visit to our church?" A white-haired woman with an open, cordial expression, and wearing a powder-blue suit with flat shoes, stood before Susanna. The woman didn't pause for Susanna to respond, no doubt believing the answer self-evident. "I'm Jessie Mueller. The pastor's wife. Welcome." They shook hands. "Would you like some cake?"

Susanna had already had dessert at her colleague's party, but she allowed herself to be led to the cake table. From another kind, white-haired woman, she accepted a slice of yellow cake with chocolate frosting. The cake was sugary but otherwise tasteless. Susanna surreptitiously covered it with a napkin and put it into the garbage bin on the far side of the room.

The minister, dressed now in a black suit with a white clerical collar, strode over to her. His responsibilities no longer seemed to weigh on him. Instead he looked exuberant and robust, a man who'd enjoyed decades of hearty food and drink and looked forward to many more.

"A newcomer! Jessie alerted me. Bach always brings the newcomers. Frank Mueller." He thrust out his hand.

"Susanna Kessler." They shook hands, he with a fervency that left her taken aback.

"And what is your faith, if may I be so bold?"

"Atheist-Jewish, I'm afraid."

"No need to apologize. Our Bach program attracts many atheist-Jews, and a lot of other kinds of Jews, too. Our Lord was a Jew, did you know? Silly question, I'm sure you know that. Nevertheless a fundamental point in our religion and always worth repeating." His expression brightened with an oddly hypereager enthusiasm. "I'm pleased to tell you that in 1994, our denomination, the Evangelical Lutheran Church in America, repudiated Martin Luther's writings against the Jews."

Susanna wasn't familiar with Martin Luther's writings against the Jews, but she could well imagine. The fact that the Evangelical Lutheran Church in America hadn't repudiated these teachings until 1994 . . . their awakening seemed a little late in coming. Judging from his rather overexcited nervousness, the Reverend Mueller might have thought so, too.

"You're always welcome here."

"Thank you."

Jessie joined them, along with several other women. "Frank, we need your advice on a question of . . ."

As they became involved in a conversation about an upcoming children's festival, Susanna stepped away. She searched for Daniel Erhardt. He was free now, on his way to the table that held coffee and cookies. He poured himself a cup of coffee. She made her way through the crowd and approached him.

"Professor Erhardt, excuse me."

He turned to her.

"My name is Susanna Kessler. I'm a visitor here." That seemed like the best opening gambit, and it did bring a smile to his face.

"Me, too. Hired to give the preconcert lecture, all expenses paid."

"Sounds like a good gig."

"It is. Especially because I love the music. Did you enjoy the cantata?"

She paused to formulate an answer. "*Enjoy* isn't exactly the right word. My background is Jewish, so I'm sure I didn't understand it properly, but—well, I thought it was staggering."

"Bach's music *is* staggering."

"I hadn't realized. Years of piano lessons when I was young, and a subscription to the local orchestra, and I never knew until now."

"I hear such things all the time."

"To me it seemed more spiritual than specifically religious."

"When the cantata begins, the music puts us into an alternate world. I believe that for Bach, God is part of the intended audience. That's what we're hearing: his call to God."

"I think I understand what you mean."

"However, Bach didn't call to a generic God. Despite how the music affects us today, Bach himself was very much of his time and place. He—okay, enough lecturing."

Professor Erhardt's light humor set her at ease. "I'm hoping you can help me," she said.

"How so?"

"Your bio in the program says you do consulting. I need to hire a consultant."

"To consult about what?"

She hesitated. "I found something . . ." She didn't want to sound deranged. "Unusual. A music manuscript."

He frowned. "What sort of music manuscript?"

"My uncle brought it back from Germany after the war. Kept it hidden all these years, and now it's come to me."

"And it's signed, I suppose."

"Yes."

"By Bach or Mozart or Beethoven?"

How quickly he dismissed her.

"That's right."

"I don't get involved in estate matters. I hear stories like this a lot. You should contact a dealer, or Sotheby's, and secure an expert appraisal. I have to warn you, though: roughly one hundred percent of these cases turn out to be false alarms. Printed sheet music used to be expensive, so music lovers often copied out pieces by hand. That's what confuses people nowadays."

"If it turns out to be an old copy, that's fine. The point is, I don't know anything about it. I don't want to show it to a dealer, or to anyone whose first thought would be to sell it. My uncle kept it hidden for a good reason, I feel certain. For now, I want only a scholar to look at it. The signature says J. S. Bach. You're a scholar of Bach." She put on her best professional manner, forthright and to the point. "Your bio says you do consulting. I'd like to hire you. I'm happy to add twenty percent to your accustomed fee, due to the unusual circumstances."

"When I do consulting, it's usually to give advice to libraries about acquiring scholarly books. Or musical advice to orchestra groups. When they're looking for a Bach piece that includes, say, one French horn, a flute, and three oboes, because those are the instrumentalists available."

He seemed to think this was funny.

"The fact is," he continued, "I don't charge them fees because they couldn't afford a fee."

"I can afford a fee."

"Dan, look who's here today!"

The Reverend Mueller pushed a wheelchair that held a frail, elderly woman dressed in a lavender suit. She wore sunglasses that curved around her temples.

"It's our own Mrs. Hoffman!" said the Reverend Mueller.

"She braved the rain to join us," Mrs. Mueller said, patting Mrs. Hoffman's shoulder.

From the Muellers' deference, Susanna inferred that Mrs. Hoffman must be a major donor to the church.

Leaning over to grasp Mrs. Hoffman's hands, Professor Erhardt asked, "Did you enjoy the cantata?"

College websites generally gave the e-mail addresses for faculty, so Susanna knew she'd have no trouble following up with him. She slipped away.

## *Chapter 6*

Daniel Erhardt pulled his car behind the others waiting on line to drop off children at the pre-K through third grade school on the campus of Granville College, outside Philadelphia. His daughter, Becky, a first grader, was buckled into her car seat in the back.

"You have your lunch and your project?" Dan said.

"Yes, Daddy. You already asked me."

As usual, Becky was impatient with his anxieties. To Dan, she seemed far older than six, although he didn't have much experience to judge by. This morning she'd dressed herself in red leggings with a white top and a short jean jacket. Julie, Dan's wife, Becky's mom, used to say that Becky had been born with a fashion sense. Two barrettes embossed with the image of a white kitten prevented Becky's silky blond hair from falling into her face.

"Sally will pick you up after school."

"You already told me." Sally was a senior at the college. "Sally picks me up every day. You don't have to keep telling me."

"Bear with me, sweetheart."

Becky shrugged. *Where is Becky, who is taking care of Becky?* This was the constant refrain of his days.

They reached the front of the line. Miss Emma, age roughly twenty-three, greeted them. "Good morning, Becky. Good morning, Mr. Erhardt." Miss Emma was forever on the verge of laughter, as if all of life were like first grade.

Becky undid her seat belt and grabbed her backpack and lunch box. "Bye, Daddy," she called as she bounded out of the car. Instinctively he reached out to her. He wasn't fast enough and didn't manage to touch her.

He felt an ache in his chest, even though rationally he knew that her ability to run off each morning showed how well she was doing. She joined her friends on the swing set. Becky's day started with recess.

As Dan drove away, Katie Reilly, the principal, waved to him. For an elementary school principal, Katie was surprisingly voluptuous, he couldn't help but notice despite his loyalty to Julie's memory. She wore a snug V-neck sweater that showed off her figure. Katie was divorced, three or four years now. Recently she'd been waving to him with an encouraging expression that he didn't want to recognize. He knew what it meant, but he still thought of himself as married. Maybe he always would. With his thumb, he turned the gold band on his ring finger. He'd been getting a lot of encouraging looks lately from unattached women. The beckoning that said, I'm here if you want to talk, or for anything else you might want to do. But he didn't want to talk. He'd done enough talking. And he wasn't prepared for more than talking.

He drove on the narrow roadways across the campus. With its sweeping lawns and hundred-year-old shade trees, the campus was looking exceptionally beautiful today. As he contemplated his morning class, he felt like two people, a public self, giving lectures and interacting smoothly with the world, and a private self, locked in mourning. He wished he could make Becky's life more fun by bringing his public self home, but he couldn't.

He found a parking space near the music building. After yesterday's rain, the air was fresh and cool. From the outside, the music building was a hideous pile of drab concrete blocks. Inside, it opened to reveal glass walls facing a forest. He walked upstairs to his office. His class was at 9:10, an awful time slot when three-quarters of the students were half asleep, but he didn't control the scheduling.

He turned on his college-issued desktop computer with its mammoth screen. He saw an e-mail from Susanna Kessler, requesting an appointment. Yesterday, when she'd told him that she'd found a Bach manuscript, he'd thought, oh no, not that: a manuscript—*autograph* was the more exacting term, if it was really in Bach's handwriting, which it wasn't—found in a closet or an attic, and an excited heir assumes it must be a lost work by the great master.

This morning, however, as he thought back on their meeting, he felt more sympathetic toward her. God alone knew how she'd come to be there, with her high heels and short skirt, amid a sea of conservative Lutheran women.

When it came to church basements, Julie had fit in perfectly. He'd often teased her, that she should have been a minister's wife. She'd lean close to him and whisper that he was her personal minister, of music, and he could bring out his instrument for her later, and she would help. She had a secret sensual side, hidden from everyone but him.

During Julie's final months, their church in Granville had united to help the Erhardts. Their fellow parishioners assured that a babysitter was always on call, so Dan never had to worry about finding someone to stay with Becky when he needed to be at the hospital with Julie. When Dan was teaching, church people made certain that someone was with Julie, reading aloud to her. In the church basement, sign-up sheets filled the bulletin board, outlining weekly care for the Erhardt family: who would cook and drop off food, do the laundry, run errands, car pool.

Pray for our beloved Julie, Pastor Mansholt intoned each week, and pray for her family. Although Dan couldn't say for certain if the prayers made a difference, he did appreciate them. The parishioners were good people, and he couldn't have managed without them. He reserved his anger for God. How could an all-powerful, all-loving God let Julie die? He hoped that someday he would come to understand God's mysterious ways. At his worst moments, Dan found himself wondering whether God did or could in fact know and watch over every person on earth.

Despite his questioning and his doubts, he had to carry on. Susanna Kessler seemed to believe that he could help her. Grief had led her into a church, a place she didn't usually visit. She'd found him and asked for his assistance. Plenty of people had been helping him lately. Maybe he ought to help her.

He replied to her e-mail message and suggested several possible meeting times.

Then he closed his eyes. In his mind he reviewed this morning's class topic: social implications in Mozart's instrumental music. Dan never wrote out lectures for his classes. Instead he reviewed the material beforehand, chose music examples, and in class let the music guide him. With luck, the immediacy made his classes more exciting, for himself and the students both. He didn't want to end up teaching the way his own professors had taught, unfolding yellowed lecture notes prepared thirty years before and delivered by rote ever since. Nowadays he faced an added challenge: to compete with Google, YouTube, texting, and whatever else was on the phone in the palm of every student's hand, teaching had to be a performance, an entertainment.

This semester's Mozart class had attracted six members of the varsity baseball team. He might be gaining a reputation for easy classes, although that was hard to believe because musical structure was like a new language for most Granville students. At any rate, he was happy to have the baseball team. They participated in discussions as if class were a game worth playing.

Picking up the stack of CDs he'd organized on Friday, he left his office, locking the door behind him. His colleague Katarina Kundera, dark-haired and motherly, was coming out of her office down the hall, holding her own stack of CDs. As usual, she was dressed in black except for a scarf tied around her neck in a complex manner she described as *French*. Today's scarf was purple. Having a colleague like Katarina was a blessing for him. She was a terrific scholar as well as brilliant and funny. An expert on the Czech composer Bedrich Smetana, she taught nineteenth- and twentieth-century music. She was married to a physics professor at the college, and her daughter and Becky often played together.

"Good morning," he said. "What's on your schedule for today?"

"*Madama Butterfly.*"

Dan cringed in spite of himself. He disliked nineteenth-century Italian opera. To his taste, the music was saccharine and the stories melodramatic.

"Many people find Italian opera cathartic," Katarina said cheerfully, well aware of his bias.

"I'm happy for them."

"What are you doing today?"

"The *Serenata notturna.*"

"You're lucky. I do love that piece."

"Yes, I *am* lucky." He was drawing a good salary essentially for ruminating upon his CD collection: a person couldn't be luckier than that.

She went into her classroom, and Dan went into his.

"Good morning, ladies and gentlemen," he said with a dash of irony to lighten the mood, so they'd be more receptive to the challenging material ahead.

"Good morning, Professor," they said in sing-song unison, responding to his tone. A few baseball mitts were stashed under chairs.

"I'm certain you've all done your listening homework"—strained laughter ensued—"so you're prepared to discuss the *Serenata notturna*. Let's begin at the end, with the third movement, which Mozart deliberately gives the French title, *Rondeau*."

"Excuse me, Professor," said Derrick Lyons, the third baseman. His gangly legs fit awkwardly under the chair's table extension. "What I want to know is, what's with the weird bit of gypsy-sounding music in the third movement? Does it make sense in there?"

Talk about cutting to the chase. This was Dan's first topic. "Interesting question, Derrick. Thank you. Let's start by considering what's happening at that spot."

## Chapter 7

Susanna sat down on a child-sized chair in the far corner of the re-
furbished library at P.S. 629. The air smelled of fresh paint and new
carpeting. Across the room, a class of second graders sat cross-legged
on the floor while Sheila Davis, the librarian, began her presentation
on a book about life on the International Space Station.

"Today's chapter is called, 'Breakfast, Lunch, and Dinner. Plus
Snacks.'"

A thin boy in a striped shirt raised his hand.

"Yes, Joshua?"

"When are we going to hear about bathrooms on the Space Station?"

Other voices rose in support of this question.

"Thank you for asking. That's the next chapter. I know we're all
excited to learn about taking a bath and doing private bathroom activities on the Space Station," she said, and the kids squirmed and
giggled, "so you'll be looking forward to library hour next week. But

first we have to learn about food. So let's begin: 'On the International Space Station, the astronauts eat three meals a day and enjoy nutritious snacks . . .'"

When Susanna had first visited this library a year ago, the paint was peeling and the windows were filthy. The overhead lights didn't work. When she'd touched the furniture, her fingers came away sticky. The air had reeked of dampness and neglect. The old library had only four shelves of nonfiction books and three shelves of storybooks. There were no computers.

"'The astronauts have the same need for good nutrition as the rest of us . . .'"

Now, murals covered the walls: birds nested in trees, lions lounged amid grasses, and a basketball player leapt into the air to make a shot. The windows were new and clean. Modern ceiling fixtures illuminated the room. Three separate reading areas had been set up, from pillows on the floor for the youngest children to study tables with computers for the older kids. The brand-new book shelves were packed with brand-new books. Special-interest displays filled the center of the room, from sports to biography to a *Who We Are* section of books that reflected the backgrounds of the kids in the school, from Asia, Africa, and the Americas.

"'The astronauts choose their food before they go into space. This way, each astronaut can enjoy the food that he or she likes best . . .'"

Along with Rob and Cornelia Barstow and representatives from the Fund for Public Schools, Susanna had been here several weeks ago for the official opening celebration. But ribbon-cutting ceremonies revealed nothing about how a project actually played out. Follow up, fly-on-the-wall style, was the most important part of Susanna's job.

"'The astronauts enjoy orange juice and lemonade.'"

Ms. Davis paused. "Do you enjoy orange juice and lemonade?" she asked the kids.

They affirmed that they did.

"I do, too," Ms. Davis said. "'For snacks, they can choose from nuts and dried fruit . . .'"

The book made the International Space Station sound appealing.

"'As you go about your day on earth, remember that just like the astronauts in space, you need to eat nutritious food in order to stay healthy and do everything you want to do at home and at school.' And that's the end of the chapter. Let's talk about what we learned. Do the astronauts choose the food they eat?"

Several kids raised their hands.

"What do you think, Emory?" Ms. Davis asked.

"Yes, they do." Emory was a serious-looking girl who wore her hair in pigtails tied with ribbons.

"That's right. What would you pick to eat, if you were going into space? Let's start with breakfast."

"I'd pick cereal," Emory said.

"I'd pick cookies," Joshua said.

"Are cookies a good breakfast?" Ms. Davis asked.

"Oatmeal cookies are. Maybe. It depends."

A spirited discussion followed on the topic of oatmeal cookies and whether they were, in fact, a type of cereal.

The bell rang, signaling the change of classes.

"I'll see you next week," Ms. Davis told the children as they stood and lined up. "And let's not forget that while we're here in the library reading about the International Space Station, the astronauts are circling the earth and doing everything we're reading about."

With their teacher, the kids filed out. Ms. Davis joined Susanna.

"This is very impressive," Susanna said. "I might have to return next week to find out about bathroom procedures on the Space Station."

"I'm eager to learn about that, too. And you're always welcome to visit us. Please tell Mr. and Mrs. Barstow how grateful the whole school is for what the foundation has done for us."

"Thank you, I will."

"For the first time in about twenty years, I feel as if I'm working in a real library."

"I'll tell them that. I know they'll appreciate hearing it."

The next class, of older kids, came in.

"I'll see you soon, I hope," Ms. Davis said to Susanna, before joining the newcomers. "Good morning, class. Let's start with everybody choosing a book to take home for the week." The kids fanned out across the room, following their interests.

Susanna positioned herself at the doorway. This afternoon she was going to Granville College to meet with Daniel Erhardt, and she had to get to Penn Station for her train. Nevertheless she lingered. The kids showed one another books and debated which to check out. After the success here, she'd be quick to recommend to Rob that the foundation fund other library renovations.

Not so fast, her pragmatic side cautioned: Rob would want to know whether reading scores on standardized tests improved at the schools with renovated libraries, including this school. She wondered, too. She'd begin gathering the statistics, even as she knew that standardized tests couldn't measure the developing minds of kids who, for example, had the opportunity to imagine themselves living on the International Space Station.

## Chapter 8

After disembarking from the local train at the Granville stop, Susanna stood on the platform. The college buildings rose in the distance, up a gentle incline. Green lawns spread before her. She waited for the music she was listening to on her phone to end.

Trying to educate herself, she'd downloaded a *Bach's Greatest Hits* collection from iTunes. Each piece was mesmerizing. Of course, that's what a greatest hits set was for, to show off the best, but nonetheless she was surprised by the buoyant charge of energy the music gave her.

She took out her earbuds and put her phone away. She seemed to hear the music still playing in her mind, its patterns spinning onward. As she got her bearings, the train departed behind her. When the clattering faded, the air was silent. She was alone on the platform. She walked up the college's ceremonial central path, beneath an arch of oak trees. When the path became steeper, a series of steps eased the way. The deserted campus was beautiful, but Susanna felt a disturbing sense of solitude. Where was everyone? She preferred a city, where people were always nearby. When she was attacked, strangers gathered to help her. If she were attacked here, no one would be close enough to notice.

At the top of the path, she made her way around the main administration building and through a series of gardens, following Daniel Erhardt's directions. She spotted the low, bunkerlike building that he'd described. When she entered it, she confronted a double-story glass wall overlooking a forest. Deer grazed amid the foliage. The sounds of practicing filled the air, piano, violin, trumpet, and voices, singing.

She walked up the stairs and found his office. Leaves pressed against his office's wall of glass.

"Welcome," he said.

"Thank you." To ease their way into conversation, she said, "This is an unusual building."

"Prizewinning modern architecture, or so we're told. Have a good trip?"

"It was faster than I expected."

"Good. I got coffee for us." He indicated the cups on his desk. "It should still be hot: from years of experience I know how long the walk takes from the station, so I timed the coffee accordingly. Took my chances and put milk in yours. Here's the sugar, if you use it." He pulled out the dictation tray of his desk and pushed a chair to the far side, for her.

"Thank you." She sat down. By now she'd googled him. She knew more about his several books and many articles, and about his work tracing music manuscripts that had disappeared at the end of World War II, appropriated by the Russian army. As she drank her coffee, she looked around the office . . . floor-to-ceiling bookcases stuffed with musical scores, shelves of CDs, a piano. Family photos covered his desk, featuring a blond woman, soft and pretty. Midwestern, Susanna decided. Some of the photos included a child, photographed from babyhood to girlhood. Susanna glanced at Dan's hand and saw his wedding ring. She made an assumption: happily married, one child.

Yes, surely this was the proper course. Susanna's intuition that Dan would be a reliable and discreet consultant had been correct. She had tried to negotiate a fee with him via e-mail, but again he'd refused.

"So." Dan sounded upbeat and positive. "Let's see this music manuscript you've inherited."

Susanna put her coffee on the far side of the desk. Opening her tote bag, she took out the manuscript. Turning it so that the title page faced Dan, she placed it on the desk's dictation tray before him.

Dan had already planned what he would say. After dropping Becky off at school, he'd formulated a response for Susanna Kessler. Words to let her know as gently as possible that what she'd discovered was a worthless copy. Nothing wrong with a handwritten copy, however. It was a nice keepsake, even if it wasn't valuable to anyone outside your family.

And yet, when he stared at the manuscript placed before him, he couldn't say those words. Instead he remembered the occasions when he'd handled the Bach autographs at the Deutsche Staatsbibliothek in Berlin, the Bach-Archiv in Leipzig, and the New York Public Library. He rubbed the wrapper, which was the name for the outside covering, and the roughness of the paper against his fingertips was just like those autographs.

The heading on the wrapper began with the indication *Dominica Exaudi: Concerto.* This meant that the piece was a cantata and had been written to be performed, or rendered (the proper term for musical works included in a religious service), on the Sunday after Ascension. Bach often called his cantatas *concertos*, which could be confusing because people didn't refer to cantatas that way anymore. The name of the piece was *Wir das Joch nicht tragen können*. This was a reference to the Bible, Dan knew without needing to look it up. Acts 15:10. The literal translation would be *We are unable to bear the yoke*. "*Of the law of Moses*" would be understood to finish the line. The cantata title was unfamiliar to him.

But that couldn't be. He knew the titles of all of Bach's 1,100 extant works, as well as their catalog numbers in the Bach-Werke-Verzeichnis. He had a good memory for such things, because he'd learned them when he was young. Same with the Bible: his parochial school had stressed Bible study, and biblical references had been imprinted in his brain.

The annotations on the wrapper indicated three separate scripts. One, listing the title and the instruments, was a handwriting he knew. He recognized it, incredibly, as Johann Sebastian Bach's.

Dan wasn't familiar with the next script, but he could read it: *Sollte nicht catalogisiert werden*, "Not to be cataloged," followed by the place and date, *Berlin, den 9. Juni 1783*.

The third hand had written, *Im Privat-Kabinett halten*, "Keep in the private cabinet."

So, concealment from early on.

He opened the wrapper. *J.J.* was written in the upper left hand corner of the first page of music. Bach almost always began his compositions with the initials *J.J.*, meaning *Jesu Juva*, "Jesus, help me." Then the title was repeated, *Wir das Joch nicht tragen können*. On the upper right was the signature, *di J. S. Bach*.

Dan could and would compare the signature to other examples illustrated in the Bach reference works on his shelves. He chose to ignore the signature for now. Any decent forger could copy a signature. Other things weren't so easy to imitate.

The piece began with a section for virtuoso solo violin accompanied by oboes, orchestral strings, and organ. This filled two pages of music.

Then the bass voice came in, declaiming, *Wir, wir, wir das Joch* . . . Dan didn't remember encountering this text or its musical setting before.

As usual in autograph cantata scores of Bach's, the words were essentially illegible to modern readers. Dan, however, had spent years reading and studying old German script. He would need to investigate the libretto carefully later, but glancing through the piece, he was able to get an overview.

No, he certainly didn't recall this text appearing in any other Bach cantata. The arias for the most part were biblical in origin. He didn't know any textual sources for the recitatives. The first recitative read, in his quick translation, *We are at fault for not striking them dead.* The second said, *Burn their synagogues . . . and bury anything that doesn't burn.* The others continued in a similar, extremely troubling vein.

He turned his attention away from the text, to the musical notations. Composers often had striking idiosyncrasies in their writing of musical noteheads, rests, clefs, and so on. Dan could identify the general characteristics of the musical handwriting of Mozart, Beethoven, Haydn. And of Bach. This looked like Bach.

The manuscript certainly had the general appearance of being old, with the ink eating into the paper and creating mirror images on the opposite side. For ink to corrode the paper like this took a fairly long time.

Indeed, the manuscript looked like a composing score, with crossouts and compositional revisions throughout. Sometimes a composing score showed scrapings where corrections had been made. As Dan turned the pages, he saw that this score had a few such scrapings, and even a small hole. Smudges showed where the composer (or the forger) touched the still-wet ink with the side of his (or her) hand. Here and there the composer (or forger) had paused for an instant, and in doing so had left a blot of ink on the paper.

In the lower margin of the third page, there was a small, rough sketch of a few measures of music, intended for the top of the next page, an *aide-memoire* for the composer (or a bit of high verisimilitude for a forger?), while he waited for the ink on this page to dry. On another page was an example of tablature, the use of letters to represent notes when space was short at the end of a line. The fourth page had a large ink spill toward the bottom.

A fantasy spun out in Dan's mind . . . Bach in his apartment in the Thomasschule, next to the Thomaskirche, in Leipzig, children and students tumbling over one another, ceaseless noise. Bach sat at his composing desk, and as usual, he was in a rush, working under what today would be called a deadline. For at least his first five years in Leipzig, he composed a masterpiece cantata for virtually every Sunday church service (except during the penitential times of year, when cantatas weren't rendered). An astonishing achievement, although Bach himself, judging from his surviving personal correspondence, may not have perceived how remarkable it was. On this particular day, a child ran over to him, breaking his train of thought. Depending on the circumstances, Bach laughed or scolded or comforted the child. In the confusion, he spilled a blob of ink onto the margin of his composing score.

Dan felt a chill as he imagined the scene.

At the end of the autograph, the letters *SDG* appeared. This meant *Soli Deo Gloria*, "To the Glory of God Alone." Bach almost always put these initials after the last bar of his compositions, liturgical and secular alike.

Dan returned to the beginning and reviewed the score again. This time, he followed only the music. He heard it in his mind. From the first notes it was vibrant and thrillingly motoric—and a piece he'd never heard before. The first chord was itself a sort of musical signature move of Bach's, a $V^7$-of-IV. At the first episode, Dan saw that the bass line, spectacularly, was an extended augmentation canon in contrary motion, set in the dense, chromatic, baroque harmonic language of, well, Johann Sebastian Bach. Most assuredly no one except Bach could pull off such a formidable compositional feat. A forger would need to be as musically brilliant as Bach himself to create this kind of music.

Dan held a sheet up to the light.

"What are you doing?" Susanna asked, startling him. He'd forgotten about her. Now he felt delighted to think that she might enjoy this next detail.

"I'm checking for the watermark. In Bach's day, paper was made with a distinctive watermark. Only very fancy paper is made this way nowadays, with words or pictures impressed into the paper and barely visible unless you hold the paper up against the light. Look." He held the sheet at an angle so she could see. He watched the recognition gradually come to her.

"A deer. With antlers. And the letters IAI."

"Watermarks are a field of study unto themselves. Let's look it up."

From the bookcase, he pulled out the *Katalog der Wasserzeichen in Bachs Originalhandschriften*, a two-volume, large-format German publication cataloging the watermarks on the various papers that Bach had used.

"We need a deer with its head in profile, and a round tail and dark eye, combined with the letters IAI, which are presumably the initials of the paper maker." Dan leafed through the book, showing Susanna pictures of leaping unicorns, knights in armor, hunters on horseback, crescent moons.

"There." She pointed.

He held up to the light a sheet from the manuscript score, and she held up the book beside it.

"You're right. A perfect match."

"What does the watermark tell us?"

"We don't know yet. This particular deer watermark is given the identification number 'six' in the catalog. So we look in the accompanying commentary volume . . ." He made his way through the charts. "Ah," he said when he found it.

"Yes?"

"It's the same, somewhat infrequently encountered watermark as for Cantata 43, a cantata for Ascension. That makes sense, because *Exaudi* is the Sunday after Ascension. And IAI apparently stands for Johann Adam Jäger, a paper maker from Bohemia. In older German spelling, the letters *I* and *J* were often interchangeable."

"So?"

"I need to think about this."

A realization swept over him, too involved to explain to Susanna, even though she gazed at him expectantly. He turned away from her and stared out the window. The fact was, the *Exaudi* cantata from Bach's third annual cantata cycle in Leipzig, the piece that would have followed Cantata 43 in the liturgical calendar, was missing. Was Susanna's manuscript the lost cantata?

"Let's move to the next step," he said, concealing his uneasiness. "We'll look up the opening measures, to make absolutely sure this music doesn't appear elsewhere among Bach's works with a different text." He pulled another book from the shelves, the *Melodic Index to the Works of Johann Sebastian Bach*, compiled by May deForest McAll. "This book organizes the opening melodic ideas of all Bach pieces by their shape."

"Their shape?"

"It puts the opening musical gestures of the pieces into a kind of alphabetical order, so you can search for them by means of the music itself. You see here," he explained an example at random, "two notes moving up the scale followed by two notes moving down, and so forth."

"I'll take your word for it."

He checked the opening phrase of the cantata and went to the required section of the book.

"This melody isn't listed," he said.

"What does that tell us?"

He didn't answer her. He faced a shocking conclusion: the manuscript might well be authentic. It probably *was* authentic. And both its music and its libretto were unknown. A wholly new discovery.

Stop: a genuine, previously unknown Bach autograph could not possibly be brought into his office on a Friday afternoon by a young woman who'd been cleaning out the home of her deceased uncle in Buffalo, New York. The chances of such a thing happening were nil.

And yet, evidently it had happened. The manuscript bore no library number or stamp. Who had written the messages on the wrapper, ordering that it be kept private? Where had it been hidden, in the many years since its creation?

Dan considered Bach's Calov Bible, lost for centuries and then found in an attic in Michigan. One day in 1934, a Lutheran minister in town for a conference stopped by the home of his cousin, and the cousin said, "I've got a big old multivolume German Bible in the attic, maybe you could take a look at it and tell us what to do with it." The Bible turned out to have Bach's signature on its various title pages and to be filled with Bach's handwritten comments.

Dan's heart was racing. He felt as if he'd gulped down five cups of coffee. This could be the most significant discovery of his career. Or if he was wrong, he'd make an everlasting fool of himself.

He turned to Susanna. "Tell me again," he said, suspicion entering his voice. He needed to keep her at an objective distance. "Where and how did you find this?"

"I was cleaning out . . ."

Dan listened to her story without interrupting. She showed him the note from her uncle. He read it. He studied her uncle's hand-drawn map. From the bookcase he pulled out an atlas of Germany. He matched the handwritten map to the atlas's map of the area in and around Weimar. He returned the note to her.

"From your uncle's letter, it appears that the manuscript was stolen. Looted after the war. Sorry to be blunt about it."

"My uncle possessed it for over sixty years. The people who owned it were probably murdered in the Holocaust."

Dan heard her defensiveness. She didn't want her uncle spoken of as a thief. "I keep up with the databases on materials stolen during the war," he said, "and I've never seen a reference to anything like this. As far as I know, it's never been reported stolen."

"I looked at those websites, too. I do realize that my uncle wouldn't have been able to know for certain, what happened to the family. If I can find any family members who survived, I'll give this back to them. But let's put the ownership question aside for now. I came to you because I'm trying to find out what this is. I need to know if it's authentic and also why my uncle was concerned about it."

She sat up straighter, appearing to Dan even more self-possessed and confident, and making him more conscious of her short skirt and black tights. He didn't intend to notice such things, especially with Julie staring out of the photos on his desk. He couldn't help himself. It was instinct. Judging from the conversations he overheard in the locker room at the gym, he was no different from most other heterosexual men in this regard.

"What do you think we've got here?" she asked.

She wasn't an expert, Dan knew. "Let me start at the beginning. It seems that Bach may have written as many as five cantata cycles."

"Which are?"

"An annual liturgical series in which music is set for the appropriate church services in the year. The purpose of a sacred cantata was to provide musical and poetic reflection on the biblical readings of the service. For unknown reasons, only three of Bach's five cantata cycles survive, and even those aren't complete."

He heard himself taking on an excessively professional tone, to ward off his increasing recognition of the attractiveness of her legs.

"There are various theories about what happened to the many cantatas that disappeared. In those days, there was no photocopying or scanning," he said, stating the obvious to provide some per-spective. "For nearly all of Bach's cantatas, the only record of them that existed in his day was the composing score, plus the separate individual orchestral and vocal parts that were copied out by Bach's students from the composing score, for the performers to use in the rehearsals and church services. When Bach died, all these materials were divided among his wife and several of his sons. From there they were sold, and some were lost, discarded in error, never seen again."

"Are you saying that this is a completely unknown piece of music by Bach?"

"Yes. Possibly." He made himself sound circumspect. "My opinion is subject to the corroboration of other experts. I don't know enough to make a definitive evaluation on my own."

"So this manuscript could be quite important?"

"If genuine, it would be tremendously important. And it could be worth millions of dollars. The smallest Bach discovery creates a sensation, and this would be major."

"What's the next step?"

"A thorough investigation. Because there will be an uproar when—if—this becomes public, every aspect of the manuscript needs to be explored. I'll need to gather as much information as I can, to develop a context. First I should tease out the full text of the libretto. That could take a few hours."

"I'll wait. I have work I can do."

"Why don't I take photos with my phone to save time?"

"No photos. At least for now."

He debated whether to challenge her on this. The lack of a re-production of the manuscript for study purposes would make the entire research process more difficult, but he could understand that she would be concerned about the possibility of digital images being spread around the world in an instant.

"Okay. With your permission, I'd like to consult with a friend who's the curator of music manuscripts at the MacLean Library in New York. Scott Schiffman. He's an expert in authenticating and dating music manuscripts through handwriting analysis. A composer's musical handwriting changes over the course of a lifetime. The way the bass clefs and the treble clefs are written, the way the beams are placed on the notes—this is Scott's expertise. Among much else. He's an expert in the history of ink, for example. I'd like him to see the manuscript so we can get his opinion."

That was a huge understatement. Anxiety was setting in as the full import of what this might be—of what it *was*—hit him.

"May I contact Scott?"

"Yes. Thank you."

"We—you—should go to Weimar, follow your uncle's map, and try to find the house he visited. If the house is still there. At least determine the address. Visit the municipal archives and learn the family's name, so you can trace survivors. And we Bach scholars would want to know if anything else significant is still to be found at the house; again, if it exists."

"That makes sense."

"In the meantime I could contact a friend at the university in Leipzig and send him a copy of the map. He could do some research to try to find the family."

"I'd like to keep this to ourselves for now. Scott Schiffman at the MacLean Library is fine, but no one else."

"In early July, I'll be attending a conference in Leipzig, not too far from Weimar. If you're not able to visit Weimar before then, I could go."

"Thank you."

"Where are you storing the manuscript?"

"In a bank vault."

"Not good." This was *really* not good, but he kept his voice measured. "It should be kept in a temperature-controlled environment. Scott can help with that. The MacLean Library would be perfect.

You should take it there today. They have terrific facilities. I can phone Scott to alert him that you'll be arriving later."

"I'm going to keep it in the bank vault for now."

"I don't like you traveling around with this and dropping it off at a bank. In fact, doing so is unconscionably reckless."

She gave him a wry smile. "I'll keep your opinion in mind."

What could he say to that? He had no standing to challenge her. He didn't want to offend her. They'd only met once before. She could easily decide to take the manuscript to another scholar, or opt to sell it. And once she understood what it was, and the reason her uncle was rightly concerned about it, she might even, God forbid, think nothing of destroying it. Nonetheless he had a responsibility to be honest with her.

"I need to explain something else." He hesitated. He didn't know where to begin. The cantata that lay on the desk between them reflected the bleak history of Europe. In the Middle Ages, Jews were expelled from England and burned at the stake in France. The Spanish Inquisition murdered tens of thousands. Pogroms were a fact of life in many parts of Europe, even into the twentieth century. The absurd so-called blood libel had recurred all over Europe, also into the twentieth century, accusing Jews of murdering Christian children to use their blood in religious ceremonies, resulting in further anti-Jewish violence. The Holocaust hadn't come out of nowhere.

Abruptly two thousand years of history became personal for him. His great-grandparents had emigrated from Germany to the United States. One of his grandmothers had been born in Germany. He had relatives who fought on the German side during the war. And Dan felt more generally implicated because of his religion. He and his family were part of the Christian biblical heritage represented by this manuscript. He shared a collective responsibility. He felt ashamed. Surely this cantata text was *not* the message that Jesus himself had taught?

She was waiting for him to continue.

But he couldn't. All of it was too close.

"With any discovery of this magnitude," he said, avoiding the issue, "the press will descend in droves. We have to be prepared. Make certain we're one hundred percent correct. After I've copied out the libretto and am able to do research on its origins, we'll have a firmer idea of what we're dealing with."

The sun had moved, and the light was dappling into the office through the trees outside the window. In the golden light, her eyes were a shade of blue that he'd never seen before, dark and deep.

"Thank you."

Where had she come from, this delicate and graceful woman, her body full beneath her sweater?

He wasn't prepared to tell her outright that the text of this cantata, powerfully supported by its musical setting, explicitly proclaimed a stark and murderous contempt for Jews. For *her*.

## Chapter 9

With the head of his walking stick, Wilhelm Friedemann Bach knocked on the palace door. Under his arm he carried an elegant presentation box tied with a white satin ribbon. The box was more expensive than he could afford, but only perfection was suitable for his beloved Sara.

When Sara opened the box, she'd find his gift: a song he'd written for her. A *Cantilena nuptiarum*, "Presented in Honor of the Marriage of Sara Itzig to Samuel Salomon Levy," as the calligrapher had inscribed upon the wrapper. The calligrapher was also more expensive than he could afford. Sara would recognize the music, which he'd originally composed as a solo keyboard piece and used in her lessons. For her marriage, he'd arranged the work for voice and harpsichord. He himself had written the poetry. This was not a typical wedding piece, intended to be performed once and put aside. No, indeed. For Sara, he had created a profound reflection on earthly struggle.

The wedding would take place at the end of the following week. The girl he loved had grown into a vivacious young woman of twenty-two. He, by contrast, had grown into a grizzled, bitter, weak, ill, decrepit man of seventy-three.

Predictably, Sara was marrying into her own class. Friedemann had met the man. Samuel Salomon Levy was a banker and a member of a banking family. Jews were skilled at banking, you could count on that. In addition the man played the flute, and rather well, Friedemann had to admit.

Friedemann knocked on the door again. These servants, they were so slow. He didn't appreciate wasting precious minutes at the door, stranded with the clatter of horses and carriages on the cobblestoned street, when he could be basking in Sara's presence.

Most likely, this was the last time Friedemann would see her. He'd declined her invitation to the nuptial celebration. He could not bear to see her married. Afterward, she would leave Berlin on a wedding journey of several months, visiting family far and wide and enjoying a stay at a spa. He, on the other hand, was dying. He doubted he'd be here when she returned.

In recent months, as he'd grown weaker, he'd been thinking a good deal about the Lord. His meditations had given him a notion that he had a good chance of going to heaven. Sara, alas, was not a *baptized* Jew, so, according to Martin Luther, she was going to hell. Herr Luther was most knowledgeable about matters of heaven and hell, and Friedemann did consider himself devout. He was proud that years ago he'd managed to express his profound Lutheran devotion by reworking into Latin two movements from his father's superb Reformation cantata on Luther's hymn *Ein feste Burg* and giving them an even greater musical grandeur through the addition of trumpets and drums. This grandeur constituted a considerable expense for his employers at the church in Halle, but it was worth every thaler. (The ignorant burghers of Halle had disagreed.)

Friedemann hated to think of Sara condemned to hell because she was a Jew. But who was he to question the ways of the Lord? The Bible was clear on this issue. Like all good Lutherans, Friedemann knew his Gospels. *Whoever believes in Him, he will not be condemned; but whoever does not believe, he is already condemned, for he does not believe in the name of the only begotten Son of God*, said the Gospel of John.

Friedemann hoped that in the end she would receive from Christ the Crown of Life. Nowadays some of her brethren were converting. He found consolation in this hope for her. In fact, he'd included a reference to Christ's Crown of Life in his wedding poem, although he felt certain that she wouldn't know the New Testament allusion, to Revelation 2:10.

At last a uniformed butler opened the door. Friedemann recognized him from previous visits. The man, slight of frame, was attired in brocades much more expensive than Friedemann's. The man's skin was olive-toned. Friedemann wondered if the butler were a Jew. He suspected so. Gossip at the tavern held that Jews were as rich as Croesus. The truth, however, seemed to be that some Jews were much less wealthy than others. Some Jews worked as servants to survive.

In his bleakest moments, Friedemann confronted the fact that when all was said and done, he, too, was a lackey.

*"Guten Tag, Herr Bach."*

Friedemann listened for any hint of a Yiddish accent, but heard none. The Itzig family spoke French, but their servants spoke German. At least to him. Friedemann wondered if he was meant to take the German as an insult. Well, he didn't have time for such games. He swept past the butler and through the doorway.

And then he confronted the steep pathway, framed by marble columns, that led to his darling. This path had become more and more difficult through the years he'd visited the palais to teach his cherished student. Now he dreaded it.

To begin, he clutched the railing to maintain his balance as he labored up the five steps into the entry vestibule. He paused, gathering his strength. He shuffled across the central gallery, with its murals of woodland scenes and its slippery marble floor. Friedemann paused again at the base of the marble stairway, which rose in a gentle curve. Sunlight filtered through the skylight and filled the stairwell with an evanescent mist. He tried to impress the scene upon his memory.

"May I carry your box, Herr Bach?"

"No, thank you, that won't be necessary." He wouldn't allow a servant to carry Sara's gift. Friedemann wished, however, that the butler would have the discernment to ask to carry his walking stick, to allow him to hold the handrail unencumbered.

"Might I take your walking stick?"

"Thank you," Friedemann said graciously, as if he were doing the servant a favor.

He began the slow journey upward. Large paintings, family portraits, hung in the stairwell. Grim-faced Jews, rendered larger than life, stared down at him. He'd come to hate these portraits. None of the ancestors resembled Sara. Because of the sun pouring through the skylight, the stairwell was hot. Friedemann felt beads of moisture forming at the back of his neck. His legs hurt. His heart raced. He was panting. He stopped to gulp in air and quite literally catch his breath. The butler stopped with him.

To occupy his mind with higher concerns while he steadied himself, Friedemann mentally reviewed the other musical compositions in the box. Sara would remunerate him handsomely for these, and he would make himself appear to accept her generosity only reluctantly. They had played this game of *politesse* on many occasions. Sara collected the works of the Bach family, almost exclusively instrumental music. They hadn't needed to discuss the reasons for her preference for instrumental rather than Christian sacred vocal music.

Today, as would be considered customary before such a momentous change in her life, he also expected to receive an honorarium for his years of faithful service. Friedemann wished he could refuse Sara's money. Alas, he could not. His debts beset him. When he died, God alone knew how his wife and his daughter, Friederica, would survive. The girl had hopelessly shamed her parents, scandalized their neighbors, and displeased the Lord by giving birth to a bastard son. The boy, Friedemann's only grandchild, was almost three years old. What would become of him? For Friederica and the child, hell might well await, the righteous judgment of the Lord.

*Not here*, Friedemann reminded himself. This was not the place to brood on the despair of his home life.

Instead, the box. It included a beautifully prepared copy of his father's *Well-Tempered Clavier I*. This would bring Sara pleasure. He allowed himself to imagine her reaction . . . her smile when she realized what it was, her gratitude toward him, her enthusiasm when she sat down to play it. Also included was a copy of Friedemann's own concerto for flute, strings, and continuo. Her future husband would take the flute part, while Sara played continuo on the harpsichord.

And finally, he'd included the score of a cantata that his father had composed for *Exaudi*. This cantata had been performed in Halle, under Friedemann's direction, before the local Philistines made Friedemann's professional position there untenable.

On the face of it, the *Exaudi* cantata was acutely inappropriate for Sara's library. The text's condemnations of the Jews went far beyond his father's settings of the Passion narrative. Murderous violence against Jews was all too frequent in German-speaking lands, hostilities enflamed even by pastors, especially at Easter. Not that this brutality had ever disturbed Friedemann earlier in his life. Knowing Sara, coming to love Sara . . . this had brought him a new perspective.

He couldn't leave the cantata to be found by his wife upon his death, sold to the highest bidder and possibly exploited. Nor could he see himself destroying both his father's composing score and the original separate performing parts for the musicians, thereby expunging all trace of this music's very existence—he wouldn't do that to the work of the great master.

Months ago he did do away with the performing parts by throwing them into the fireplace in his home. He had decided to save the composing score as the only remnant of the cantata, and today he would give the composing score to Sara. He trusted she would conceal and protect it because it was the work of Johann Sebastian Bach. He also trusted that—if not immediately, then by and by—she'd feel honored to be the cantata's guardian. During their hour together today, he would explain his reasoning to her. He hadn't yet formulated precisely what he would say. It was an awful task, to risk causing her pain, but this once, he must.

He resumed the journey up the stairs, the servant keeping pace beside him. In a certain way of thinking, he concluded as he gripped the handrail while hoping to give the impression that he merely touched it lightly, this cantata was the greatest gift he could give Sara. The giving of this gift reflected his infinite respect and admiration for her: *she* was the one he had chosen to safeguard this baleful masterpiece by Johann Sebastian Bach. Who better to entrust with the responsibility than his Jewish protégée?

He, Wilhelm Friedemann Bach, had never been disturbed by the fact that Sara Itzig was a Jew. They'd never even mentioned it, all these years. Whenever their lesson times were adjusted due to her family's peculiar holiday celebrations, they'd tacitly ignored the reason. Her musical gifts ennobled her, and therefore ennobled him as her teacher, no matter what her background. The Lord surely would not forsake her.

The top of the staircase was within sight. Six steps remained. The sunlight became oppressive. His head and shoulders swayed. Dizziness overcame him. He was losing his balance. He was about to fall backward down the stairs. He clutched at the handrail to stop himself from falling, but he didn't have the strength.

The servant grasped his arm and placed a strong hand upon his back. "Allow me, Herr Bach," the servant said with utmost deference.

Thus entwined, Friedemann's walking stick safely stowed under the butler's arm, they took the final steps. Together they crossed the landing to the antechamber. Friedemann regained his equilibrium. The antechamber was shadowed and cool, and Friedemann felt himself revive. They reached the entry to the music room.

She was playing the harpsichord. It was one of the fugues he had composed for her. She performed it to perfection, elucidating every subtlety.

Taking his walking stick, he shook off the servant's support. He would never enter her music room on the arm of a servant. He took a long breath and summoned up his remaining strength to face her. He stood with his shoulders back and made his walking stick into an affectation, rather than the necessity it was.

The servant knocked on the door. The music ceased.

"*Entrez.*" Her voice, exquisite to him, bid him forward. The servant opened the door.

She stood beside the harpsichord, waiting for him. She wore a low-cut gauzy dress, suitable for summer, a silken shawl draped around her shoulders. Her hair was pulled back and swept up. Some might label her features less than perfect, in fact might label her features *Jewish*, but she would always be his gorgeous, precious beloved.

He stepped into the room as the servant closed the door behind him. He stopped approximately eight paces from her, as he'd planned, and said the words he'd prepared. "My dear student, I have brought my wedding gift to you, a *Cantilena nuptiarum* that I have written to celebrate your past and your future."

Sara listened to him with a smile at the edges of her lips. She understood the game of courtesy that he played.

"Do not open the box until later, for it contains other compositions in addition to my wedding gift. I wish you to discover and study these compositions one by one, with your fiancé. My gift is for him, also. Indeed, the box includes one of my own compositions, a concerto for flute, strings, and keyboard continuo, for you and your future husband to play together."

Friedemann could not bring himself to tell her about the *Exaudi* cantata now. He didn't want to upset her. He'd tell her toward the end of their visit.

With a touching formality, she replied, "Thank you, my esteemed teacher. I shall always be grateful for your generosity, your insight, and the sense of discipline that you have instilled in me. Each time I perform for my family and friends, and each time I practice, I shall think of you and hope that I meet the high standards you have set for me."

She walked forward and accepted the presentation box. And then, utterly and completely unexpectedly, she leaned forward and kissed him on the cheek.

As if nothing noteworthy had occurred, she turned away and said, "Monsieur Bach, sit down, please, for coffee."

He followed her instruction, even as he continued to feel her kiss.

The silver coffee service was already arrayed on the table, the same thin-legged table where they'd taken refreshment twice each week for so many years, years that nonetheless felt like the merest instant of time. The long windows were open to the cooling breeze. For once, the governess was nowhere to be seen. He pulled out a chair. Keeping one hand on the chair and one on his walking stick, he sat down with care, praying his knees wouldn't lock in pain. He leaned the stick against the wall.

She placed his presentation box on the desk in the corner, and she joined him. She poured the coffee into the dainty cups. They looked at each other, she still with a smile at the edges of her lips, as if secrets were passing between them. How gracious she'd become. She displayed the height of good manners. Of deferential courtesy.

She was twenty-two, and she conducted herself with the refinement of her position.

Today he did not feel at ease amid such courtesies. What little nothings could they discuss? Every topic was simultaneously fraught and frivolous. Finally he said, "Even when you are married, you must practice every day. Every single day."

"I will," she responded. "I promise. Would you like some cake?"

*I will. I promise. Would you like some cake?* Each word was burdened. This was the last time she'd pour him coffee, the last time she'd offer him cake.

Samuel Salomon Levy. Friedemann assumed the marriage had been arranged, as marriages typically were among the wealthy. Samuel Salomon Levy seemed like a nice enough young man, although not nearly good enough for her. A few weeks ago, during one of Friedemann's visits, Samuel Salomon Levy had joined Sara to play a flute and harpsichord sonata by Johann Joachim Quantz. A pleasant diversion, Quantz, but not suitable for Sara's prodigious gifts.

Friedemann ate the cake she served him, although his mouth was dry. He had to do something, after all, to fill the charged emptiness around them. When she asked to refill his coffee cup, he could not refuse. He tried to impress onto his memory every detail of this room. Every detail of her face.

"When Monsieur Levy and I return from our wedding tour, we will perform for you the concerto you have given us today."

"I shall look forward to it." He was jarred by a horrifying vision of her burning in hell, her skin melting from her face until only the bones remained.

"Are you quite well, Monsieur Bach?"

The vision was too strong, too terrifying, for him to respond.

"Are you composing in your mind?"

He shook his head sharply, breaking the image. "Yes. Precisely." He forced himself to smile. "How well you know me."

"I like to think that I know you," she said with an expression of such gentle indulgence that he wanted to reach across the table and take her hands.

Of course he didn't. To approach her in this way would be inappropriate. An unforgiveable breach.

He must tell her about the *Exaudi* cantata in the box. He inhaled, to prepare himself to begin. I have brought you a hateful work that was composed by my father. I give this work to you, to guard. Because I trust you. Because I love you.

He could not bring himself to speak.

Too soon, the ormolu clock chimed the hour. The time had come for him to depart.

Did she know that they would never see each other again?

He rose. "The clock tells me that I must be leaving."

"No, no, Monsieur Bach. Please, sit down."

But she, too, rose. "I'll play for you." She rubbed her hands together to warm her fingers. "I've prepared a piece especially. I've been practicing all afternoon."

"Not today, Mademoiselle. I have another appointment."

He did not have another appointment.

"Monsieur Levy will be here soon. He'd like to see you."

"Most kind. Please do give him my regrets. He is—" What precisely was Samuel Salomon Levy? "He is an *honorable* man. I'm certain you will be happy with him."

Her cheeks reddened. "Do you think so?" She treated him to a shy smile.

Could it be that she loved Monsieur Levy? Friedemann loved Sara enough to hope that she did. "I *know* you will be happy with him. And share with him a long and fruitful marriage."

Please, don't go forward with this, he told her within himself. Don't imprison yourself with marriage and a dozen children. Do not choose family over music. Over me. I beg you.

He said, "I comprehended the unity of your spirits the moment I heard the two of you perform together."

"Thank you, Monsieur Bach. Thank you so very much." She gazed at him with a vulnerability that caught him by surprise. "Your opinion means more to me than, well, than anyone's."

He sensed she needed to be consoled. He wanted to press his hands upon her shoulders to reassure her as she faced her future. But he didn't dare. Instead he replied, "Your kind and generous words have touched my heart."

"I'll call for the carriage to take you to your next appointment."

She must have intuited his physical weakness.

"No need, the walk will do me good." He was going home—he was too weak even for the tavern—and he wouldn't allow her coachman to see where he lived. Sara might question the coachman afterward and learn details of his private life that he'd steadfastly concealed from her. And if Friederica came outside to show the coach to the eager, curious child, whose behavior betrayed no awareness of the curse of its birth . . . the shame was too dreadful to contemplate. "I'm not so elderly that I must trouble your coachman!" he said with a good humor that sounded, to him at least, sincere.

"As you wish." From the desk, she retrieved a leather pouch. She took his hand. She turned his hand palm upward. She placed the pouch upon his palm. "For you, my teacher, in gratitude for all you have given me, these many years."

He didn't need to open the pouch to know what was within. The weight alone told him. Far more than the honorarium for his years of loyal service and the generous fee he'd expected for the compositions. She folded his fingers around the pouch and pressed their hands together. He could not speak, for the pressure in his throat.

"Goodbye, my dearest," he finally managed, disengaging their hands and bowing to her.

With that, he retrieved his walking stick and left her, closing the door behind him.

━━━━

Sara stared at the door. She fought an urge to follow him, to pull him back and resume their traditional places: she at the harpsichord, he standing behind her, Madame Goldberg watching from her chair at the window.

The urge, Sara knew, was a reflection of this moment in her life, one part of her wanting to return to her youth, to the blissful, unencumbered hours of practicing the harpsichord and playing for her teacher, the other part looking forward to marriage and to a home of her own, and the responsibilities these required. She was determined to go forward. *To every thing there is a season*, as she knew from the Bible.

Sara turned to check the time—Samuel would arrive at any moment—and she saw the presentation box with its white satin ribbons upon the desk. Impetuously, she decided not to wait for Samuel. She went to the desk and untied the ribbons. She opened the box.

The composition in honor of her marriage was first. The title read, *Herz, mein Herz, sei ruhig*. "Heart, my heart, be at peace."

When she was with Samuel, her heart was, indeed, at peace. Her teacher's understanding moved her. She leafed through the composition, hearing it in her mind. She knew this music. She'd played a solo keyboard version of it in her lessons. For her wedding, Monsieur Bach had transformed it into a vocal piece. He'd combined her past and her future into one gift. The poem was uncredited, so perhaps her teacher himself had written it. It was a melancholy meditation on the travails of life from beginning to end. Odd fare, for a wedding.

She wasn't surprised that her teacher would do something so unconventional. Wilhelm Friedemann Bach was a brilliant and extraordinary man. He'd tried to hide from her his difficult circumstances, but more than once, secretly, she'd sent servants to follow him home and to question the local shopkeepers, as well as the tavern owners. She knew how things stood with Monsieur Bach. She also knew his pride. She tried to help him, but she would never allow her help to embarrass him.

*Heart, my heart, be at peace.* She reviewed the practicalities of performance. The song could be presented at the supper after the marriage ceremony. Perhaps she herself should play the keyboard accompaniment. No, she mustn't add another element of strain to the questions of dress, food, and table arrangements. Instead, two of her siblings could perform the piece. She would discuss this idea with Samuel.

Sara and Samuel considered themselves fortunate: their marriage had been arranged, in the tradition of their community, but they'd grown to love each other. They enjoyed many mutual interests, as their parents had known when they made the choice. Like Sara, Samuel had been well educated by tutors. Together they'd vowed never to convert to Christianity. They embraced the beliefs of the Haskalah movement, championed by the philosopher Moses Mendelssohn, who urged Jews to adapt to the customs of the countries in which they'd settled while keeping the faith of their forebears. Sara and Samuel practiced charity, supporting the *Freischule,* the Free School, which provided education for the poor. They shared a passion for the music of Bach, Haydn, and Mozart. Because Samuel was a talented musician himself, he understood the joy and fulfillment that music brought to Sara.

She allowed herself to daydream, imagining the children they would have together. She had no desire for the fifteen siblings of her own family, with their constant squabbling. Five or six would be the perfect number. She saw her children gathered around her, pulling on her dress. She visualized them in this very room. The eldest, a girl, about ten, played the harpsichord for Sara's parents, while Sara held the youngest, a baby boy, against her shoulder and gently rubbed his back to soothe him. The in-betweens, as she thought of them, played on the floor with their toy soldiers or with their dolls. *Soon this will be my life.* How she yearned for it.

Putting aside the wedding composition, she returned to the box and came upon a timeworn manuscript of *The Well-Tempered Clavier I*—this was marvelous and rare. Virtually everywhere in Berlin except in this house, Johann Sebastian Bach's musical style was considered passé. Sara's parents, however, had intense admiration for his work, and Sara and her siblings had grown up with it. Sara especially felt drawn to this music, to the complex harmonies and to the intricacies of the counterpoint.

Next, she found her teacher's promised concerto for flute, strings, and keyboard continuo. She and Samuel would begin work on it immediately, and she'd recruit several of her brothers to take up the string parts.

At the bottom of the box, Sara found a composition in its original wrapper. She read the title. *Dominica Exaudi: Concerto Wir das Joch nicht tragen können.* She saw Johann Sebastian Bach's signature. She leafed through the piece. His handwriting wasn't easily legible, but from what she could parse out . . .

Disappointment and revulsion grew within her. She knew Bach's church cantatas were Christian works, and that on religious beliefs and practices Christians didn't agree with Jews, but she couldn't have imagined that Bach's cantatas could be *hateful* toward Jews and show *contempt* for Jews—not the work of the revered master.

Although her parents had tried to shelter her from anti-Jewish hostility, she was aware it existed. Her brothers told her about the wider world. She knew that Jews were not granted citizenship in Prussia, and that certain professions were closed to them. She was familiar with the oppressive regulations governing every aspect of life for the Jews of Berlin. Aware, too, of the recurring outbreaks of violence against Jews. These injustices were part of the fabric of daily life. At least she'd never felt personally threatened.

Now she confronted something she'd known all along, but never focused on: because of her father's many services to the king, the monarch had granted her father and his family special privileges and protections. These had shielded her.

A knock at the door.

She slipped the cantata into the top drawer of the desk. *"Entrez,"* she called.

The door opened. Samuel. Her *bashert.* Her soul mate. She tried to put her concerns aside.

*"Ma chérie,"* Samuel said.

How handsome he was. He forever surprised her, merely by his presence. Thick black hair. Brown eyes. He strode across the music room and wrapped her in a hug, lifting her off her feet. She wrapped her arms around his neck and kissed him once, twice, three times across his cheeks. His freshly shaven skin felt soft against her lips.

"I've brought a drawing of our library stamp," he said.

They'd been working on the stamp together, seeking to combine their initials with elegance and grace. The library stamp represented their future . . . the children they would have, and the children of their children, their library of books and music passing from generation to generation.

Samuel took out the drawing the artist had done based on their sketches. "You see, our initials close together, almost merged but not completely."

"Yes." The stamp was precisely what they'd envisioned. But her thoughts were elsewhere.

"You seem worried, my dear."

"No."

"Truly?"

Already he could read her moods. "I must show you what Monsieur Bach has given me today." She led him to the desk. "First, an unusual composition for our wedding."

He read the title. "*Heart, my heart, be at peace* . . . that's exactly how I feel about you."

She felt herself blushing, so she turned quickly to the next piece. "Also this."

"*The Well-Tempered Clavier, Book One*. Extraordinary."

"Yes."

"As soon as the stamp is prepared, we'll officially begin our library with this masterpiece." When she didn't reply, he said, "What's disturbing you, my dearest?"

Their library stamp would never adorn the cantata for *Exaudi*.

"What is it?"

"Monsieur Bach brought another composition. A church cantata by his father."

She gave him the autograph. He studied it. His expression turned hard.

"Have you ever seen such—I don't even know what to call it."

"Yes, I'm sorry to say, I have seen such things."

"Why did he bring this to me?" She felt as if their years together had been a lie. "Is he punishing me for being myself?"

"Punishing you?" Samuel reflected. "I don't think he wants to punish you."

"What then?"

"He admires you. Loves you, even. I've seen how he looks at you—not in a lewd way. With respect. He's ill. He must see the end of his life at hand. What would happen to this music, if you didn't have it? Who could he give it to?"

Sara didn't respond, remembering her many conversations with her teacher. Even when she was young, he'd spoken to her as if she were an adult and an equal. During their lessons, he'd paid her compliments only after she'd earned them. His praise was always genuine.

"How would we feel if he *hadn't* given it to you? If it were performed after his death and were to provide an angry preacher a powerful way to breed contempt and possibly even incite violence?"

"If that's what he was thinking, why didn't he tell me?"

"He must not have known the words to explain, or couldn't bring himself to say the words. Because he cares for you."

Wilhelm Friedemann Bach. Her teacher. She felt bound to him in trust and affection. Yet so much had remained unspoken between them. The realization was heartbreaking.

"He's a good man," Samuel said.

Yes, Sara thought. Her teacher *was* a good man.

She leaned her head against Samuel's shoulder, and he embraced her.

## Chapter 10

At 4:15 on Sunday morning, Dan sat at the kitchen table, sipping coffee. As usual, he'd woken up at 4:00, feeling alert. If he lay in bed, the demons came back, the terrible memories, so he got up, made coffee, and read or worked downstairs, trying not to disturb Becky.

The kitchen was *cheerful*. At least that was the word Julie had used to describe it. Yellow walls, white cabinets, yellow-and-white checked curtains, Becky's artwork (he tried to keep it updated) covering the refrigerator. He'd never particularly noticed the décor until he began to spend the early mornings here. He tried to convince himself that the room was indeed cheerful, and that's how he should feel as he sat here, but each day *cheerful* turned into dismal once more.

This morning, accompanied by his laptop computer and a variety of German dictionaries and reference works, he was preparing a translation of the libretto from the cantata that Susanna Kessler had brought him. He'd grasped the gist of it in his office, but now he needed to do the hard slog of getting every detail correct. The process was made more difficult because the meaning of certain German words had evolved over the centuries, and he needed to reconstruct the meaning of the words in Bach's day. For the biblical references, he kept in mind that Bach and his contemporaries had used Bibles that retained Martin Luther's sixteenth-century wording but updated its spellings. Over the years, he'd been asked to vet countless academic articles that made the basic mistake of using the modern, heavily revised version of the Luther Bible that was published in 1984 (or worse, using a modern Bible in English), rendering many scholarly conclusions incorrect.

As part of his research, he also wanted to find out where the libretto came from, and if possible, confirm that it had existed in the eighteenth century and was available for Bach to use.

So, the first line, *Wir das Joch nicht tragen können*, an allusion to Acts 15:10.

For a quick start, he put the line, surrounded by quotation marks, into Google.

Nothing.

Next line. *Doch nicht auf der Halse wollen*. Also an allusion to Acts 15:10.

He tried this exact phrase in Google, too. No results. He repeated the process through the first aria. When he reached the first recitative, he decided that the time had come for more coffee.

A few years ago, for their anniversary, Julie had treated them to a technologically advanced espresso maker that ground coffee beans, made coffee, and heated milk. It was an extravagance he enjoyed every day. The grinding of the beans was loud but had never yet awakened Becky. The aroma was fantastic, like a pure nectar of coffee, and he inhaled it greedily.

Fortified with his second cup, he returned to the kitchen table.

He considered the German text for the first recitative phrase in the cantata, *So ist's auch unsere Schuld, daß wir sie nicht todschlagen.* "We are at fault for not striking them dead."

Who had written this bit of inflammatory rhetoric? Hope triumphing over experience once again, he typed, *So ist's auch unsere Schuld,* surrounded by quotation marks, into Google.

A handful of hits came up. According to Google, at least, the phrase appeared in Martin Luther's infamous 1543 treatise, *On the Jews and Their Lies.*

Was this possible? Dan didn't believe it. He checked the *Weimarer Ausgabe,* the standard scholarly edition of Luther's works, available digitized online. *On the Jews and Their Lies* was printed within volume 53 of the collection. He skimmed through Luther's appalling screed. Although some branches of Lutheranism had repudiated this work, his own branch, the Wisconsin Evangelical Lutheran Synod, had not done so, as far as Dan knew.

And there it was, at lines 8–12 on page 522: *So ist's auch unsere Schuld, daß wir . . . sie nicht todschlagen.* "We are at fault for . . . not striking them dead."

The cantata's second recitative read, *Ihre Synagogen mit Feuer anstecke und, was nicht verbrennen will, mit Erden überhäufe.* "Burn their synagogues and bury anything that doesn't burn."

This he found on page 523, at lines 1–3.

---

Later that day, Dan sat in his Granville church with Becky and waited for the service to begin. She should have been downstairs attending Sunday school, but after Julie's death, Becky had asked to stay at the service with him, and he allowed it. She was quiet. She followed along, sang the hymns, and took a nap when she was bored.

"Blessed are they that gather in the name of the Lord," Pastor Mansholt intoned from the entryway, before the introit. Dan and

Becky stood. "We offer our prayer to God . . ." Pastor Mansholt pro-
cessed past them in his robes of white, his face serene.

This church was smaller and simpler in design than the Church
of the Holy Shepherd in New York. No soaring Gothic columns here,
no pipe organ or stained glass, merely rows of plain, hard pews, an
electronic organ, and clear, leaded glass.

"The Lord be with you," the pastor chanted.

"And also with you," the rest of the congregation responded.

Dan was shaken by his Luther discovery of early this morning.
As the service followed its usual course, with its prayers and hymns,
Dan's thoughts wandered to the cantata and to Susanna Kessler. She
was a Jew. She didn't believe in Jesus. He'd always been taught that,
therefore, according to the historical doctrines of his church, she was
going to hell. Not a figurative or metaphorical hell, but an actual,
burning, punishing hell. *The unbelieving shall have their part in the lake
which burneth with fire*, according to Revelation 21:8.

Dan wasn't sure how many people in his church still accepted this
as true. He did suspect, however, that in addition to entrenched prejudice, this up-to-then-traditional teaching had contributed during the
Nazi era to the indifference that many otherwise upstanding European Christians had felt toward the rounding up of Jews. If those
millions of Jews who hadn't converted to Christianity were going to
hell anyway, what was the point of risking one's own life to fight for
their survival on earth? Alas, not many voices were raised to try to
protect those Jews who had converted, either.

Dan and Becky joined the congregation in standing to sing the
Lutheran versification of the Nicene Creed. *We all believe in one True
God* . . .

Dan had grown up in a small town in Wisconsin, in a family that
belonged to the most conservative of the larger Lutheran denomina-
tions in America. His father worked at a hardware store that served
the farmers in the surrounding area, and he rose to be store manager.

His mother took care of the children at home and volunteered at church, the center of their lives. To an outsider, the religious beliefs Dan grew up with might appear oppressive, but for an insider, the church put everything into a God-given slot and presented a world that made sense.

This was also a narrow world, which saw life in terms of black and white, either/or. With us or against us. *Jew them down, cheap as a Jew*—these were commonly used phrases. Jews, Dan's childhood pastor explained to his congregation each year at Easter, had murdered our Lord and Savior, and ever since, Jews had continued to bring down condemnation on themselves by refusing to accept Jesus as the Messiah.

Was this still preached? Dan hadn't heard Pastor Mansholt express this view, and he didn't know what was said in Protestant churches elsewhere. Presumably in Catholic churches the teachings had changed after the Second Vatican Council's *Nostra Aetate* in 1965, but of course Protestant churches by definition didn't look to the Vatican for guidance.

Dan couldn't recall even meeting a Jew until he went to graduate school at Yale. Now he had many Jewish friends and colleagues. He was ashamed to realize, though, that before his discovery this morning—of Luther's hatred of Jews placed into a Bach cantata—the fate that his conservative religion had in store for Jews had been only abstract to him. He'd heard the doctrines repeated in church and in his parochial schools, but he hadn't reflected on their meaning.

He supposed that like many of his fellow parishioners, he'd cherry-picked his religion, choosing which beliefs and practices to take seriously and ignoring the rest. Meeting Susanna Kessler also seemed somehow to make the fate of Jews concrete and particular—this singular individual, who'd approached him in a church basement and spent an afternoon in his office, *she* was the one who'd supposedly be burning in hell, *she* was the one who would have been shot, gassed, or starved to death if she'd been in Europe during World War II.

Pastor Mansholt went to the lectern. Becky knew what this meant, and making a pillow with her hands, she rested her head against Dan's arm. "Brothers and sisters in Christ, as the Lord tells us in Psalm 139, 'For you created my inmost being . . .'"

Dan hated the New International Version of the Bible, which had taken all the poetry out of the text. In his mind, he heard the King James Version:

*For thou hast possessed my reins:*
*Thou hast covered me in my mother's womb.*
*I will praise thee, for I am fearfully and wonderfully made.*

Becky closed her eyes.

"'You knit me together in my mother's womb. I praise you because I am fearfully and wonderfully made,'" the pastor continued with the NIV. "My dear friends, could our Lord be any clearer in the value He places on life, especially on the lives of the helpless unborn?"

The word *unborn* caught Dan's attention, and he concentrated on what the minister was telling them—instructing them, because a sermon was supposed to expound upon the true Word of the Lord.

"A Holocaust taking place in this country, a Holocaust of the unborn," Pastor Mansholt said. "The Lord requires us to make our communities our front line as we fight the sacred battle for life . . ."

Dan thought: Who in God's name was Pastor Mansholt to speak of a Holocaust, and to proclaim what the Lord wanted concerning the unborn? If Julie had heeded science instead of Pastor Mansholt's religion, she'd be here with him and Becky today. She'd be alive. Wouldn't the Lord have wanted that?

Julie had received a diagnosis of breast cancer when she was twenty-five, during the fourth year of their marriage, just when they were thinking about having children. She had surgery and chemotherapy and went into remission. The experts advised them not to have children. After five years had passed cancer-free, however, Julie wanted a baby. Dan did, too. So they took a risk—or rather, they put their faith in God. They were blessed with Becky. Julie's cancer did not return.

When Becky was five and still the cancer did not return, Julie wanted another child. Again her doctor said no, the rush of hormones could bring the cancer back. You have a wonderful daughter. Don't tempt chance, the doctor said.

It's not chance, Julie said. We're in God's hands.

*God's hands.* She convinced Dan. Her confidence convinced him. She became pregnant the first month—a sure sign of God's love and protection, she said. Dan couldn't disagree. But at three months, she discovered a lump under her left arm and another in her left breast.

A series of excellent physicians at the University of Pennsylvania Medical Center discussed with them the issues of chemotherapy during pregnancy. Some therapeutic agents appeared not to harm the fetus, one physician said. Consider having an abortion, another said, ever so gently. Then you can do the full course of chemotherapy, with stronger medications.

God will provide, Julie said. She wouldn't consider an abortion. She would never choose between herself and the new life within her. Dan begged her to have an abortion. God would understand. Just this once. The life of the mother: that's always the exception. The *legal* exception, Julie said. Not God's exception. Dan fought with her, the worst fights they'd ever had: do the abortion, take the full course of therapy with the stronger medications, save your life. So Becky will have a mother. So we can grow old together. What about your responsibility to Becky and me? Doesn't God value that?

God would never condone abortion, she said.

How do you know what God would or wouldn't condone? he asked. How can any of us truly know God's will?

We have proof, she said: God has let us conceive this child.

Dan couldn't force her. So Dan, too, put his faith in God. She took the chemotherapy that was supposed to be well tolerated during pregnancy. Groups formed here at the church to pray for her.

Pastor Mansholt continued from the pulpit, "We cannot compromise. Compromise is the temptation of the Devil."

By the time she'd carried the baby to eight months, Julie was dying. She was kept alive by technology, only to serve the fetus within her. Seeing the baby in distress, the doctors opted for a caesarean three weeks early.

Their son weighed five pounds, nine ounces, and was perfect in every way except that his heart had stopped beating. The Lord had taken him home, as the saying went. Who are we to question the ways of the Lord? They named him Martin, after Julie's father. Pastor Mansholt came to the hospital and prayed over Martin's body. *Suffer the little children to come unto me.*

Dan remembered holding his newborn son. He felt again the small, perfect body resting upon his arm, pressed against his chest. Martin's soft head, with its blond fuzz, nestled in the palm of his hand. The gray-blue eyes, frozen open. The eyelashes, full and pale. The tiny, perfect feet. Dan sensed that Martin had been alive moments before. His skin was still warm. At that moment, Dan decided that Julie was right not to have aborted him. And yet . . . Dan wanted it both ways, wanted it all ways, wanted it *his* way—to have his son and his wife, both.

He'd been left with neither.

I'm sorry, the pediatrician said after Martin died. The doctor was crying. The *doctor*, crying.

We tried our best, said Julie's oncologist. Our very best. He shook his head and shuffled out of the hospital room.

One week after their son died, Julie died. Fifteen months ago. Like yesterday. *It was God's will*—these words of comfort were offered to him again and again by family and friends. God had willed these terrible events. Was this supposed to make him feel better? Was it meant to give him a consoling perception of order in the midst of apparent chaos?

Dan was finding no consolation in the notion of God's will. During the fraught days after Martin and Julie died, his fellow parishioners— his friends—seemed to be jumping through hoops as they struggled to find meaning in their deaths. Dan came to wonder if maybe there was no meaning.

He met several times with a pastoral counselor. She told him that he was entitled to feel angry at God, but time would bring him to understanding and acceptance. He must bow before the will of God.

This reasoning seemed so facile that Dan stopped the sessions. He began to question whether God had a plan for his life, and to wonder whether all existence was in fact, as secularists maintained, nothing but a series of random events.

Today, looking at the candles on the altar, at the minister preaching his fanatical convictions, Dan thought, if there really were a God looking after them, Julie would at least have died believing her son had survived. Martin would have lived one week, until Julie died. She wouldn't have had to torment herself over whether parents can presume God's salvation of children who die before baptism. She would have thought the sacrifice of her own life was worthwhile, to leave her child behind. This one act of mercy, God would not give: that Julie, His faithful servant, would die before her infant son. Seeing Martin dead . . . from that moment, she'd looked at everyone, even Becky, even Dan, with a vacancy in her eyes. Dan held her, he talked to her, but she was absent.

"We must rescue this nation from the terrible sin of murder," Mansholt thundered on.

Right then and there on this October morning, in church no less, the edifice of faith that Dan had been raised with, that he'd remained loyal to throughout his adulthood, that had guided his life, collapsed around him. The clarity of his reverse epiphany—*there is no God*—left him shattered. He'd been a fool, all these years, coming here, praying, singing hymns, serving on church committees with their endless, often futile discussions. He felt an inverse of the faith message in the hymn "Amazing Grace": for years, he'd been blind, but now he could see.

The minister prepared for communion. He chanted, "The Lord be with you." The congregation responded, "And with your spirit." The minister then said the words of consecration over the bread and wine, by which they were transformed into a sacramental union where the body and the blood of Christ are *truly and substantially present in, with, and under* the forms of the communion elements. Or so the minister reminded the congregants.

Dan felt ill.

The minister said, "The gifts of God for the people of God."

Around him, Dan's friends stood, walked toward the altar, and waited in line.

Dan wouldn't, couldn't, take communion. A cataclysm had taken place within him. As he looked around, however, everything outside himself appeared normal. Friends nodded, some with a smile as they passed and saw Becky asleep, cradled against his arm. They didn't expect him to disturb her by getting up for communion, not after all she'd been through.

What were these people doing here, Dan wondered. Was Karl Marx right, and religion nothing but an opiate? Or was it just a habit: from childhood, you've attended church, so you keep going as an adult whether you believe in the teachings or not. Whether you even pay attention to the teachings. And then you have your children do it because you did it. If Dan took a poll, how many of those standing in line for communion would say that they truly believed that the bread and wine had also become the actual physical body and blood of Christ, as their Lutheranism taught?

Dan felt as if he'd been living in a trance. For fifteen months, since Julie and Martin died, he'd been struggling to abide within a lifelong frame of reference. Today the framework had disintegrated. Why this particular day? The accumulation of Pastor Mansholt's convictions, Luther's writings, Susanna Kessler and her Bach cantata, Julie and Martin . . . today these reached a breaking point for the certainties of his life.

Dan thought back to Julie's funeral, held here fifteen months ago, ten days after Martin's. Pastor Mansholt had said, our Julie is happy now. Her pain has ceased. Her soul is at peace.

Yes, her physical pain had ceased, that much was true.

For the funeral, Julie's childhood friend George Graff had traveled from Wisconsin to sing the bass aria "Mache dich, mein Herze, rein" from Bach's *St. Matthew Passion*.

The aria's music and text, a metaphor for the Sacrament of Communion, began to run through Dan's mind . . . *Mache dich, mein Herze, rein, Ich will Jesum selbst begraben. Denn er soll nunmehr in mir.* "Make yourself pure, my heart, I wish to bury Jesus himself within me." The aria consumed him with longing for Julie, and for the faith that had abandoned him.

*Mache dich, mein Herze, rein* . . . The oboe lines, with their parallelisms and insistent appoggiaturas, expressed a desolate yearning, but also a comfort. After Julie died, Dan had listened to the aria over and over at home at night after Becky had fallen asleep. He had buried himself in the music just as the singer begged that Jesus be buried within his heart.

The aria continued to sweep through him, as it had at Julie's burial, her body in its box lowered into the earth, beside Martin's grave, leaving Dan bereft. *Make yourself pure, my heart, I wish to bury Jesus himself within me* . . .

Once, Dan had believed that the transcendence of Bach's music proved the objective truth of Bach's faith, which was also Dan's faith. Faith had drawn Dan to Bach, and Bach had drawn Dan to faith, a perfect circle.

He still felt the aria's spiritual consolation, even though he'd lost its doctrinal meaning.

When the service was finally over, Dan woke Becky. He helped her to her feet. As always after a nap, she was groggy, clinging to his jacket with one hand, rubbing her eyes with the other. They waited their turn to join the procession out of the church.

Dan shook hands with Pastor Mansholt as if everything were the same as when he'd entered the sanctuary an hour or so before. With a mock bow, the pastor shook hands with Becky. Awake now, she giggled and curtsied. So sweet, she was. Again the music was in his mind, filling him, *Mache dich, mein Herze, rein* . . . assailing him with the tragedy of his and Julie's life together. He no longer understood his place within the scheme of things.

He and Becky walked into the autumn sunshine, into a grove of sugar maples exploding in red and orange, hurting his eyes. Dan was dazed. He didn't know where to go next. He couldn't summon the motivation to step forward.

"Daddy," Becky said, pulling on his hand to get his attention. "Wake up, Daddy." She tugged at him. "I'm hungry. Let's have lunch."

# Chapter 11

On Sunday afternoon, the day after Susanna received her divorce decree in the mail, she and her friend Miriam Krieger reclined on Adirondack chairs in the garden of the Peabody Episcopal Seminary in Chelsea. Susanna's apartment building, a renovated Victorian mansion, was on the seminary grounds.

"Susanna, I have to ask you: Why are you living here?"

Miriam spoke bluntly to all her friends. She was a small woman, well toned from the gym, her hair cut short and turning prematurely gray. She was an attorney specializing in trusts and estates.

"I just don't get it," Miriam continued. "There's a church in your garden."

"I know. Isn't it lovely?" St. Anselm's was a Victorian Gothic chapel, a jewel in their midst.

"I have to tell you the truth: it's so . . . *Christian* here."

"Of course it's Christian. It's a *seminary close*."

"Listen to you—you've learned phrases that don't even make sense."

Most of Susanna's friends, Jewish and Christian both, were mystified when Susanna moved here. While she was apartment hunting, she'd seen an advertisement for the building in a real-estate insert in *The New York Times*. In addition to the promises of EIK and WBF, the photos showed a historic community of gracious seclusion. After being shown a string of apartments that she couldn't imagine living in because they were so much like the home she'd shared with Alan, she remembered the Victorian mansion.

From the moment she moved in, she felt more like her old self. She rarely noticed the religious aspect of the setting. For her, St. Anselm's simply added to the peaceful atmosphere. The seminary owned the entire block, and the inner garden, hidden from the street, was a park-like refuge. The tranquillity and safety were exactly what she needed after the attack. The seminary provided its faculty with accommodation in town houses that opened onto the close, and the children in the garden, the chapel bells, and the regular pattern of students going to classes created a steady rhythm to Susanna's own days.

On this sunny afternoon, families played hide-and-seek around the trees. Children chased dogs across the grass and vice versa. The sounds of laughter, barking, and mild parental admonishments drifted on the breeze.

"You haven't answered my question: Why are you living here?"

"I like it. It's a big city and a small village simultaneously." She paused, feeling she owed Miriam more. "I feel safe here."

Miriam studied her with a frown of suspicion. "No place is safe. Not forever. Not completely."

"This is the best I can do right now. Besides, I like the people." Among the dozen residents of her building, she'd become close to the gay architect who lived on the ground floor with his partner, raising the two disabled boys they'd adopted. She'd also befriended a long-married couple, both professors of church history, who lived on the second floor. Their grandchildren visited on holiday weekends, rushing up and down the stairs and piling into Susanna's apartment for hot chocolate. "I've been elected head of the building's tenants' committee." With light irony Susanna added, "So you see, I have the beginning of a power base."

"A power base is good, I do understand that." Miriam was the director of the board at her co-op uptown. "But you're not going to convert, are you?"

"Convert to what?"

"Don't pretend to be dense. You're not going to become a Christian?"

Susanna couldn't help but laugh. "Doubtful."

"You have doubts?"

Miriam was being oddly serious today.

"No, Miriam." Susanna couldn't imagine herself practicing any religion. "It's just history and real estate, all of this."

"Okay, so what about the divorce decree? How are you feeling, now that you finally have the decree?"

"What is this, gang-up-on-Susanna day?"

"It's my job as your friend to make sure you're okay."

And Miriam *was* a good friend. She'd come to the emergency room after the attack and spoken to nurses and to Detective Lazetera when Susanna and Alan were too upset to think rationally. She'd accompanied Susanna to her therapy sessions when she was too frightened to go out of the house alone and Alan had to be at work. Susanna felt a responsibility to give Miriam an honest answer.

"Put it this way: I'm not glad I was attacked, but I *am* glad not to be married to Alan anymore." For Miriam, she tried to sound strong, even though part of her was still mourning for the life she'd once led, for the closeness she and Alan had shared, and the pleasure they'd experienced together each day. "Not after what he—" He was tortured, too, Susanna knew, because he'd told her this. Her anger toward him seemed, sometimes, ungenerous. "After what he decided he had to do."

"He was a complete jerk."

"Please don't say anything bad about him."

"I don't understand why you defend him."

Susanna knew exactly why: she'd loved him for years. They'd hoped to have a child together. Had he been *a complete jerk* the entire time? She tried to put herself into his shoes, to imagine the violation he felt. Her sympathy for him didn't go very far but even so, she didn't like her friends to criticize him. That was *her* prerogative. By judging him, they were judging her.

"I have the decree, so it's all in the past now."

"That's a healthy attitude."

"Thank you. Good of you to approve."

She could see Miriam internally debating whether to continue pressing the issue. To deflect the conversation away from herself, Susanna asked, "How are the girls?" Miriam and her husband, Ben, had two daughters, Helen and Nicole.

"Fine." Miriam stopped.

"And?"

"The fact is." Miriam stopped again. "You are not going to believe this."

Susanna sensed that Miriam was about to deliver a long and complicated story, most likely funny, and her own tension eased.

"As you know—and you'd better be saving the date—Helen will make her bat mitzvah next September. Last week, completely out of nowhere, she announced that she's going to give a speech about being a Jew who doesn't believe in God. She's calling her speech 'How to Be a Good Atheist and a Good Jew.'"

"Excellent title. I think a lot of people will be interested in that topic. *I'm* interested. The rabbi approved it?"

"He said it was perfect, thought-provoking, the height of creativity and self-knowledge."

"I have to agree, it *is* perfect, thought-provoking, et cetera."

"Don't tease."

"I'm not teasing."

"Helen's creativity and self-knowledge aren't the problem."

"So what's the problem?"

"It's Gran: she should live so long to hear the speech. What will she think? We haven't told her yet, but eventually we'll have to."

Miriam's grandmother Sofia was ninety-four, slow on her feet but mentally sharp. Somehow she'd survived the war, hidden in a neighbor's barn. She was a tough-minded woman who shrewdly examined everything and everyone.

Susanna said, "Atheism and Judaism aren't mutually exclusive, as I can attest. Sofia might be an atheist. Have you asked her?"

"She lights candles every Friday night. She covers her eyes and prays. Does that sound like an atheist?"

"She might enjoy doing it because her own mother did it, and she doesn't even think about whether it has broader meaning or not."

"I don't think so. She actually murmurs the prayers. Anyway—" Miriam's voice constricted, and she inhaled sharply. "I'm trying not to encourage Helen by discouraging her, if you see what I mean. She's stubborn and says exactly what she thinks. She can be impossible when she thinks someone is trying to cross her."

Susanna refrained from saying that Helen was much like her mother.

"Ben is livid and lets her know every day. They're barely speaking. He thinks she's being disrespectful."

"Instead of keeping it secret, Helen should talk to Sofia about the topic of the speech. Include her great-grandmother's reaction, the opinion of a survivor."

"That might work," Miriam conceded.

"They can figure it out between the two of them."

Miriam thought this through. "Okay, I'll try. Enough of that. I have another question for you: What's the situation with the house in Buffalo?"

Susanna brought Miriam up to date. Henry and Greta's apartment was finally empty, and legal matters were on track for Jenna and Diane, the upstairs renters, to buy the house.

"Find anything interesting when you cleaned out the apartment?"

Susanna stiffened. "What do you mean?" She wasn't ready to tell anyone about the manuscript, beyond the scholars who could potentially help her.

"When Gran dies—thirty or forty years from now and not a minute sooner, I wonder if we'll find anything in her apartment."

"What sort of anything?"

"Oh, I don't know." Miriam seemed to be making an effort to be nonchalant. "Letters, photos, documents. Anything. About Gran's family. Which is our family, of course. We don't know anything about her family from before the war. Her parents, her brothers and sisters. She won't talk about them. I don't even know where the family was from. Austro-Hungary, that's all she says. Do you know how big Austro-Hungary was?"

"Yes, I do know." Susanna remembered standing outside doorways when she was young, listening to conversations. *Susanna looks like her.*

"There are so many websites nowadays, where you can do research to try to find out what happened to people, but unless you have at least a few details, it's useless. There are millions of entries. Sometimes I wonder if Gran's trying to cover up some crime that her family committed. Incest or murder or an illicit love affair, God knows what. Maybe they were professional thieves. Or Gran's father, my great-grandfather, was in prison."

Once Susanna had thought such things about her own relatives, speculating that a scandal stopped Henry and Evelyn from telling her the truth. Now she believed that the simplest explanation was also the most likely: they were murdered during the war. Did the exact details matter? Yes. But Susanna had never allowed herself to search for those details. The whispered secrets of her childhood had filled her with dread.

"When Gran does answer my questions, her replies are meaningless, like *those places don't exist anymore*, or *the records were destroyed*. Once she said, 'What family are you talking about?' As if I were a fool."

"I'm sorry. Maybe Helen will be able to discover something."

"I hope so." Signaling that she didn't want to talk about this anymore, Miriam leaned back in her chair, closed her eyes, and let the sun bathe her face.

Later, after Miriam went home, Susanna put together a salad for dinner. Her kitchen was newly renovated, with granite countertops and lighting under the cabinets, but Susanna didn't feel inspired to cook. She and Alan had enjoyed experimenting with unusual recipes. Nowadays Susanna kept her meals simple.

She took the salad to the dining table in the living room. The apartment was sparsely furnished. Apart from her books, clothes, and other personal items, she'd left everything behind when she moved out of the home she'd shared with Alan. She'd started afresh, going to Room & Board to purchase the necessities. On the wall behind the dining table, she'd placed a Japanese woodblock print by Hiroshi Yoshida that she'd found at last year's print fair at the Armory. It was a scene of a boat on a lake, the air turning pink after a rainstorm. Its serene mood soothed her.

After dinner, she washed the dishes. Then she sat at her desk by the window, intending to respond to several work-related e-mails and get a head start on the coming week. She opened her laptop.

Miriam had said, *There are so many websites . . .*

A familiar sense of menace began to creep into her. She felt compelled to fight it, at least this once. She typed *Holocaust database* into
Google. Nearly a million links came up. She scrolled through the first
few pages of results. She didn't know where to begin. She returned to
the top and clicked on the first link. This was for Yad Vashem, the
Holocaust memorial center in Israel.

A page came up, with a form requesting information. A photo
on the left side of the page showed a family: a nattily dressed man in
a suit and tie, a woman wearing a stylish, pleated dress, and a child
held up between them, a girl of about four dressed in white, her arms
around both her parents, uniting them. The family was standing on
a boat. If you clicked on the photo, the website indicated, you could
learn about the people. Susanna clicked. The family was from Hun-
gary. The little girl died at Auschwitz. The caption did not include
information about the girl's parents.

Susanna returned to the previous page, with its form requesting
information. *Family name/maiden name, first name, location.*

She summoned her memories. *Family name.* When Susanna was
eleven or twelve, she'd stumbled upon a document relating to her
mother . . . she couldn't remember exactly what it was, possibly Evelyn's birth certificate. Susanna had been looking through her mother's
desk when Evelyn was at the supermarket and she was supposed to
be doing homework. The document asked for *mother's maiden name*—
that is, the maiden name of Evelyn and Henry's mother, Susanna's
grandmother. According to Susanna's recollection, the name written
into this space on the document was Altschuler.

Susanna typed it into the online form. She had nothing to write
into the space for *First Name.*

*Location.* She tried to remember a long-ago conversation, overheard.
Someone had asked Henry how he came to be fluent enough in German
to be an Army translator. He'd replied that his father was from East
Prussia and his mother was from the Sudetenland. She typed.

When she clicked on the search button, a wave of nausea swept over her, for what she might learn.

*We're sorry, but we can't find any results that fit your query.*

She pressed the BACK button, returning to the initial page with its request for information. A different photo came up on the left. A man in a suit, sitting and reading with his young son. The boy wore a velvet tunic. Susanna tried to ignore their image, even though it tugged at her. She wanted to focus on her own family, not the families of others.

She thought about the *Location* line. Maybe she needed an actual town. She googled "towns in the Sudetenland." Leitmeritz, to use the German name, Litoměřice in Czech, was a good-sized town. She returned to the Yad Vashem form and entered Leitmeritz into the *Location* field and pressed the search button.

A family name appeared: Altucher, with a list of individuals. But Abraham, Isak, and Henie Altucher of Leitmeritz were not her family. Or were they? She tried using the Czech name, Litoměřice, and the same individuals appeared.

*Back.* This time, the photo on the left showed a wide-eyed young woman of about seventeen or eighteen, her hair in braids. The young woman smiled for the photograph.

Susanna tried another town. Komotau had become Chomutov. She tried both.

Altschueler. Berta, Elsa. Not Susanna's family. Or were they?

Maybe she needed a bigger place. *Back.* The photo on the left was of a man with thick glasses, shirt sleeves rolled up, tossing a giggling baby in the air. Because of the baby, Susanna couldn't help herself: she clicked on the photo. Mother, father, baby . . . murdered at Treblinka in 1942.

Susanna tried Aussig, now called Ústí nad Labem. This seemed to be the biggest town in the region.

*Altschul, Max.* Was this the name she was looking for? Or had the family name been changed when Susanna's grandmother entered America? An hour ago, the family name had seemed like a concrete fact. Now it had turned elusive.

She tried a dozen more towns. Incredibly, she found no one by the name of Altschuler.

*Please bear in mind that the Central Database only has about half of the Jews who died in the Shoah,* the Yad Vashem website cautioned. And the website did not include survivors. Could it be that her family had survived? If so, where were they now?

*Back.* The photo on the left showed a dark-haired young woman holding a baby. Susanna clicked on it. The woman had been rounded up and shot in Poland at the age of thirty-seven. The fate of the baby was unknown.

*Back.* A boy in a sailor suit, looking into the distance with expectation. This boy was murdered when he was four years old.

Susanna experienced a kind of hypnotic trance. Click on a picture, read the story of an individual who was murdered.

A severe-looking woman with her two children, a stiffly posed boy in a suit and tie, and a girl who wore a large bow in her light-colored hair.

Susanna felt like a voyeur. But she couldn't stop. Click and read. Click and read.

A beautiful young woman with stylish, wavy hair, leaning her head on the shoulder of her handsome husband. The young woman was taken from her home in 1941 and shot.

A middle-aged couple, bourgeois, from Frankfurt. They died at Theresienstadt.

Couples dressed formally in clothes provided, perhaps, by the photographer, posing for portraits marking their engagements. Couples on their wedding day. Parents showing off their children. Children photographed alone, in close-up. Photos made to be sent to family living far away, even as far away as America.

A little girl with ribbons in her hair.

Each story was different, and yet each was the same. The search became a compulsion, these strangers replacing Susanna's own murdered family, and merging with the family in Weimar that had owned the cantata.

An elderly couple sitting side by side on straight-backed chairs.

Susanna possessed a knowledge of these individuals that they didn't have at the moment of their weddings, engagements, and dressing up their children for photographs. Susanna knew their fates.

Gradually the individuals shown in the photos began to look eerily familiar, especially the young women. With their curly hair, deep eyes, and dark eyebrows, with their expressions of hope—of looking into a future that Susanna knew they wouldn't live to experience— they began to remind her of someone.

They began to remind her of herself.

## *Chapter 12*

PALAIS LEVY
HINTER DEM NEUEN PACKHOF 3
BERLIN, PRUSSIA

*June 1796*

This afternoon, Herr Ludwig van Beethoven was to perform in a private concert at Sara Levy's musical salon.

As Sara looked around the room, she felt an intoxicating mixture of pleasure and anxiety. Family, friends, and acquaintances crowded the reception room. Activity near the entryway drew her attention.

The butler announced Jakob and Amalia Beer. Sara went to greet them. Amalia was a close friend. Jakob joined Samuel, and Amalia pulled Sara off to the side, grasping her hands.

"How lovely you look," Amalia said.

Amalia, with her porcelain skin, striking figure, and large brown eyes, was among the great beauties of Berlin. Sara knew that she herself was most definitely *not* among the great beauties of Berlin, but she appreciated Amalia's kindness.

"Thank you. You're looking lovely, too," Sara said.

"Thank you. What a crowd this is."

"Yes."

A *frisson* of expectation and excitement filled the air. Each time the butler entered the reception room to announce a newcomer, the guests paused, wondering if *he* had arrived.

"And what a gorgeous day."

The French doors were thrown open. Guests made their way onto the terrace and to the garden.

"Have you practiced?" Amalia asked, teasing, knowing full well that Sara had been practicing for weeks.

"I've practiced too much." The concert would begin with Wilhelm Friedemann Bach's Concerto in D Major for flute and strings, which her teacher had given her upon her marriage. Sara would play the fortepiano, Samuel the flute, and other friends would take the string parts. To Sara's regret, she and Samuel had never been able to perform this piece for Monsieur Bach. He had died by the time they returned to Berlin after their wedding journey.

"You know the concerto so well, you can simply let the notes flow through you."

"I do hope so."

After the concerto, Herr Beethoven would perform from his newly published op. 2 piano sonatas, and he'd also promised to treat them to an improvisation.

The voice of Sara's older sister Fanny Arnstein, Viennese hostess *extraordinaire*—as Fanny would be the first to tell you—reached them from the far side of the room. "Oh, yes, I know Herr Beethoven well. He's lived in my home . . ." Fanny held the rapt attention of a circle of young men. She was visiting from Vienna for this concert and staying for a month. Not with Sara, luckily. Fanny projected a Viennese sophistication, curls surrounding her face, the rest of her hair pulled tightly back. Her pearls shone with a pink hue that suited her pale skin and dark hair. Berlin was nothing but a backwater compared with Vienna, cultural center of the world. Mozart, too, had lived at her opulent home.

"I heard some dreadful gossip," Amalia said.

Sara absolutely did not approve of gossip, but she was always happy to hear it.

"I heard that in Vienna, Fanny is considered hopelessly Prussian."

Sara turned away to conceal her smile. How well Amalia understood Sara's charged kinship with her glamorous older sister.

"I'd best say hello to her."

"Yes, you should."

Amalia crossed the room to greet Fanny, who made a fuss over her. Amalia's father was among the richest men in Berlin (rumor held that he was wealthier even than Sara's father). Amalia's husband was also among the richest men in Berlin. People often made a fuss over Amalia. To her credit, Amalia had no illusions about the reasons for her wide appeal.

"Madame Levy." Prince Anton Heinrich Radziwill presented himself with a sharp bow. He was married to Princess Louise of Prussia, who was a niece of Frederick the Great and a cousin of the current king, Frederick William II, who'd ruled for a decade. Radziwill, in his early twenties, cut a handsome, modern figure, his hair worn shoulder-length and miraculously windswept despite the lack of a breeze in the reception room. Although his features were boyish, his eyes were astute. Music was among his special interests. He wore civilian clothes, with an extravagant bow tied around his neck.

"*Bonjour, mon prince*, you honor me with your presence." Privately Sara thought Prince Radziwill was a bit too confident of both his good looks and his position, but his presence bestowed the highest aristocratic validation on the afternoon.

"The honor is mine, as always."

They were joined by Prince Louis Ferdinand of Prussia, a nephew of Frederick the Great and a talented musician. Louis Ferdinand bestowed an equal if not surpassing imprimatur as that of Radziwill, who was his brother-in-law. "Madame, my respects and gratitude."

Louis Ferdinand wore a military dress uniform, its red collar accentuating his blond hair, which was pulled back into a style called a soldier's queue. With his brown eyes and blond hair, he, too, was a striking figure.

"The gratitude is mine," Sara said.

Guests crowded around the two princes and their entourage. Sara was pleased to see the princes politely ignore the admiring throng and instead join her aging father, who'd seated himself near the windows. Sara's older sister Babette kept him company. Daniel Itzig was still an influential banker, and Sara appreciated the recognition the princes accorded her father on account of his many labors for Prussia.

Other members of the nobility arrived. Samuel was the banker for several of the Prussian noblemen here today. A half dozen of Sara and Samuel's nieces swarmed around the aristocrats. Wealthy young Jewish women were increasingly converting in order to marry impoverished Christian noblemen, exchanging money and religion for a title, a regrettable development Sara didn't like to see abetted in her own home.

"Tante!" Her niece Lea was beside her.

"Lea, I'm so glad you could join us."

"Thank you for including me."

Lea, Babette's daughter, was nineteen. With her oval face and big eyes, she was innocently lovely. She had multiple gifts, for music, drawing, and languages, including even classical Greek, commonly considered too taxing for the female temperament. Lea was utterly unaware that her many accomplishments made her exceptional.

"I've been practicing *The Well-Tempered Clavier* from the copy you lent me. I'll play it for you. On a quieter day," she added mischievously.

"That would make me happy."

"Madame Levy, such a pleasure." Baron Wilhelm von Humboldt, philosopher and statesman, bowed before her. Lea left them.

Long and jowly, Humboldt's face was most unattractive, but his high, smooth forehead had inspired a universal belief that he was a genius. On this issue, Sara was willing to give Wilhelm von Humboldt the benefit of the doubt.

"The pleasure is mine." Such a refined game of courtesy they played.

Count Carl Gustav von Brinkmann, the Swedish diplomat, slipped to their sides. He was a hearty, amiable man. White hair and thick, dark eyebrows defined his round face. "Good to see you, Madame Levy. You, too, Humboldt. Such an intriguing crowd today. Even by your standards, Madame Levy." Brinkmann was the kindest man Sara knew.

"If that is true, then you yourself are responsible, because of the many fascinating guests that you have brought here over the years."

"My friends are always impressed with the music and the company *chez* Levy."

A group of French aristocrats, exiled by the French Revolution and the Terror, entered the room. They exuded the oversophistication and heavy condescension they used as weapons against their diminished (if not vanished) status. Duc, Marquis, Marquise, noses literally held high, cheeks painted. Sara really did try to remember their names, and all they had lost, but frankly they annoyed her with their pompous airs. No one in Berlin knew what to make of them, with their perfumes and powder, their gaudy clothing and headgear that became shabbier by the month.

"Do excuse me," Brinkmann said. "The French contingent has arrived. I must do my diplomatic duty."

"Herr Johann Christoph Friedrich Schiller," the butler announced.

Could it be? Receiving Schiller—philosopher, playwright, poet—was almost the equivalent of receiving Goethe.

Samuel reached him first. "Welcome, Herr Schiller."

Samuel was superb. As others greeted Schiller, Samuel caught

Sara's eye. They shared a secret smile in satisfaction at the arrival of their esteemed guest, as well as a harkening to what would happen between them later, in private.

"Napoleon?" someone said behind Sara. "I don't believe it, not even of Napoleon."

"Goethe said . . ." began another man, in a different group.

"Kant wrote to me . . ."

The literary, the political, the philosophical group. Sara circulated to make certain everyone felt welcomed.

"Judaism must continue to reform itself . . ." David Friedlander, banker, philosopher, and Sara's brother-in-law, waxed eloquent upon his favorite topic to a small group that included the Protestant theologian Friedrich Schleiermacher, who kept his eyes upon the sole woman standing with them: beautiful Henriette Herz, one of Sara's childhood friends, her face drawn into a frown of concentration. Schleiermacher was rumored to be in love with Henriette.

"Ignore anything you hear to the contrary: Herr Beethoven is a true gentleman . . ." Fanny described to a different collection of eager young men the solicitous, domestic Beethoven whom only she understood. "Mozart lived at my home for several months also . . ."

Ah, Fanny.

"Haydn, too, has graced us with his presence," Fanny continued.

Sara would have much to discuss with Amalia later, even though Fanny was only speaking the truth: Sara had met both Haydn and Mozart during her visits to Fanny's home in Vienna.

Sara stepped to the side of the reception room, toward the French doors that opened onto the terrace, the garden, and the river. The moment had come when everything clicked into place and nothing more remained for Sara to do. Her guests mingled effortlessly. The staff served drinks and canapés in a flowing dance. Even if Sara departed, all would be well. She observed her visitors. Young, old. Christian, Jew. Nobility and commoner. Wealthy and middle class. A generation ago, this would have been impossible in Berlin. Now it was a way of life, not simply at her home, but at a half-dozen salons across the city. In the new Germany, everyone lived together in a spirit of mutual respect.

She went into the performance room. The chairs were lined up in perfect order. For the third time today, she checked the music on the stands . . . Samuel's flute part. The continuo part. The music for the violins, viola, and violone. All was ready.

She stepped through the French doors and onto the veranda. She loved this house, with its veranda on three sides. Sara's younger nieces and nephews strolled and cavorted in the garden. The boys skimmed rocks into the river. The girls chatted in tight groupings, their hair flowing loose down their backs, catching the sun. Lea was among them, although at nineteen Lea was becoming too old for such pursuits. Better this, however, than hovering around the Prussian nobility in the reception room. Sara hoped the music would lure the young back to the veranda. She knew the music would lure Lea, who was already a virtuoso at the keyboard and reminded Sara of—well, of Sara herself.

As her nieces and nephews walked farther along the river, Sara stepped around the corner of the veranda so that she might continue to observe the enjoyment they found in their simple diversions.

Sara was thirty-five this year. She had no children. She possessed this grand home, filled with paintings and with the shimmering reflections of sunlight upon the Spree. She nurtured this peaceful garden, with its mature shade trees. She organized musical soirées each week for a glittering assembly of friends and acquaintances. She herself performed on the harpsichord or fortepiano at these gatherings. She had everything she could desire.

Except children.

Samuel was successful in business. They supported an array of charities, focusing on education for the poor.

She and Samuel loved each other.

But they had no children.

She never spoke to anyone about her sorrow. She never mentioned it to Amalia, who was several years younger than Sara and already the mother of two sons. Nor did Amalia refer to it. Sara's interfering sisters, who had opinions on every topic, said nothing to her about it, although she felt certain they discussed it among themselves: *Poor Sara has no children.*

Remarkably, Sara and Samuel never discussed it, despite their passion and their intimacy. Despite their conversations, late into the night, as they lay linked together.

A woman's most important task, and she had not fulfilled it. The only babies she'd soothed against her shoulder were her nieces and her nephews, and Amalia's boys. The suite of rooms in the *palais* dedicated to the nursery was empty. She was *unfruchtbar*. Barren. The ugly word made her flinch.

"Well, well, this is quite a gathering today," Sara overhead a man saying around the corner of the veranda, where Sara had stood a few moments before. "These Jews certainly know how to entertain."

She recognized the sonorous voice of Wilhelm von Humboldt. Was it an insult? She and Samuel were indeed Jews, and they did, indeed, know how to entertain.

"Such a lovely setting." His brother, Alexander, the naturalist and explorer. Sara adored Alexander, who was gracious, gentle, and curious.

"The Jews have taken possession of the most beautiful properties along the river."

"And look how exquisitely they're preserving them . . . these trees, this garden."

"They offer up Herr Beethoven and the finest refreshments as lures to fill their salons."

"And here we are, my dear brother, enjoying both. What does that say about us?"

Wilhelm's response was to laugh.

What did his laughter mean?

"What's left in Prussia that Jewish money can't buy?" Wilhelm asked.

Now Alexander laughed. "As long as they're the bankers, I suppose everything is up for sale to them, sooner or later. For myself, I'm more than happy to enjoy the fruits of their financial labors. They've been good to me, as bankers go. What would any of us do without them? Where would Prussia be, without Daniel Itzig? I noticed that the two princes who've blessed us with their presence today are well aware of his achievements."

"How right you are. Let us toast Frederick the Great's Jew— Daniel Itzig, son of a horse trader."

Their glasses clinked. Then, silence. They must have returned inside. Sara felt blunt pain. She pressed her hand upon the wall of her home to steady herself.

Had she in fact lured her guests to be here today? She'd never considered the music of Beethoven to be a bribe. The Humboldt brothers were here virtually every week, Beethoven or no. They were her friends.

She gazed at the river. Along the shore, the branches of the willow trees arched down to brush the water. Yes, they were her friends. She'd misinterpreted their words. Her garden was beautiful. Beethoven visited her home. Her father had been Frederick the Great's banker, and he'd served as Master of the Mint. Her grandfather had been a horse trader. The Humboldt brothers couldn't be faulted for telling the truth. The fault must be that she'd heard a malicious tone where none was intended. Something to guard herself against in future. She wouldn't let them know that she'd overheard their conversation. To do so would be discourteous.

The footman was at her side, no doubt sent by the butler to find her. He gave a quick nod. Herr Beethoven had arrived. The butler would be with him at the entry vestibule, delaying him with offers of the cloakroom and refreshment, to allow a moment of organization so that Sara and Samuel could greet him properly.

Music and Samuel . . . these were her fulfillments. And a house filled with nieces and nephews.

She straightened her posture, as if preparing for a performance. She walked around the veranda and into the reception room. Conversation ceased. Her visitors sensed that the moment had come. They looked to her for guidance. As she swept through the crowd, along the aisle that opened before her, she smiled to her guests. She saw expectation upon their faces. Her sister Fanny nodded at Sara in encouragement. Her father stood nearby, pride on his face—pride in *her*. His approval filled Sara with happiness. Beside him was his granddaughter Lea, her hands pressed together in a silent clapping of excitement. Amalia offered her support. The Humboldt brothers were at Amalia's side, and they, too, regarded Sara with anticipation.

Samuel waited for her. How handsome he was. Her *bashert*. She reached him. He took her hand and squeezed it. Together they turned toward the entryway. At last the butler appeared and announced with a flourish, "Herr Ludwig van Beethoven."

The renowned composer—unruly hair, broad forehead, probing eyes—entered the room.

Sara stepped forward. "Greetings, Herr Beethoven. Welcome to our home."

## Chapter 13

Scott Schiffman put out his hand to Susanna Kessler as Dan introduced them. He could be polite, even when his time was being wasted. "Good to meet you. Welcome to the MacLean Library."

Although Dan had briefed him by phone, Scott wasn't ready to believe that Susanna Kessler had found an authentic J. S. Bach cantata autograph in—where was it?—a piano bench in Buffalo. Well-meaning individuals turned up at the MacLean all the time, claiming to have found unknown novels by Jane Austen or letters that were absolutely, unequivocally written by William Shakespeare. Dan must have let himself be seduced by wishful thinking, or more likely by admiration for the woman who got off the elevator with him.

He'd arranged to meet them in the MacLean's conservation center, upstairs from his office. This way, he could conveniently insist on taking high-resolution digital photographs of the manuscript, if that proved necessary. Which it wouldn't.

He led Dan and Susanna across the center's laboratory and toward the conference room, where they could speak privately. He loved the lab, and he was happy to show it off. The place was a combination of spaceship and barn, high-tech venting tubes paired with rough-hewn wooden beams that crisscrossed the ceiling. Staff members, three men and one woman, sat at long tables, beneath high-intensity lights. Scott paused so that Dan and Susanna, and he himself, who never tired of scrutinizing such exacting work, could observe his colleagues: they were repairing the torn pages of books and documents with an ultrathin fabric that seemed to disappear when a touch of glue was applied to it.

"Amazing," Susanna Kessler whispered to him.

"Yes, it is." Her reaction pleased him, even though she was wasting his time.

The conference room was Scandinavian-inspired, all sleek, pale wood. After they were seated, Susanna said, "Thank you for meeting with me today. I'm grateful. I'm also grateful to have the chance to go backstage at the MacLean Library. I've been to dozens of exhibitions here, and to see the areas that are closed to the public—well, this is a thrill for me."

"Glad to have you." An icy rain lashed the windows. Despite her compliments, he wanted to keep his focus on business. "So . . ." he began.

He stopped as Susanna took the manuscript out of a plastic bag, or more correctly two plastic bags placed crosswise to each other. He glanced at Dan in recognition of the absurdity of this (if by chance they were in fact dealing with a priceless Bach autograph), but Dan was watching Susanna.

"Here it is," she said. "Hidden by my uncle for sixty-five years."

Scott took the manuscript from her. He placed it on the table. To begin, he ran his fingers over it, feeling the paper. Opening the wrapper, he studied the score page by page. He lifted a sheet to inspect the watermark.

What had sounded crazy when he spoke with Dan on the phone didn't sound so crazy now. Good God, Scott thought when he reached the end—was Dan actually right?

"I have to admit, when you first told me about this, I was skeptical."

"Good," Dan said. "I wanted a fresh pair of eyes. Assuming for a moment, then, that it *is* authentic, what are your initial thoughts on when the music would have been notated?"

"As an educated guess, pending more research, I'm thinking the 1720s. I'd need to make some comparisons to verify that."

"It would make sense, if this is in fact the missing *Exaudi* cantata from the third Leipzig cycle."

"Agreed."

Dan passed his transcription of the German libretto and his translation across the table to Scott, who read through them.

"The poetry could be Neumeister, don't you think?" Scott asked Dan.

"That's a strong possibility."

Susanna asked, "What does the text say?"

Dan didn't answer her.

Was he trying to protect her? Scott wondered. She didn't look like the sort of person who needed protection. Scott said, "The text of the opening aria says:

"'*Wir das Joch nicht tragen können,*
*Doch nicht auf der Halse wollen.*
*All die mördrisch lügend Juden*
*Hätten Christum glauben sollen.*'"

Dan said, "The first two lines are adapted from Acts 15:10, and the second two lines are adapted from John 8:44."

"As to what the text means," Scott continued, "Dan has translated, with commentary, the first aria thusly:

"'*We*'—that means the followers of Jesus, as well as all human beings in general—'*are unable to bear the yoke*'—understood to mean the yoke of the Law of Moses—'*certainly don't want it on our necks.*
*All the murderous lying Jews*
*should have believed Christ.*'"

"The libretto goes on from there," Dan said, "through two recitatives, two arias, and a hymn stanza. I'm sorry to say the polemical sentiments intensify throughout the piece."

"By *polemical* he means anti-Jewish," Scott said to Susanna.

"Granted," Dan said.

"The recitatives are especially offensive," Scott said.

This was a nasty piece of work, and talking about it in circles, trying to smooth everything over, wasn't helpful. In fact, doing so was destructive. Scott believed in facing facts, even facts that were tough to accept.

Scott continued, "'*Burn their synagogues . . . We are at fault for not striking them dead,*' lots more along those lines. Dan has helpfully discovered that these recitatives are direct quotes from a book by Martin Luther called *On the Jews and Their Lies*. This treatise was reprinted in various multivolume sets of Luther's collected works that a writer of church cantata poetry could readily enough have consulted, and even Bach owned two of these collections."

Scott saw Susanna frown in disbelief.

"So this work of art is anti-Semitic?" she said.

"Yes," Scott said.

"And that's the reason my uncle kept it hidden?"

Scott understood that she wasn't really expecting him to know the answer, but he said, "I assume so."

"Who did you say put this together?"

"We don't know, but one possibility is Erdmann Neumeister. He was a clergyman in Hamburg. A contemporary of Bach's," Dan said.

Scott added, "Neumeister is known to have successfully incited anti-Jewish rioting in Hamburg in the 1730s through his sermons in church. Bach set several of his poems to music. Cantatas 18 and 61, among others."

"As far as we know right now, however, this could have been written by any of Bach's librettists, who were typically anonymous."

"As to the wrapper," Scott said, "apart from the lines that appear to be written by Bach himself, the person who wrote, '*Sollte nicht catalogisiert werden, Berlin, den 9. Juni 1783*,' clearly owned the manuscript in the late eighteenth century, because of the date. '*Im Privat-Kabinett halten*' . . . that handwriting is from the early-to-mid-nineteenth century."

"How can you possibly know such a thing?" Susanna said.

"Based on years of reading all sorts of scrawl like this."

"But how exactly?"

Was she doubting him? "I have clues I look for. I took a special course on old German scripts at Moravian College to learn how to do it. You could take the course, too, if you're interested."

"I'll take a rain check on the course, but it's kind of terrific, that you can do that."

"It *is* terrific, I agree with you." His job was fantastic, no sense being modest about it.

"What are your thoughts about the ink?" said Dan, forever serious.

"Iron-gall ink. The level of *Tintenfrass* is about what I'd expect, given the estimated age."

"*Tintenfrass*?" Susanna asked.

"It's a German word for corrosion. I use it for fun. I like the way it sounds."

"What does it mean in this context?"

"Iron-gall ink eventually eats into paper. That's why it appears to bleed through to the other side of the page. It's also why the lines are thick and blurry. When the words were first written, they were clear and sharp. The German word for the effect is *Tintenfrass*."

"Don't you actually have to do scientific proofs to tell us whether this manuscript is authentic or forged, and to confirm the dates and analyze the ink and the paper? Like on TV shows? Radiocarbon dating? Investigations with X-rays?"

"We don't do those types of tests here. When we need such tests, we send items to bigger labs, like the one at the Metropolitan Museum. In this case, however, the tests wouldn't be necessary or relevant. Say we did a test and confirmed that the paper is old. Well, we do already know the paper is old, that's obvious by looking at it, and the unusual water-mark fits with papers Bach used. But unused old paper with this very watermark might have been sitting in a box in a closet somewhere until a forger got his hands on it—although this is rather unlikely, I admit. X-ray fluorescence spectrometry might show that the ink is identical to inks used by Bach, which would be great, or it might *not* show identical chemical content for the ink, which in turn would only tell us that Bach might have used more inks than the ones discovered thus far."

As Scott listened to himself he thought, *Am I turning into a complete and total bore to outsiders?* Yes, he was. No help for it, however. This was his world, his arena of battle. If she wanted to understand, she had to be willing to listen. If she didn't want to understand, fine. He continued:

"This manuscript shows the characteristic physical signs of Bach autographs. These signs, however, don't in themselves prove that this manuscript was notated by Bach. If the cantata were written with a ballpoint pen on photocopying paper, we'd know for certain that it *wasn't* prepared by Bach, because those items didn't exist in Bach's day. But to prove that it *was* notated by Bach, and that the music was *composed* by him, to prove the positive instead of the negative, the context is crucial."

"Thank you for explaining," Susanna said. "That was helpful."

She sounded sincere. Scott went on, "We have to trace the provenance. As you can read about in the trusty Christoph Wolff biography of Bach, the autograph scores and some particular performing parts from the third Leipzig cantata cycle went primarily to Carl Philipp Emanuel Bach."

"With the exception of some pieces for certain liturgical occasions, which Wilhelm Friedemann, the eldest brother, was allowed to take. *Exaudi* being one of those occasions," Dan said. "I looked into this in some detail. For the Ascension cantata rendered during the previous week, we do know that Wilhelm Friedemann had both the score and the performing parts, although so far we have no specific proof that Friedemann would have had this particular *Exaudi* cantata. What we do know for certain," Dan turned to Susanna, "is that Carl Philipp Emanuel took good care of his father's works, and Wilhelm Friedemann was a notoriously bad caretaker."

"According to scholarly wisdom," Scott said, "Friedemann suffered from alcoholism, manic depression, stress-anxiety from the pressure of being his father's eldest son—you have to feel for the guy. He couldn't hold on to a job. Therefore, logic dictates that this cantata, if authentic, should more likely have been among those materials that went to Carl Philipp Emanuel, and that he, as we'd expect, took good care of it."

"Logic dictates, but that's not proof," Dan added.

This conversation was turning into a pissing contest, Scott thought, the kind he'd literally had with his brother during their youthful summers in Maine. That's what came of showing off for a girl. Correction, woman. The good part was that Scott and Dan could keep up with each other. Scott always enjoyed their repartee.

"I don't suppose," Scott said, "that you entered the melody into the theme-finder websites, to see if someone other than Bach might have written it?"

"I had to leave something for you to do," Dan said.

"Happy to oblige." The theme-finder databases were notoriously incomplete, but nonetheless, Scott would check them later. "Speaking of good caretaking," he said to Susanna, "I heard a rumor that you're storing this manuscript in a safe deposit box at your local bank."

"Yes."

"You should allow me to keep it here for you. It would be in a secure, climate-controlled facility, much better than a bank."

"He's right, Susanna," Dan said.

"I'll hold on to it for now," she said.

Unbelievable. He tried a different tack: "I need to do a full set of high-resolution digital photographs for study purposes. This would allow me to put the musical and verbal handwriting side by side with other examples, to work out the context I was talking about. I'll also need images as I work to identify the nineteenth-century handwriting on the wrapper."

"As I've said to Dan, I want to wait on the photographs until we know what we're dealing with."

"We already have a pretty solid idea of what we're dealing with," Scott said. "Frankly, it's stupid, not to—"

"But it's your call, Susanna," Dan interrupted.

Scott paused. "Absolutely. Your call. The truth is, however, that Dan and I have every reason to keep this confidential. For us, it could be the discovery of a lifetime. The apex of our careers. We don't want anyone else to publish on it before we do. Just like you, we don't want the evidence spread around the world in the blink of an eye. I have to say, your approach to this is incomprehensible to me."

Susanna gazed at him unperturbed.

Doing his best to sound conciliatory, Scott said, "May I at least photograph the wrapper and the first several pages?"

"The wrapper and the first three pages only." She sounded matter-of-fact and much more professional than he did. He was accustomed to being in charge, and she'd thrown him.

Scott stood and retrieved a stainless-steel tray from a cabinet and placed the cantata on it. With Susanna and Dan following, he carried the manuscript out of the conference room and toward the far side of the laboratory. On the way, they passed broad sinks where documents floated in tubs of clear liquid.

"What's this?" Susanna asked.

"It's an ethanol bath. To clean the paper. Actually, this is really cool." Scott stopped beside the sinks to explain. "These particular documents also happen to be written in iron-gall ink, which is indelible. The sulfuric acid in the ink burns through the paper, so the ink can't be washed away." He felt a spark of—what, exactly? The sheer pleasure of his work, replacing his previous irritation. "That's why we're able to soak the paper to clean it without ruining the document."

"Hmm, iron-gall ink is indelible. Good to know," Susanna said.

"I probably shouldn't have told you."

"That was a definite miscalculation on your part."

Maybe he could grow to like her despite her exasperating attitude.

In the narrow photography room, Scott sensed Susanna watching his every move, as if looking for mistakes. Not that she'd recognize an error even if he made one, but he felt an urge to finish as fast as possible. He'd brought his own memory card for the camera, and he loaded it. He positioned the manuscript on the stand beneath the elevated camera and made adjustments page by page. He would transfer the images onto the computer in his office later.

Task completed. He put the memory card into his shirt pocket and returned the manuscript to the tray. Susanna and Dan followed him back to the conference room.

"That's it for today?" Susanna said.

"As far as I'm concerned," Scott said.

He watched her rewrap the cantata in the same two plastic bags she'd brought it in. She returned the package to her tote bag and patted the bag in reassurance, of herself or of the cantata, Scott wasn't certain. What was wrong with her? Why was she so irrational?

"What happens if you leave the cantata in a taxi?" he said.

"I take full responsibility."

"What if there's a flood at the bank?"

"No more likely than here at the MacLean."

"This is crazy." He turned to Dan for support, but Dan shook his head to tell him to stop. Scott wasn't prepared to stop. "Here at the MacLean, as I've said, we have state-of-the-art—"

"You've made your point." She placed the tote bag over her shoulder. "I need to get going."

"Dan, do you want to stay so we can start planning the next steps in the research?"

"I'm giving a lecture later, so I'd better go, too."

Scott was surprised, but he walked them to the elevator without further comment.

As the elevator door opened, they shook hands. "Thank you again," Susanna said.

———

Dan and Susanna returned their visitors' passes to the security desk, and the guard checked their names off his list.

"Let's leave through the new atrium," Susanna said. "I haven't been here since the renovation."

The atrium, with its trees and soaring glass ceiling, was dreary in the December rain. At least it didn't leak, or not yet. Dan watched Susanna as she looked around the space.

"Maybe we have to see it on a sunny day," she said.

"I've been here on sunny days."

"And?"

"With the sun beating down, it's hot."

"I can well imagine."

They headed toward the Madison Avenue exit. Dan felt increasingly tense walking beside someone who carried what might well be a priceless Bach autograph in her tote bag. But if they were going to work together, he had to appear to respect her position. He put the issue aside and focused instead on asking her to have a cup of coffee with him. Asking her to have a cup of coffee had become a fixation for him these past few days, and now it was close to becoming a paralysis.

The MacLean had a café, but it was staid and expensive, and he also wanted to escape the professional atmosphere that the MacLean represented. By chance he'd noticed a Starbucks one block south, on Madison between Thirty-fifth and Thirty-sixth Streets. Okay, he hadn't noticed it by chance. He'd done a Google search and located the closest Starbucks to the MacLean. Before the meeting today, he'd walked by to make certain it had an adequate seating area.

In a little over an hour, he had to be uptown to attend the opening reception of a Lutheran organists' conference. He was giving a speech during the dinner that followed. He'd return to Granville late tonight. Becky had seemed happy enough at the prospect of a sleepover at the home of his colleague Katarina Kundera. He was lucky that Becky and Katarina's daughter, Lizzie, had become close friends.

Possibly he didn't have time for coffee, after all.

As they walked out of the museum, pedestrians hurried past, their umbrellas angled across their faces against the lashing rain.

Susanna stopped about ten feet from the front doors of the MacLean. Beneath her open umbrella, her face seemed illuminated. To ask her to coffee, or not to ask? And why her, instead of the other women he knew? She was so different from Julie, that must be the reason. He wouldn't be betraying Julie's memory. Besides, it was only coffee.

"I need to get to the bank before it closes," she said.

"That's a good idea." He was simultaneously relieved and disappointed that the coffee question had been resolved. "You know, though, you can still take the manuscript back inside for Scott to store. The MacLean really is the safest place."

"I appreciate your advice, but as far as I'm concerned, the safest place right now is with me. I'm still trying to figure out what my uncle would have wanted."

"Okay, I understand." Before they parted, he felt pressed to explain himself: "Look, I'm sorry I wasn't frank with you at the beginning. About the subject matter. I wanted to be, but I couldn't. It's not easy—"

"I have to think about what I learned today. I wasn't expecting . . . well, what you discovered about the subject matter."

"I wasn't expecting it, either."

"I'm sure you weren't. And don't worry, talking about these things isn't easy for any of us."

"Your family?"

"A story like many others."

"I'm sorry."

"Thank you. And thank you for introducing me to Scott."

"Sometimes Scott can be testy, but he knows what he's doing."

"I could see that. In spite of the testiness." She checked her watch. He sensed her wanting to be polite. "Have your wife and daughter come to New York for the weekend?"

"I'm not married," he said, startled.

"Forgive me. I'd assumed. Since you wear a wedding ring."

He glanced at the ring. "Yes, I do. It's been there for so long I tend to forget about it." He didn't want to begin their first personal conversation by explaining about Julie. "I'm not married anymore, though."

"Me, neither. My divorce was finalized just recently. How long have you been apart from your wife?"

"It's a long story." To shift the focus away from himself, he asked, "What about you?"

"A long story, too. Oh, I meant to tell you," she said, changing the subject. He sensed that she, too, was concealing experiences too difficult to talk about here on the sidewalk in the rain. "I'm trying to educate myself. I downloaded a set of Bach's greatest hits from iTunes."

This put him on firmer ground. "How are you liking it?"

"It's terrific."

"Who are the performers?"

"I don't know. I mean, I don't recognize the names. And some of the pieces aren't complete; only individual movements are included."

"I might be able to help you to find a collection that's better."

"Thank you, I'd like that. It's not easy to reconcile such astonishing music with what we've been discussing today."

"No, it isn't."

She gazed at him steadily, as if expecting more. He said nothing. Nothing seemed sufficient.

"I'd better go."

"And I should sit down somewhere and figure out what I'm going to say to the Lutheran organists I'm lecturing to this evening."

This provoked an unexpectedly warm smile from her. "That sounds like a good idea. And thank you again for your help."

"We'll talk soon," he said.

She put out her hand to him, and he shook it.

With this recognition of gratitude and budding friendship, she turned. Dan watched her as she headed off uptown.

# Chapter 14

Today, a cold, quiet Sunday morning, Scott Schiffman decided to stay home and do the research he'd been itching to get to since his meeting with Susanna Kessler two days before. He made coffee and went to his desk.

Because of his family's wealth, Scott was able to make choices. Most of his peers lived on their salaries, meager in comparison with his own resources. He never wanted them to feel ill at ease in his presence, so he made certain his choices appeared ordinary even when they were very fine. He kept his clothing simple. He limited what he discussed at work. His terrific vacations, including his family's yearly reunion between Christmas and New Year's at Caneel Bay on St. John, in the Virgin Islands, and the annual ski trip to Jackson Hole, Wyoming, in March with his siblings, their spouses and children, remained unmentioned.

When it came to his apartment, however, concealing his resources was impossible. The apartment was his private refuge anyway, and he was glad to give himself an excuse to keep it that way. He invited only close friends to visit him. Dan stayed in the guest room on occasion. Now and then Scott's girlfriends stayed over, although in general Scott preferred to stay at their apartments so he could make a graceful exit at breakfast time and be home alone in the morning.

Scott lived in Greenwich Village, a neighborhood chosen primarily because it was far from his family's town house on the Upper East Side. He'd picked a postwar building because he'd grown up in a historic one. He'd opted for modern décor because upholstered antiques had filled his family home. His apartment was an expansive three-bedroom (one of the bedrooms served as his study) on a high floor facing north, with an open view of midtown Manhattan. Because he'd grown up in a town house, with views of the street in front and of a walled, carefully cultivated garden in back, the open view from this apartment was among its attractions for him.

Astonishingly, from his desk he could see both the Empire State Building and the Chrysler Building. As he now became absorbed in his work, however, he rarely looked up and when he did, he didn't notice the view. From his computer at home, he had immediate access via the Internet to Bach Digital, a site that provided scanned images of the autograph scores and original performing parts of Bach's works. Another site supplied a searchable database of the texts to Bach's vocal works in their original languages. These resources provided a good beginning, and their very existence was terrific and exciting. Nevertheless, some questions could be researched only in major libraries, which he'd need to visit in due course.

He wanted to compare both the musical and verbal scripts in the cantata that Susanna Kessler had discovered with those of Bach's works from the 1720s and 1730s. He opened several windows showing the works of the 1720s, so that he could move easily among them. He cautioned himself that he must keep a critical eye. After several hours of work, he was forced to conclude that the scripts in the *Exaudi* cantata really did appear exactly the same as those in Bach's works of the late 1720s.

So where did that put matters? The *Tintenfrass*—such a great word—that he'd observed at the MacLean had shown that the manuscript, with its rare watermark pairing of the deer and the initials IAI, must indeed be old, and now the handwriting analysis showed that the cantata had most probably been notated by Bach.

Next, he needed to determine identifications for the handwriting on the wrapper (the handwriting that didn't appear to be Bach's, that is). This was a needle-in-a-haystack assignment of laughable magnitude.

Or was it? Only a limited number of people would have had access to the autograph, and those who did were, obviously, German-speakers. The two writers were educated, Scott concluded from the fact that their script was fluid. Most likely they were upper class, because they'd gained possession of the autograph and had the luxury of concealing it, rather than needing to sell it. *Berlin, den 9. Juni 1783* gave Scott a starting point for one of the early owners. Because of the reference to cataloging, this owner might have possessed a noteworthy private music library.

Scott loved puzzling out stories from the past. Who in Berlin had collected Bach cantata autographs in the late eighteenth and early-to-mid-nineteenth centuries? And who there, furthermore, might have indicated *not* to catalog this cantata? Of the two most noteworthy German collectors, Georg Poelchau moved to Berlin later, in 1813, and in any event was only ten years old in 1783; and Franz Hauser, who never lived in Berlin, wasn't born until a decade later. Conceivably one of them might have written the subsequent inscription, *keep in the private cabinet.* In Bach Digital, Scott checked the entry for Franz Hauser (Poelchau didn't have an entry) under the advanced search category *Schriftproben*, handwriting samples. Nothing matched. Scott looked forward to following up in an actual library—and he loved a big library, filled with, yes, books. Stocked with potential discoveries.

Scott paused. Now he did look out and study the view. Much of the day had passed. The winter sun cast precise shadows that accentuated the architectural details of the cityscape before him. The Empire State Building and the Chrysler Building took on a glamour that reminded him of the music of George Gershwin. He couldn't imagine anyplace he'd rather be than right here.

Yesterday, he'd attended the bar mitzvah of his nephew Greg. Scott had two older sisters and an older brother, and he'd gradually acquired nine nieces and nephews. Remarkably, he managed to remember their names—which was good, because every one of them had attended Greg's bar mitzvah. The ceremony was held at Rodeph Sholom, where Scott himself had his bar mitzvah years before. Most of his parents' Jewish friends went to Temple Emanu-El on Fifth Avenue, but Scott's father (no doubt trying to escape his own father) favored Rodeph Sholom.

Scott hadn't been to synagogue in a few years (not since the bar mitzvah of his nephew Eric), and he was surprised by the general good feeling of the place. Yesterday he'd paid closer attention to the service than he had the last time. It was affecting, especially the part when Greg, a shy, mild-mannered boy, carried the Torah around the sanctuary and the congregants, whether elderly, middle-aged, or young, reached to touch it with their prayer books. Most kissed their prayers books afterward. The scene had left him feeling a little choked up.

During the service, Scott sat next to his mother. She'd been born in Germany, and both her parents were killed during the war. She'd escaped to Britain and then Canada via the Kindertransport when she was only four years old. Decades later, through a remarkable set of circumstances, she was surprised to learn from a survivor that her father had taken his pocket score of Bach's *St. Matthew Passion* with him on the train from Theresienstadt to Auschwitz, where he died. Where he was murdered.

Why the *St. Matthew Passion*, Scott wondered, of all the compositions by Bach? He might have chosen *The Well-Tempered Clavier*, or *The Art of Fugue*, or one of the violin concertos. Secular pieces. Scott couldn't comprehend why his grandfather would embrace above all a composition about the crucifixion of Jesus. And yet . . . Scott knew from his own experience that one didn't have to accept Christian doctrine to be moved by the emotional content of Bach's liturgical music. He'd been soothed often enough himself by the transcendent opening movement from Cantata 170. The *St. Matthew Passion* especially evoked a sense of promise within despair. Scott hoped his grandfather had felt the music's consolation when he was pushed into the cattle car of his final journey.

And here Scott was, a Jew focusing his research on the music of Bach, in addition to his daily curatorial duties at the MacLean. He'd taken years of piano lessons without developing the skill to be a professional performer. He didn't have the instinctive generosity and patience needed to be a teacher of undergraduate music history courses. He considered himself a historian and scientist. His position at the MacLean was a perfect fit for him.

If the cantata proved to be authentic Bach, he wanted it to be entrusted to the MacLean. Down the road, as the situation developed—and if Susanna Kessler was able to prove that she did, indeed, own the cantata—he would approach the MacLean's director about making her an offer. He needed to remain in Susanna's good graces, or more correctly get himself into her good graces, to smooth his way on this. If only he'd had the foresight to be nicer to her. He'd said a few things that were way out of line. At this point, who could say what she would do with the manuscript. He couldn't dismiss from his thoughts the idea that she might even destroy it. He'd have to start afresh with her. Apart from the fact that she'd found the manuscript in her family home in Buffalo, Dan had told him nothing about her. He'd do some Internet research. Once he discovered where she worked, where she'd gone to school, where she lived, he'd find their mutual connections.

His thoughts leapt ahead. The MacLean had fantastic Web designers on staff, and when the time came to go public, they could take the discovery in several dozen directions. He imagined the Web pages they'd create . . . link after link of visual, aural, and textual material aimed at a wide audience. With the new exhibition techniques, you could clink on a link and hear only the oboe line extracted from the recording of a piece, or only the violin line.

As Scott worked through this, his rational side kicked in to warn him: the manuscript could turn out to be a spectacular forgery, perhaps even produced by the Nazis. If he allowed himself to be seduced by a forgery, he could end up humiliating himself in a way that would ruin his career.

On the other hand, if he and Dan kept their wits about them, they could get an interesting, if minor, article out of a Nazi forgery, too. So in a sense this was a win-win situation. Professionally speaking, that is. And personally? Forged, authentic . . . either way, the cantata was grim, hideous, and bleak. It concerned a topic he preferred not to think about, one that was far too close to home. This must be part of Susanna Kessler's family history, as well: Kessler was predominantly a Jewish last name, and indulging in common stereotyping, Scott would have to say that she looked Jewish, too. Judging from Dan's reticence, the cantata's unsettling topic touched his family history, too. From the other side.

As a Jew, maybe he should refuse to work on this piece, with its gruesome text. Maybe he should tell Susanna Kessler to suppress it. Had he been letting scholarly enthusiasm take priority over loyalty to his heritage?

He thought this out. He'd always advocated the opposite of suppression in regard to uncomfortable truths. That was still the right path. In fact, he concluded, as a Jew he had a special responsibility to bring the cantata into public knowledge, to promote discussion and understanding of the dismal history that the cantata represented. He hated the word *transparency*, but he believed in the concept.

Back to work. The authenticity question remained.

When all was said and done, the music would be its own proof of authenticity. On the theme-finder sites, he typed in the letters that represented the first six notes of the opening. True, the sites weren't definitive, but there was always a chance of a hit.

Nothing.

He printed out his digital photographs of the cantata's first pages of music. He took them to the piano in the living room. He had a Steinway baby grand. He still took lessons, nowadays from a delightful woman on the Upper West Side who taught only adults. He played in recitals with her other students, attendance forbidden to friends and family, which suited him because he didn't take the lessons in order to perform for family and friends. He took them because of the Zen-like state he entered when he practiced, clearing his head of all distractions except the notes. This year in his lessons he was inching his way through the third movement of Beethoven's op. 110 sonata.

He opened the keyboard, sat down, and arranged what little he had of the cantata score on the stand. He played the *basso continuo* part with his left hand and as much of the string parts as he could manage with his right hand. And he was caught. Captured by the rich harmonies and the formidably complex counterpoint.

This was music by a true master. If not Johann Sebastian Bach, who?

## Chapter 15

BERLIN, PRUSSIA,
UNDER FRENCH OCCUPATION DURING
THE NAPOLEONIC WARS

*1808*

In the performance hall of the Sing-Akademie, Sara placed her hands into position above the keyboard. She waited for the conductor to give the signal to begin. On this gray afternoon, and despite the large windows, little natural light filtered into the hall. Candles, guttering, were attached to the music stands. Given the intricacies of her part, Sara had memorized the music so she need not struggle to read it in the inadequate light.

For two years, Napoleon's forces had occupied Berlin. Frederick William III was still king, but the royal family had fled Berlin. Prussia had essentially become a vassal state of France, subject to outrageous monetary demands. In the audience today, the festive uniforms of French officers contrasted with the shabby clothing of Berlin's citizens. As the occupation dragged on, financial hardship had forced some of Sara's friends to sell their homes and leave the city. Resentment toward the occupiers was ever-present.

This concert was a form of resistance, or so Sara viewed it. Bach's music was a paean for an independent Prussia. And to represent their cause, Carl Friedrich Zelter, director of the Sing-Akademie, had chosen Sara Levy to play the brilliant harpsichord part in Bach's Concerto in D Major for flute, violin, obbligato harpsichord, and strings.

This was a public concert. The audience had purchased tickets. For the first time in her life, Sara was performing as a professional musician.

How could this be, that an upper-class woman was performing music as a professional?

Sara knew the answer: she was a widow, and she had no children.

Because Samuel was not among the stalwart Berliners sitting in the audience, keeping their cloaks upon their shoulders in defense against the cold, and because she was barren, she'd been able to escape certain rigid bonds of society. Two years had passed since Samuel's death. He was only forty-six. He died the same month the French marched through the city gates, October 1806. The occupation and his death were forever linked in her mind. The pain of missing him was piercing, and she never wanted to stop missing him.

Zelter coughed to gain the ensemble's attention. Sara sat up straight. She met his eyes. He was an arresting presence, with his shock of white hair, sharp nose, and narrow chin. She nodded. He raised his hands.

They began. She played continuo with the string ensemble as they performed the concerto's insistent ritornello. Soon the violin and flute were interacting as if they were partners in a dance. Their dance became an interweaving duet of love. Sara's continuo part moved smoothly in the background, before gradually coming to the fore, her right hand first playing chords, then obbligato, then onward to the section of arpeggios, in preparation for her long unaccompanied solo.

She'd practiced this piece for months, for years, playing at home with friends, Samuel on the flute. This piece was part of her very being.

A return to D major, as if the piece were about to end, and the music jars the listener with a C natural in the bass line and returns to material from the movement's beginning. Then once more one senses that the piece is going to end, but the music plays another trick, not an A to D in the bass line but an A to F-sharp—the beginning of the accompanied bravura lead-in to a wildly virtuosic extended solo.

She leapt into the solo, abandoning herself, the phrases ever more complex, faster, frenzied, a feast of notes. She closed her eyes. She saw the keyboard within her mind. Breathe, she told herself. She missed a note. Don't think about it. *Keep playing*, she heard her teacher's voice. *Don't stop.* Joy filled her in the sheer pleasure of the notes. Nothing else mattered but this music, here, now.

And then the herculean solo was over. The movement ended. She opened her eyes. She'd done it. The rest of the concerto was easy, at least in comparison. Zelter began the second movement. Her continuo part resumed. She was damp with sweat. The violin and flute took over, while she maintained the continuo line, keeping the beat. Slow down, she cautioned herself.

Would there be cake at the reception later? *Focus.* The second movement came to the end. On to the third. She was becoming tired. Where was her energy?

*There*, her vigor returned as the flute line became the main voice, their parts intermingling, the flutist lifting his eyes to hers. He might have been Samuel, standing beside her.

The concerto concluded. She lifted her hands from the keyboard. Yet she remained frozen within the music.

She heard applause. The audience. She'd forgotten them. She wasn't ready to face the crowd. She sensed the other musicians standing up and bowing.

She, too, must stand and bow. She rose. She turned toward the audience. She looked out upon them. She felt dazed. The throng shouted their approval. She couldn't identify individuals. She knew that her vast family, at once infuriating and encouraging, was here, along with her many friends. Also here were people she didn't know, strangers, concertgoers, French officers from the occupation force, drawn to this event by the program. By the music of Johann Sebastian Bach. The hall gleamed in the candlelight. She'd fulfilled the promise of her girlhood.

Zelter made a special recognition of her to the audience. As she bowed alone, the applause swelled. The musicians bowed together once more. They left the stage. They returned to the stage. Seeing the French officers in their colorful uniforms, Sara knew that some of the applause, which continued far longer than she or her colleagues had any right to expect, was because of those French uniforms. The music of Bach rebuked the French army, saying, you may occupy our city, but you have no power compared with the force of our culture. You may defeat our armies, but we will endure.

The applause subsided and ceased. Sara and her fellow performers left the stage. In the anteroom, the musicians shook hands, praising and congratulating one another with two-handed grips. She, too, received this two-handed gripping handshake. Instruments were put away, clothing adjusted. Sara and her colleagues walked down the hallway and joined the reception. The high-ceilinged room, with its arched windows, was crowded with her countrymen, not a single French uniform among them.

Amalia was the first friend to reach her. "My dearest, you were wonderful."

Next, Brinkmann. "You are my heroine," he whispered. "How proud I am, of you."

Others gathered, congratulating her. She felt a wave of affection sweeping over her.

A pause. She looked around.

Carl Friedrich Zelter approached. She steeled herself for his critique. He was renowned for his blunt honesty. If she were lucky, he'd offer only a sentence or two about what she could do to improve. He almost never gave praise. He might very well deliver an extended lecture on her faults, right here in front of her family and friends. Whatever he said, he'd be correct.

"My dear Frau Levy." Since the occupation, she was *Frau* instead of *Madame*. He took her hands in his, like a father. "A splendid performance." He nodded sagely, fulfilling the role of the wise man he believed himself to be. "Exactly as I expected. Next week we shall begin work on Bach's magnificent Concerto in G Minor. That is all I have to say to you."

He dropped her hands and walked away.

She felt alone, even though she was surrounded by people, everyone talking, praising. Amid the din, she couldn't make out exactly what anyone said.

"Tante, Tante."

Some French words would never be replaced, and cut through any clamor. Sara turned. Could it be?

"I wanted to surprise you."

Lea, her dearest niece. The daughter she might have had. "You were brilliant."

Lea lived in Hamburg, married to Abraham Mendelssohn, son of the philosopher Moses Mendelssohn. Abraham was a banker, partnered with his brother Joseph in the internationally successful Mendelssohn bank. Every member of Sara's family agreed that Abraham wasn't good enough for Lea, but she would have him and no other.

"It means the world to me—" Sara's voice caught "—to see you here." Hamburg was a long journey.

"I *had* to be here."

"You could play the piece I performed today. All you have to do is practice."

"And *don't stop*." Lea was as much of a tease as Sara herself once had been. They'd often had fun together, before Lea's marriage and her move to Hamburg, Sara as teacher, Lea as student.

"By now you know all my good advice."

"I should hope so."

"When did you arrive in Berlin?"

"Last night. Mother promised to keep my visit a secret. She didn't give you so much as a hint, did she?"

"No, not even a hint. How is your little one?" My granddaughter, Sara wished she could say. Fanny was three years old.

"Thriving. Already she sits on a pillow and tries the keyboard. Her hands are perfect. She has fingers for playing fugues."

"She hears her mother creating beautiful music, and she wants to do the same."

"Oh, Tante." Lea blushed, still a girl herself, despite her husband and child.

"And when she's older," Sara said, "we shall teach her the music of Bach."

## Chapter 16

On a Thursday morning in December, Susanna stood on the rooftop of the Booker T. Washington High School in Brooklyn. She tried without success to ignore how cold she was. Anita Randolph, the school principal, and Raffie Espinal, a science teacher, stood beside her. The rooftop was wide, empty, and blackened by soot.

"I know it's freezing out here, Ms. Kessler," said Raffie. "The winds of Brooklyn are blowing. I'd tell you to hold on to your hat, if you were wearing one." Raffie was in his mid-thirties, a small, lean man who, despite his thick parka, moved like a dancer. "It might be winter on our roof, but here's what I'm seeing." He gestured expansively. "Lettuce over there. Carrots over here. Cherry tomatoes. Kale, even."

From his enthusiasm, Susanna saw the garden, too. Other New York City schools had established green roofs with combined support from private foundations and city funds, but this would be a first for the Barstow Foundation. According to reports she'd read, green roof projects could easily cost upward of a million dollars, more than her board would allocate for this, but Susanna felt confident that once the project was moving forward, she could coordinate donations from other foundations as well.

"This is the time for us to order the tubs, the soil, the seeds. Think of the potential. Every class will be involved: science, mathematics, poetry workshops. Art classes, making paintings and drawings of what's growing."

"We're proud that we still have an art program here," said Mrs. Randolph. She was a severe-looking woman whose stout body was like a bulwark against the wind.

"The only reason we still have it after the budget cuts is that Mrs. Randolph fought for it. And keeps on fighting," Raffie said. "For our kids."

"I want you and your foundation to know," Mrs. Randolph said, "that everyone in the school is on board with the green roof project. Teachers, administrators, students, as well as the maintenance and custodial staff."

"The students especially," Raffie said. "But don't take my word for it. What's that sound I hear?" he said loudly, signaling to unseen companions.

A group of about two dozen students made their way up the stairs, clapping their hands and stamping their feet in a unified rhythm. They arrayed themselves across the roof. They wore matching green scarves around their necks. As they began to sing, Susanna took out her phone to film the performance:

It looks bad now but don't despair,
We just need time and money to prepare.
We're making plans,
Can't grow pecans . . .

The song progressed through multiple verses.

*. . . Stories to write,*
*Poetry to recite . . .*

The group joined hands and raised their arms as they approached the end:

*And we hope that soon you'll say*
*Hey, hey, this is the way!*

They dissolved into laughter.

"That was fantastic," Susanna said.

"Well done, students," Mrs. Randolph said, clapping.

"Okay, now listen to this," Susanna said to the students, who gathered around. She resisted the urge to speak in a rap rhythm herself. "You've given me a terrific presentation, but I need more than a presentation. I need forms filled out." Groans. "I know it's boring, but if you want the money, you do the work. That's part of the project, too." From her tote bag, she took a copy of the standard grant application and gave it to Mrs. Randolph, who gave it to Raffie. "If it were up to me, I'd give you an A-plus-plus and all the money you need. But the foundation has a board, and the board has a director, and they're the ones who make the decision."

Glancing through the papers, Raffie said to the kids, "I see we've got a tough job ahead. Back to the classroom to get started."

With their energy and enthusiasm, the kids seemed to glide down the stairs.

Susanna said to Raffie and Mrs. Randolph, "Let me know if you need help with this from people who've worked on similar projects. Your best first step is to apply for enough money to hire a consultant and an engineer. I've heard that city regulations can make this process more complicated than you'd ever think possible. Questions of handi-capped access, insurance, safety issues. The list goes on and on."

"We can deal with the city regulations," Mrs. Randolph said, "but I want the kids driving this as much as possible, learning as they go. They may be young, but they have to own the project. I don't want this to turn into just another bunch of rich do-gooders pushing stuff onto us. No offense meant."

"None taken," Susanna said. "I try my best not to give rich do-gooders a bad name. I try to give rich do-gooders a *good* name."

This earned a smile from Mrs. Randolph, pleasing Susanna im-mensely.

Later that day, Susanna studied the Matisse above the fireplace at Rob and Cornelia's apartment on Fifth Avenue in the Seventies. The painting portrayed a young woman sitting at a table reading amid a profusion of multicolored flowers.

Susanna happened to know—because it had been appraised recently with an eye toward either donating it to the Metropolitan Museum or selling it for the benefit of the foundation—that the painting was worth $23 million. What even 1 percent of that money could do to help Raffie and his students . . . Susanna stopped her imagination from going any farther in that direction. Large amounts of money dropped onto even the most worthy causes tended to be wasted, frittered away in confusion. Incremental steps were the only way to make lasting progress.

Even so, she felt the gap between the kids who'd performed for her this morning and the crowd gathering in Rob's apartment for a dinner to celebrate his mother's ninety-fifth birthday. The guest of honor received well-wishers from her wheelchair near the windows. She wore a red Chanel suit that looked not simply vintage but orig-inal, purchased sixty or seventy years earlier. Mrs. Barstow had a public reputation as a liberal firebrand and civil rights activist going back to the 1950s and '60s.

Cornelia Barstow greeted guests on the opposite side of the room, as if mother-in-law and daughter-in-law held separate spheres of influence. Cornelia wore an Asian-style, high-buttoned embroidered silk jacket over trousers. Rob stood in the middle, the mediator between the two. The vast apartment, on two floors, combined coffered ceilings and mahogany wainscoting with starkly modern furniture and modern paintings.

Susanna had been invited to many such events at the Barstow home. Cornelia and Rob were proud of what they accomplished through the foundation. A cynic might say that Susanna was a trophy being shown off to their friends, but in the realm of rich people's trophies—yachts, Maseratis, basketball teams—foundation director wasn't so bad.

Soon Susanna would be traveling to Buffalo for the closing on the two-family home on Lynfield Street where she'd grown up. From Lynfield Street to Fifth Avenue and Seventy-seventh Street . . . the distance still astonished her. When Susanna first began visiting Rob and Cornelia's home, she'd felt ill at ease. She'd worried about her clothes, her shoes, her jewelry; about what to say and how to say it. To learn the subtleties of good manners, she'd surreptitiously studied Cornelia. Step by step she'd trained herself to fit in, to look elegant and polished, to create a façade that made her appear as if she belonged.

"Susanna, I was hoping you'd be here," said Ina Freeman, joining her. Ina was Susanna's mentor and had given Susanna her first job after business school, at Rockefeller Philanthropy Advisors. When Rob was looking for a foundation director, Ina had recommended Susanna. With her slate-gray hair brushed back and her tailored suit, Ina was impeccably turned out, as usual. In the realm of refined self-presentation, Ina was an inspiration. Ina's father had worked on the factory floor of a GM facility outside Detroit. Susanna had noticed over the years that many foundation directors and staffers came from far different backgrounds than their board members. "How are you?" Ina said.

"Good. Work is going well."

From the look of concern on Ina's face, Susanna suspected that Ina was on the verge of asking about nonwork matters. Susanna didn't give her the opportunity.

"Today the students at a high school in Brooklyn treated me to a hip-hop performance. They're hoping to build a green roof. Tremendous curriculum potential."

"I've heard that constructing green roofs on public schools is a bureaucratic morass."

"I warned them, but the teachers and administration, not to mention the students, are fully committed."

"Keep me posted. It might be something we could become involved in, down the road."

Well, this was good news: she certainly would keep Ina informed.

Ina was drawn into another conversation, and Susanna went to the windows facing Fifth Avenue and Central Park. The towers of the San Remo and the Majestic, on Central Park West, glimmered in the distance. Hoover, Rob and Cornelia's overweight cat, reclined on the radiator cover. With effort, he maneuvered himself onto his back, as if inviting Susanna to caress his tummy, which she did. Because of the radiator heat, his fur felt especially dense and silken.

"Hello."

She turned.

Scott Schiffman was standing before her. Meeting him here, she saw him anew: he was dark-eyed and attractive. He didn't fit with Susanna's idea of a man who spent his days studying handwriting on old documents.

"You may not remember me. We met at the MacLean Library."

"Of course I remember you. It was only last week."

"I'd like you to forgive me for my impatience that day."

"Were you impatient?"

"You know I was. In fact, I was rude. The angry way I spoke to you was completely out of line."

He had a winning grin.

"Put it down to the shock and trauma of discovery," he continued. "It's not every day that a young woman . . . I won't say more in this relatively public place, but I trust you understand what I mean."

"I do understand." The content of the cantata ought to be enough to make any sensible person angry. She felt certain, however, that his anger had actually been prompted by her refusal to leave the manuscript with him. "What brings you here?"

"First tell me you forgive me." He seemed utterly at ease, to the manor born.

"I forgive you."

"Thank you. I'm here because my mother is an old friend of Mrs. Barstow's. They used to go on civil rights marches together, back in the '60s. My mother was in her twenties, and Mrs. Barstow was . . . older. My mom carried Mrs. Barstow's suitcase. Shared a room with her. Got arrested with her."

"That's fascinating."

"Anyway, I'm a last-minute addition for the dinner: my mother's usual escort, an entertaining confirmed bachelor who accompanies her everywhere, came down with the flu."

Susanna noticed that he didn't ask her what *she* was doing here. She sensed, uneasily, that he already knew a good deal about her. He couldn't know about the rape, however: the court records were sealed, and her name appeared nowhere. She'd done an Internet search on herself (several searches) and found nothing relating to it.

"I haven't been to this apartment in years," Scott said. "I'd forgotten the Matisse. You come here often?"

"I do."

"It's a long way from Buffalo."

"Yes."

"I've been to Buffalo," he added, as if not wanting to offend her, "and I can assure you it's not as bad as it's generally made out to be."

"I agree with you. What took you to Buffalo?"

"The Albright-Knox Art Gallery. It has a terrific collection."

She was beginning to like him. "I agree with you on that, too."

The group was moving into the dining room.

"I should find my mother. Help her to her seat. And I already checked, your table isn't my table. But I'm glad we saw each other and had a chance to talk."

"Me, too."

And Susanna *was* pleased to see him. But if he had some scheme to entice her into giving up control of the cantata, she thought as she took her place in the dining room, she wasn't falling for it.

## Chapter 17

Dan and his colleague Katarina sat in the playground bundled in coats and scarves while the girls romped from the jungle gym to the swings.

"What are you doing over Christmas break?" Katarina said.

"Visiting family. One week with my family, one week with Julie's. Becky will have fun playing with her cousins. I'll try to get some sleep."

He regretted saying that. It felt too personal for the playground. As usual, he'd woken up at 4:00 a.m. He'd tried to fall back to sleep, but he was haunted by Julie's vacant stare after Martin died, and by Martin in his little coffin. This morning, too, he'd felt his spiritual emptiness more acutely than usual.

He didn't want to reveal this to Katarina, or to anyone, so he masked it with chitchat.

"What about you? What are your plans?"

"We'll be with my mom and grandmom in Pittsburgh."

"What's your routine there?" He wasn't genuinely interested, but he wanted to keep her talking.

"Cooking, cleaning, home repair. Changing the lightbulbs they can't reach. This year will be special, though: I finally convinced my grandmother to do an oral history. I'll ask her questions and record her answers. We're going to do the interview in Czech, so she'll feel more relaxed."

Katarina and her mother had been born in America, but her grandmother came from Bohemia and had spent the war years there. She'd been a kitchen worker for the SS administrators at Theresienstadt. Katarina had shared the basic facts with him long ago.

Dan said, "Forgive me for prying, but how does your family deal with your grandmother's . . ."

"Job. That's what we call it. Her job. She was a young woman alone. She needed a job. That was the job available. She could have turned it down and starved. How many people can be heroes?"

She was silent. Then, "Even though she agreed to do the oral history, Grandmom keeps saying she can't remember anything. Sometimes I wonder if her story is plausible. Wouldn't the SS have used prisoners to do kitchen work? Maybe Grandmom created the story to cover up something else that happened to her. Something she thought was worse. Maybe she was in fact a prisoner. I just don't know. I'll have to consult with experts to see if the details of her story pan out."

She shook her head, as if to cast off her doubts. "In case her story does pan out, I'm planning ahead for a book. I'm thinking big: *I Was a Chef at Theresienstadt*, how's that for a memoir title? Or *Concentration Camp Cook*. That has alliteration. Although a recipe for, say, Bohemian potato-peel soup garnished with dandelions may not qualify her as a chef, or even a cook, exactly. And she might only have washed dishes. But the situation does bring the idea of fresh local foods, the whole locavore movement, into a new perspective."

Dan was accustomed to Katarina's black humor.

"If her story is true, does she bear responsibility for what happened at Theresienstadt? Being a cook, or even a dishwasher, wasn't the same as being a guard. Or was it? Maybe she smuggled the SS officers' food to the prisoners. Or maybe she didn't. I'm hoping that if I ask her under the guise of doing an interview, everything will be less personal and emotional, and we'll be able to discuss things that we wouldn't say otherwise."

In Dan's own family, forgetfulness was the rule regarding relatives who'd been in Germany during the war years. His relatives, of course, were on the other side. The side of the aggressors.

"My mother and grandmother made certain that I grew up speaking German and Czech both. Czech in case the Americans ever sent us back, German in case *they* came looking for me. The threat of an amorphous *they* was big in my childhood. It's stupid, I know, but I applied for a passport for Lizzie right after she was born."

Becky didn't have a passport.

"When I look at Lizzie, I wonder what languages I should be teaching her." The girls were going up and down on the seesaw, Becky leaning back and forth in heedless delight. "What language will *they* be speaking next time? Chinese? Arabic? Hindi? Never too early to start defensive planning."

The wind picked up. Katarina pulled her hat down over her forehead. "I've had just about enough of sitting in the cold watching children play. But before we go home, forgive me for bringing up a sensitive topic: Are you ready yet to start dating?"

The shift took him by surprise.

"I only ask because I have a line of women-in-waiting."

"Thank you, but I don't think so."

"It's been a year and a half. That might be enough time for you. Or it might not. Frankly, that's not my concern. Don't start dating for *them.* Or even for yourself. Start dating for *me.* These women don't give me a minute's peace. You've got to help me make them stop bothering me. I've got a daughter, a husband, a mother, and a grand-mother. I've got terrific and demanding students. I've got research to do and books to write. I can't afford to spend my precious time contending with women who'd like to get to know you better. What should I tell them?"

"You could say—" He wanted to make a joke of it, but he wasn't able to muster any humor. "I don't know, Katarina." He struggled to remain impassive in front of his colleague.

She stared at him. "All right. I'll accept no for now, with the stipulation that I'll ask you again when I've determined the time is right."

She stood and walked toward the girls, who were running to the slide. "One turn down the slide for each of you, and then we leave."

With Becky safe in her room hosting a tea party for her dolls, Dan sat at the desk in his study and stared out the window instead of reading term papers. Julie's desire to make everything in the house cozy had led to a Persian carpet in shades of red and velvety curtains to frame his staring bouts. Floor-to-ceiling CDs lined one wall. Books lined another. As he whiled away his time not grading term papers, Bach's viola da gamba sonatas were playing on his stereo system. The sonatas filled the room with a joie de vivre that Dan didn't feel.

He'd made a good number of scholarly breakthroughs, such as they were, staring out this window. He glanced at the stack of term papers. His guilt about them led him to reflect once again on how fortunate he was. This was his *work*, and excellent it was, compared with the labors of most people in the world, including himself in previous years. One summer in college he'd cleaned gutters. Another summer, he'd done roofing. Every November and December week-end during his teenage years, from midnight until 6:00 a.m., he and his brother worked at a turkey farm, grabbing unruly birds by the legs, turning them upside down, and loading them into a truck.

Dan had never looked at Thanksgiving or Christmas dinner the same way after that.

The term papers began to take on an accusatory edge.

He remembered his promise to Susanna Kessler, that he'd help her do better than the set of Bach's greatest hits she'd downloaded. He'd devoted his life to Bach's music, and he wanted to prove to her that there was a lot more to the repertory than the cantata she'd found.

He decided to let himself be impulsive. He'd order for her a collection of five CDs of Bach's instrumental music. He sensed she was younger than he was, so maybe she no longer listened to music on CDs. He still thought in terms of CDs and saw their merits, however, so they'd have to do. He logged on to the Internet music site Arkiv. Five CDs suitable for a desert island.

As he went through the website, debating the repertoire and performances, the project became absorbing and moving. Most likely Susanna wouldn't realize how much it meant to him. But she'd surely be excited to receive the package. She'd open it, she'd maybe play the CDs several times over the following week . . . he liked imagining her doing this.

While he reviewed the options, he kept his eye on the time. He needed to start dinner at 5:30. That meant he soon needed to turn on the oven and put in a casserole dish of—he didn't know what. Every Friday afternoon, in return for expenses and a modest fee, a retired woman from church arrived at the house with several bags of groceries and cooked meals for the coming week, putting each day's dish into the freezer, labeled by date. Each morning he transferred the designated container from the freezer to the refrigerator, in preparation for baking in the evening. He felt awkward about essentially hiring a personal cook, but at least this way Becky always had a hot and healthy dinner, with daily variety. Left to his own devices, he and Becky would have eaten pizza with onions, pineapple, and pepperoni (drawing from three basic food groups) every night, and they'd have enjoyed it, too. But Julie wouldn't have been happy about it.

He had only twenty minutes remaining to review the Arkiv site. He didn't want to leave this for later, when he might not be feeling as impetuous as he felt now. Okay, decisions: the oboe concertos with Marcel Ponseele, that was a must. So many good performances of the cello suites . . . let's go with Jean-Guihen Queyras. The violin concertos—Amandine Beyer. The first of Pierre Hantaï's two excellent recordings of the Goldberg Variations. The lute music for sure, but with Jakob Lindberg or Hopkinson Smith? A tough call. The Lindberg was perhaps a bit more introspective; Susanna might appreciate that.

He had his five. But so much was missing, even without the sacred music. How about the Brandenburg Concertos? He loved them, but they'd become overused. The last time he arrived at New York's Penn Station, they were blaring over the loudspeaker system. The local mall in Granville played them at the holidays. He'd read studies indicating that classical music in shopping malls and transportation terminals discouraged teenagers from congregating. The justly renowned Brandenburg Concertos had become a weapon in the battle against loitering teenagers.

Nonetheless he'd add one more disk to make it six. The viola da gamba sonatas, the same recording he was listening to now. Vittorio Ghielmi on gamba and Lorenzo Ghielmi on the fortepiano. He loved this recording for its clarity, and for its combination of melancholy and high spirits.

At 5:17, he pressed the ORDER tab. He was asked for the shipping address. With a quick bit of online sleuthing, he was able to find her home address. The site asked if he wanted to write a gift card. This he hadn't planned for. He might not need a gift card. The CDs were self-explanatory.

Yet he didn't want anything misconstrued, so maybe he did need a gift note. He tried some examples. Belated Happy Hanukkah. Happy New Year. These didn't sound right.

Maxim, the cat, stared at him from the armrest of the old sofa that Dan and Julie had put into his study when they bought a new one for the living room. Julie had added a variety of pillows and something called *throws* to conceal the sofa's shabbiness. Maxim liked to use this sofa as a scratching post. He also took a perverse pleasure in rolling over it, spreading his fur. Thus Dan never sat on the sofa. Maxim's fur was black, with accents (as Julie called them) of white on his paws and chest.

Julie had adopted Maxim when an elderly woman from church died and the pastor's wife e-mailed the congregation to find a home for a grieving cat. This was exactly the type of cat Julie liked, a grieving cat who needed a home. Maxim had been named after the main character in the novel *Rebecca*. Although Dan hadn't read the book, he'd seen the movie, and the cat's original owner must have been lonely indeed to name her cat Maxim. Julie went to meet Maxim, and it was love at first sight for them both. They became inseparable. During Julie's last days, spent here at home with hospice nurses, Maxim had never left her bed except to eat and do his business. Dan had found Maxim licking Julie's face after she died, before the undertaker arrived.

Dan had never liked Maxim. Because of this, he'd never stopped to consider how Maxim was taking Julie's death. Dan supplied the cat with food and water, and cleaned the litter box, but he'd made no effort to pay attention to Maxim, despite what Julie would have wanted. Since Julie's death, Maxim had slept on Becky's bed.

Unblinking, Maxim continued to eye Dan, passing some inscrutable judgment as Dan prepared to send CDs to a woman not his wife.

To hell with that accusing cat. Dan looked again at the Arkiv request for a gift card. Keep it innocuous. *Thought you'd enjoy these.* Dan clicked on the SEND button.

## Chapter 18

After the real estate closing in downtown Buffalo, Susanna felt wrapped in sadness. With her childhood home sold, and her high school friends scattered around the country, when would she ever return to this city?

She and her mother bid a temporary farewell to Diane and Jenna for the short drive to the art museum, where the four of them planned to share a celebratory lunch. Heading to the parking lot where they'd left their rental car, Susanna and Evelyn walked along sidewalks defined by snow mounds. The city's nineteenth-century architectural landmarks rose around them with a resplendent grandeur. The air itself seemed to shimmer, the wind across Lake Erie carrying ice crystals that sparkled in the winter sun.

Snow began to fall, even as the sun was shining . . . a light snowfall of fat, floating flakes. The combination of snow and sunshine turned Susanna's much-maligned hometown into a place of enchantment.

Evelyn stopped walking. "This is so beautiful," she said. "You want to know something surprising, Susanna? I'm going to miss that house. Even though I never really liked it."

Evelyn's eyes were watering—from the cold, or was her mother crying? Snowflakes accumulated on her mother's hat and scarf, accentuating her Florida tan. Everything about her, from her stylish short haircut to her suede boots, seemed well thought out, as if now, in retirement, she finally had both the time and money to become the type of person she'd always hoped to be.

"I never thought I'd spend so much of my life in this city. But now that we'll probably never come back, I feel, I don't know, like I never looked at it before. After your father died and we were alone . . ." Her words drifted off.

Evelyn had never spoken about herself to Susanna. These fragments of her mother's thoughts felt precious, like an entry into who she really was, behind the parental façade she put on for Susanna.

"Of course, if we'd moved somewhere else, I never would have met Jack." Before his retirement, Jack had been an attorney at the law firm where Evelyn worked as a secretary. After his wife died, they began dating. "So everything turned out okay in the end." Evelyn wiped her eyes and tightened her scarf. "We should get going. Diane and Jenna will wonder what's become of us."

The moment of confidences was gone. Nonetheless, Evelyn's few revelations gave Susanna courage: "Mom, I've been trying to find out what happened to our family in Europe."

"What family in Europe?"

They turned onto Washington Street. The parking lot was up ahead, at Swan Street.

"We don't have any family in Europe," Evelyn added.

"From before the war. Your aunts and uncles and their families. Your cousins." When Evelyn said nothing, Susanna felt compelled to ask, "Remember?"

"Not really," Evelyn said, as if they were discussing something insignificant, like a mislaid pair of gloves.

"There are websites now where you can trace people who were caught up in the war. Not everyone is listed, but many are."

"Oh, honey, why stir up the past?"

"After the war, did Grandma try to find our relatives?"

"I think there were ways to find people, right after the war. If they were alive. I was young then, so I don't really remember. Your grandparents didn't talk about it. At least not to me."

"Didn't you wonder about your lost relatives?" Susanna's questions felt even more pressing after what she'd learned about the text of Henry's cantata manuscript.

"Why should I? I was young. I had other things to think about."

"You must have wondered."

"It wasn't something we ever talked about."

To Susanna, Evelyn's reaction sounded rehearsed, long kept in reserve for a moment like this.

"I don't believe you." Immediately Susanna regretted this, feeling she'd overstepped a boundary. No going back now, however. "I overheard you and Henry whispering."

"Whether you believe me or not, that's what happened. And we may have been whispering, but not about that. Most likely about *you*," she added with what sounded like affection.

"An entire family . . . you mean you pretended they never even existed?"

"We didn't have to pretend or not pretend. It was what it was. The relatives had our address and if they survived they could have found us, if they wanted to."

"What if the kids were the only ones who survived? Did the kids know where you were or even who you were?"

"Susanna, it's seventy years since the war started. They're all dead by now anyway. What does it matter?"

"Are you dead? Am I dead?" She didn't want to goad Evelyn, but she couldn't help herself. "Don't you wonder if you have cousins, even living in this country? They could have ended up here in Buffalo. They might be ordering lattes at Spot Coffee right now."

"You should let it go."

"Is it so awful, to want to know about my own family?"

Evelyn said nothing.

"I need to confirm the spelling of your mother's maiden name."

"What for?"

"For the Internet search. There are a lot of variations in the spelling of last names."

They turned into the entryway of the parking garage. They walked up the grease-stained incline to the second level. The noxious odor of gasoline filled the air.

"There's the car," Evelyn said, spotting it up ahead, a well-scrubbed white Nissan. "Jack says we're going to need a new car next year. This might be a good choice. A level up from the Honda, but I think we can swing it. Why don't I drive to the art gallery. See how it feels."

Susanna found the keys in her purse and passed them to her mother. Susanna got into the passenger side of the car.

"I wonder what's on the menu these days at the restaurant at the Albright." Evelyn adjusted her seat and the mirrors. "I hope we'll have time to look at the art. Remember how you used to volunteer with the young kids in the art classes, and how you loved seeing the paintings?"

Susanna did remember. Sunday afternoons at the museum . . . splashes of colors across giant canvases. The Albright specialized in abstract expressionism.

"I should have checked on the special exhibitions," Evelyn said. "What with worrying about the closing for the house, it went completely out of my mind."

They drove out of the parking lot. When they reached Delaware Avenue, they made a right, and they drove past City Hall, majestic in its Art Deco splendor. Snow and sunshine still surrounded them.

"I like the way this car handles," Evelyn said. "Nice and easy."

Susanna tried again: "Mom, I know I shouldn't have done this, but once when I was a kid, I looked through your desk, and I saw a document that gave Altschuler as your mother's maiden name." She spelled it. "Is that correct?"

She didn't tell Evelyn that she'd already tried this name and found nothing. She didn't want to give Evelyn the opportunity to say, *You see—I told you so.*

"The websites offer alternate spellings," Susanna said, "but the search will be easier if I have the closest spelling I can get. That's how a computer works."

"I know how a computer works."

Susanna felt foolish. Evelyn's law firm had organized computer classes for the staff, to bring them up to date on software advances.

She tried another question: "What was the family's profession?"

"I have no idea."

Susanna tried not to sigh like a surly teenager. "How big was the family?"

"I'm sure it was huge."

"What makes you say that?"

"All families were large in those days."

"What about the name of the town or village they came from?" Susanna insisted, sounding like a child even to herself, slipping into the role that Evelyn set for her. "Did Grandma ever mention the name? Did you ever see the return address on the letters?"

"Susanna, I was young. My guess is the place doesn't even exist anymore. The Sudetenland, Czechoslovakia, the Czech Republic. How can you figure anything out?"

"It must have had a name."

"I do remember my mother saying it was outside one of those spa towns. Marienbad, maybe. Or Karlsbad. I remember my mother talking once about going to Marienbad, or Karlsbad, when she was little, to see the emperor ride his horse in a parade. I think it was the emperor. The Austrian Jews loved Emperor Franz-Joseph, I do remember her saying that. He gave the Jews freedoms they'd never had before. But it may have been just a prince or an archduke that she saw."

"How far away was Marienbad, or Karlsbad, from her town? Did she have to stay overnight, was it that far away from her home?"

"This happened to your grandmother a hundred years ago. Before the *First* World War. Your grandmother wanted to forget all that. Look what a wonderful country this is: your grandparents came to this country with nothing, and here you are, working for a family so rich they might as well be the Rockefellers. Helping them give money to charity. Doing *mitzvahs* every day. For complete strangers. That couldn't happen anyplace except in America. Henry was so proud of you."

Susanna knew this was true.

After several minutes passed, Evelyn said, as if offhandedly, "By the way, it's Alshue."

"Pardon?"

"My mother's maiden name. Alshue." Evelyn spelled it. Susanna found a pen and paper in her purse and wrote it down.

"A-L-S-H-U-E?" Susana asked doubtfully, looking at what she'd written.

"Yes, that's right. I don't know what document you saw, or imagined you saw, years ago, but the name is Alshue."

Susanna wondered if this was only half a name. Still, it was more than she'd had before.

They rounded Gates Circle and drove onto Chapin Parkway, a broad boulevard with six rows of trees across it and well-kept homes on either side. Snow dusted the branches.

"Since you're so eager to learn about the past, Susanna, I should tell you that even in America things weren't easy for Jews when I was young. I don't know what happened to our family in Europe, but I do know why more Jews didn't end up in America: because America wouldn't take them. America didn't want any more of their kind. Our kind. The immigration quotas were low, but even the low quotas weren't filled because supposedly there weren't enough people who were acceptable to be future Americans."

Susanna did already know this. When she was an undergraduate at Columbia, she'd taken a history course on America between World War I and World War II. She'd learned about the anti-Jewish radio tirades of Father Coughlin. About the hatred promulgated by Henry Ford, who received a medal from Hitler. The negative sentiments expressed even by Eleanor Roosevelt, in her younger days. The rise of the pro-Nazi German American Bund. The quotas on university admissions. Susanna had seen photographs of signs posted outside country clubs and hotels: *No Hebrews*. Sometimes the signs said, *No Hebrews, no dogs*.

But the history course had covered many topics of American life between the wars, and Susanna had never thought specifically about her own family when she learned American history. She'd never taken the history personally. Besides, other minority groups, especially African Americans, had faced much more difficult discrimination.

"The war ruined my mother's life. She lost her family, and she couldn't find out what happened to them. She was nervous all the time, ready to snap. She worried about every little thing. Each morning when I left for school, she was afraid that I wouldn't come home at the end of the day, because *they* would take me away. She never specified who *they* were. I couldn't wait to get away from her. And Henry—the war ruined his life, too. I don't even know everything that happened to him. He wouldn't tell me. He was tortured inside himself."

"So that's why—"

"You think the war is over, Susanna? It isn't over. Don't you understand why so many of the survivors don't want to talk about it? Oh, yes, the fighting stopped and everybody declared peace, but the war, what it did to people, goes on and on and still hasn't stopped and probably won't ever stop. Look at you, seventy years later and you're still asking questions."

Susanna stared at Evelyn. Evelyn stared at the road. She took the curve around Soldier's Place. They were only a few blocks from Lynfield Street and their old home. As if to avoid Lynfield and its memories, Evelyn made a right onto Lincoln Parkway, with its regimented rows of trees. The snow had stopped.

"This car is so smooth. When I get home, I'm going to tell Jack to arrange to do a test drive."

They drove past a row of mansions, and the street opened into a magnificent vista of Delaware Park. On their left was the Albright-Knox Art Gallery with its columns and caryatids evoking the Parthenon. In the distance was the neoclassical Historical Society. On their right was the park lake, frozen and covered with snow.

## Chapter 19

The June weather was exquisite. Sara's formally attired guests walked along the river, or gathered in shifting groups across the lawn. In her role as hostess, Sara stood at the open doors leading from the house onto the veranda. She greeted newcomers as they arrived.

Although the French occupation continued and Prussia remained a vassal state, the political situation in Berlin had stabilized. The royal family had been allowed to return to the city. In large measure, the soldiers who had once patrolled the streets had been withdrawn. Sara's gatherings of music and conversation had resumed, although not in their former splendor. Friends who had left the city because of financial difficulties had not returned. Friends killed in battle would never return.

Alexander von Humboldt was here this afternoon. Karl Gustav von Brinkmann. Carl Friedrich Zelter. And a new generation had begun to visit her salon, men and women in their twenties. With their commitment and determination, they gave Sara hope for the future. In recent years, Sara had become a mother of sorts: young poets, writers, and artists stayed at her home (hardly an imposition considering the size of the house, entire wings unused). She introduced them to society, listened to their romantic torments, and urged them to complete their musical compositions, their books and plays, their essays and poems.

"Bettina, Countess von Arnim," the butler announced.

Sara crossed the reception room to greet her. "My dear Bettina, welcome."

Twenty-six-year-old Bettina von Arnim, *geborene* Brentano, was a writer. She was striking in a disturbing way, plain and stolid, her eyes too big for her face. Her husband, Count Ludwig Achim von Arnim, was an essayist, and he had lived here at Sara's home for a time. In fact, Arnim had proposed to Bettina in Sara's garden. The two were only recently married.

"Thank you for inviting me, Frau Levy." Because of their age difference, Sara called Bettina by her given name, and Bettina called Sara by her family name. Bettina seemed to hold back from Sara today, uncharacteristically timid.

"I'm so very glad you're here." Sara had heard a report from her nephew Moritz Itzig, who studied philosophy at the university, that recently Count von Arnim had delivered a lecture filled with anti-Jewish invective. Military defeat and economic hardship often brought out such nonsense. The presence of French soldiers in the streets had led many to idealize German history and folktales, and to yearn for a mythical German purity.

After Napoleon was defeated, as someday he must be, these misguided passions would dissipate, Sara felt certain.

"Will Count von Arnim be joining us?" Sara had invited them both, despite the report she'd heard from Moritz. To invite Bettina to this gathering without her spouse would be rude.

"I don't know." Bettina seemed nervous. "Perhaps later."

"No matter," Sara said, trying to find a way to set Bettina at ease. "You'll find many friends in the garden." Regardless of what happened in the harsh world outside, Bettina would always be welcome here. "Please, enjoy this lovely day."

Other newcomers joined them, and Bettina slipped away. When Sara next looked out at the garden, she saw that Bettina had indeed met several friends, and she sat with them upon a bench by the water. Amalia Beer and Alexander von Humboldt walked along the river. Alexander appeared to be pointing out to Amalia a bird hiding amid the rushes.

This afternoon Amalia's son Jacob would be performing for them. He was rehearsing in the concert salon, and the sound of his virtuoso scales and arpeggios reached Sara with hints of what was to come. Jacob Meyerbeer, as he called himself (having put together the surnames of his grandfathers), was the twenty-year-old prodigy in their midst. He'd been performing in public since he was eleven.

"Hello, Tante." It was Lea.

"There you are, my darling."

Lea had moved back to Berlin with her family because of increasing tensions with the French in Hamburg.

"I hope you don't mind: I've brought Fanny to hear the music."

The girl, six years old, stood behind her mother. She gripped her mother's gown. In her formal clothes, Fanny looked like Lea in miniature.

"I'm always delighted to see Fanny." Sara leaned down toward her. "Welcome to the party, Fanny."

The girl curtsied. "Thank you for including me," she recited in a light, precise voice.

"Fanny, you may play in the garden now," Lea said. "But don't go far. I'll be watching you."

Fanny ran off with abandon, her hair and its ribbons tossing.

From a distance, Sara could see the difference in the height of her shoulders. Fanny shared with her grandfather Moses Mendelssohn a deformity of the back, severe for the philosopher, slight for Fanny, and never mentioned.

"How are your little ones?" Sara asked.

Felix was two, and Rebecka was a newborn.

"They are thriving. You must see them again soon. Tomorrow would be perfect."

"Thank you. I'll visit you tomorrow. Meanwhile today, you should stroll by the water and enjoy the sunshine."

"You must come outside, too, not stay here to greet the stragglers."

"That's my role as hostess: to greet the stragglers."

"I'll return for you in ten minutes. Anyone who arrives after that doesn't deserve to find you waiting."

"Thank you."

Sara watched Lea cross the lawn. Fanny ran to her and took her hand. Together they walked toward the river.

"Count Ludwig Achim von Arnim," announced the butler.

Count von Arnim was dashing and handsome, a Romantic figure in the best sense. Sara approached him cordially, ignoring what Moritz had told her. Arnim was dressed in street clothes rather than the formal attire the others wore. Undoubtedly he'd come from pressing endeavors. Men nowadays . . . one couldn't expect them to be devoted to the intricacies of dress. The world was changing, and the rules of society must change, too.

"Welcome, my friend," she said.

He ignored her. He walked onto the veranda.

"Greetings, everyone. Is Countess von Arnim here?" he said to the general group.

Sara was confused. She followed him outside.

"Has anyone seen my wife?"

Studying him more closely, Sara saw that his cravat was askew, his skin reddened. He was an attractive man, but today dark circles ringed his eyes. He must be inebriated.

"Count von Arnim," she said, approaching him once more. "Some refreshment?"

She motioned to the food, presented buffet-style. Most likely he'd missed his lunch. Drinking without food was always ill-advised. Recently she'd heard, as one did in society, that he was suffering from financial problems, that he was in debt and at the mercy of his bankers. After the pressures of the occupation, many noblemen were in similar positions. She must be kind to him.

"Ah, Zelter," Arnim called, spotting the director of the Sing-Akademie amid the crowd. "I must tell you, I heard a superb joke today: Why do Jews have big noses?"

Zelter stared at his plate.

"Because the air is free!" Arnim thundered forth.

Zelter turned away as if he hadn't heard.

Sara knew about Arnim's penchant for such supposed witticisms. Heretofore he'd kept this penchant in check during his frequent visits to her home. He'd always been a gentleman here. Sara thought back on the day that Arnim and Bettina had become engaged. They'd been sitting in close conversation, holding hands, on the same bench where Bettina sat now. When they'd returned to the terrace, Bettina whispered the news to Sara. Delighted, Sara called for champagne. Arnim made the announcement to the gathered guests, and everyone had toasted the new couple.

"What is that smell?" Arnim asked the crowd.

"The garden is in bloom," Sara said.

Without looking at her, he said, "I do not refer to the sweet fragrance of nature. I mean the other smell. The stench. The *foetor Judaicus*."

And then he laughed. His laughter was cutting, bitter, and cruel.

*Foetor Judaicus*, the stench of Jews. An ancient slur.

Conversation on the terrace ceased. Sara's guests looked to her for guidance. She knew her duty: to coddle Arnim back to his proper self. "Even if you dined earlier, my dear Count, you must dine again with me." She went to the sideboard to prepare a plate for him. "I recall you have a fondness for apricot preserves."

"I'm here to fetch my wife. Where is she?"

"Arnim, how are things at your estate in the country?" Count Gustav von Brinkmann was with him now, steering him to the side of the terrace, out of the way. Count von Brinkmann had been serving as Swedish ambassador to London, and he was visiting Berlin only for a short time. How Sara had missed him. "Are you preparing for the planting?"

No doubt the planting was over by now. Brinkmann was grasping at a way to distract their inebriated friend. Brinkmann—how she loved him.

"I haven't been in the country. I've been in the city. Clemens Brentano and I have been busy." Clemens Brentano, Bettina's brother, was a poet.

"Good, good," Brinkmann said. "A man needs solid work to focus his mind. I've been in England, so I haven't heard—what have you two been doing?"

"We've created a dining and study club," Arnim said, his expression turning sly. "A *Christlich-deutsche Tischgesellschaft*. With strict rules." He looked around, eyes narrowed, as if measuring those who might challenge him. "No women, no French, no Jews. We Germans must have some standards."

The gentlemen formed an isolating circle around him, a conspicuous warning to him, in the confines of their refined society. Sara felt as if she were witnessing the fulfillment of a stage direction in a play: *The gentlemen stand in a circle around him.*

"Countess von Arnim!" he called, spotting her.

Bettina was hurrying across the lawn. She reached him.

"Bettina—I smell the stench of the Jewish banker, snatching up everything that's good and right in Prussia."

His financial troubles must be worse than the rumors said. Why hadn't he come to her for help? Samuel had left her financially well protected. She would have assisted Arnim, if only she'd known. She'd helped others through the challenges of the occupation.

"Arnim," said Brinkmann, placing a cautioning hand upon his shoulder. "You're not yourself today."

"Let's stop all the politeness and recognize what we've known for years. The Jews are destroying Prussia. They're stealing the very best of our nation."

Her nephew Moritz pushed himself through the circle of gentlemen. "How dare you visit my aunt's house and insult her with your disgraceful attire and your aggressive words?"

"Ah, the *foetor* becomes stronger as you come closer, young man. Now I know the source of it."

"For these insults to my family, I demand satisfaction."

"The Jewboy imagines that he will defend his honor?"

"Yes, I do, sir."

All understood that Moritz had challenged Arnim to a duel. Traditionally in Prussia, duels were the prerogative of the nobility, not of Jews.

The afternoon was spinning dangerously away from Sara.

"I say that a Jew has no honor to defend," Arnim said.

Bettina said, "Dearest, please, silence now." She pulled at his arm. "Let us depart."

The desperation in Bettina's voice. Sara's heart went out to her.

"Don't bother me, woman." After calling for her, now he was shaking her off.

"That's quite enough," said Alexander von Humboldt. He'd settled in Paris but visited Berlin regularly. He was Sara's friend, her savior. Amalia was beside him. "Let me see you to a coach, Arnim, since you're unwell today. I will return shortly, Frau Levy. Please don't begin the music until then. And do me the honor of reserving a seat for me, beside you."

Sara understood: this was his way of saying to everyone present (and those many who were not present, but would hear of it later), *I am with you.*

"I want to hear our young Berliner perform," Humboldt continued. "Now there's a Prussian spirit to be proud of, our Jacob Meyerbeer."

Humboldt took one of Arnim's arms, and Brinkmann took the other. Bettina followed, head down.

"Let go of me," Arnim said, trying to break loose.

They grasped him more tightly. They led him away.

"He'll regret this," Moritz said. "I will fight him."

"Hush, Moritz," said Amalia, as if scolding a child.

And then: silence.

Sara was at a loss. Glancing around, she saw Lea and Fanny standing at the side of the veranda. She wouldn't allow these events to cause them distress.

Gathering her composure, she said to the group, "We have a special guest with us today. My grandniece, Fanny Mendelssohn. As we gather in the music room for the recital, let us leave places for her and her mother in the front row, so that Fanny may be inspired by our brilliant Meyerbeer."

Sara opened the French doors into the music room. Jacob leapt from his chair, apparently so absorbed in rehearsing that he hadn't heard the commotion or been aware of the passage of time. How like his mother he was, with his thick dark hair and large dark eyes.

Amalia went to him, touching his shoulder and speaking to him in reassurance.

Sara said, "Everyone, please take your seats."

Jacob went outside so he could make a proper entrance after he'd been introduced.

The guests sat down. Sara stood by the fortepiano and reviewed the brief remarks she'd prepared.

No, she was too shaken to read them. She'd ask Humboldt to read them for her. She couldn't trust herself: she wouldn't allow her guests, especially Lea and Fanny, to see her upset.

While she waited for the gentlemen to return, alternate scenarios pushed into her mind, words she might have said to Arnim, things she might have done, to make everything turn out differently. Anger and pain warred within her, first telling her to lash out, then telling her to weep.

She would allow herself to do neither. The rules of society held her like a vise. She took control of herself. She had a job to do: to keep this grand occasion of her salon flowing smoothly.

In a few hours, these sordid events would no doubt be discussed at evening meals across the city. Friends and family members who weren't here today would learn what had happened and visit Sara tomorrow with the sole purpose of inquiring about it. Amalia would want to review all the details, everything she'd missed while strolling along the river with Humboldt. This would be the *cause célèbre* of the summer. Of the year.

As Sara saw to it that everyone was comfortable, she made her resolution: she would not allow her life, and her future, to be defined by this incident.

She would practice and perform her music, nurture her honorary children and grandchildren, and strive to be someone her friends could trust and rely upon.

And she would never speak of this day again.

Already she knew that Arnim's mockery of her family heritage, and his savage and brutal laughter, would smolder within her forever.

## Chapter 20

As Rob and Susanna walked out of the lobby of the glass office tower and onto East Forty-fifth Street between Madison and Park, the wind whipped around them. Rob didn't notice.

"I'm thrilled," he said.

At the meeting they'd just attended, an old friend of Rob's had proposed that the Barstow Family Foundation donate a new building, complete with a theater as well as rehearsal, production, and administrative facilities, to Rob's beloved Gilbert and Sullivan troupe. This would require the foundation to go into principal to make a lump-sum donation of $25 million to get the process started.

"What fun!"

"No," Susanna said.

She confronted a line of black cars with waiting drivers. The cars shielded billionaires from the world they'd created.

"Let's set up a meeting with the architect."

"No."

"It's cultural, it's educational, it's everything we do."

"No."

Oscar, Rob's driver, was in one of the black cars lined up before them. Susanna texted him.

"I do so love Gilbert and Sullivan," Rob said with a wistful sigh.

"That's not relevant."

Oscar emerged from a car halfway down the block.

"What an opportunity. I'm grateful. Honored. The Barstow Foundation can guarantee Gilbert and Sullivan in New York City for generations to come."

"Rob—"

"Did he mention a costume shop? I don't think he did. He's not as alert to production issues as I am. Put the costume shop on the list for the architects."

"*Rob*—enough." She grabbed his arm to gain his attention. "Can you honestly say that providing a place for rich people to put on Gilbert and Sullivan productions is the best fulfillment of the foundation's mission?"

He gazed at her in bewilderment. "Gilbert and Sullivan operettas aren't just for rich people. All types of people enjoy Gilbert and Sullivan."

"If you want to support musical theater, why don't we expand the foundation's involvement in existing public school programs? As you well know, many public schools offer no music or drama at all."

"I've been involved with this Gilbert and Sullivan troupe for fifty years. I've been offered a remarkable opportunity to assure its future."

"And I hope you're involved with it for fifty more years. With your own, personal funds. It's not the mission of the Barstow Family Foundation to build a Gilbert and Sullivan center."

"Flexibility is key in running a family foundation."

"Flexibility within limits. The foundation is a kind of public trust."

"You think I'm treating the foundation as a piggy bank for indulging my personal whims?"

"I wouldn't put it so starkly."

"I should hope not."

"You'll need the support of the board." The foundation board was composed of Rob, his mother, his wife, their four children (the youngest was nearing forty), and the children's spouses, along with two nonfamily financial advisers. The family members were divided almost equally between participating in Gilbert and Sullivan productions and rolling their eyes at any mention of Gilbert and Sullivan. Susanna didn't know the views of the financial advisers. "Approval won't be easy," she said with what she hoped sounded like conviction.

"I wouldn't be so certain of that," Rob said.

"If they do approve it, I'll resign."

What had she said? The words had leapt from her without forethought.

"Obviously you have to do what you believe is right," Rob said.

"Yes."

In silence, they walked toward Oscar. When they reached him, Oscar evaluated them astutely. "Hello, my friends," he said. "We're in a wind tunnel. Let's get out of it." Oscar wore a gray suit that accentuated his lithe body. His tightly curled gray hair was turning white. He spoke with a clipped accent. "I've kept the car heated for you."

"Thank you, Oscar," Rob said. "You take the car, Susanna."

She had two meetings uptown.

"I'll walk back to the office," he said.

"No problem to drop you off, sir," Oscar said.

"Ms. Kessler and I have had a disagreement. Not certain I want to continue it in the backseat of my car."

"Whatever the disagreement is, no sense you catching cold over it. Ms. Kessler's just doing her job, I'm sure, Mr. Barstow."

"No doubt you're right, Oscar."

"Thank you, Mr. Barstow. Much appreciated."

"Even so, I'll walk."

"As you wish. Allow me, Ms. Kessler." Oscar opened the car door for her.

"Thank you, Oscar." Susanna slid onto the soft leather. The car smelled of Cornelia's perfume, Chanel No. 5. Was Rob really going to walk? "Plenty of room for you, Rob. We can put business aside for ten minutes."

"Farewell," Rob said in his best melodramatic Gilbert and Sullivan fashion, waving goodbye with a sweep of his arm as if he were the Pirate King.

They watched him head up the block.

"Sounds like you two had a tough discussion," Oscar said.

"I couldn't go along with something he wants."

"That's called doing your duty."

"I hope so, Oscar."

"He'll recover."

"We'll see."

"Part of your job is to protect him from himself. I've done the same over the years."

"Thank you for saying."

"There're some M and Ms in the covered candy tray. Mrs. Barstow always says, *M and Ms after a tough meeting.*"

"She's insightful, isn't she? I'm sure she's had a lot of experience with tough discussions." Cornelia Barstow sat on many nonprofit boards.

"I've observed that she has special expertise in protecting Mr. Barstow from himself. Well then, on to our next stop."

Oscar eased the car into Midtown traffic, and they headed uptown. The skyscrapers reflected the clouds, as if she and Oscar were traveling through a cloud forest. She didn't want any M&Ms.

She felt the impact of what she'd said, and it cut her with anxiety. She'd stood up for what was right, but that would be small consolation if she did, in fact, lose her job.

———

At St. George's Church, Amsterdam and Ninety-ninth Street, Susanna sat in the book-filled office of the Reverend Karen Duncan. Karen's dark blond hair, worn loose, reached her waist, and despite her clerical clothes, Karen seemed more like a retro hippie than a devout religious professional. She was heavily pregnant. In addition to being the pastor of St. George's, Karen taught at the Peabody Seminary and was the administrator of Susanna's apartment building. As head of the tenants' committee, Susanna was about to go through its list of concerns. To avoid bringing discord into the peace of the seminary close, Susanna and Karen held their every-other-month meeting in Karen's office.

"How are you feeling?" Susanna asked.

"Ready for this pregnancy to be over," Karen said, laughing. The baby, due in three weeks, dominated her body. This would be her second child. "Still, it's worth it. Just barely."

"I'm sorry to take up your time with my constituency's issues."

"I'm happy for any distraction."

"In that case, glad to be of service. First: the heat. There's too much heat on the upper floors and not enough heat on the lower floors."

"Too much heat, not enough, the story of my days. These old buildings. The engineers assure me that they're planning a new system of thermostats for the entire seminary complex."

"When will that be, do you think? I don't mean to press, but the tenants will demand to know."

"I'll confirm a date and e-mail you." Karen made a note on her yellow pad.

"And our heating problems right now?"

"I'll arrange for an engineer to visit as soon as possible."

"And?"

"I'll have the engineer be in touch with you directly."

"Thank you. Next: apartment 2A continues to have a water leak under the kitchen sink, reported two weeks ago and still unaddressed . . ." And so it went, through the checklist. Finally, "Now about the garbage."

"You always save the garbage for last."

"Seems appropriate. As you know, 1B has approached the maintenance department repeatedly about whether the garbage bins beneath their windows can be moved." A new tenant was an amateur chef, and his culinary experiments made for exceptionally odoriferous garbage.

"The tenants have my permission to move the garbage bins anywhere they deem appropriate, except into the garden itself. I'll let the maintenance staff know, so they can adjust accordingly."

"Thank you. Also, we'd like the garbage picked up every other day, not every three days."

"Agreed." Karen noted it. "Garbage is among my easiest challenges."

"For me, too." Susanna closed her notebook. She had another meeting to go to, but today she felt a need to reach beyond the mundane conversations that she and Karen usually shared. No one seemed to be waiting for Karen's time. Over the past months of coming here, Susanna had often wondered about Karen's calling, if that was the right way to describe her faith and her profession. "Forgive me for asking, Karen, and please don't answer if you prefer not to, but what made you decide to become a minister?"

"A priest. Episcopalians use the word *priest*. And your question is an easy one. I wanted to serve God."

Susanna must have looked skeptical without intending to, because Karen added, "Really. I did. And I do. Serve God. Everything seems simple to me."

"Forgive me again for being frank, but you actually do believe all of this?" Susanna motioned to the crucifix on the wall behind Karen's desk, and to the theology books lining the shelves. "I just want to understand."

"I'm happy to talk about it. I know some people struggle—I know because they tell me—but I never have."

"What about . . . *evil*, for lack of a better word? Rape, murder, the Holocaust?"

"I believe that God suffers along with humanity. And you?"

"Pardon?" Susanna asked.

"Are you familiar with the writings of Abraham Joshua Heschel? He said God loves his people so much that He, too, suffers for their actions."

Susanna didn't know anything about Abraham Heschel beyond his name, and judging from Karen's description, Susanna thought his beliefs sounded far-fetched, an attempt to get God off the hook. "I wasn't raised with faith. It isn't part of my frame of reference."

"That's sad," Karen said with what sounded like genuine pity.

"Perhaps." Susanna shrugged. "Some years ago, when I lived on the Upper West Side, a young woman was murdered a few blocks from my apartment. Stabbed to death by a man who was insane. At the memorial service in a nearby church, I think it was Episcopalian, the priest said, don't worry, she's happy, she's in heaven and looking down at us. Was that supposed to make everyone feel better?"

"I remember when that happened," Karen said.

"Do you think the priest really believed that the murdered woman was literally looking down from heaven and that she was happy? Or did he mean it as a metaphor?"

Karen didn't answer, instead gazing out the window at the winter-bare garden. The sun was behind the clouds. "I believe the woman was in a better place. *Is* in a better place, looking down from eternity. Her suffering is over." Karen was silent. Then, "What brought you to our community, beyond the great apartment?"

An urge came over Susanna to test Karen, to see if Karen could give her any consolation. "A few years ago, I was raped. Right on my own block on the Upper West Side. My husband couldn't handle it, and our marriage broke up."

Karen studied her. "I'm so sorry. That isn't what I expected to hear."

"What did you expect?"

"I'm not certain. But not violence."

"I thought the seminary close would bring me a sense of safety," Susanna said.

"Has it?"

"Yes."

"The Lord works in mysterious ways."

"There's a gate and a twenty-four-hour guard."

"That, too," Karen said with her easy laughter.

Susanna rose. She felt embarrassed, as if she'd challenged Karen unfairly. She wanted the conversation to end. "I need to get to another appointment."

"Take a minute to look at the sanctuary on your way out. Our Tiffany windows are back. We missed them during the renovation. If the sun comes out again, they'll be gorgeous at this hour."

"Will do," Susanna said. "See you at home."

"Thanks for coming uptown."

"My fellow tenants and I appreciate your time."

After these courtesies, Susanna left Karen's office. She walked along the Victorian-Gothic passageway, with its vaulted ceiling, that led to the sanctuary. Her footsteps echoed against the stone floor. When she entered the sanctuary, the windows were dark. She sat in a pew halfway back.

If she'd believed in God, would God have stopped the man from choosing *her* to rape beside the garbage cans? Or was the fact that the man didn't also murder her a sign of God's mercy?

The questions were absurd. Dark thoughts spiraled: she'd never fully recover from the rape. Never find someone to share her life. She'd lose her job.

As she sat in the pew and looked around the sanctuary, sunlight gradually spread across the stained glass. The windows seemed ablaze. It was the most beautiful sight Susanna had ever seen. It filled her with a perception of hope and promise. Basking in it, she began to cry.

She heard footsteps behind her, but she didn't turn. More footsteps followed. A whispered conversation.

She felt a hand on her shoulder. "Susanna, are you all right?"

She looked up. It was Karen, concerned. Behind Karen was an array of white-haired church ladies, uniformly worried. Ten steps back, a muscled security guard regarded her with sympathy. As if they were surprised by her reaction. Susanna would have expected that any person seeing the sun pouring through these stained-glass windows for the first time, or the hundredth time, would dissolve into tears.

"Oh, for goodness sake." She'd almost said *for God's sake*, but she caught herself. She managed to speak lightly, showing that she was fine, they shouldn't worry, she was coping, she could even be whimsical: "Honestly, can't anyone cry around here in peace?"

---

"How about the top letter? Can you read that one for me?" said Jessie Fuller, optometrist. Jessie was about Susanna's age, her hair done in cornrows with multicolored beads. She wore a white lab coat, yet with her relaxed manner, she seemed wrapped in an aura of fun.

"E," said Monique, a fidgety second grader in a red plaid jumper, her chin-length black hair falling straight around her face.

"How about the second row?"

Monique sat on her hands. "F and P."

"Great job! Now the third row."

She leaned forward, squinting. "D, O, T."

The third row was T, O, and Z.

"Let's skip to the fifth row."

"You're playing a trick on me—there isn't a fifth row."

"Okay, we'll figure out if I'm playing a trick or not."

Susanna stood in the gym of an elementary school in Washington Heights. Today eighty second graders were having their eyes checked and were being fitted with glasses, if necessary. The kids were brought to the gym in small groups, and while they waited their turns, they played tag or jumped rope. After Jessie determined the need for corrective lenses, her colleague, Mrs. Ortega, showed the kids the choice of frames.

The Barstow Foundation paid for everything from the initial exam to the finished glasses.

"Now I'm going to use this big weird machine to test different lenses on you." The machine dwarfed Monique as Jessie moved it toward her. "It's called a *phoropter.* I have to take a long time with each person, and everyone has to sit very still."

Monique seemed to disappear behind the phoropter. Her feet, in pink sneakers, moved back and forth, up and down, as if they were dancing.

"Can you have a contest with your feet, to see which one can stay still the longest?"

"I can try." Monique pressed her feet against the chair.

While Jessie tested different lenses, Susanna remembered her own first pair of glasses. She was eight years old when her teacher said that she needed to have her eyes checked. Evelyn took an afternoon off from work, and they went to a shop on Hertel Avenue. Susanna's eyes were checked by an optometrist who patiently cajoled her to sit still. The following week, Evelyn and Susanna returned. The optometrist handed Susanna a pair of glasses and checked the fit when she put them on. Now you can look out the window, he'd told her. Susanna looked—and the world outside went from being a blurry wash to being sharp. Clear. The leaves on the trees were like the pictures in science books. She could read the street signs. The view onto Hertel Avenue wasn't anything remarkable, simply cars, small shops, grocery stores. It became remarkable because for the first time, Susanna could see the details.

She'd been fortunate. Her vision problems were recognized and dealt with early. From that point on, the point when she could see, Susanna had loved school. She wore contact lenses now. Glasses had changed her life.

"Which is better, this one—or," Jessie said, switching the lens, "this one."

"Second one."

"And this one, or this one?"

"They look the same," Monique said.

"Good. Now, take a look at the chart. Is there a line marked number five?"

"Yes!"

"So I wasn't playing a trick. Number five is too easy for you now. Let's skip down to the line marked number eight."

Monique read the letters.

"Excellent. One hundred percent correct. Now we'll do the other eye, from the beginning." Jessie took Monique through the testing of the left eye.

Studies showed that more than 20 percent of public school kids had uncorrected vision problems. How could kids learn if they couldn't see?

"Hold on just a minute more." Pushing the phoropter away from Monique, Jessie double-checked the information on the machine and made notes. She put the required lenses into an awkward-looking metal frame. "We call this a *trial frame*," Jessie said. "It gives me an exact idea of how your new glasses are going to work for you."

On Monique's oval face, the contraption looked appropriate for characters in a horror movie.

"Before I have you read the chart again," Jessie said, "why don't you look around the room."

Monique turned toward her friends playing jump rope on the far side of the gym. Her smile was tremendous. "Wow!"

*Exactly*, Susanna thought.

⸺

"Hi, Mr. Edgerton," Susanna greeted the guard when she arrived at the seminary gate. She was still delighting in the look on Monique's face when the girl first saw the world through corrective lenses.

"Hello, miss." Mr. Edgerton was from Jamaica and had old-school manners. His voice carried a lovely lilt. "I tell you, miss, this cold gets in my bones."

"Mine, too."

"I do believe you have a package." He went into the office to retrieve it, and she followed him and signed the log for it.

"I didn't order anything," she said, examining the box.

"Someone's sending you a present. I'm sure you receive a lot of those."

"Not as many as I'd like," she joked.

"Isn't that true for all of us," he said. "Except for my granddaughter. She has eight presents on her Christmas list this year, and I suspect she's going to receive every one."

"And I suspect that you've already bought them for her."

He turned sheepish. "I'm up to six."

"I'm sure you'll find the others."

"God knows I'm trying."

"Good luck with your shopping. And thanks for the package. See you tomorrow."

"Good night, miss."

As she made her way across the garden, toward the Victorian mansion that was her home, the sharp purity of the air and the crunching of snow underneath her feet reminded Susanna of the winters of her childhood.

She heard an insistent voice inside herself: withdraw your threat to resign. Don't take the risk. You could lose everything you've worked for. Life is a succession of compromises. Do what Rob wants. It's his money, after all.

Except it wasn't his money. The money belonged to the foundation, and the foundation was for the children it helped. If she had to leave her job, she had enough savings to hold on to her apartment for about a year. Eventually she'd find another job. Wouldn't she?

*Everything is going to be okay*, she said to herself, repeating a kind of mantra she'd used in the days after the rape.

She unlocked the mansion's outside door. As she walked up the staircase, with its carved, wooden banister, she heard the muffled, comforting sounds of conversation, television, and music in other apartments. Their newest neighbor, the amateur chef, was cooking, and a tantalizing aroma filled the air . . . *boeuf bourguignon*, Susanna determined.

Unlocking her front door, switching on the light, she did an automatic check: everything fine. Undisturbed since this morning.

She went to the windows, closed the blinds, and pulled shut the curtains. She changed out of her business suit into leggings and a soft sweater. Her apartment was among the overheated ones, which she appreciated this evening. She opened the package that Mr. Edgerton had given her. Six Bach CDs from Daniel Erhardt . . . how generous and thoughtful. Straightaway she sent Dan an e-mail, saying she was grateful for his gift and would be back in touch after she'd listened to the discs.

At random, she put on the CD of violin concertos. The music filled the room with a sense of unbridled joy that became her own as she went into the kitchen and contemplated dinner.

## *Chapter 21*

Scott Schiffman pushed a book cart out of the elevator, through the vestibule, and toward the lower-level reading room of the Beinecke Rare Book and Manuscript Library at Yale. The cart held not only rare books but also several gray boxes of uncataloged materials. On top were his own manila file folders, organizing his research. This was his third day of work, and he was tired and frustrated. He'd taken an early lunch because the morning had seemed a year long, and he doubtless faced a similar afternoon. He was searching through undigitized collections of eighteenth-century German cantata poetry, hoping to authenticate the libretto used in Susanna's cantata.

The Beinecke was a hideous building. He wished an architectural critic would come out and admit it. From the outside, it looked like dozens of television sets arranged in a patchwork. The pseudo–TV screens were made from translucent marble. When the sun was shining and light poured through the marble, the interior, at least, was beautiful.

Today the sun was not shining. On such a day as this, working at the Beinecke was like laboring in a futuristic bunker, especially because the reading room was underground.

Because Scott had done his graduate work at Yale, and because he'd made it his business to ingratiate himself with the librarians (going to the extent of getting a part-time job here even though he didn't need the money), he had special privileges when it came to research materials. He still had his staff ID. He didn't have to wait in the reading room as others did, while librarians fetched requested materials. Instead, he found what he needed himself. In this way, he avoided the gnawing worry about whether the book or manuscript *next* to the one he'd requested was in fact the single book or manuscript that would answer every question and solve every problem. Even better, he was allowed to examine as-yet-uncataloged materials. This prospect had excited him when he began his career years ago. Sometimes it still did.

The Yale libraries specialized in German literature, so theoretically this excursion could have productive results. Realistically, however, its main purpose was in the general effort to climb every mountain—alas, that saccharine song was stuck in his head. This past Sunday, during a snowstorm, he'd visited Rachel, the younger of his two sisters, her husband, and their children, Josie and Lily, ages nine and eleven respectively. The girls had forced him to watch a DVD of *The Sound of Music.* "Uncle Scott, you have to watch with us, you *have* to!" they'd said. He was unable to resist their demand. So he'd watched it with them. Twice.

He forced his concentration back to the Beinecke. Even if this jaunt to New Haven wasn't productive professionally, he would telephone Susanna Kessler afterward, relate what he'd found or hadn't found, and ask her to dinner. Ever since the party given by the Barstows, he'd found his thoughts wandering to her.

Distracted by aesthetic contemplation of his mental image of Susanna Kessler, Scott wasn't paying full attention to his surroundings. If he had been, he would have promptly returned to the stacks or slipped into the restroom.

Instead he faced an inescapable problem looming fifteen feet before him: Centennial Professor Frederic Augustus Fournier, Scott's erstwhile mentor and present-day nemesis, galumphing down the stairs. Professor Fournier was the doyen and the scourge of Bach scholars around the world. He'd also been Scott's and Dan's thesis adviser for their PhDs. In scholarship, the relationship of adviser to advisee never completely went away, no matter how hard one tried. Scott had tried.

Freddy (as Scott and Dan called him privately) was round of face, round of head, round of body—okay, Scott was prejudiced—and more energetic than seemed possible given both the roundness and the fluffy (possibly *tufty* was the better word) sprigs of white hair upon his head. Today a handful of earnest young men and women accompanied him. At the bottom of the stairs, they regrouped, following closely behind their leader. They stared at Freddy as if their professional futures depended on him. Who were they? Doctoral candidates applying to begin their studies next year? Visiting scholars hoping for grants or other professional advancements?

As they came closer, Scott heard them speaking French. Freddy loved to show off his knowledge of languages. The young women did indeed look French, with their tight jackets, short skirts, and black tights.

"Ah, *voilà*, what a surprise," Freddy said, switching to English. "Here approaches one of my best students. Scott Schiffman, curator of music manuscripts at the MacLean Library. Travels the world to authenticate autographs. What brings you here today, young man?"

"Research." Scott kept his tone lighthearted.

"Naturally. Scott, these are my fledgling associates from the Sorbonne," Freddy said by way of introduction. "I'll be commuting to Paris next semester to work with them."

Scott felt compelled to acknowledge this news, which was in fact impressive. "Excellent."

"*Mes amis*, let's see if we can do a little sleuthing from the titles Mr. Schiffman has collected here."

Freddy was fast. That's what forever astonished Scott. He could disarm in an instant. Memorize at a glance.

"'Susanna Kessler, Buffalo, New York,'" he read off the tab on the top file folder.

Freddy didn't ask who she was, doubtless figuring that he could discover her identity himself in no time. Mercifully, Scott had labeled the folder with her name rather than calling it *Possible unknown cantata by Bach, found in Buffalo*.

"And all these books of old German poetry. And look here, uncat-aloged volumes, too. What could this project be, I wonder," Freddy said affably, as if he really did want to encourage his former student. But Scott recognized the gleam that signaled more greedy desires. "Here's a folder labeled 'BWV 46, 42, 18, 126, librettos.' That's cu-rious."

Freddy would know immediately that the element uniting these four cantatas was their religious polemic, their ranting against Ca-tholicism, Islam, Judaism.

"And this one says, 'Digital photos.' Digital photos of what, I wonder." Freddy stared at but refrained from picking up the file.

Possibly on account of his three days of frustration, Scott experi-enced an irresistible urge to tease Centennial Professor Frederic Au-gustus Fournier in front of his French graduate students.

"It's a secret, Professor," Scott said. "One of those 'Grandpa brought something home from the war' stories—except this one might pan out."

The students were impressed. Eyes widening, they stared at Scott, no doubt thinking, *Yes, this will happen to me, someday I will make the discovery of a lifetime.*

"Controversial subject matter, too."

"Is that so? Well, well." Freddy seemed to lick his lips in expectation. "I look forward to reviewing the fruits of your labors."

Embarrassment washed over Scott. He felt himself blushing. He'd risen to the bait. Why, *why* couldn't he remember that everything Freddy said was designed to entrap? Scott should have simply said hello and gone about his business. Instead he'd played directly into Freddy's devious hand.

"I see one of these folders is labeled 'Dan,'" Freddy continued. "That would refer to Daniel Erhardt, another of my success stories." How long would it be before these French students were calling him Freddy, or some French version thereof, behind his back? "Three books and more than a dozen journal articles to his credit, and he's not even forty years old."

The French students nodded in appreciation. Scott heard a few French exclamations, almost *ooh-la-la*, although not quite. This was yet another dig at Scott, because he'd chosen a different path and had only eleven articles and no books to his credit. Scott well knew, however, that Freddy could readily denigrate Dan's work if he saw the need. Freddy was an equal-opportunity denigrator.

"Yes, Dan's taking a look at some of the issues." Scott tried to sound blasé. Dan's involvement would signal to Freddy that the issue had a religious aspect, Dan's specialty. Of course, Freddy would know that already from the file label with its list of polemical cantatas, but this would drive the point home. Scott girded himself for Freddy's reply, but the centennial professor appeared to lose interest.

"Alas, we must be on our way, Dr. Schiffman." Freddy had the ability to make even the use of Scott's title and family name sound like a put-down. "Much more to show these fine young people."

Chastising himself, Scott watched them continue down the corridor. After they disappeared through the door into the multilevel stacks, he pushed his cart of research materials to an empty table near the back of the reading room. With its low ceiling, the reading room created a feeling that the weight of recorded history, held on the stacks on the floors above, was about to pancake onto the heads of the scholars gathered here. He sat down wearily. Most people opted to sit near the windows, to take advantage of the small degree of natural light that reached the underground room from the moat, as Scott called it, outside the reading room's floor-to-ceiling windows. Modernist sculpture, covered with snow, filled the moat. All right, the moat was beautiful in its way. Nonetheless, Scott preferred the privacy at the back of the reading room.

He'd have to brief Dan on the disastrous conversation with Freddy. They'd need to increase their vigilance. Freddy had a way of inserting himself into projects and guiding their direction. German academic tradition called a senior professor who advised students on PhD research a *Doktor-Vater*. Freddy was about as unfatherly as it was possible to be, unless he was the evil father in a Freudian nightmare.

Another afternoon to be spent searching for eighteenth-century poetic hate speech. Best get started. As he alternated between the cataloged and uncataloged materials, hoping the variety would keep his attention from flagging, family memories began to fill his thoughts. He had a lot to live up to. His mother's family, murdered during the war. His father's family: they'd gone from textile manufacturing to real estate development. His brother was the head of the company and happily married, with four children. His sisters had both become physicians, and they'd managed to marry, raise children, and work full-time.

One could say they were a traditional, old-fashioned Jewish family that valued learning, achievement, and liberal causes. All they were missing was a wife and children for Scott. Increasingly, Scott was feeling that lack, too.

In his office at Yale's Stoeckel Hall, Frederic Fournier said farewell
to Robertson Barstow and put down the phone. He'd taken the visiting French students to a luncheon hosted by the French department,
where they could spend time with their own kind. He was allowed to
say this because he was part French. He'd begged off the invitation for
himself, pleading work. Which was simply the truth.

He was feeling smug, he couldn't deny it. He'd always been lucky
in his friends and in his students. Interesting tidbits of information
had a habit of making their way to him.

The first step was to meet the heretofore unknown Susanna Kessler. Happily, research wasn't what it used to be, hour after hour, day
after day, weeks to months to years of meticulous labor. No more!
Frederic had googled Susanna Kessler.

How marvelous to be alive at a moment in time when a stranger
could be googled. From a wedding photo and brief accompanying
article in the *Times*, he learned that a Susanna Kessler originally from
Buffalo now lived in New York City. Another site described her as
the executive director of the Cornelia and Robertson Barstow Family
Foundation. Google didn't list any other women named Susanna
Kessler with a Buffalo connection.

Frederic already knew that Robertson Barstow was heir to the
Barstow Process of oil refining. Frederic had attended Harvard, and
Harvard boasted a Cornelia and Robertson Barstow Scholarship
Fund for the Sciences. Furthermore, Frederic knew from his avid
reading of the Harvard alumni magazine, a veritable gold mine of potentially useful information, that he and Robertson Barstow had both
lived in Lowell House. They didn't overlap (Frederic was younger),
but the Harvard houses inspired lifelong loyalty.

Frederic had picked up the phone and called old Rob just like
that, with the excuse of soliciting a donation for their alma mater.
Several years before, Frederic had assisted the development office in

this way, so he knew what to say. Much to Frederic's surprise, Rob promised a substantial contribution.

After settling this bit of business in a most satisfying way, they discussed their lives, Rob's retirement, Frederic's ever-fascinating career, and before you knew it, Rob had invited Frederic to an afternoon garden party at the family estate in Tarrytown in May, to celebrate the blooming of the lilacs in his mother's famed garden. The party, Rob had noted, would take place whether the lilacs were blooming or not. Frederic surmised that this party was an annual event, but he could hardly torture himself about not receiving previous invitations in view of the fact that he hadn't spoken to Robertson Barstow in . . . had he ever spoken to Robertson Barstow? Not to Frederic's recollection.

He hoped Susanna Kessler would be at the party, but of course he couldn't inquire. He had a toehold, which was all he needed.

By May, with any luck, Dan and Scott, his intrepid students, would be finished with their research and have a journal article or two sketched out, as well as the outline of both a book and a critical edition of whatever this Bach piece was. Might as well let them take care of the heavy lifting.

A new cantata by Johann Sebastian Bach. It was like finding a new play by Shakespeare. The first live performance would sell out months in advance, and subsequently the piece would be performed in churches and in concert halls around the world. Thousands of printed scores would be sold. The first recording, the prestigious *World Premiere Recording*, would garner enormous attention.

Momentous questions arose: Who would be the first conductor, the first orchestra, the first music publisher?

And who better than Frederic to ponder these questions?

Frederic was grateful to the cosmos for his good fortune. He was a public intellectual, not a stuffy academic. He wrote essays for *The New York Review of Books* and the *Times Literary Supplement*. He'd also written

or edited more than a dozen scholarly books about Johann Sebastian
Bach. He was the perfect man to deal with whatever Susanna Kessler
had stumbled upon. After all, the discovery would have political ram-
ifications. The cantata numbers listed on Scott's manila folder were
46, 42, 18, 126 (Frederic was lucky in his near-photographic memory).
What these pieces had in common was inflammatory religious content.

Kessler was a Jewish name, wasn't it? Frederic felt certain it was.
He reached a preliminary conclusion that the discovery most likely
concerned Jewish issues. More specifically, *anti*-Jewish issues. Why not
take advantage of the controversy? He'd contact Elie Wiesel, bring
him on board. The first performance should be in Israel, to highlight
the moral problems of the piece and thereby garner even more attention. Perhaps the Bach Collegium Japan was the proper choice for
the debut concert and recording—yes, a Japanese group, performing
in Israel, to emphasize the global significance of the discovery. Their
recordings were sublime. Such thoughtful work deserved to be rewarded. As to the other musical groups understandably competing
for his patronage, he'd find some bone to throw them later.

Where would the manuscript go, once its authenticity was proven?
Surely Yale had the best facilities to care for it. Frederic would persuade
some wealthy Yale donors to make Susanna Kessler an offer—if, that
is, she could prove legal ownership. She might well *not* be able to
prove legal ownership. Furthermore the German government might
make a fuss, their national patrimony and all that *Quatsch*, but the
Jewish element was a powerful weapon to use against the German
government. He'd dealt with the German government before, on previous, less spectacular discoveries. Frederic was not intimidated by
the German government. Germans remained transfixed by guilt—as
well they should—for the crimes committed by their parents and
grandparents. Frederic knew how to exploit their guilt and felt no
need to apologize.

As to the descendants of the original European owners, if any were still alive . . . he'd keep them in mind as the situation evolved, so that they, too, would be prepared to see the autograph go to Yale, one way or another.

Although Frederic had never told anyone, Daniel Erhardt and Scott Schiffman were the best students he'd ever taught. They had a gift for bringing diverse evidence together into a coherent, illuminating whole. But Dan pushed his religious obsessions too far. From Frederic's perspective, Bach's true concerns were always and only aesthetic, even in an anti-Jewish cantata. Bach's official duties at the Thomaskirche paid the bills for Bach's overflowing family, and in Frederic's learned opinion, that's as far as Bach's religious faith went. Bach had composed for the future, for eternal, universal artistic contemplation, separate from the trivialities of religion, politics, and any specific time or place.

Initially, Frederic had been taken aback when Dan brought to his attention the evidence that Bach had often signed up to take communion soon after one of his children died. Astonishing, that such records had survived, and also that parishioners actually had to sign up in advance for communion, the demand being so strong. But Frederic himself took communion every now and again, at his son's wedding mass, for example, and in and of itself it didn't necessarily mean a thing. Not in terms of faith, at least.

Dan also harped on the fact that Bach had owned an extensive library of theological books, including a Bible commentary whose margins were filled with annotations written by Bach himself. Someday Frederic might have to take a look at these books.

The phone rang. He glanced at it.

Despite all rational evidence to the contrary, Frederic Fournier knew God existed. Caller ID proved it. He knew when his wife was calling, or his son, or one of his graduate-student flirtations.

The incoming call was international. Must be the result of an e-mail he'd sent to Sotheby's in London a half hour ago, requesting a conversation. Sotheby's, London, was the place where musical auto-graphs were most often sold—not that Susanna Kessler was going to sell the cantata at auction—but Frederic was stirring the pot. Getting the buzz going. Putting himself at the center of attention.

"Frederic! Good to hear your voice," said Ian McCloud, director of books and manuscripts at Sotheby's. Music manuscripts were Mc-Cloud's special expertise.

"And yours, Ian."

"Received your e-mail," McCloud said. "Piqued the curiosity."

"And rightly so. I've run across something potentially rather in-teresting. Johann Sebastian Bach, as it happens. Sacred music. I'm waiting for confirmation from my junior colleagues. Might take sev-eral months to cross all the *t*'s and dot all the *i*'s. But I'm hopeful. No, *hopeful* is overstating the situation," he corrected, remembering that understatement was essential when speaking with an Englishman. "Look, we'll see. I've said too much. Don't like to get people's expec-tations up, only to dash them. Step by step. No premature headlines. You know what the press is like."

"Unfortunately, yes."

"Don't want to fall off a cliff and bring you with me." Frederic pretended to chuckle. "Still, I wanted you to know."

"Thank you very much."

Perfect, McCloud had taken the bait.

"A rare opportunity here—although I can't promise you a sale. Who knows what the present owner may decide to do with the ma-terials."

"Understood. Keep me in the loop."

"Will do, Ian."

They bid farewell and hung up. Life was good. Yes, it was. Classi-cal music dying, as Philistines so often claimed? Not a chance.

*Be prepared* was a motto Frederic was happy to share with the Boy Scouts.

Poor Susanna Kessler. She wasn't prepared. Despite her sophisticated job, she didn't understand the pressures that would be brought to bear on her from the likes of dealers, performers, recording companies, foreign governments, possible descendants, archivists. Even the IRS, coming to claim unpaid estate taxes, if in fact her family owned this priceless artifact. She didn't comprehend the exhausting demand for newspaper interviews, TV, radio, and so on. A PBS documentary. An over-the-top History Channel program complete with costumed actors reenacting Bach et al.

Susanna Kessler would need someone experienced in these matters to guide her. She'd need a mature, steady hand. She would need Centennial Professor Frederic Augustus Fournier.

## Chapter 22

Alshue, the family name Evelyn had given her. And an unnamed village, near Karlsbad or Marienbad. Susanna wanted to see a photo, read a ledger, find something, anything, to fill out the meager information that Evelyn had provided.

She went onto Google Street View and toured Karlsbad, now called Karlovy Vary, a town of fanciful medieval churches and eighteenth-century houses painted in pastel colors. She toured Marienbad, now Mariánské Lázne, with its ornate spa hotels and baths.

She went to the Yad Vashem website and entered *Alshue*.

Nothing.

She moved on to the extensive Web links at jewishgen.org. Each link led to another and another, in an endless chain. But each time she filled in the requested information and pressed the search function, she came up with nothing. Alshue may once have been Alshu, or Altshu, or—it could have been anything.

She studied a map, locating the small towns and villages around Karlsbad and Marienbad, their names listed in German and Czech. Lázne Frantiskovy, once called Franzensbad. Cheb, once called Eger. Haslov, formerly Haslau. She tried them all.

Nothing.

She couldn't say to Evelyn, you lied to me.

Susanna leaned back in her chair and turned to stare out the window. It was Saturday afternoon. A light snow was falling.

These past few weeks at the office, Rob had treated her with an absolute correctness that was like a line drawn between them. He'd asked her to coordinate a substantial donation, from his own funds, to Harvard, which she was pleased to do. No mention was made of the Gilbert and Sullivan proposal. She assumed he was discussing it privately with the foundation board.

The snow became heavier. Years ago, on a similar snowy Saturday, she and Henry had filled the afternoon by watching a movie on TV, *The Train*, starring Burt Lancaster. The story was about a train filled with crates of looted French paintings that the Nazis were taking to Germany. After a variety of plot twists and a good deal of shooting, Burt Lancaster stopped the train. Many German soldiers, as well as hostages and French Resistance fighters, were killed in the effort. At the end of the movie, crates of paintings were strewn on the ground beside the derailed train. The camera panned across their labels . . . Manet, Monet, Renoir. The film seemed to imply, at least to Susanna, that the paintings were more valuable than the lives lost saving them, and that the heroic French Resistance fighters had sacrificed themselves to the noble cause of preserving and honoring French culture.

Henry had been moved by the film, but Susanna had been offended by it. She didn't believe then, and she still didn't believe, that a painting and a human life were equivalent in value. Nor did she believe the ludicrous adage that beauty is truth, or that beauty would save the world. Yes, beauty existed and was personally moving: she recalled her experience when the sunlight poured through the stained-glass windows at St. George's Church. But her reaction made no difference outside her own narrow sphere. By all accounts Hitler had admired art immensely, ordering his cronies to steal it from across Europe. His admiration of beauty hadn't put a stop to his murderous plans.

The CD that Daniel Erhardt had sent her of the Bach sonatas for viola da gamba was playing on her stereo. With their lilting dances, the sonatas managed to be simultaneously poignant and electrifying. She'd listened to this CD several times during the past week.

A hypothetical but relevant ethical question entered her mind: Would she give her life to protect the world's only material record of Bach's viola da gamba sonatas? No, she wouldn't. The reverse was true, too. She would willingly destroy the world's only copy of the viola da gamba sonatas, if somehow this might save one person's life. How about the only material record of Beethoven's Ninth Symphony? She felt the same.

She could easily destroy the manuscript Henry had left her, if she decided this was the best option. Apparently (if authentic) it was a great work of art, but it was also the product of a dismal tradition that had brought lethal consequences for her forebears.

And yet . . . Henry had guarded it. It was part of his legacy to her. She also felt a responsibility to the original owners, to learn if any family members were still alive and if so, return it to them.

The proper path eluded her.

She went back to the computer. She tried smaller towns and villages. Nothing.

Finally she took the opposite approach. She tried Prague, a teeming city, even though it wasn't in the Sudetenland. The family might have gone to Prague after the German occupation of their hometown, and therefore they'd appear in the records as citizens of Prague.

She found nothing.

## *Chapter 23*

LUISENHOF GARDENS, NEAR SCHLESISCHES TOR
BERLIN, PRUSSIA

*Summer 1816*

Peace reigned. Napoleon had been defeated at Waterloo a year ago.

On this lovely day, Sara sensed the air itself trembling with life. Fountains tossed spray into the sunlight, creating rainbows. Geometric-patterned flower beds bloomed in a wash of color. Statues of Greek and Roman mythological figures stood on plinths arranged in a procession: Diana the Huntress, Daphne becoming a laurel tree, Leda and the swan. In the near distance, stands of lime trees framed the scene.

When Sara's father bought these acres years ago, he hired the royal gardener to design them. The landscape had grown to resemble the gardens surrounding the royal palace of Sans Souci. The family possessed another garden, too, a wild, rustic retreat that was their summer estate, outside the city gates: the Bartholdy Meierei, with its *petite palais* and broad meadows, its dairy farm and windmill. But the Luisenhof was the place that her father had loved best. Once when

Sara was eleven or twelve, he had brought her here (his valet following at a distance, the coachman waiting at the garden gate). He'd shown her the view from the *orangerie*. She'd stood beside him during his meeting with the gardener. She'd shared his company throughout the afternoon. Those hours were the longest time she'd ever spent alone with him.

She could still sense her father's presence, today as she walked with Lea. Lea's children fanned out around them. The group was like an Oriental caravan making its progress across the landscape: Sara herself and her maid, who maintained a suitable distance behind her; Lea and Lea's maid, also at a suitable distance; and the four children . . . Fanny, almost eleven, with her tutor; Felix, seven, with his tutor; Rebecka, five, with her nanny; and Paul, almost four, with his nanny.

"Mama, Mama!" Rebecka, braids bouncing, ran across the lawn toward Lea and Sara. "Paul pushed me, he pushed me," she shrieked as her nanny chased her. "And he hit me."

The girl stood before them. "Now, Rebecka," Lea said, "that sounds unlikely."

"Fräulein Rebecka," said the nanny, catching up, panting in the heat, squinting from the sun, "you know very well that *you* were the one who pushed Paul, and hit him, too."

Paul was crying in his nanny's arms amid the faux-Greco-Roman statues.

"You must apologize to your brother," Lea said.

"I will not."

"Rebecka," Lea cautioned.

"I won't."

"Nanny can take you home if necessary."

"Come with me, Fräulein Rebecka," said the nanny. "You apologize to Paul now, or home we go." The nanny took Rebecka by the hand and led her to her brother, who wailed as she approached.

"Ten times a day, this happens," Lea said.

What could Sara say? Lea had the proverbial patience of a Christian saint. Sara had longed for children, but the daily bickering, which went on despite the nannies and the tutors, would have been a strain to her. As she grasped this fact, she laughed at herself.

"What is it?" Lea asked. "What makes you laugh?"

"Ah, dearest." She wouldn't share the truth with Lea. "Your children are marvels. And you're a marvelous mother to them."

Lea smiled, her expression combining happiness, pride, and a hint of wistfulness. "They can be little monsters, I'm not blind to that. But thank you."

"I think of them as my own grandchildren. Fanny, Felix, Rebecka, Paul. Each one dear to me."

That was an overstatement. Sara felt little empathy with Felix and Rebecka, and Paul was too young to have much personality. Fanny was the child she felt drawn to—Fanny, gazing at a lily while her tutor appeared to be explaining to her some fact of botany. Fanny, brilliant at her music and her studies, one shoulder higher than the other, her features heavy.

"You must always consider them your grandchildren. That's what I expect. And what I want."

How earnest Lea was. How concerned. Sara wished never to be a source of worry for Lea. "Thank you, my dear. The day is gorgeous, let us walk."

Arms linked, they continued their promenade. Behind them, Felix called to his siblings for a game of hide-and-seek.

Sara and Lea reached the welcome shade of the allée beneath the giant plane trees. On the far side, visible through the trees, was the open-air theater where Sara and her siblings had performed theatricals for their parents. Soon Lea's children would do the same.

And so it would be, throughout the generations.

"Is the garden different now, from when you were young?" asked Lea.

"It's exactly the same, except more magical, more beckoning."

They reached the octagonal garden house, half-hidden by peach trees. Its wide-windowed room held a piano, comfortable chairs, books, and a stack of notebooks going back decades, recording the names of the birds observed within the garden.

"The garden house meant so much to me when I was a girl," Lea said. "It was my little paradise. My imagination took flight here."

"And what did you imagine?"

"My future."

"Has your future matched your imaginings?"

"Yes, it has. My husband and I are most happy together."

Sara's private opinion of Abraham Mendelssohn, that he was unworthy of Lea, hadn't changed over the years, but Lea's contentment made his unworthiness acceptable.

"A happy marriage illuminates life," Sara said. "I felt such fulfillment with Samuel. I feel it still, in his memory. Our happiness has been the unwavering center of my life."

"I understand," Lea said.

The children's game of hide-and-seek continued, with shouts of surprise and triumph.

"My children exceed my imaginings. Everything I've read and studied, the piano pieces I've played—all this I now teach to them. Tante," Lea squeezed Sara's hand. "I must speak with you in confidence."

"Yes?" Sara feigned surprise. She'd suspected that a secret needed to be discussed today. The formality of the invitation had alerted her. A note, delivered this morning by Lea's footman, requesting a rendezvous, suggesting this meeting place. Perhaps Lea was once more *enceinte* . . . another pregnancy, *that* would warrant a formal invitation.

"You mustn't tell my mother."

Yes, probably a pregnancy. Babette worried terribly.

"You must promise not to say anything to her. Not yet."

With the request repeated, Sara wondered if it was disturbing news that Lea was determined to protect. Was Abraham Mendelssohn's work with the bank taking him away? Were they leaving Berlin, moving to a foreign city? This would be a blow to Babette. And to Sara.

"I've always spoken to you more . . . frankly than I've been able to talk to my mother."

Sara couldn't deny that this pleased her.

"I want your blessing."

"My blessing? For what, my darling?"

Lea stopped walking. The shifting shadows of the sunlight through the trees softened the anguish on Lea's face.

"What is it, Lea?"

"Several months ago, we had the children baptized."

"Pardon?"

"We had them baptized."

"I don't understand."

"As Christians. They're Christians now."

Sara still couldn't grasp what Lea was saying. "They're only children."

"Children can be baptized."

"That's not what I mean."

Of everything Sara had expected to hear, she hadn't expected this. More than once, Sara had heard Lea express disdain for friends and family who'd converted.

"Shouldn't your children be allowed to choose for themselves, when they're grown?"

"They have to be raised as Christians. Educated that way. So they'll really *be* that way, and have no regrets, no past to look back to."

"But why?"

"You must already know why."

"I don't."

"First, because of people like Arnim. Because of what he did and said at your home."

Sara was silent. She didn't think about that afternoon much anymore, but in the months immediately afterward, the memory of it had returned to her in waves of horror.

"His words expressed an ever-more-common view in Prussia."

"That was long ago, Lea." It wasn't long ago, even though Sara tried to convince herself that it was. "And it had nothing to do with your children and everything to do with Arnim himself."

"It was only five years ago. Fanny was there, remember? I told her that the shouting man was ill and had to be taken home. I don't think she understood what he was saying. I don't like to call attention to it by pursuing what she did or didn't comprehend."

Sara said nothing.

"If she'd been a few years older, she would have understood," Lea said.

*The other smell*, Arnim had said. *The stench.* The *foetor Judaicus.* Once more Sara heard his brutal, cutting laughter.

"I know you never talk about it."

And Sara wouldn't discuss it now. Within herself, she raged. She felt sick with humiliation and revulsion. But Sara wouldn't burden Lea with these feelings.

"The rest of the family, the rest of the city—we discuss it for you."

Sara knew this was true. The notorious Itzig and Arnim affair. Newspaper articles, essays, even a play centered on it. There had been a sensational judicial case, because her nephew Moritz had attacked Arnim on the street, beating him with a stick, and Moritz was arrested for it.

The grand irony was that the judge, as well as Arnim's peers in the nobility, sided against him. Arnim was discredited. Dishonored. During Prussia's final battles against Napoleon, the army wouldn't accept him. The nobleman who'd refused to duel a Jew had spent months holed up at his country estate, while the Jew died as a hero fighting for Prussia in the Battle of Lützen in 1813.

Sara would rather have Moritz alive than dead in the glory of battle.

"Yes, the nobility did side *against* Arnim," Lea said, as if they heard each other's thoughts, "but that doesn't mean they sided *with* us."

Staring at Lea, Sara felt the gulf between them that her own silence had created.

"I don't want that kind of hatred to be directed toward my children. Talk like that, where does it lead?"

Sara couldn't contradict her: anti-Jewish violence recurred again and again.

"And for the boys . . . Abraham and I have to think about their professional futures. As Christians they'll have the full rights of citizens. Felix's profession, Paul's, whatever they choose, they'll be able to pursue."

Lea was right about this. Even the much-heralded (among Jews, at least) Emancipation Edict of 1812 had changed little for the Jews of Prussia. They still didn't have full citizenship. Certain professions remained closed. And alas, most of the edict's provisions had been withdrawn by the Prussian king after the defeat of Napoleon.

"In order to have a future in this country, they must be Christians. That's what Abraham says."

"And you?"

"I must keep them safe."

"Your brother—"

"That's why we can't tell mother."

About fifteen years before, Lea's brother Jacob had converted to Christianity and changed his name from Salomon to Bartholdy, taking the name of the family's rustic retreat outside the city gates. Afterward, Babette had disinherited him.

Sara said, "*This* is why I must promise not to tell your mother—my

sister—something so important? So that you won't be disinherited?
*Money* is the reason you ask me to betray my duty to her?"

"My mother lives in the past. She would never understand."

This was true. Babette was only twelve years older than Sara, but
she seemed to belong to a different generation.

"You live in the world as it is, Tante. What about *my* duty—to
safeguard my children?"

"You think converting will shield them? You think no one will remember that they were born Jews? That their grandfather was Moses
Mendelssohn, the philosopher? You think baptism will give them
blond hair and blue eyes?"

"I have to do whatever I can. To try to keep them safe. To give them a
future. And besides, Christianity teaches morality, and ethics. It teaches
everything good and fine, everything we Jews can believe in, too."

"In theory, yes. But in practice? How ethical are today's Christians, really, if Jews need to be protected from them? I regret to say
that many Christians have strayed far from the teachings of their
Lord."

Lea turned and hastened away. Was she crying? Sara suspected
she was. Sara felt tears, too, for Lea's rejection of their heritage. Sara
and Samuel had fulfilled their early vow never to convert. Each week,
Sara joined her family and friends at the synagogue. Even so, Sara
knew that many of their brethren felt compelled by the society around
them to make the choice that Lea and Abraham had made.

After giving Lea a few moments to herself, Sara followed her,
waving off their ladies' maids. She found Lea sitting upon a secluded
bench beside a lily pond. Purple hydrangeas surrounded the pond,
and a stone nymph emerged from the flowers.

Sara sat down beside her as Lea wept. The laughter and shouts of
the children reached them from a distance, on the other side of the
copse.

After a time, Lea composed herself.

"Lea," Sara said gently, "have you and Abraham converted, too?"

"No. Only the children."

"But someday you might."

"Someday. To keep the family together. What choice do we have?"

*"Over here,"* Fanny's voice reached them as she called to her siblings.

"Tante, I hope you'll still love me, after what Abraham and I have done."

They'd arrived at the moment of choice. Sara's choice. The moment of saying, I promise not to tell my sister. And, you have my blessing.

Sara's love for Lea was stronger than her disapproval. Lea and her children would live in a future that Sara would never see. Lea had to do what she believed was right.

Misinterpreting Sara's silence, Lea said, "If you can't give me your blessing, please say you don't despise me for what I've done."

Sara made her resolution. She'd mourn Lea's choice later, in private, alone.

"Lea Salomon Mendelssohn, now you have truly shocked me. You and your husband must always do what you believe is best for your children. That is indeed your duty as parents. And *you*, my own dearest niece—my cherished niece, from the time you were little—you could never do anything that would cause me to stop loving you."

## Chapter 24

Dan took the curve on the gravel road, and the forest opened to reveal a modern Georgian-style mansion surrounded by expansive lawns. He was ten miles outside Princeton, New Jersey. A heavy rain had given way to fog.

As he pulled up to the front door, two men uniformed in gray-and-green striped vests and dark trousers emerged from the house, ready to unload his luggage and park his car in a garage hidden amid the trees.

"Good afternoon, sir," the older of the two men said. "Mr. Kranich is in the hall."

"Thank you."

Surrendering his car and its keys as well as his overnight bag to the—*footmen*, would that be the proper term?—Dan felt a touch exposed. He wasn't accustomed to strangers looking after him. He entered the house. The front entryway led into a reception area with a broad staircase. Upstairs he'd find a well-appointed bedroom with bathroom en suite, his overnight bag conveniently placed in the closet. His confirmation letter for the conference had noted that he'd been assigned the same bedroom he'd had last time, here in the main house rather than the nearby guesthouse. This placement was a sign of the approval of their host, Jonathan Kranich.

"Dan, welcome," Jon greeted him.

Jon wore a conservative suit in the style of his longtime profession, banker. He was in his early seventies and seemed to relish his role in bringing the group together. A glance into the dining room showed that many of Dan's colleagues had already arrived.

"We've got some terrific events planned for the weekend," Jon said.

Jon had never married, and Dan assumed he was gay, but if he was, it had never been discussed.

"I'm glad to be here."

Jon said in mock confidentiality, "I wonder if we'll witness any fisticuffs."

This biennial gathering, Friday to Sunday, brought together scholars, religious leaders, and church musicians from Europe and America to discuss Lutheran theology as illuminated by the work of Johann Sebastian Bach. The group tended to be argumentative, and passions often ran high.

"A good quarrel always livens things up, and you're an astute referee," Dan said.

"Kind of you to notice." He guided Dan into the dining room. Jon engaged in lavish display, beginning with the buffet table. "Lobster thermidor. A hot lunch for a chilly day. Don't overlook the dessert table."

"I can't recall ever overlooking dessert."

"Something we have in common." Jon left him to greet another arriving guest.

Dan had never tried lobster thermidor (indeed had never heard of it until this moment), and he allowed the uniformed server to fill his plate. Yes, he enjoyed being here. Luxury was seductive. No wonder so many conservative clergymen railed against it—while partaking of it fully. For his health's sake, Dan added salad to the side of his plate.

Chairs were grouped around a half-dozen tables. Dan found a place at a table that included Reverend Mueller from the Church of the Holy Shepherd in New York.

Mueller was saying, "When it comes to dogs, golden retrievers are incomparable."

If they were discussing dogs, no doubt they'd already attempted a scholarly discussion that had devolved into an ugly argument. Like their host, Mueller was good at defusing conflict.

*"Ja, Sie haben recht,"* said Dietrich Bauer, *Yes, you are correct,* as if Bauer were granting judgment from on high. Which, in the context of this meeting, he was. Bauer was a professor at the University of Heidelberg with chairs in music and theology. He was their senior colleague in both age and professional stature. He must be well into his eighties by now. Bauer had been a bon vivant in his younger days, the life of any party, but today he looked overly thin and elongated, as if turning into a cadaver before their eyes. When Dan sat down beside him, Bauer wearily lifted his hand from the table in greeting.

*"Ich hätte eher den Retriever als auch den Schäferhund,"* Bauer continued. *I prefer the retriever even to the German shepherd.* He didn't trouble himself to speak English, although his English was perfectly good. Bauer must have assumed that anyone worthy of hearing his canine insights would speak German. *"Sie sind außerordentlich treu."* *They are exceptionally loyal.*

"Yes, yes, I agree totally," Mueller said.

*"Die Hündchen sind niedlich."* *The puppies are adorable.* From Bauer's

tone, this wasn't only ardent praise but also today's final word on the subject.

A young man sitting opposite Dan put down his fork. "Dachshunds are nice dogs." This young man, Mark van Ostrand, according to his name tag, was new to the group. He was meticulously turned out for this particular crowd, wearing chinos, a white shirt, an understated tie and tweed jacket, his pale brown hair cut a tad too short. A pen protruded from his jacket pocket, as if he'd placed it there after due consideration, believing it made him look more serious and mature. "Especially miniature dachshunds."

With immense, frowning effort, Herr Professor Bauer turned in his chair and stared at the newcomer.

"I mean, dachshunds are the ideal *small* dog," Van Ostrand added.

Bauer's look had nothing to do with dogs and everything to do with a young person offering an opinion, unasked. Dan remembered the same expression on his father's face, when he or one of his siblings provided an unsought opinion. Conservative Lutheranism was strictly hierarchical. The opinions of children counted for nothing.

*"Kleine Hunde gefallen mir nicht,"* Bauer said. *I don't like small dogs.*

After an awkward pause, Reverend Mueller said, "Anyone read the essay in last month's *Harvard Theological Review* about Pietism in Bach's vocal works?"

Mercifully, the two Scandinavian churchmen at the table had read it and now gave full expression to their views, which Bauer did not contradict.

Dan was content to enjoy his lunch in silence. The lobster thermidor was delicious. He had no particular view on the dog issue (he'd never had a dog), and he considered overvalued the perennial question of Lutheran Pietism versus Orthodoxy in Bach's vocal works. He made room at the table for Bauer's younger (although well into her sixties) wife, Gudrun Bauer, professor of musicology at the University of Heidelberg and author of several learned tomes. Frau Professor

Bauer was elegant but too angular for Dan's taste, her hair cut in a severe bob that didn't suit her, and her clothes—he caught and chastised himself at his automatic evaluation of a female scholar for her appearance instead of her accomplishments.

"Herr Kranich has asked my husband to deliver the sermon on Sunday," she shared with him, pride unmistakable in her voice.

This was a gathering of the religiously devout, and Dan used to fit right in. Today he felt like an interloper. Nonetheless he needed to be here: more than other scholars, these colleagues had an understanding of the contextual background to the cantata Susanna had discovered. With careful probing, he might learn something useful without revealing anything about his own work.

Jon had built a chapel on the grounds of the estate, and guests were expected to be present at Sunday morning Eucharist. Dan could plead illness as an acceptable excuse for not attending. If he did end up going, he'd simply be following along to get by.

"I look forward to hearing it," Dan said.

⸻

"Rejoicing about death is key in Bach," said Mark van Ostrand, the unfortunate dachshund lover. Since their first lunch the day before, Dan had learned that Van Ostrand was from Iowa and had recently been awarded a joint PhD degree in music and theology at the University of Utrecht, which was a true achievement. "Bach's Cantatas 56, 83, and 161 reveal a joyful desire for the end of this earthly life, and they are the subject of my paper this afternoon . . ."

The meetings were held in the mansion's ornate library, done up with the most advanced audiovisual technology. About twenty-five colleagues were gathered around the table. Outside, a misty rain fell.

"Bach's beliefs are revealed by the sprightly dance rhythms which accompany the text. Rather than the somber melodies one might expect, given the subject matter, Bach . . ."

Dan was surprised by the presentation. Van Ostrand's approach was plodding and abstract, as if the earnest young man, untempered by personal experience, didn't understand the import of his subject—which was *death*, after all: real, actual, physical death, not a theory about death.

"Thank you, Mr. Van Ostrand," Jon said when Van Ostrand had finished his presentation. "Who will begin the discussion?"

Anna Carlson, a theologian at Vanderbilt University Divinity School, raised her hand. Anna presented herself as everyone's grandmother, complete with white hair in a bun, knitted shawl, and wire-rimmed reading glasses, but her outward demeanor concealed a piercing intellect. She'd published five or six books, Dan had lost track.

"Professor Carlson," Jon said.

"Thank you, Jon. Mr. Van Ostrand, welcome to our gathering. Do you believe the views on the grave in the cantatas you've discussed truly or only superficially differ from the energetic melancholia associated with the anticipating of death at the closing aria with chorale from Bach's Cantata 58?"

*What?* Dan was relieved for Van Ostrand's sake that the young man was familiar with Cantata 58 and able to jump into an extended theological discussion with Carlson and the others.

When this finally concluded, Jon said, "Next, twenty minutes for discussion of open research questions. Daniel Erhardt, professor at Granville College, has requested time."

"Thank you, Jon." Dan looked around the table as he addressed his colleagues. "I'd like your guidance. I'm looking into the origins and repercussions of the anti-Jewish polemics in several cantatas, including 42 and 44, among others. The difficult truth, long ignored, is that Bach's church cantatas do at times take an explicit contemptuous stance against Jews. Theological Bach research has not come to terms with this, and it ought to. Are any of you working on this or on similar topics? Do you have any thoughts on the subject?"

Silence.

At last Anna Carlson's hand went up. "Whatever the texts of these cantatas, Bach did not write them, so we can't hold him responsible."

This misguided knee-jerk point of view was forever frustrating to Dan, since it was well documented that Bach had been ordained as a minister of music and was responsible for choosing the texts he used, whether he wrote them or not. However, Dan wasn't interested right now in Bach's biography. "In the end, my research is not about what Bach himself personally believed, or what he was held responsible for. The church cantatas aren't about self-expression. They're about reflecting and promoting the religious beliefs of Bach's milieu. That's what I'm trying to learn about."

"If you're looking for context," said Ronald Schultz, a faculty member at Dan's alma mater, Wisconsin Lutheran College, "you should know that when it comes to anti-Jewish vitriol, the vocal music of other composers was much worse. Telemann, for example. Fux, Freislich, Keiser. In this context, Bach's work isn't all that bad."

Dan said, "Yes, but what does it really matter now if Fux, Keiser, or Freislich wrote anti-Jewish works? Hardly anyone listens to them. Many, many people listen to Bach. Bach's work actually matters."

"But none of Bach's cantatas call for the extermination of world Jewry," Anna Carlson said. "So I don't understand what the issue is here. Bach was no Nazi."

Dan was startled. "Are you saying that something is anti-Jewish only if it calls for mass murder?"

"I wouldn't put it so bluntly, but since you do, yes."

Others chimed in now, repeating Anna Carlson's viewpoint and continuing, despite Dan's earlier objection, to defend Bach the person.

When the discussion finally ebbed, Dietrich Bauer got up. With his old-fashioned ways, he no doubt believed that standing was the respectful way to make important professional points. Bauer's height and thin frame gave him a grandeur and gravitas. His white hair was brushed back in a style that most likely he hadn't changed in fifty or sixty years.

"You've raised an interesting and important issue, Professor Erhardt."

Bauer spoke in English and gave Dan his title, both signs of respect. Dan couldn't help but appreciate the compliment. Bauer seemed
more animated now than he'd been at any point in the conference.

"One must always remember, however . . ." Bauer paused.
"These are *Jews* that Bach is talking about in the cantatas. They're
punished because they refuse to accept Jesus as God's Messiah. *This*
is the message that Bach is bringing us. Now, surely we agree that
murder goes too far," he said smoothly, looking around for confirmation, which was readily given in affirmative nods. "Rather, the
Jews can be taught to see the error of their ways. Always there is
hope of them acknowledging Christ. As long as they remain Jews,
alas, they are condemned, along with everyone who hasn't seen the
wisdom of Christ's proper path. Muslims, it goes without saying.
Catholics, too, are condemned, Luther tells us, because of their sin
of believing in works righteousness—a grievous sin the Catholics
share with the Jews, as everyone here well knows. Only the un-
merited gift of proper Christian faith, not good works, justifies our
salvation: this is the message of the gospel, restored through Martin
Luther. And Luther has the only truth." With one hand grasping
the back of his chair and the other holding the edge of the table,
Bauer eased himself down.

After a moment, Jon said, "With all due respect, Professor, officially, at least, American Lutherans have progressed far beyond your
point of view. Justification by faith alone, that of course will never
change. But most leading Lutheran church bodies would no longer
claim that Lutherans hold the only truth."

Dan felt sure his colleagues realized that Jon's view wasn't precisely correct, in terms of official Lutheran church teaching: after a
major 9/11 memorial service at Yankee Stadium, a pastor in the Lutheran Church–Missouri Synod had been famously suspended from

his job for sitting on a stage and praying with a Catholic cardinal, a rabbi, an imam, and Sikh and Hindu holy men.

Before anyone could comment, Jon continued, "On that optimistic note, we arrive at our afternoon repast, to be taken in the conservatory. Viennese coffee and *Apfelstrudel* fresh from the oven. I urge us to put aside our cares and bask in those eternal cure-alls, coffee and dessert."

Dan stood outside. The rain had stopped, but a damp chill seeped into him.

He'd just finished a brief conversation with Becky. She was visiting Disney World with Dan's sister and her family for spring break. Becky had been eager to get off the phone.

Dan was seething. Not about Becky. He was happy that she was having fun at Disney World. He was appalled by the discussion he'd elicited. Maybe he'd deserved it. He'd come here knowing he was no longer truly part of the group, and that his question might provoke them. In a certain sense, he'd baited them. So who was he to feel angry? Nonetheless, what had been said was horrifying to him, as was his own reluctance to confront them.

What to do now? Leaving in protest would be self-defeating. They'd just take his departure as confirming their righteousness.

Maybe he should advise Susanna to destroy the cantata. Wouldn't the world be better off without such an artifact?

He caught himself: he was a scholar. His role was to study, not censor.

Reverend Mueller made his way down the steps, joining Dan. "Had to have a smoke, *Apfelstrudel* or no. Did you know that I smoke?" He shook a cigarette out of his pack and lit it, inhaling. He held his breath for a moment, then exhaled. "That's better. Would you like one?"

"No, thank you."

"Didn't think so. Yes, I smoke, and I'm overweight, too. As you may have noticed. And I drink. German beer—how I love it. So easy to buy in America nowadays. Becks. Warsteiner. I try to curb my desires, but I can't. I'm weak."

Despite his mood, Dan found himself laughing.

"What's a man of God to do? What sort of example am I to my flock?"

"Judging from the crowds you draw at Sunday services, the best example," Dan said.

"They see a sinner, and they can't resist." Another long drag on the cigarette. A pause. A long exhale. "You seem perturbed, Dan."

"Yes."

"I can guess why, but tell me directly."

"The intolerance, to begin with."

"Ah, yes."

"It's shameful."

"The trick at these conferences is to take away what's useful for your own work, for your own soul, and ignore the rest."

Dan felt a need to gain the wisdom of Mueller's counsel. He chose his words with care. "Reverend Mueller, what would you say if a scholar discovered a lost work . . . a work that was morally disturbing, and which should be condemned, but was composed by Bach, Mozart, or Beethoven? Or written by Shakespeare? Or painted by Raphael, Michelangelo, or Leonardo?" Dan attempted to make the question sound hypothetical. "Do we suppress the work? Or do we bring it out for public scrutiny and discussion?" Dan was taking a risk: he hoped Mueller wouldn't, with his long experience as a pastor, notice the old tactic of *a friend of mine has this problem*.

"A scholar's role is to pursue knowledge wherever it leads," Mueller said. "My role is different."

"That's what I'm asking: How do you see it?"

"My role is to promote my religion. I can't answer in specifics without knowing more."

He waited for Dan to respond, but Dan didn't want to tell him more.

"These issues seem very personal for you."

Dan said nothing.

"I'm always here to talk."

"Thank you."

"Have you ever wondered why I attend conferences like these?" Mueller asked.

"Love of Bach's music. Is any other explanation needed?"

"In my case there is a further explanation. For me, Bach's cantatas and Passion settings are not museum pieces. They're a living part of the liturgy. They teach my flock today very much as they taught the Lutherans of Bach's day. I need to understand them, even if some of their messages are troubling."

He stopped, clearly hoping Dan would engage with him on this issue, but Dan looked out across the bare meadows.

"How long is it, since Julie passed?"

It was a year and nine months, but Dan didn't want to say it.

"Work, that's the ticket," Mueller said as if giving a cheer at a football game.

Mueller must have misinterpreted Dan's silence for despair.

"Johann Sebastian Bach worked nonstop, even though he must have felt discouragement enough for all of us. His first wife died, ten of his children died, he was orphaned when he was young. Still he found a way to keep going."

Dan felt compelled to respond, to maintain at least a semblance of courtesy toward this man he'd known for years, this man who was trying, in his own way, to help him. "That's right."

"He felt joy, also. Joy in faith." Warming to his theme, Mueller continued, "Excluding our Lord, who was divine, Johann Sebastian

Bach was the greatest genius in the history of humanity. He enjoyed beer, rich food, a good smoke, and strong coffee, with a coffee cantata to prove it. And he enjoyed sex, too, with twenty children to prove that. I'd advise you to remember this. You're still young. You have another lifetime ahead of you."

Mueller took a drag on his cigarette.

"This is my advice to you today: live in the image of our hero, no matter what modern medicine has to say. Rich food, strong tobacco, stronger coffee, good German beer, and frequent sex—within the sanctity of marriage, of course."

"I suppose we could do worse," Dan said.

The bell rang, calling them back for the next session.

## Chapter 25

On Friday evening, Scott Schiffman sat on the balcony of the Metropolitan Museum and enjoyed a mojito. He'd arrived early and secured a terrific table, at the balustrade on the left side, from which perch he could look down on the Great Hall and watch people coming and going. Monumental, shadowed, airy, this was most romantic place in Manhattan for a drink, especially at the beginning of a relationship. Scott said this with authority, having investigated many such places over the years. He'd arranged this meeting to bring Susanna up to date on his research. He also wanted to encourage in her a sense of connection to the MacLean.

Who was he kidding? He wanted to get to know her better. She'd sparked his interest.

There she was, walking across the Great Hall toward the central stairway. He willed her to turn and look up, to see him waiting. He stood. She did turn, scanning the balcony. He waved.

She didn't see him. She joined the admissions line and disappeared from his view.

"Hello."

She was before him. She put out her hand, deflecting his instinctive move to give her a hug. He shook her hand.

"Hope you didn't have trouble finding me," he said.

"Not at all. You're exactly where you said you'd be."

Scott wondered if he might have done better to sit somewhere else and keep her guessing. A black-clad server arrived to take their drinks order. Susanna asked for white wine, and Scott, a second mojito.

Susanna perused the menu. "Let's try the 'Cabrales blue-cheese-stuffed Medjool dates with Serrano ham, roasted almonds.' That sounds great."

Precisely the type of adventuresome choice that boded well for the evening, in every way. A woman who was attracted to Cabrales blue-cheese-stuffed Medjool dates with Serrano ham and roasted almonds—God alone knew what else she'd enjoy. Scott's imagination took flight.

"I'm glad you suggested that we meet here," she said. "I used to be a docent on the weekends until . . ." He heard the odd pause in her phrasing. "My divorce. I'd like to begin again. Now that . . ." Again the pause. "It's resolved."

"I grew up a few blocks away," Scott said, joining her in covering over whatever she wasn't saying.

"Did you take the museum for granted, growing up nearby?"

"My sisters were constantly bringing me here when they were theoretically babysitting me. They'd sit outside smoking and gossiping with their friends while I was supposed to wear myself out by walking up and down the front steps."

"Could be fun."

"I heard a lot of foreign languages, I'll say that. I was under strict instructions never to tell our mother about these excursions, under penalty of death by pinching."

The conversation flowed from there, lighthearted, stressless, like a dozen conversations he'd enjoyed here in the past. Their appetizer was even more luscious than Scott had expected. After finishing their drinks and splitting the check (at her insistence), they went to see a much-heralded Picasso exhibition. Scott didn't like it. The exhibit was too large, without a central organizing principle. The MacLean did better with its exhibitions, creating small presentations focused on one narrow topic.

He didn't say this, however, because Susanna appeared to be, if not exactly enjoying the show, examining the paintings with interest. As they neared the end, Susanna circled back to a grim portrait of a woman laundress bent over an ironing board. *Woman Ironing*, painted in 1901. Scott stood beside her, but Susanna didn't seem to be present to him anymore. She studied the woman's face, which to Scott held a dreamlike expression. The woman might be bent double from her burdens, but in her mind, she was far off, in another, better world.

"I think we've seen enough of this show," Susanna said, walking toward the exit with a resolve that made Scott fear she'd seen enough of him, too. Once they were out in the main corridor, she seemed to revive. "Whenever I'm here, I like to visit my favorite painting."

From her ease, Scott understood that she wasn't annoyed with him. "Which is?"

"You'll see," she said in a playful tone that pleased him.

"I'd love to be introduced to your favorite painting." Scott heard himself sounding a little too eager, but she rewarded him with a smile.

Off they went, through a maze of large rooms overflowing with European paintings and sculpture . . . Ingres, Toulouse-Lautrec, Redon, Degas, bronzes and paintings of ballet dancers wherever he turned. He wondered if she'd lost her way, but no, she strode before him with confidence. They entered a smaller, darkened room. The painting in the far corner seemed to glow, drawing him close.

"Here it is," she said. *"Moonlight, Strandgade 30.* It was done by a Danish painter, Vilhelm Hammershøi."

The painting measured about sixteen by twenty. The palette was in shades of gray. The image showed a nineteenth-century interior, with moonlight pouring through a long window. Disturbingly, there was no view out the window. Scott read the label, which described Hammershøi as *a painter of silence and light.* The window, according to the label, looked out onto a loggia.

"It's so lonely," Scott said.

"It's peaceful," Susanna said.

"The window doesn't open onto the outside."

"But the room is filled with light."

Scott certainly wouldn't have chosen this as the one he liked best.

"I always expect to see a woman in the painting," Susanna said. "A woman with her back to us, staring at the moonlight—that's how I see the painting in my memory. One day I realized that *I'm* the woman missing from the painting. Not me personally. Everyone who views the painting inhabits that room."

"I don't think I do," Scott said.

"The question for me is, how does an artist portray our inner lives? Like this, I think: by creating a place of peaceful reflection."

Scott sensed a sadness in her that the painting comforted.

He wanted to comfort her, too.

The room was deserted. Even the guard, a stout woman, stood at the entry to the next room. Scott decided to take a risk. Not a wild or outrageous risk. In fact, it wasn't a risk at all. It was a normal step along a road he'd traveled many times. They were standing side by side, and gently he put his arm around her shoulder and pulled her close to him. She turned toward him, as he expected.

And pushed him away.

"What are you doing?" she said in a museum whisper filled with anger. She stepped back and held her hands up, as if to defend herself from him.

"Hey, it's okay."

"Don't touch me."

"I'm sorry."

"Who gave you the right?" She looked shocked, whether from what he'd done or from her own reaction, he couldn't tell. "Stay away from me."

"Okay, I will."

This had never happened to him before. He had no idea what he'd done wrong. He hadn't been aggressive. He'd put his arm around an available woman. Plenty of women had responded positively to this move over the years, and the ones who hadn't—a simple step away sufficed to show that his advance wasn't welcome and no hard feelings either way. Susanna's reaction was way overblown. Scott couldn't understand it. She didn't look like an innocent. Far from it. And besides, he hadn't even meant the gesture in a sexual way. "I didn't mean to upset you."

"You did upset me."

"Hey, all you have to do is say *no.*" Now he put his hands up, defending himself. "*No* is *no.*"

"I trusted you."

"It's not like I attacked you."

"You're right. Thank you for not attacking me."

Scott was flummoxed. *Thank you for not attacking me?* "I don't need to attack you or any other woman. To be frank, the problem is usually the other way around."

This made her laugh. "I can well imagine." She had a gentle laugh, and she looked even more lovely now that she wasn't frightened. Yes, frightened—that's what she'd been. This worldly woman had been frightened of him. Why?

"We're in a public place. There's a guard at the door." Scott gestured toward the entryway, and as if on cue, the guard turned, her eyes glancing over them as she scanned the room.

"Yes, a public place. I know." Susanna spoke more calmly now. "I think we'd better go."

She walked back the way they'd come, toward the central corridor, ignoring the artistic masterpieces crowded around them. He hastened to join her.

When they were side by side, she said, "I need to apologize." She stared ahead. "The problem is I *was* attacked, about a year and a half ago."

"What do you mean?"

"I was raped."

He was horrified. He wanted to grab her arm, bring her to a stop, and ask for a full explanation. But clearly she didn't want that. "Did you know the guy?" He regretted the question and didn't know why he asked it, except it was the first thing that came to his mind. What happened was terrible whether she knew the guy or not.

"He was a stranger. He grabbed me on the street, on the same block where I lived then. Not long afterward, my husband left me."

Her voice carried a savagery that Scott had never expected from her. She seemed to be defending herself from her own pain, as if the brutal tone set up a barrier between what she'd suffered and her real self.

"I'm sorry about what happened to you," he said. "I'm sorry I surprised you. Thank you for explaining."

They reached the museum's central stairway. Scott had a vision of himself at four or five years old, proudly walking down the stairs by himself, hand on the railing, his mother following behind him. As he stood next to Susanna, the memory saddened him, both because of the passage of time and because his life had been so easy, so innocent.

"So you see," Susanna said, taking on an objective tone, "my reaction had nothing to do with you personally. It's a problem I'm work-

ing on, not appropriate for discussion during a visit to the museum.
We should continue our evening as if nothing happened."

"That's what you want to do? Pretend it never happened?"

"Yes."

But that wasn't right, Scott thought as they walked down the steps.

"Let's tour the Greek and Roman wing," she said, taking charge,
reminding him of his elder sister, Lara, during her head-girl phase at
prep school.

He wasn't going to press her to discuss what she didn't want to discuss, but as they walked across the Great Hall, his regret increased.

The Greek and Roman galleries were filled with images of naked
men and women: stiff Archaic-period sculptures of nudes; sensuous
painted nudes decorating terra-cotta vases; bronze nudes holding up
incense burners; idealized, voluptuous Hellenistic nudes in polished
marble. Scott felt awkward, and wondered if she did, too. Evidently not.

"Greek and Roman art was one of my specialty areas when I was
a docent," Susanna said. "I've always loved this part of the museum."

Scott stood beside her as they gazed at a more-than-life-sized
statue of Aphrodite, a Roman copy of a Greek original. The marble
was so smooth he felt an urge to run his fingertips over it. To caress
the sculpted breasts.

Glancing at Susanna, who appeared to be reviewing the descrip-
tive label with genuine interest, he felt an unexpected desire to protect
her. Even as he maintained the distance that he'd determined to be
correct, approximately fifteen inches away, he felt close to her, closer
than he'd felt to a half-dozen women at least, around whom he'd in-
vitingly wrapped his arm while touring these very halls.

## Chapter 26

LEIPZIGERSTRASSE 3
BERLIN, PRUSSIA

*September 1826*

Seeking solitude, Sara left the reception on Lea's terrace. She was in an odd mood, and she wanted be on her own. Her life was filled with too much talk. Because she knew essentially everyone at Lea's gathering today (indeed had hosted many of them at her own home last night), Sara felt a freedom to wander alone, trusting no one would take offense. Refusing the refreshments offered by the hovering footmen, she followed the paths that meandered among the shade trees.

When Lea and Abraham bought this estate, with its *palais* and seven-acre garden, the house had been in a shambles. They'd spent a fortune rebuilding it. The estate was in an undeveloped section of the city, near the Royal Porcelain Factory. The factory's chimneys rose in the distance.

With thick shrubbery now lining the paths, Sara could no longer hear the merriment on the terrace. A clearing opened before her.

And there they were, Lea's children, although they were hardly children anymore. Each held a book, and as Sara drew closer, she realized they were reciting Shakespeare.

"*Fare thee well, nymph. Ere he do leave this grove, / Thou shalt fly him, and he shall seek thy love,*" said Paul, a dark-haired, serious boy who would turn fourteen this year.

"*Re-enter Puck.*" Rebecka gave the stage direction succinctly. At fifteen, Rebecka was plump and sweet-tempered.

They were performing *Ein Sommernachtstraum, A Midsummer Night's Dream.* Shakespeare was *en vogue* since the recent publication of the collected plays translated into German by August Wilhelm Schlegel, the brother-in-law of the children's aunt on their father's side; such was their tightly knit community.

"You play Oberon now," Paul said to Felix. "I want to be Puck."

"No, I'm playing Puck." At seventeen, Felix seemed young for his years. His formal clothes looked too large for him, as if they were a theatrical costume.

"You were Puck before," Paul said.

Fanny, almost twenty-one and apparently filling the role of director, stepped forward: "Felix, you'll play Oberon now." As the eldest, Fanny was generally the sibling in charge of their games. *Poor Fanny* was a phrase that Sara often heard whispered at gatherings. Even Lea privately admitted that her eldest daughter didn't meet society's standard for prettiness.

"Oh, all right." Felix found the lines: "*Hast thou the flower there? Welcome, wanderer.*"

"*Ay, there it is,*" Paul said.

"*I pray thee give it me,*" Felix said, continuing: "*I know a bank where the wild thyme blows, / Where oxlips and the nodding violet grows . . .*"

"Tante!" Fanny interrupted her brother. "Come and join us. You can play Titania."

Sara walked closer. "I don't think so, my dear."

"We need you. My sister is hopeless as Titania."

"It's true," Rebecka said. "But only because I am the perfect Helena. I've also performed Peaseblossom, Cobweb, Moth, and Mustardseed, all to great acclaim," she added with a dramatic gesture of her hand.

"You are kind to ask, but I cannot play Titania." At her elevated age, sixty-five this year, Sara felt self-conscious performing theatricals. Nonetheless she was flattered by the invitation. "Why don't you play Titania yourself, Fanny?"

"I'm the director," Fanny said.

"Tante, you absolutely can play Titania if you want to," said Paul. "Don't be scared. It's just us. I was scared when I first began acting, but not anymore."

What a lovely boy. "I don't enjoy acting," Sara said. "For myself, I mean. I like it in others."

"In that case, why don't you be the audience?" said Rebecka. "We never have a proper audience."

"That, too, is a kind invitation, and I thank you. I'm rather occupied at the moment, however: I left the reception to walk alone in the garden."

"That's also important," Felix said with earnest consideration. "You will experience the *Waldeinsamkeit*."

"Indeed." *Waldeinsamkeit*: the enrapturing loneliness and peace of the forest.

"Tante, since you appreciate the garden," Felix asked, "have you read the latest edition of our newspaper, the *Gartenzeitung*?" The *Garden Times*.

"No, I haven't."

"You must." Felix ran to retrieve it from a box positioned on the nearby sundial. He gave it to her.

"Thank you, Felix. I shall find a secluded bench and delight in reading it."

"Thank *you*, Tante," he said with a solemnity that left Sara embarrassed. She'd been speaking ironically. He paused, looking worried. "It's our only copy."

"I'll take good care of it. I'll return it before the concert."

"Thank you."

"I'll say farewell for now," Sara said.

"Farewell, Tante," they said in unison as she walked away.

Then Fanny instructed: "Pray continue, Felix."

"Where was I?" Felix said. "I have it: *Lulled in these flowers with dances and delight . . .*"

As Sara continued along the paths, their words faded behind her. The children were charming. Nonetheless Sara found something a bit too precious, a bit too isolated about them, here in their walled garden. Lea and Abraham doted on them endlessly. Sara couldn't remember herself being doted upon. She could count only a few occasions when she'd experienced her father's or her mother's undivided attention. Admittedly, fifteen children growing up in one household was rather different from four.

But Fanny, Felix, Rebecka, and Paul weren't precisely children anymore. Fanny was an adult. Lea had sent away the one suitor who'd thus far pursued Fanny—sent him away not for one year, which might be considered a suitable waiting period, but for five years. Fanny would be twenty-three when he returned. *If* he returned. He was a gifted artist. Sara suspected that Lea's true quarrel with him was not his relative financial poverty but that Fanny's marriage would break the dreamlike spell that held the family close. Fanny was a talented keyboardist with a particular gift for the works of Beethoven. She also composed music. Her pieces were skilled and pleasing, if somewhat lacking in originality. Her work was improving, however, and Sara had great hopes for her.

Finding a shaded bench beneath an arbor of white roses, Sara sat down. The handwritten *Gartenzeitung* was filled with drawings of the house and garden, poems, and humorous articles on the concerns of the city. Amusing? Whimsical? Sara sighed.

The bell rang, calling her to the concert. Today's event was one in a series of midday Sunday concerts that Sara had attended here, the social and cultural élite, Christian and Jewish, brought together harmoniously by music. As Sara returned to the house, she greeted friends along the way.

The *palais* had an unusual design feature, not visible from the street: a long rear wing, called the *Gartenhaus*, or garden house. This rustic structure had a dozen rooms, several kitchens, and, most crucially, a columned performance hall, called the *Gartensaal*, that could accommodate a sizable crowd, well over a hundred, especially on days like today, when the weather permitted its series of French doors to be opened.

When she reached the terrace, Abraham Mendelssohn, looking dapper in his fashionable cravat, was saying to one of their distant relations, a cousin from Pomerania who'd called on Sara the day before, "Yes, yes, my daughter Fanny will perform today. Music is the ideal ornament for her. Never to replace her true calling as a wife and mother, of course."

This was a constant refrain from Abraham: Fanny was awaiting her true calling (even though her suitor had been sent away). With his ready smile, Abraham was forever kind toward Sara, and she chided herself for her stubbornly negative opinion of him, but he did rule the family like a dictator. Nonetheless he made Lea happy, or so Lea persistently claimed.

"As to Felix," Abraham continued, "*he's* the master in the making."

Always Felix, never Fanny. Felix was the one who'd accompanied his father on a recent trip to Paris. Felix, the one who'd visited Goethe in Weimar not once but several times. Felix, who'd already had his music published, and who performed in public, not simply in the family's private *Gartensaal*.

"Felix will take his place among the greatest composers in German history. Already he's being compared to Mozart . . ."

No, Sara could never bring herself to like Abraham Mendelssohn.

"Tante." Lea was at her side. "I've reserved a seat for you near the front on the left, so you can see the keyboard."

"Thank you, my dear. And let me give you the *Gartenzeitung.* I promised the children I'd take good care of it."

"Ah, the *Gartenzeitung* . . . the ways they find to amuse themselves." Her tone was at once exasperated and indulgent. "I'll make certain it's returned safely to its box."

"Thank you."

Finding her seat, Sara glanced around. How the *Gartensaal* came to be built, years ago, she couldn't imagine. The central cupola provided a soft, filtered light. Surreptitiously Sara counted her fellow guests, giving up at seventy.

String players, including a violinist, violist, and cellist, gathered at the front of the room, around the fortepiano. They began tuning their instruments. When required, Abraham employed professionals from the royal orchestra for the Sunday concerts. Fanny took her place at the piano.

At a nod from the violinist, Fanny rose. She announced, "As the first piece on our program today, we will perform the Piano Quartet number 2 in F Minor, opus 2, composed by Felix Mendelssohn Bartholdy in 1823, in honor of his teacher, Carl Friedrich Zelter."

*Bartholdy* . . . this was the name by which the family styled itself nowadays. Abraham seemed to believe that the addition of the name of the family dairy farm would downplay the memory of his father, the renowned philosopher Moses Mendelssohn.

Fanny gave the signal, and the music began. The quartet was a solid effort, especially in view of the fact that it had been written when Felix was fourteen. Yes, thought Sara, it was workmanlike, occasionally bombastic, derivative of Beethoven. A few moments in the adagio movement touched her. But overall the piece wasn't worthy of comparison to Mozart, or to Beethoven for that matter.

In due course the piece concluded, and Sara did not regret its passing.

The string players dispersed. Paul, carrying his cello, joined his sister. After a moment of tuning and adjustment, Fanny rose once more. "Next, the *Andante con variazioni* in D major for piano and cello, a stunning new work, not yet fully completed, by Felix Mendelssohn Bartholdy, composed in honor of Paul Mendelssohn Bartholdy."

Young Paul . . . the piece had a technical complexity that he easily managed. Sara leaned forward and focused her attention. His performance was poignant and filled with melancholy. He made the music reveal emotions beyond his years. Sara was moved. Judging from the applause when he finished, others shared her opinion.

With an appealing diffidence, Paul bowed and left the performance area before the applause ended. Why had she never heard talk from Abraham about a musical career for Paul? She'd love to hear Paul perform Beethoven's third and fourth cello sonatas, written in Beethoven's earlier style, free of his later harangues.

When the audience quieted, Fanny rose and said in a mischievous tone, "And now our final piece for today: the concert overture *A Midsummer Night's Dream* by Felix Mendelssohn Bartholdy, a brilliant composition for piano four hands."

Sara had heard about this piece from Lea. Felix had been laboring over it for months.

Felix joined Fanny. Brother and sister sat side by side. They exchanged impish grins. They were unusually close. Too close for their own good, perhaps.

As the piece unfolded, Sara felt herself transported into another realm, ethereal and enchanted . . . *I know a bank where the wild thyme blows, Where oxlips and the nodding violet grows* . . .

Sara was amazed, and awed, by the preternatural originality of the music. Fanny and Felix played their parts as if they were of one mind, performing the intricate piece from memory.

As the closing chords lingered in the air, the two siblings raised their hands from the keyboard. The applause began. Fanny and Felix rose, laughing. They embraced.

All at once Sara understood: Abraham had not exaggerated. He and Lea did not indulge Felix. The children did not lead lives of empty charm. Felix Mendelssohn (God help her, she'd never add the absurd *Bartholdy*) was indeed another Mozart. In fact, he was greater than another Mozart. He was himself, fully and completely.

Fanny stood behind Felix as he bowed, so that the attention was focused on him. He looked back at her, as if for support and approval, which she gave him through a quick hug, but then she stepped aside once more.

Sara realized that Fanny, too, understood: Felix was much more than her younger brother. The wildly enthusiastic applause continued. Felix bowed again. He was an awkward, modest, gangly boy in formal clothes, a boy not yet grown into manhood, not even fully comprehending what he had already accomplished.

The future was open to him. How would he fill it?

## Chapter 27

Seven a.m., and Reverend Frank Mueller was settled on the rectory roof with his morning coffee and his *New York Times*. His iPod was fully charged, and he wore his headphones. This morning he was listening to J. S. Bach's Goldberg Variations, on piano, the astonishing Simone Dinnerstein performance. He never listened to Glenn Gould. For him, Gould was eccentric and self-indulgent, too much Gould and not enough Bach.

Whenever the weather cooperated, he enjoyed his rooftop morning ritual. He defined *weather cooperating* as neither raining nor snowing and a temperature above 45 degrees Fahrenheit. He was happy to wear a coat and long underwear, as he did today. He made adjustments to his timing in accordance with the ebb and flow of daylight over the course of the year. He liked to arrive soon after dawn, when the sky was lavender, and stay until the sun was above the buildings on Fifth Avenue. On roof mornings, he prepared his coffee *mit Schlag*, with sweet whipped cream. Because he rose before his dear wife, she didn't have to confront him on this. She was obsessively concerned about his diet. He, too, was concerned about his diet, but his priorities were different. He'd happily pass up any number of grilled tenderloins with brandy peppercorn sauce (and God knew he loved *that*) for the privilege of sitting on his rooftop each morning to enjoy his coffee *mit Schlag* in the peace of the Lord's own dawning day.

From his rooftop perch, Central Park and the apartment buildings of Fifth Avenue spread to the east. To the west, the Hudson River and the cliffs of New Jersey. He had much to be grateful for. God had been good to him. Thankfulness filled his heart each morning when he sat down on the roof with his *New York Times* and his coffee.

Today, as usual, he began the paper with the news summary on page 2. How he loved his newspaper. He prayed—yes, God help him, he prayed—that the physical newspaper would continue to exist throughout his lifetime, despite the profligate waste of lumber to produce newsprint, the worrying reduction in readership, and the proliferation of electronic devices. Bringing his computer, tablet, or phone up here in the morning to read the digital version of what was supposed to be a *newspaper* just would not be the same.

So, the news summary . . . the usual political viciousness in America and violent upheavals around the globe. The Arts section was his reward for slogging through the world's miseries, and he always read the Arts summary last.

Musicologist and theologian arrested in Heidelberg, Germany, for crimes against humanity, page A5.

What? Had he read this correctly? He tried again. The words were the same.

He turned to page A5. He saw a black-and-white photo of several stalwart SS men standing beside a mass grave. In the mass grave, limbs jutted out at unnatural angles. The SS men smoked and laughed together. The thin young man in the middle of the group, taller than the others . . . could it be, as the article claimed, Dietrich Bauer? The line of the jaw, the angle of the nose, these were similar. The height, too, was familiar, as was the mien, the self-importance.

But the person in the photo was young. Dietrich Bauer was old.

*In 1941 in what is now the western Ukraine . . .*

Mueller didn't want to read this. The thought of mass graves overseen by a personal acquaintance cast down his soul.

He forced himself to continue: *953 men, women, and children were taken from a group of villages . . .* He made himself read even as bile rose within him. *They were beaten along the road to keep them moving . . .*

The Goldberg Variations in their sacred glory continued singing in his ears. He, Frank Mueller, had often sat with Dietrich Bauer over a few beers and discussed the music of Johann Sebastian Bach. They'd broken bread together.

Mueller had never suspected. Never once. Okay, Bauer made some surprising references to Jews, but those references came under the category of *harmless cranky old men not subject to political correctness.* Or so Mueller had decided years ago. And last month in Princeton, Bauer had affirmed that Christian chastisement of Jews should not extend to the taking of life.

*. . . children who couldn't keep up were lifted by the feet and swung against . . .*

Justice dictated that Bauer was innocent until proven guilty, but Mueller had to assume that the old man wasn't arrested without probable cause. Again he studied the photo. The strong chin, the well-trained body, the precise uniform. The smile as he and his buddies relaxed with cigarettes beside the trench filled with naked bodies, some no doubt still clinging to life.

How old was Bauer in 1941? The article said he was eighty-seven now. Mueller wished he had his phone with him, for the calculator.

He created a picture of the numbers in his mind and did the math. Bauer was nineteen in the photo.

At nineteen, Bauer was essentially a child. People change as they grow older. At least Mueller believed they did. Faith had called to Bauer, and he'd matured into a theologian. His many devotional writings . . . Mueller had read them all. Nonetheless, Mueller felt a dread growing within himself: Could Bauer possibly have believed that he'd been doing the Lord's work during the war? On the other hand, Bauer might have thought of his career as a kind of penance for his actions in the war.

*. . . forced to dig their own graves . . .*

Where was the merciful all-powerful God, while Dietrich Bauer smoked and laughed beside a trench of naked, dead, and dying humans?

Mueller couldn't understand. Personal evil, institutional evil—did God allow Himself to wait for the good people in the world to rise up to defeat it?

So many questions, tugging at him. Did the persistent survival of Judaism open the possibility that Jesus wasn't the Messiah—was that why Christian anxiety lapsed into violence against Jews? Was it because Christians historically blamed Jews for the Crucifixion, even though they believed the Crucifixion had to take place in order for Jesus to fulfill His mission on earth?

Although Mueller didn't like to focus on it, several members of his own family had been members of the Nazi party. It was a way to get ahead. He refused to consider that it was more to them than a social necessity. He would not countenance that his relatives might have believed in the tenets of Nazism in the same way that he, for example, believed in the tenets of Lutheranism. When the war was over, his grandmother said that all their family members in Germany during the war had been members of the resistance, risking their lives every day to defeat the Nazis and to shelter Jews.

This was the improbable if not blatantly false story that Mueller had been raised on.

Years later, when he was helping to clean out his grandmother's home after she died, Mueller had found photos sent from the family in Germany before the war. Family members dressed in Nazi uniforms. Giving the salute. He'd hidden these photos, ashamed to show them to his parents or to his cousins. He still had them, in a shoe box under the bed. Even his dear wife had never seen them. Someday, when he himself was gone, his children, Chrissy, Pam, and Tom, would find the photos, and they'd have to figure out what to do with them, and how to understand them.

The strains of the Goldberg Variations, aching with longing, tugged at him.

Dan had been trying to tell him something in Princeton. After his many years counseling the needy, Mueller liked to think that he could always spot the my-friend-has-this-problem trick. Dan must have discovered something important and problematic. Mueller needed to stay alert, to find out what it was.

The recording reached the remarkable twenty-eighth variation. Dietrich Bauer liked this movement, too. They'd discussed it two years ago, over breakfast during a conference in Bad Arolsen, Germany.

Mass murder. The Goldberg Variations. Johann Sebastian Bach composed for the Lord, dedicating his compositions, every one, *to the glory of God alone.*

Mueller's brain was teeming. He slowed himself down. He focused on the music, the Lord's own music, emanating from a rectangular, flat machine that fit into Mueller's shirt pocket. This amazing little gadget held all of Bach's music, in the performances that Mueller liked best. Mueller let the music of God suffuse his mind. He'd always been certain of its sacred truth and power. It calmed and steadied him.

The Quodlibet began. Traditionally this section was described as a medley of frivolous folk tunes, tacked onto the end of the Goldberg Variations as a learned joke. In an epiphany, however, as if the Lord were indeed manifestly with him, Mueller heard the affinity of the Quodlibet's main theme with the hymn *Was Gott tut, das ist wohlgetan,* "What God does is done well."

Beams of sunlight silhouetted the buildings of the Upper East Side. The Lord was all around him. Mueller could have wept. He tried to do God's work each day, in small ways and large. He would attempt to discern the message that the Lord wanted him to take from the arrest of Dietrich Bauer.

He resolved to devote his Sunday sermon to these issues that weighed so heavily upon him.

At 8:55 a.m., at Granville College, Dan opened his e-mail. He had fifteen minutes before his morning class—Bach, this semester—and he was fully prepared, so he allowed himself to check e-mail. Seventy-three new messages. That seemed excessive for a Tuesday morning. His account must have suffered a spam attack.

But no. At least thirty of the messages were links from friends to an article in today's *New York Times.* The others were from his Bach listserv, with an initial announcement referencing the *Times* article and then a series of reply messages from list members commenting on the story.

Dan went to the *Times* website. He found the article. He saw the photo.

Dan remembered Bauer at the conference in Princeton. The severity. The old-world propriety.

Dan figured out that in the photo Dietrich Bauer was nineteen, the same age as many of Dan's students who were gathering in the hallway now, greeting one another with jocular complaints about the dining-hall breakfast and about how hard it was to get up in the morning after a late night of studying and/or carousing followed by various intimacies and indiscretions.

What would it take to turn them into murderers?

The music library downstairs had copies of Bauer's books. Should the books be removed from the shelves? He'd discuss the question later with the librarian.

"Hey, Professor."

It was Derrick Lyons, the third baseman. Derrick had proven himself to be among Dan's best students and was now taking the Bach course. Dan tried to imagine Derrick, with his open, eager expression, a wayward lock of hair continually falling over his forehead, in a military uniform, a rifle slung over his shoulder. Derrick as not only a soldier but also a murderer of civilians. The image struck Dan with its force.

"What do you think about this music guy who got arrested? Do you know him?"

Derrick, lifting the rifle to murder a woman or a child who stood naked on a plank over a pit.

"Aren't we reading some of his stuff later in the term?"

Derrick, ordering the next victim onto the plank.

"I did know him. I *do* know him."

Derrick, turning the rifle on Dan himself. Except most likely Dan, tall and blond, with his perfect Aryan heritage, would be among the senior officers. He'd be Derrick's teacher in a far different educational endeavor.

"What's he like?"

"Go into class, Derrick. I'll be there in a moment."

Derrick looked startled. Hurt.

"I'm sorry to be abrupt. I just found out. I'm trying to work this out myself. We'll discuss it in class. Would you be willing to check in with your classmates and make a list of questions for us to consider?"

With this bit of responsibility, Derrick seemed to brighten. "Okay." He went down the hall.

Dan pushed aside the stack of CDs he'd prepared for class. He made notes for discussion points that he hoped would be meaningful to his students, to add to Derrick's list. Dan's first question for his students was whether they thought he should remove Dietrich Bauer's writings from their assignments for the semester, yes or no and explain your position.

## Chapter 28

Susanna sat at her dining table after dinner and reviewed the proposal submitted by Raffie Espinal and his students for a green roof at their school. Four thousand dollars for planters. Two thousand for plants. Six for an irrigation system.

Where were they getting these figures? Were they guessing?

She put down her pen in frustration. The engineer's feasibility report was positive, so they were ready to move to the next step. They had laudable ambitions, but turning dreams into quantifiable details wasn't easy. In a proposal like this, listing two thousand dollars for plants was meaningless. They needed to determine what type of plants, affirm that the plants were suited to the conditions on the site, and note where they were going to buy the plants. This degree of specificity was required for every purchase. Building a green roof was a multiyear project, and unfortunately the current students would graduate before it was completed.

Taking a break, she pushed the proposal aside. She still hadn't heard anything from Rob on the issue of the Gilbert and Sullivan center. Most likely nothing would be resolved until the next board meeting, in a few months.

She picked up the newspaper, which she'd left half-read this morning. As she leafed through it, she glanced over an article about Dietrich Bauer. His story seemed very much in line with his era and didn't surprise her. She assumed that Dan and Scott must know him. She turned the page.

The CDs, she recalled. She'd acknowledged the gift when she received it before Christmas, but she'd never thanked Dan properly. On his salary, six CDs probably constituted a good deal of money. Damn. It was after 9 p.m., so she could leave a message on his office answering machine and assuage her guilt. Tomorrow she'd write a snail-mail thank-you note to him. She found his card on her desk and dialed the number.

"Hello?"

Oh, hell. She couldn't very well hang up; his phone doubtless had caller ID, so he was looking at her phone number if not her name. "It's Susanna Kessler."

"You're calling because you read about Dietrich Bauer?"

"No. Although I did read about him. Do you know him?"

"I do. I never suspected."

"You *really* never suspected?"

"Point taken. I always do wonder, Germans of that age. But I let myself not wonder too closely in this case."

"Because of his scholarly achievements and his theology degree?"

"I suppose so."

She didn't want to discuss Dietrich Bauer. Best get right to it: "I'm calling because I've been remiss. I haven't suitably thanked you for the CDs. I've listened to them often. I appreciate you sending them."

"I'm glad."

"I especially like the viola da gamba sonatas."

"I like those pieces, too."

She wanted to give him a specific detail, to show that she had indeed listened carefully. "I love the sound of the old piano."

"The fortepiano."

"The sound is so . . ." She felt at a loss, without the language to describe to him, an expert, what made the music compelling. "Beckoning."

"I understand what you mean."

To cover her awkwardness, she reverted to chitchat. "You're working late."

"Becky, my daughter, is at a pageant rehearsal and sleepover tonight."

"What kind of pageant?"

"I believe it has something to do with addition and subtraction. Much excitement about it in the first grade."

"If I'd taken part in a math pageant in first grade, I'm certain I'd still be able to add and subtract without a calculator."

"Me, too. Anyway, she talked me into allowing her to have a sleepover at a friend's house after the rehearsal and go directly to school tomorrow from her friend's. I'm sure she's fine, but it doesn't seem right somehow."

"Based on my extensive babysitting experience when I was a teenager, it sounds reasonable enough."

"Thank you. I've got a lot of e-mails to answer about the Bauer situation, and I'm trying to write some reflections about it, too, if only for my students. No one waiting at home, so I have a lot of free time for work."

Sensing the grief beneath his forced jocularity, she said gently, "What happened to you and your wife?"

"It's a sad story."

"I thought it might be. Don't worry, though. You can tell me."

And he did, narrating his experiences matter-of-factly, as though they had happened to someone else.

As he was reaching the end, Susanna heard the pain coming into his voice.

"I keep remembering," he said, "I mean I keep feeling, how soft Martin's skin was. And his perfect tiny fingers and toes, even though he . . ."

*Was dead*, Susanna heard, although he didn't say it and neither did she.

"What about you?" he asked.

The immediate segue, before she could respond to what he'd said, shifting the conversation away from himself . . . she'd reacted this way often enough, too, in order to avoid further probing questions. Nevertheless his query raised her hackles and made her feel she had to defend herself.

"What do you mean?" she asked.

She hoped Scott hadn't shared with him the details of their evening at the museum. Her reaction that night had surprised her. She'd experienced such an immediate and instinctive recoiling from him. Poor man, he hadn't deserved the torrent of outrage that had come down on him. He'd done nothing out of the ordinary. A visceral, involuntary part of herself had taken over, and she'd lashed out in fear and panic. She didn't want any repetition of that.

"What you mentioned when we were standing outside the MacLean."

So no, Scott hadn't said anything.

"I've been wondering about it."

Dan was a sympathetic voice at the end of a phone connection. He wasn't here in her living room. She could allow herself to confide in him.

"A few years ago, when I was walking home from work . . ." She told the story slowly, skipping no details.

When she reached the end, he said, "That's not what I expected you to say."

"That's what everyone tells me. What exactly do people expect?" She didn't mean to rebuke him; it wasn't his fault. She went to the window and looked out at the close. Moonlight illuminated the trees.

"The phrase is only a placeholder," he said, apparently not hearing her anger. "It gives people time to recover and think of something better. Now that I've thought of something better, I'll say it: I'm sorry."

"Thank you."

"I think we'd both like to talk about something else now," he said.

"Yes."

"I'll start: I don't know exactly what your job is."

"I help a wealthy family to give away its money."

"People need help with that?"

"It depends on how much they're giving away."

"How much is this family giving away?"

"A minimum of ten million dollars a year."

"That's a lot."

"Yes, it *is* a lot."

"My family never had that kind of problem," he said.

"Neither did mine."

And so their conversation flowed.

## Chapter 29

Frederic Fournier stood on the upper-level terrace of Robertson Barstow's family home and gazed across the lilac gardens to the Hudson
River beyond. The house behind him screamed imitation English
aristocracy. His host was circulating through the gardens below,
making certain his guests were adequately supplied with canapés and
champagne.

Frederic knew he was lucky to be invited here today, yet he noticed that many others had been similarly lucky. The garden was
vast, and it was crowded. The terrace around him was packed. The
reception rooms on the main floor of the house ("house" was a euphemism) were also crowded. From his position on the terrace, for-
tuitously poised between inside and out, he recognized more than a
few famous faces. He even saw his former student Scott Schiffman (*he*
wasn't famous) squiring an older lady, his mother, from the look of
her, as she strolled amid the fountains and the lilacs.

No sign of Susanna Kessler, however. Her wedding photo from the *Times* was impressed upon his memory.

A waiter offered him another glass of champagne, and as Frederic turned to take it—there she was. Not ten feet from him. Looking exactly like her photograph. She wore a sleeveless, form-fitting dress. She was chatting with several well-turned-out youngsters, and from her ease among them, and vice versa, Frederic concluded that they must be Rob's grandchildren.

He was nervous. He, Frederic Fournier, man of the world. His brow turned damp.

What to do? He adjusted his tie, although it was already perfect. His suit jacket was impeccably cut and it smoothed over his imperfections. Now he simply had to await his opportunity. But what would he say to her? His mind grasped for the speech he'd memorized. *We haven't had the pleasure, I'm a college friend of Rob's. How do you know Rob?*

How foolish it sounded, playing in his mind while he contemplated the flesh-and-blood Susanna several steps away from him.

No, no, he reassured himself, he could do this. He'd pulled off greater social challenges. And she'd be bound by *politesse*, he being (or rather, claiming to be) a friend of Rob's.

The group of youngsters loosened as a uniformed server appeared carrying a tray of—he couldn't see what. This was his opportunity. He took the ten steps to Susanna Kessler's side as if he had nothing but food on his mind.

"Rob certainly has an excellent caterer," he said to Susanna as he took a sampling of—it turned out to be a strip of roast chicken on a skewer accompanied by some type of sauce on the side. He hated roast chicken on a skewer, he hated sauce on the side, but what could he do?

"Yes," she said politely. "He does." She herself did not take a skewer.

"I don't believe we've met." Balancing both his champagne glass and the skewer in his left hand, he put out his right hand. "Frederic Fournier. Rob and I know each other from Harvard."

"Susanna Kessler." She shook his hand. Sensing the start of an intelligent conversation, the youngsters moved away and regrouped.

"How do you know Rob?"

"I work for him."

"Do you, then. I'm sure he must be quite the taskmaster."

A sweet laugh. "He'd like to believe that he works us hard, but mostly he leaves us to our own devices."

"The mark of a confident and creative boss. He knows how to get the best out of people. That's my philosophy, too."

"What do you do?"

The perfect transition. "I teach at Yale. Centennial professor, as a matter of fact," he added with feigned modesty.

"What's your field?"

"Music history. A specialty in the music of Johann Sebastian Bach." He spoke with a nonchalance that he'd rehearsed throughout the previous week. This was the moment when she was supposed to exclaim, *Music history? Specialty in Johann Sebastian Bach? I found an unknown Bach cantata in the basement (or attic or wherever).*

Instead of leaning toward him in excitement, she stepped back, as if to gain a better view of him. She stared steadily. Her gaze made him feel as if she were stripping him, and not in a good way.

"I've written four monographs on Bach, including what I must confess is widely considered the definitive study of Bach's compositional process in the writing of fugues."

Still she stared, saying nothing, and he felt compelled to fill the silence.

"Yes, my work has led me to some unusual places. Last year I organized the first Bach festival in China. Four cities in two weeks. And to follow up . . ."

He realized he was trying too hard. Slow down, he told himself.

*Shut up.* But like a desperate kid on his first job interview, he couldn't make himself stop. "And a few years ago in Cracow, a young fellow stumbled upon an old painting of a group of musicians and hadn't the least idea of what it was, so he went through the usual channels, and when the lawyers came calling"—important to mention lawyers, so she'd know he had experience dealing with unreasonable lawyers, in case any turned up to challenge her possession of the cantata—"as they always do, in these situations, you can count on the lawyers to find an opening . . ."

When would someone, anyone, come to rescue him?

---

In the garden, Scott Schiffman stood beside his mother as she talked with Robertson Barstow's mother.

"Isn't this a lovely spot?" Mrs. Barstow said. She used a walker instead of a wheelchair today.

"Yes, lovely," Scott's mother said. With her white hair pulled into a chignon, she was looking very well, Scott thought. He hadn't seen her in a while. Or rather, he'd seen her, but he hadn't actually looked at her. She was as chic and gracious as ever.

"We ladies should stay right here," said Mrs. Barstow. "Claim the best view for ourselves." She glanced to her right, and instantly a butler was at her side. She gave her instructions. Soon, two wrought-iron garden chairs with green-and-pink striped cushions appeared. Mrs. Barstow sat down. Scott's mother sat down. A large umbrella was set up to shelter them. A table was brought over and a tier of tea sandwiches was placed upon it.

"I think I'll excuse myself for a moment, Mother." Scott hoped to find a gin and tonic. He didn't like champagne in the afternoon.

"Yes, dear. You go find some younger ladies to talk to."

Scott felt a familiar sting. What she was actually saying was *why aren't you married like your brother and your sisters?* Nonetheless, as impatient as he sometimes became with her, he was glad his mother had friends, her mind was intact, and she took pleasure in the world.

A waiter told him that the bar was on the terrace. He walked up the stairs and saw the bar on his left. He also saw Susanna Kessler. He'd been hoping to run into her at this event. In fact, he'd offered to escort his mother (who attended the lilac fete every year) for the sole purpose of seeking out Susanna and trying to regain her trust.

Who was she talking to? Could it be? It was: Freddy Fournier, lecturing her, leaning close to make his points. Susanna looked as if she were downright allergic to him. Scott could imagine how she felt, not wanting to offend him yet desperate to escape.

Steeling himself for battle, Scott walked across the terrace and joined them. "Susanna, good to see you."

Freddy looked as if he'd witnessed a miraculous apparition. "Miss Kessler, have you met my prized student, Scott Schiffman?"

Was Freddy introducing them right after Scott had addressed her by name, proving that they already knew each other? Freddy must be way off his game.

"Yes, we've met. How good to see you again, Mr. Schiffman."

Scott noticed her teasing smile as she addressed him formally.

Freddy said, "Mr. Schiffman has done very well for himself, I take some pride in saying."

"I agree," Susanna said.

"Well, well, I'd best be moving along," Freddy said. "So many friends to greet, so little time." He turned and disappeared into the crowd.

"Who was that?" Susanna asked Scott.

"Oh, just the foremost Bach scholar in America, or rather the second foremost, after Christoph Wolff of Harvard."

"Are we working with him?"

Scott liked hearing the word *we*. "Not at the moment, but we may need to at some point in the future. Although Freddy has become more of an impresario than a scholar."

"An impresario?"

For Susanna's benefit, Scott reviewed Freddy's dazzling array of accomplishments in the classical music world.

"Do I want to get to know him?"

"Someday. Possibly."

"By the way, what are you doing here?" Susanna said.

"Escorting my mother, once again. She's sitting with Mrs. Barstow down below. Bit of an odd couple, though."

"How so?"

"Mrs. Barstow is the genuine article: an American aristocrat of high WASP origins. My mother, on the other hand, was—is—a Jew from Darmstadt. A refugee. Came here when she was young. She was lucky enough to marry well." Immediately he regretted his disloyalty to his parents. "She had family in New York to sponsor her, and so . . ."

He stopped. Her family in America was well-to-do. She met Scott's father at a wedding. Scott's father's family was, in its own way, part of the American aristocracy, the type of people about whom he'd heard the whispered opinion that they were so rich, it didn't matter that they were Jews.

"You seem upset," Susanna said quietly.

With embarrassment, Scott realized that he'd been staring at the river. "Oh," he pretended to shrug it off, "I don't like to talk about the past."

"You're in an odd profession for someone who doesn't like to talk about the past."

"I mean the personal past."

"I know the feeling."

He felt a bond with her. Their evening at the Met seemed now to rest between them like a shared difficulty that unites people rather than divides them. Nonetheless he wanted to change the subject to something less fraught for them both. He noticed the sweet scent around them. "What is that awful smell?"

"The lilacs. This is a lilac fete, remember?"

He felt back on solid ground, engaging in repartee with an attractive woman. "Right: a lilac fete."

"I love that smell."

"Then this is clearly the party for you. I'm searching for a gin and tonic. Can I bring you another glass of champagne?"

"Thank you. Very kind of you."

Excellent. He was redeeming himself. The afternoon was moving along in an altogether pleasing way.

———————

Frederic Fournier, bloodied but unbowed, watched them from the lawn below. Was a romantic link developing between those two? If so, it could prove useful. He'd monitor the situation.

When a server passed bearing a tray of scallops wrapped in bacon, Frederic placed three on a napkin. He would enjoy them, indeed he would. He took himself to an arbor covered with grapevines. Standing in the arbor's shade, he relished the canapés one after the other. When he finished, he cleared his palate with another glass of champagne provided by a conveniently passing server.

As expected, his strength returned. Susanna Kessler still needed him. She needed his knowledge and his experience. Nothing had changed. They'd met, the details didn't matter. Eventually she would wake up to the fact that with Dan and Scott, she was dealing with rookies.

He simply had to be patient until she came to her senses.

## Chapter 30

Was this the cure for heartache?

Sara stood in the central courtyard of Berlin's Jewish orphanage. She watched a dozen or so boys, dressed alike, hair cut alike, as they kicked balls, played catch, and organized footraces. They wore sturdy shoes.

For several years, Baruch Auerbach, the leader of the Jewish Freischule, had been gathering funds to expand the orphanage. He was filled with dreams: a new, larger building to accommodate more boys. A separate, connected facility for girls. More classrooms, music and art lessons, an infirmary and a live-in nurse. Sara gave generously.

Today, however, Herr Auerbach wanted something different from her. He wanted time. Love. He was searching for *Ehrenmütter*, "honorary mothers," as he called them, to give the orphaned boys a semblance of family. To help guide their lives.

Herr Auerbach believed she would be a good candidate. Or so

he said. She didn't know whether she could entirely trust him on this question. She was, truth be told, the largest contributor to the orphanage. Naturally he would want to keep her close by. At seventy-six, she might be too old for the role he suggested.

Nonetheless, she'd agreed to come here today, with several of her friends, to tour the orphanage and share the midday meal with the boys.

A teacher rang a bell. The boys lined up and proceeded in an orderly fashion to the washroom. Soon after, they were seated at tables in the refectory.

Herr Auerbach was a stout, balding man who rarely smiled. "I've given you a group of nine-year-olds," he said as he led Sara to a table. He announced to them, "Boys, this is Frau Levy."

"Good afternoon, Frau Levy," the four boys said.

Herr Auerbach had them well trained. He departed. Sara sat down.

The boys stared at her. Sara stared at them. They looked endearing in their tidy identical uniforms. Their hair, mussed during their games, was now neatly combed. All four boys had dark hair, brown eyes, and pale skin. They were neither thin nor fat. They looked healthy. Well fed and well exercised.

Kitchen maids served the food table by table, starting at the opposite end of the room. Sara glanced at her friend Amalia Beer, sitting nearby. Amalia already had the four boys at her table engaged in conversation, eagerly responding to her questions. Amalia had a gift with children.

At Sara's table, the boys continued to stare at her in silence. She didn't know what to say to them. She had no trouble talking to Lea's children, but they were family, with an abundance of shared experiences. Finally a topic came to her:

"What are you studying?"

No reply.

She turned to the boy on her right. "Are you studying history?"

The boy looked away as he responded. "We're learning about Frederick the Great."

She should have asked their names first.

"What's your name?" she said to this boy.

"Daniel."

"My—" She was about to say that her father's name was Daniel, but she stopped herself. She didn't want to elicit sad memories from the boys. "So, Daniel, tell me about Frederick the Great."

He looked at her now. "He won the battles of Hohenfriedberg, Rossbach, and Leuthen."

"That's right." *I was born when Frederick the Great was king,* she thought but didn't say. Would they find this fact about her interesting? Would it make the past more alive for them? She had to say something. "When I was born, Frederick the Great was king."

"Did you know him?" said the boy on the far left, his eyes widening.

"No, I—please, tell me your name."

"Georg."

"Well, Georg, I never met him, but he was the king, so in a kind of magical way, people felt they knew him even if they didn't." Where had this bit of wisdom come from? She hoped it was true.

"I think I know him, even though I don't. Didn't," said Daniel. "After all, he won the battles of Hohenfriedberg, Rossbach, and Leuthen."

"Frau Levy, please tell us something else about Frederick the Great," said Georg.

Sara pondered. "He liked to speak French. Because of that, when he was king, many children were taught how to speak French. I know how to speak French, for example."

Quietly the boy on her left said, "I can speak French."

"And what's your name?"

"Carl."

"How did you learn to speak French?"

"My mother." He stopped.

No one said anything. What had happened to their parents? Sara didn't need to ask. Death in childbirth, disease, poverty, desertion . . . there were many reasons for children to be here. And these children were the lucky ones, not living on the street as beggars, filthy and barefoot, sleeping in alleyways, starving.

"Carl, say something in French," said Daniel.

"*Parlez-vous français?* That means, 'Do you speak French?'"

The boys laughed. Sara laughed, too.

"Your accent is perfect, Carl," Sara said.

"*Merci.*"

"I know two words of French," said the boy on her far right. "Elias, that's me," he said before she could ask. He patted a finger against his chest. "*Mais oui.* That means, 'but yes.'"

"Very impressive," Sara said.

"How do you say 'I'm hungry' in French?" asked Elias.

"*J'ai faim,*" Sara replied. As their conversation continued, their food arrived, a goulash soup with fresh bread, rather delicious, in Sara's opinion, and the boys appeared to agree, finishing their portions. In response to their queries, Sara taught the boys—not Carl, who already knew and helped the others with pronunciation—the French words for bread, beef, carrots, onions, and potatoes. The kitchen staff returned and distributed second portions, which the boys enjoyed.

Too soon, it seemed to Sara, a teacher again rang a bell. Time for afternoon classes.

The boys stood. Sara stood. As the boys waited their turn to join the line leaving the refectory, Daniel said, "You'll visit us again next week, Frau Levy? Teach us more French?"

"Yes, I will."

Her boys took their places on the line and marched out with their teachers. Sara joined the other ladies in the center of the room, but she barely heard their exclamations—*adorable boys, so polite, so well-behaved.* All these ladies had children of their own. Most had grand-children.

Herr Auerbach said, "If I may impose upon your time for a brief discussion . . ." He led them to a meeting room. He presented his plans for the orphanage. Sara had heard all this before, and she didn't focus on it. Instead she tried to recall the details her father had told her about his meetings with Frederick the Great. Sixty, seventy years ago, that was. Her father had visited the royal palace of Sans Souci more than once. How had he described it? If only she could remember. She wanted to have something special to share with the boys next week.

At the end of the meeting, Herr Auerbach walked the ladies out. Sara's carriage was waiting up the block. Her driver spotted her and approached.

*Goodbye, goodbye* . . . Sara went through the required rituals with these women who'd been her friends for decades. Amalia drew her aside to confirm an outing they'd arranged for tomorrow and then climbed into her own carriage and was driven away.

Sara's driver helped her into her carriage, and they set off.

She turned to stare back at the building. She wondered if an adult would sit with her boys at supper this evening. If they woke up in the night in the dark, if they had bad dreams, who would comfort them?

———

Today was Wednesday, and on Wednesday afternoons, Sara visited Lea for tea. The day being pleasant, they sat at a table on the terrace. The footmen arrayed miniature cakes and a silver tea service before them. The sound of piano music reached them . . . Fanny was in her study in the nearby *Gartenhaus*. She played a few phrases, stopped, and tried the phrases again in a slightly different configuration. She was composing.

Fanny's seven-year-old son, Sebastian, raced across the lawn chasing his father, the irresistible Wilhelm Hensel. Hensel (as everyone called him, even Fanny) was kind, considerate, and filled with high spirits. He was the suitor who'd been sent away for five years. He'd returned on schedule to marry Fanny.

Hensel pretended to be caught by his son. They turned, and now Hensel chased the boy, who laughed as he ran. Sebastian was a blond-haired, angelic child. His bright eyes seemed forever animated by happiness. Father and son resembled each other, Hensel more weathered, but the link was clear. Hensel was a Christian, and Sebastian was being raised Christian.

Noticing Sara, Hensel said, "All right, my boy, let's say hello to Tante Levy." Hensel straightened Sebastian's shirt and his own, and they approached the terrace.

"Good afternoon, Tante," Sebastian said with great seriousness, as if he'd been practicing the art of proper greetings.

"Good afternoon, Sebastian."

"Wonderful to see you, Tante," Hensel said.

"And you, Hensel."

In recent years, Hensel's reputation as an artist had grown. Commissions in various states of progress filled his studio. He created captivating portraits of the family, pictures filled with spontaneity and vivacity.

Upon Fanny and Hensel's marriage, Abraham had ordered an art studio for Hensel to be built as an extension of the *Gartenhaus*. Thus Fanny had never left her parents' home. Lea's other children had scattered. Rebecka was married and had two children. Felix and Paul were both married, but had no children yet. Despite Paul's talents as a cellist, he'd become a banker, joining the Mendelssohn bank. London, Paris, Hamburg . . . business took him everywhere, and he'd experienced great success.

"Papa and I are playing tag," Sebastian said.

"And you must continue," Sara said.

"Thank you." Sebastian ran off. "Try to catch me, Papa," he called over his shoulder.

"Please, do excuse me," Hensel said, bowing.

"Of course," Sara said.

Off he went in pursuit.

Sipping their tea, Sara and Lea watched them until the game of tag turned into hide-and-seek and Sebastian and Hensel disappeared from view, into the farther corners of the garden.

Lea seemed preoccupied. She'd faced much sadness in recent years. Abraham had died. Fanny had lost two babies when she was far along in pregnancy, the second only a few months before. Lea herself had been unwell over the winter.

"You seem subdued today, my dear," Sara said.

"Yes."

Sara didn't want to press her.

Fanny played a longer segment, the haunting melody drifting around them.

"This music is gorgeous," Sara said. "What is it?"

"It's one of Fanny's new pieces for solo piano." Lea sat up, anger evident on her face. "I must tell you: once again, Felix has written to Fanny refusing to give his permission for her to publish her compositions."

So this was the issue preoccupying Lea. The debate about whether Fanny should be allowed to publish her music had been going on within the family for some time.

"Just this morning, I told Fanny to go forward without Felix's approval. I'm sorry to say I raised my voice to her, as if she were still a child. I hate to take sides when my children disagree, but in this case, I must. I will write to Felix, to urge him to reconsider. I hate to grant him such power over her. But he seems to have that power anyway."

Almost eleven years had passed since Sara had seen the siblings perform Felix's *Midsummer Night's Dream* overture on the piano. Since then, Felix had been hailed as the greatest composer of the era. He'd garnered international renown. *Our Mozart,* he was called. His compositions were performed everywhere, from the courts of royalty to concert halls, to the homes of admirers who played his music from inexpensive mass-produced piano editions. He was based in Leipzig and traveled constantly. Meanwhile Fanny stayed home, caring for her family, composing, organizing Sunday gatherings, and writing an endless stream of letters to her brother.

That Felix should forbid Fanny to publish her work was outrageous to Sara. She'd said this to Lea more than once, but she wouldn't remind her niece of past discussions. As if starting afresh, she said, "What concern is it of his? If anyone else's opinion were necessary, and I don't think it is, surely her husband's would be the crucial one."

"Hensel supports her wholeheartedly. Encourages her in every way."

"Well, then."

"She continues to value her brother's opinion above all."

"But Fanny's work has been published before, and under Felix's name, as you well know."

Sara regretted her tone, but the issue enraged her. Everyone in the family knew that six of Fanny's songs, with their ethereal beauty, had been included in Felix's published sets of lieder—not simply included, but presented under his name. Disgracefully, Fanny had assisted in the technical aspects of the publication of the collections, preparing the manuscripts for the printer while Felix journeyed across Europe conducting his orchestral compositions and receiving extravagant acclaim.

"What exactly does Felix say now, to justify himself? Wait, I will tell you: he says that publication would be inappropriate for a woman of her elevated position in society. That she should devote herself to the needs of her husband and son, and to the supervision of her cook and butler."

"How well you know him."

The dictates of society were strict and harsh, as Sara herself was well aware. And yet, sometimes rules could be circumvented. In this case, Sara believed, Fanny's talents were such that she could and should transgress society's rules.

"The issue is complex," Lea said, lowering her voice. "Maybe the truth is that apart from those half-dozen songs published under his name, Felix dislikes her work. He told her as much, about her sacred music. He encouraged her to focus on piano compositions. And with these new pieces for piano, I believe she's reached a very high level of accomplishment. But still Felix won't change his mind about publication. When Fanny and I discussed the matter this morning, I fully realized the anguish that Felix's decision causes her, and it breaks my heart. She is desperate for his approval."

"How does she find the inspiration to continue with her composing?"

"She is compelled from inside herself. She seems to hope that somehow, someday, she'll create a piece that her brother admires so much that he'll allow her to publish it under her own name. Oh, Tante, I should have done something years ago, to separate them."

Sara took her niece's hand. "You mustn't blame yourself."

Sara thought, *I, too, have been remiss. I should have found a way to do more to help Fanny.*

The melancholy strains of music continued.

"I despair for her," Lea said.

"Would it be all right if I spoke with her?"

"Of course." Lea's mood shifted, to concern for Sara. "You don't need my permission to speak to my children. You must always seek them out."

"Thank you."

Sara walked across the terrace to Fanny's study. With Fanny concentrating, Sara was able to slip silently into the room and sit on a chair near the windows. She wouldn't interrupt; she'd wait for Fanny to notice her. Fanny was still hollow-eyed from her illness and her grief following her baby's death a few months before. Nonetheless, her expression held a fierce focus, as if she composed out of anger, or out of a desperation to prove her worth.

To prove her worth to whom?

The situation between the siblings was difficult to make sense of. It wasn't Felix's prerogative to exercise societal authority over his married sister. And in any event, even if the publication of Fanny's work under her own name did indeed cause any scandal in society— well, the Mendelssohn bank wouldn't collapse, the family wouldn't lose its home, Felix's concert commitments across Europe wouldn't be canceled.

Fanny reached the end of the section. She lifted her hands from the keyboard. "Hello, Tante," she said with her usual warmth.

"Hello, Fanny. Sebastian is looking well."

"Isn't he marvelous?" She glanced downward for an instant, as if caught expressing an opinion that, as Sebastian's mother, she should properly keep to herself.

"Hensel, too. They're very much alike, aren't they?"

"I think so. Thank you for noticing. I'm very glad to see you, Tante—but tell me the truth, did my mother send you to talk to me?"

"No. I sent myself. After she told me about your disagreement this morning. I want you to know that I join your mother and your husband in supporting your endeavors."

"I'm grateful."

"Then why is Felix's opinion the one that counts above all for you?"

"We are close," she said with an open sincerity. "We always have been."

"When you were children. You were close when you were children. You're adults now. You're both married. Felix lives far away."

"We are united in spirit."

"You are *not* united in spirit."

Fanny appeared to flinch, hearing these words.

"You must forgive me for speaking bluntly," Sara said. "I'm your elderly aunt who loves you, so I can say things other people might not feel able to say. I will say it again: you and your brother are *not* united in spirit."

"He wants the best for me, as I do for him. We are honest with each other."

"He may think he wants the best for you, but that doesn't mean what he wants actually *is* best for you."

"We've always looked after each other."

"When you were children."

They were talking in circles. Hadn't Fanny ever grown up? Was she still, despite her husband, son, and the deaths of two babies, metaphorically as well as literally living in the enchanted garden of her childhood? And what about Felix . . . might he have fled his family home struggling to escape what may have felt to him like the suffocation of Fanny's love or obsession, or whatever the right word was to describe the intensity of her regard for him? Did her constant pleading for approval make him, in the midst of his many professional achievements and commitments, impatient and annoyed?

These possibilities didn't excuse his cruelty, but they might reveal a facet of the fraught emotions between them.

"I don't want to discuss this anymore," Fanny said, but she said it lightheartedly, putting on a shield of amusement. "Shall I play for you the piece as I have it so far, from the beginning?"

They'd reach no resolution today. "Thank you, Fanny. I'd like that very much."

And so Fanny Mendelssohn Hensel, composer, performed for Sara an exquisitely beautiful piano solo, filled with yearning.

Would anyone outside this private garden ever hear it?

## Chapter 31

As they took their seats for the concert, Scott was at a loss: he was the one who'd secured the house tickets for this performance of the Bach Collegium Japan at Zankel Hall, on the lower level of Carnegie Hall; he was the one who'd invited them, first Dan, who was in town for something or other and staying with him, and then Susanna, thinking this would be a low-stress way to spend time with her—and now Susanna had ended up sitting on the far side of him, with Dan in the middle. Dan and Susanna were chatting, and Scott was left to admire the woodwork of Zankel Hall, the perfection of it . . . yes, he'd respond if anyone asked him, the design of the hall was exceptional, such that audience members weren't even disturbed by the subway running nearby.

Had his sin been so egregious, that evening at the Met? He didn't think so. Susanna should be sitting next to him.

This evening she wore a black, remarkably feminine suit. She sat with her legs crossed, and her skirt had hiked its way up her thighs. Her high heels seemed to elongate her already long legs.

Had Dan noticed this? Apparently not. Dan was reviewing the program with uncalled-for seriousness and filling Susanna in on the details. " . . . And the second piece is the Concerto in D Minor for two violins."

"Isn't that the piece Balanchine choreographed as *Concerto Barocco?*" Susanna asked.

"Yes, it is."

"I love that ballet, especially when the two principal dancers take the solo violin lines and create a kind of love duet."

Scott wondered whether something was going on between these two behind his back. No, the idea was absurd, he reassured himself. Dan wasn't the type. Judging from Julie, Dan liked farm girls from Iowa. Or was it Wisconsin?

"And next is the Fifth Brandenburg," Dan was saying. "In that piece Bach includes a wild harpsichord solo at the end of the first movement."

Dan couldn't handle a woman like Susanna. The worlds they came from were too different. Dan was the genius from the farmland, the brilliant hick. He was not the one who was supposed to get the city girl.

"With the gut strings and the one-and-two-keyed wooden flutes and oboes, these early music groups have really transformed the way we hear the music of Bach . . ."

Could she really be falling for this? Most likely she was just being polite. Scott still had a chance.

The orchestra walked onto the stage, which happily forced Dan and Susanna to stop talking.

═══════

During the intermission, Japanese women in kimonos circulated through the lobby.

"Do the Japanese have a special interest in Bach?" Susanna asked.

"Not only Bach, but all Western classical music," Scott said. He could play the scholarly game, too. "In Japan . . ." and he continued with an exposition on the adoration of not simply Bach but also Beethoven, particularly Beethoven, among the Japanese, proven by the fact that several orchestras in Japan existed solely to tour the country performing one piece of music, Beethoven's Ninth Symphony.

Even though Dan and Susanna stood apart from each other and appeared riveted by his explanation of Japanese veneration of Beethoven's Ninth, Scott sensed that they weren't quite present with him. Where their thoughts were instead, he didn't want to contemplate.

"Scott, Dan, there you are," said Jeremy Meyers, frowning as usual behind thick glasses. Jeremy, a musicologist at Cornell University, was short in stature, tall in brains (to borrow a quip of his older sister's). "What do you think they're going to do in the Suite in B Minor? Will they double-dot the rhythm during the first movement?"

Oh, boy . . . with friends like these, Susanna was going to think he was a complete geek. Worse than a geek. A total bore. The double-dotting issue was what passed for an earth-shattering controversy in some early-music circles. What made Jeremy's question worse was that Scott himself had been wondering about this.

Luckily Scott didn't have to reply, because all at once colleagues were approaching them from every direction, eager to discuss this or that aspect of the performance, this or that piece of gossip, share details of the upcoming Bach conference in Leipzig as well as the recent news about Dietrich Bauer, the name whispered everywhere. Drawn into these discussions, Scott turned away from Dan and Susanna. He spotted Frederic Fournier in the distance with his wife, but the crowd was tight and Freddy appeared not to notice him.

As they returned to their seats at the end of the intermission, Scott observed that Dan didn't touch Susanna, didn't position himself closer to her, didn't brush her hand with his, or touch his knee to her leg, even accidentally on purpose. If anything was going on, it was beyond his understanding.

---

"Shall we go out for a drink?" Scott said as they stood on Seventh Avenue after the concert.

"I need to get home," Susanna said. "I have an important meeting in the morning."

"I'll accompany Susanna home," Dan said.

"Thank you," Susanna said. "That's kind of you."

Even their diction was trying his patience. Scott had expected they'd go out as a threesome for a drink, with himself as top dog. But he could see he wasn't wanted. Dan had his own key to the apartment. They didn't have to stick together.

Scott reconsidered his activities for the evening. He wasn't accustomed to feeling like the odd man out. To hell with it, he decided angrily. The bar at Trattoria Dell'Arte was always lively after a concert. Or he could attend the cast party, so to speak, for the orchestra. He could attach himself to someone who was going to the party and slip in despite his lack of an invitation. He glanced around. Where, where were his colleagues when he needed them?

"See you later," Scott said. He turned away. Ah, there was Jeremy Meyers, walking with a purpose, maybe to the party. Scott hurried to catch up with him.

## *Chapter 32*

Dan said, "You can see the stars from here. I never thought I'd be able to see the stars from Manhattan."

What an inane remark, he thought. But they couldn't sit here in silence. And anyway, he *was* surprised. His preconceptions of the city were being overturned one by one. When they'd arrived at the gates of the Peabody Seminary, she'd invited him inside to see the close. She did not include her apartment in the invitation, which was a disappointment and also a relief; one less possibility to worry about. Entering the seminary gardens, he found himself in a haven of greenery and quiet. Episcopalians always seemed to place a high value on gracious tranquillity. Even the air was different, sweeter than the world outside the gates. They sat in the Adirondack chairs on the lawn. They'd pulled the chairs side by side but not touching, and that's how they sat, side by side but not touching.

"A few years ago," she said, "I attended a stargazing event in Central Park. I saw the rings of Saturn."

He sensed a shyness in her, a reluctance similar to his own, which simultaneously drew them together and kept them apart.

"I loved the concert," she said.

"I did, too." The air cooled as the night deepened. He sensed wildlife around them, an owl cooing.

"I wish I could figure out the right words to describe how, or why, the music is so affecting. What words would you use? Describe to me what makes it so beautiful."

He paused, thinking. "The fact is, the music exists outside words. It's like asking, why do you love someone? You just love them. When a man describes a woman as having, say, a spark in her eyes and a warm smile, he notices those things *because* he loves her. Those things don't explain *why* he loves her. The *why*—that can't be explained."

Where had this disquisition come from? He believed what he'd said, but was surprised to hear himself express it.

"I understand," Susanna said.

He felt compelled to step back from such . . . *intimacy*, was that the right word? To return to the arena of practicalities. "I'm looking ahead to my trip to Germany, for the conference in Leipzig in early July. I'll try to go to Weimar, to get some leads on the family that owned the cantata."

He wanted to say, *You should come with me.*

"I'll make a photocopy of my uncle's map for you."

"Thank you."

No, he couldn't bring himself to suggest that she join him. With luck she'd come to the idea on her own. He hoped so.

She rested her head against the back of the chair. She closed her eyes. Her body was at ease. How easily he could reach over and caress her hand, and open a different type of conversation between them. He longed for this, but didn't know how to approach it. He'd married young. The courtship scenes in movies had always passed him by. Now he wished he'd paid attention, so he'd know what to do. *Shall I take her hand?* he asked himself. Better not. Maybe simply put his hand over hers. But he didn't want to jeopardize their friendship.

He pushed himself to the edge of his chair. "It's late. I should get going."

She opened her eyes. "Yes, that's right." She sounded as if she were trying to convince herself. She stood when he did.

"My building is over there."

He followed her to the mansion where she lived. She walked up the five steps that led to the front door. He stayed at the bottom of the stairs. She unlocked the door into the dimly lit vestibule. She turned. She waited. For what? He wasn't certain. He didn't know what to do. He couldn't risk making the wrong guess. "Good night, then," he said from the bottom of the stairs. "I'll be in touch."

"I hope so."

And she was gone. The heavy wooden door shut behind her. Dan walked away from the house and turned to gaze at the building, hoping to see her lights go on, even though he hadn't asked if her apartment faced the garden. There—lights *did* go on, and she came to the window. With the light behind her, he couldn't see her face, but he saw her silhouette, and her silhouetted hand waved to him. He waved in return.

Now that she was safe, he turned and walked toward the gate, feeling or at least imagining that he felt—he willed himself not to turn around to check—her gaze upon his back.

When he reached Ninth Avenue, the sidewalks were crowded, as if the time were noon instead of midnight. New York City . . . always alive, its energy flowing and never ending, drawing him into its stream.

Dan decided to do something he'd never done before. This felt, in its own small way, more daring than anything he'd ever contemplated, a precursor to even more daring acts he might commit in the future. It was something he had observed in movies and on TV shows, and something he'd watched Susanna do after the concert this evening.

He stepped off the curb, raised his arm, and hailed a taxi.

# Chapter 33

Susanna arrived at the office early. The foundation board would meet at 10:00 a.m. Last week, she'd distributed her summary report of the foundation's activities in the past six months, along with her recommendations for future grants. She'd come in early today in case any board members wanted to speak with her before the meeting. And she had come in early to prepare herself to resign.

Still holding his briefcase, Rob stopped at her office door. "Susanna, good morning. Join me in five minutes, would you?"

"Of course."

She changed into her high heels. She checked her watch. As she went to Rob's office, she felt an unexpected sense of peace.

Rob motioned her to sit, and she did.

"Before we go into the meeting, I felt I owed it to you to let you know what's been going on. I've been holding discussions with the board privately, to avoid any awkwardness for you. Yesterday I put the issue to a vote. The board has rejected the Gilbert and Sullivan Center. In addition, the board has made clear that they consider you indispensible."

Susanna said nothing. She experienced a realization that she didn't have to stay with the Barstow Foundation. If she wanted to, she *could* find another position. The job-hunting process would be difficult, but she did have a choice in the matter.

"I'm sorry to have to tell you that the board has threatened to fire me."

He was trying to make her laugh, but she didn't find him funny. Instead she recalled the gap between them. He could talk about being fired as if it were a joke.

"Unlike you, I'm at the mercy of the board's demands: Cornelia refuses to have me at home all day, and my beloved mother feels the same."

His game was meaningless. Almost insulting, from her perspective. Whether or not he served on the foundation board, he'd still be the head of the family, he'd still control a large and ever-increasing fortune. He waited for her to reply, ostensibly assuming or hoping that they could resume their usual repartee.

"So the burden is on me," he said, "to get things back on track between us."

Her silence seemed to make him nervous. Make him squirm, even. She was glad of it.

"What . . . what can I do," he said, spreading his arms, "to achieve our reconciliation?"

"Tell me the details of the board's vote."

"You'll be amazed. Shocked." He paused for dramatic effect. "After months of lobbying, not one, not one single vote, apart from my own, in favor of supporting a Cornelia and Robertson Barstow Family Foundation Center for Gilbert and Sullivan. I was embarrassed. Humiliated."

Susanna decided to stay. At least for now. "If you'd listened to my advice in the first place, this never would have happened to you."

"I know, I know. I've been hoist with my own petard," he said with his usual theatrical flair. Then he looked at her with an odd flatness, and she felt as if she were seeing him as he really was, gray, aging, weakening. "It will never happen again, believe me."

Several hours later, Susanna sat on a bench in Central Park. She was surrounded by runners, bicyclists, and strolling tourists. She held a latte. A large chocolate cookie with chocolate chips, from a French bakery near her office, was in a bag on her lap. She broke off small pieces of the cookie one by one, to make it last longer. It was crispy. The chocolate flavor was intense and pure. The chips were luscious, melting.

She was trying to revive herself. She felt exhausted from the praise heaped on her at the board meeting, with more praise at the luncheon that followed.

The board members (apart from Rob) seemed to believe that she'd achieved a victory, but if it was a victory, she felt no satisfaction from it. She'd done her job. She'd preserved the foundation's mandate. She'd refused to be swayed by Rob's whims.

She'd taken a risk, and she'd come through it. During the past few years, her focus had been on protecting herself; she'd become a passive recipient of her own life. Now, with this issue at work, she'd been able to make a choice, and take a step forward.

A class of five- or six-year-olds, arranged in two rows, filed past with their teachers. Each child wore a white hat. An older couple walked by, guidebooks in hand.

She remembered last night, sitting beside Dan in the close. After being fearful for so long, she'd hoped that he would take her hand, would pull her toward him. She'd imagined him doing this. Later she'd stood at the doorway and waited for him to join her. But he hadn't. Maybe he didn't want to. Or maybe he was waiting for her to give him permission. She was ready to give him permission.

*One risk after another for me these days*, she thought, and she was glad to realize that she could laugh at herself again. She was becoming more like the person she used to be.

With summer approaching, she was due for a vacation. She could go to Germany with Dan, find the house, trace the family that had owned the cantata. She had a duty to her uncle, to follow through herself, rather than delegate the task to someone else. She could trust Dan, at the very least as a traveling companion. She hoped as more.

Now that she knew she had a job, she could begin making plans.

## Chapter 34

Dan had an hour to kill before meeting a colleague for lunch at a café on Sixteenth Street off Union Square. He figured he could fill the time by perusing the used classical CDs at his favorite New York City shop, Academy Records on Eighteenth between Fifth and Sixth. He walked up Sixth Avenue from Scott's apartment.

When he reached Sixteenth Street, he decided he'd better find the café before he went to the CD shop. He didn't want to be late for lunch. Halfway down the street, he saw a building called the Center for Jewish History. He'd never heard of it. A poster advertised the current exhibition: *The History of Jewish Philanthropy in America*. Susanna would want to know about the exhibit. It provided an excellent excuse for phoning her.

Feeling the pull of locating the café, he looked down the block. He thought he spotted its sign. A quick check on the map on his phone confirmed it. He was three minutes away at most. He went into the building.

The Center for Jewish History turned out to be a combination of library and museum, with exhibitions on two floors. The presentation on Jewish philanthropy was on the main floor and began with the Colonial era. It was extensive, filled with family names he recognized—Guggenheim, Lehman—and many more he didn't recognize, with accompanying photographs of hospitals, museums, and synagogues. The name Schiffman appeared in a photograph of a dormitory at Barnard College, but Dan didn't know if this was Scott's family. Scott had never mentioned it.

Returning to the entry corridor, he checked his watch. He still had time to spare. He looked at the listing of other exhibitions. *Jews of Morocco* could be interesting, but not for him. *A Refugee in Shanghai: One Woman's Story*—no. On the second floor, in Gallery B, *Jewish Stammbücher of 18th and 19th Century Germany*.

Now *this* did sound interesting. Dan knew that in eighteenth- and nineteenth-century Germany, people of the middle and upper classes kept *Stammbücher*. The closest modern equivalent were visiting books, but *Stammbücher* were much more. It was never enough to write, *Thanks for the great party. See you soon.* You had to leave a message that was memorable. Guests tried to outdo one another. Some wrote poems. Others created drawings, from caricatures to portraits of pets to botanical studies. Composers wrote brief musical sketches into *Stammbücher*. Dan had seen such entries by both Bach and Beethoven. The books were treasure troves of cultural history. And they were fun.

He walked up the stairs and found the exhibition room. The lights were turned down. The exhibit was small, two glass-topped tables containing eight books in each. A note on the wall said that pages would be turned each week. The lighting was kept low to preserve the fragile paper.

After Dan's eyes adjusted, he was hooked. The books were delightful. One page showed a drawing of a playful dragon. Another had a poem about the glories of beer. Some guests wrote in English, some in French. He saw a greeting in Russian, with a sketch of a mock-fierce bear beneath it. He saw a script he thought might be Turkish. The handwriting of the entries was remarkably graceful, as if every educated person of that era were the modern-day equivalent of a professional calligrapher.

When he finished examining the books in the glass cases, he spotted a sign on the wall next to a computer screen: *Explore the digital collection.*

And so he did, choosing the albums from the list at random, leafing from page to page, or more correctly, doing the computerized equivalent.

He reached the *Stammbuch* of Mirjam Itzig, born Oppenheimer, the wife of Moses Daniel Itzig. His fascination continued. Wasn't Itzig the family name of Fanny and Felix Mendelssohn's grandmother? One guest had written a note in the shape of a circular maze. Another page featured a silhouette of a lovely woman, seen in profile.

He clicked to the next page. A three-line message and signature caught his attention. On this page, in Berlin on June 18, 1784, Sara Levy *geborene* Itzig had written, *Laßen Sie Theuerste! weder Zeit noch Abwesenheit aus Ihrem Herzen verdrängen Ihre Sie stets schätzende und aufrichtigst liebende Schwester,* which basically translated as, "My most precious one! Let neither time nor absence push out of your heart the sister who cherishes and sincerely adores you."

Sara Itzig Levy. He'd occasionally come upon that name over the years. She was a skilled harpsichordist, evidently the only Berlin student of Wilhelm Friedemann Bach. She was also the great-aunt of Fanny and Felix Mendelssohn, an intriguing footnote in the story of the famous siblings. And she collected manuscripts of the Bach family, not simply Johann Sebastian, but also his sons Wilhelm Friedemann, Carl Philipp Emanuel, and Johann Christian. She must

have been the sister-in-law of this *Stammbuch*'s owner, Mirjam Oppenheimer Itzig.

On the next page, with the same date, was the following:

*Ich werde mich bemühen Ihnen durch . . .* In Dan's rough translation
of the extravagant prose of the era: "I shall endeavor to show you
through more than words that there will be neither far-offness of
place nor far-offness of friendship; this I, your friend and brother,
assure you." *Samuel Salomon Levy. Berlin, June 18, 1784.*

The fat, triangular *B*. The looping precision of the *S*. The distinct
clarity of the *m* and the *n*. This handwriting looked curiously familiar,
as if it had been pressed onto his memory without him even realizing.

An improbable hunch became a conviction within him. He
punched his password into his phone. Scott had sent him the digital
photographs that Susanna had allowed, of the first several pages of
the cantata manuscript.

The handwriting of Samuel Salomon Levy's message in the visiting book looked like it matched some of the unknown writing on the
wrapper of Susanna's cantata.

He needed to share this with Scott. He took a photo of the
*Stammbuch* page on the computer screen before him. He sent it to
Scott.

When he finished lunch, he had a text from Scott confirming the
match.

By dinnertime, Dan was back in Granville, trying to maintain
Becky's usual routine even as his discovery and its implications . . .
well, to say they electrified him wasn't too strong a term. As soon as
Becky was asleep, he would begin researching the lives of Sara and
Samuel Levy.

By 8:15, after three adjustments of her night-light and two adjustments of the curtain, Becky was settled and he was free to go to his

study. He checked his phone on the way. Susanna had left a voice message, asking him to call her. This was a happy surprise.

"Hi, I received your message," he said when she answered.

"Thank you for calling back."

Was she actually worried that he might not? "I made a discovery today." Damn. He hadn't intended to tell her yet. He wanted to know more before he said anything.

"That's exciting." When he didn't continue, she said, "And?"

"I shouldn't have said anything. Enthusiasm got the better of me. Once I've done more research, we'll talk about it. Once I have more of a context."

"*Context*—always the crucial word."

"Yes."

"I'm calling because I realized that I have some vacation time coming up. I've decided to join you in Germany. If traveling together is okay with you. It's my responsibility, to try to locate the house in Weimar where my uncle found the cantata, so I can find out who lived there and whether any of their family has survived. Also I want to go to Buchenwald, because my uncle was there. And I've never been to Berlin."

"Well, that's great, that you can make the trip. Berlin is a ter-rific city." In a rush, he began telling her about his many experiences there, his love for the place—all this a cover for everything he wasn't saying about how thrilled he was by her news. He didn't want her to feel threatened, or smothered, by his feelings. "The energy and cre-ativity, in the old eastern sector especially. Of course we should travel together. I'm going anyway."

The discussion turned to practicalities. The specifics of dates, air-planes, travel from city to city.

"In Berlin I always stay with the family that's hosted me for years, since I was a graduate student." In Leipzig, he'd be at the confer-ence hotel. He hoped against hope that they would end up staying together, but he didn't want her to think that he was reading more into her plan than she'd intended.

"That's fine. I'll make my own reservations. I . . ." She paused, and he sensed her searching for the correct words. "I enjoyed our time together in the close last night."

"Me, too. Very much."

"So we'll stay in touch?"

This sounded almost plaintive, as if she needed reassurance from him, he was taken aback to realize. "Definitely."

"I'm glad."

They said good night.

## Chapter 35

LEIPZIGERSTRASSE 3
BERLIN, PRUSSIA

*June 1846*

Sara rested on a bench in Lea's garden, gathering her strength for the challenge ahead: she was about to perform in one of Fanny's Sunday concerts. She closed her eyes and reviewed the piece in her mind. She was hoping Lea—

Lea was dead, Sara reminded herself. Even now, four years later, Sara found herself automatically looking forward to seeing her niece; to sharing meals with her, to discussing questions, concerns, gossip. Lea had been only sixty-five when she died. She'd been fine that day four years ago, her usual self, or so Sara had thought when she arrived at noontime to help Lea prepare for a gathering. By evening Lea had collapsed. By morning, she was gone. The doctors called it a stroke.

How Sara missed her. She was eighty-five this year, older than she had any right to be, when Lea was already dead. This morning she'd woken up feeling stiff and confused, and for a frightening moment, she hadn't known where she was.

Because of this, she'd felt compelled after breakfast to review her last will and testament, to make certain all was accounted for. The cantata her teacher had given to her was not, of course, listed in her will. For years she'd put off deciding who to give it to, as if by pretending that it didn't exist, she could make it disappear. Now she must quickly determine its future, while she was lucid enough to choose wisely, and still capable of explaining what it was. Her nephew Felix was the logical choice, but given his drive and ambition, she didn't trust him to keep it secret.

She opened her eyes and looked around.

Elias was with her today. Yes, Elias, one of her original orphan boys. He was speaking with Alexander von Humboldt, stooped and white-haired. Elias was too young to receive the burden of the cantata. Alexander was too old. Elias glanced her way continually; he kept watch over her even though they both maintained the fiction that she was self-reliant. Elias had grown to be tall and lanky. She paid his fees at university, where he studied Classics. Of her other first boys, Carl, who'd spoken French that day, had been claimed by a cousin in Freiburg, and Sara had lost touch with him. Georg had died of a fever when he was twelve. Often she mused about the man he might have grown to become. Daniel, who'd admired Frederick the Great, was studying history, and Sara paid his fees, as well. They were the first of nearly a decade of orphans who'd touched her life. She had been the honorary mother for as many as she could.

So although she herself was *unfruchtbar*, barren, she'd bettered the lives of many children.

"Tante. Are you ready?" Sebastian stood before her. He was sixteen this year, and he looked like a winsome angel still. "Mother sent me to find you. The concert will soon begin."

"Thank you, Sebastian." She roused herself, and with his help, she stood.

"More than two hundred people are attending today," he said.

"Astounding." She suspected Sebastian exaggerated, but she'd credit at least a hundred and fifty.

"May I hold your arm?"

"How thoughtful of you, Sebastian."

Seeing her rise, Elias hastened to join them.

"May I assist you, Frau Levy?" To Sebastian, Elias said, "I'm happy to accompany Frau Levy to the performance salon."

"I have her arm already," Sebastian said, squeezing it as if to prove his point.

Were these two young men actually fighting over her?

"With today's heat," Sara said, "I feel I must have support on each arm."

Thus arranged, they walked to the *Gartenhaus*.

"Ah, here she is, safe and sound," said Hensel when he spotted them.

"Thank you, boys," Sara said, indicating she no longer required their help. She could most certainly walk by herself to the front of the salon for her performance, in the first piece of today's program.

The audience was gathering. *Tout le monde* attended Fanny's Sunday concerts. Today the guests included the rather ferocious-looking Giacomo (as he now styled himself) Meyerbeer, who'd experienced fantastic success composing operas in the French style. He accompanied his mother, dear Amalia. From Jacob Beer to Giacomo Meyerbeer . . . he'd changed his name but abided with the faith of his heritage. Sara could give the cantata to him. But could she trust him to keep it secret? He'd become a man of moods and high drama, at least by Sara's reckoning. No, she couldn't trust him.

She took her place, greeted Fanny, and once again reviewed the music in her mind: the Concerto in D Minor for three harpsichords and strings, by Johann Sebastian Bach. Today it would be performed with three pianos. Although she felt most at home with the harpsichord, Sara found switching between piano and harpsichord to be effortless. For today's performance, she would be joining Fanny and a young friend of hers, a talented musician in his early twenties.

"Frau Levy, an exciting day for us," said this friend as he took his place. He was a handsome and good-humored man, and he had ambitions to join the diplomatic corps. Sara had been introduced to him several times during the past week as they rehearsed, but she simply could not remember his name. She wouldn't reveal her forgetfulness by asking yet again. Fanny announced the piece.

And so they began. Sara might not remember the young man's name, but she remembered this piece, every note, and she played it from memory. What a joy it was . . . the sense of proportion, the balance among the three pianos, the astonishing profusion of trills and runs.

All too soon, it was over. The applause was sustained. Afterward, Sebastian, with polished poise, escorted her to an empty seat in the audience, next to Alexander von Humboldt.

"I saved this spot for you," Alexander said, patting the chair. "You were brilliant, by the way. As usual. Exactly as I expected."

"Thank you." She felt herself reddening, as if she were a girl.

"Blushing, for me? After all these years?"

She tried to think of a witty rejoinder, but nothing came to her. What a life Alexander had led, as a scientist and diplomat, exploring such places as South America and eastern Russia. But he was still and always her kind, gentle friend. She leaned against his shoulder for an instant, a gesture allowed them within society because of their elevated ages, and he responded with a quick wrap of his arm around her shoulder.

The next piece on the program was Robert Schumann's *Andante and Variations*, op. 46, for two pianos, performed by Fanny and her friend. After only a few bars, Sara found herself mystified: Why had Fanny paired a Bach masterpiece with such a work as this erratic Schumann? It was technically virtuosic, but tiresome. It jumped from style to style. It led nowhere.

Why hadn't Fanny selected one of her own pieces to perform with her friend? Sara had heard Fanny play her superb four-hand compositions with friends at private dinners here at Leipzigerstrasse 3. Could Fanny actually believe that *this*, this bizarre Schumann duet, was more worthwhile than her own compositions? Sara was barely able to conceal her instinctive cringing at several sour, screechy dissonances.

When the music finally concluded, the applause was tumultuous. Clearly the younger generation disagreed with Sara's opinion. She caught Alexander's eye. He raised his eyebrows, revealing that he shared her point of view.

After a break for conversation and refreshment, the audience reassembled for the final work of the afternoon, Johann Sebastian Bach's cantata *Gottes Zeit ist die allerbeste Zeit*, "God's Time is the Very Best Time." Fanny conducted the choir and instrumental ensemble from the piano.

The opening bars were among the most beautiful music Sara had ever heard. Two flutes seemed to sing above two cellos, while a steady ticking rhythm from the bass line created a recognition of the passage of time, of earthly time subsumed into eternity.

Fanny brought the work to life in all its fullness and complexity. Fanny . . . she'd lived her life mostly in the seclusion of the garden. Sara felt close to her, through bonds of both family and friendship. If she were to ask something important of Fanny, Sara felt certain that the girl would understand and respect her aunt's wishes.

And then Sara knew: Fanny Mendelssohn Hensel must be the next custodian of the J. S. Bach cantata that her teacher had given to her so long ago.

———

Several days later, Fanny sat opposite her at the tea table in Sara's morning room. "Thank you for visiting me today," Sara said.

"No need to thank me." The girl's liveliness glowed from her dark eyes. Sara perceived how Hensel, in his drawings, transformed her into a saint, a goddess, a muse. "You said in your note that you needed to discuss something with me—but *I* need to discuss something with you. I think the two might be the same."

As if it were yesterday, Sara remembered Fanny as a child, racing across the garden. Time had became a tidal stream, carrying Sara backward and forward.

"Would you like some tea, Tante?"

Here she was, Lea's daughter, grown up and taking the role of hostess in Sara's home.

"Yes. Thank you."

Fanny poured the tea.

"Cake?"

The cake was chocolate with layers of marzipan, a combination Sara loved. Fanny was kind to bring it.

"Most definitely cake, Lea." The tidal stream. "Forgive me: thank you, Fanny."

"I'm glad I remind you of my mother." Fanny cut a good-sized slice for Sara and the same for herself.

The chocolate was dense, the marzipan intensely sweet. They ate in companionable silence. This was a cake that deserved their full attention.

"The cake is outstanding," Sara said.

"I agree. Shall we have more?"

"Only to make certain we weren't mistaken in our initial conclusions."

Fanny refilled their plates.

When she finished her second slice, Sara said, "I was surprised you performed the Schumann variations on Sunday instead of one of your own works."

"I would never compare my work to Robert Schumann's." Fanny licked the frosting from her fork. "He's a great genius."

"That Schumann piece," Sara said, dismissing it. "Irksome and boring."

Sara caught the look on Fanny's face, the indulgent smile that said, *Aged Aunt Sara, what will she say next?*

"Fanny," Sara said, as if to wake the girl up. "Your piano music is brilliant. Surely you recognize this? After a lifetime of music, you must understand your own merit."

"Sometimes." Fanny had a winning smile. "When my friends and family force me to." She cut a sliver of cake for herself and another for Sara. "I have a surprise for you in that regard. Two publishers have approached me. They're competing with each other to publish a collection of my lieder. With more publications to follow, or so they promise. I've decided to accept one of the offers. What do you think of that?"

"Oh, Fanny. I'm so very pleased."

"Thank you. I suspected you would be."

"And what does Felix say about this?"

A pause. "I haven't told him. But I will."

"You'll go forward regardless of his opinion?"

"Yes. I'm resolved."

"What made you change your mind?"

"I'm getting old."

"Old?" Fanny was only about forty. "You're not old. You're not as old as *me*, for example."

"Very few people can claim to be as old as *you*, Tante."

"And a good thing, too. But truly—what changed for you?"

"I suppose I finally began to hear what Hensel, and you, and my friends have been telling me for years. And Mother, too. Felix's opinion began to seem unjust."

"I must agree."

"So, have I robbed you of the reason for your invitation today?"

"Pardon?"

"Isn't this what you wanted to discuss with me? To urge me once more to put myself forward?"

"I'm sorry to say, that isn't what I wanted to discuss today."

Fanny reached across the table to take Sara's hand. "You're not ill, are you?"

"Ill?"

"You didn't invite me here to share some awful news, so that Hensel, Sebastian, and I can prepare ourselves?"

How worried the girl looked.

"No, nothing like that. But nothing good, either."

Asking Fanny to retrieve the manuscript from the sideboard, Sara began the sad task of explaining to her what it was.

---

Home again. Fanny sat at her desk in her study in the *Gartenhaus*. She loved this room, especially the tall windows overlooking the trees. Her husband's paintings, and Felix's watercolors, covered the walls. Here was her piano and her library of musical scores.

Often in the past, Fanny would look out these windows and watch her mother walking in the garden. How sorrowful was life, that her mother was dead and Tante Levy lived on. This was a mean-spirited thought, Fanny knew, but she couldn't help herself. Nevertheless, to honor her mother, Fanny was attentive to her formidable great-aunt. Fanny genuinely cared for Sara, too. Sara had always been encouraging toward her.

Therefore, Fanny would follow Sara's wish and preserve in secret the Bach cantata that rested now upon her desk. The libretto was indeed a shock. Over the years Fanny had often felt pulled like a pendulum . . . baptized and confirmed as a Protestant, studying and believing Protestant tenets, yet living in a society that considered her Jewish. She'd never been able to find a steady path between the two parts of herself. In the end, she'd simply put the conundrum out of her mind.

She'd put God out of her mind, too, after her babies died. She'd had three children, Sebastian who had lived, and the two who had died yet survived in her thoughts: when they were small, they'd raced across the garden playing tag with their big brother. Fanny had instructed them at the piano. Hensel had taught them how to draw. In her imaginings.

Fanny rubbed her hands together. So cold, she was, despite the fine June weather. She was always cold. She hadn't been joking, when she told Sara that she was getting old, although she should have phrased it differently. She *felt* she was getting old. Sometimes she experienced numbness in her hands, and in her arms. She felt the passage of time pressing against her. This, too, made her more willing to listen to the advice of Hensel and of her friends, that she publish her compositions.

She lit the candle on her desk. She examined the cantata manuscript. On the wrapper, someone other than Sara (Fanny knew her great-aunt's handwriting) had written *Sollte nicht catalogisiert werden*, Not to be cataloged, and a date. Perhaps Sara's husband had done this. Sara still wore her wedding ring, and she'd never remarried. She must have loved her husband very much. Fanny tried, without success, to picture Tante Levy as a young woman in love.

*Especially don't tell Felix*, Sara had said this afternoon, as she urged her to keep the cantata concealed. When Fanny asked her why, Sara had replied that Felix wouldn't be able to resist performing it in public. Sara was probably right about this.

Keeping a secret from Felix would have been impossible for Fanny when they were younger, but it would be easy now. More and more, Fanny didn't tell Felix what was most important to her. To maintain an illusion of their closeness, she kept her letters to him filled with amusing stories and witty (she hoped) turns of phrase. When they were young and he went on travels with their father to visit Goethe, and to stay in Paris, Felix had written to her at length, sharing his observations, thoughts, and feelings through pages and pages of prose, so she felt as if she were right beside him on his adventures. Nowadays he rarely wrote, and when he did, he shared little of himself.

Nonetheless she must write to him soon, to tell him that she was going against his wishes and publishing her work. She'd ask for his blessing, although she didn't expect to receive it. She dreaded writing this letter and had been putting it off. She dreaded also the wait for his response. But she was resolved on her course.

She checked the clock. Household responsibilities pressed upon her. A dozen friends were expected at dinner. Afterward, another dozen would join them for music-making. Fanny needed to consult with the housekeeper and the butler to make certain all was prepared. She wanted to speak with Sebastian, to learn how he'd spent his day. She must also write to her brother Paul, who handled the family's finances, to request an advance on next month's disbursement.

Felix never had to trouble himself over household matters at his home in Leipzig. Apart from correspondence with Paul relating to expenses, Felix's wife, Cécile, took care of everything. Fanny had never felt at ease with Cécile, and she sensed Cécile felt the same toward her. Felix composed, conducted, traveled across Europe, met with royalty, published his work, spent time with his children when the mood struck him, and Cécile did the rest. Such was the way of the world, no sense complaining, especially when Fanny herself employed a full complement of servants.

Opening the ink bottle, she dipped her pen. *Im Privat-Kabinett halten*, she wrote on the wrapper of the cantata that Sara had given her. Keep in the private cabinet.

She put the manuscript into the cabinet where she kept the compositions she was in the midst of working on, those she wasn't ready for anyone, not even Hensel, to see.

Taking the candle with her, closing the study door behind her, she headed toward her dressing room to change for dinner. Since her mother's death, Fanny was the hostess at Leipzigerstrasse 3, and soon their evening would begin.

## Chapter 36

On Monday afternoon, in preparation for a curators' meeting on Thursday, Scott received a draft report on proposed exhibitions for the next several years.

One proposal in particular caught his attention: *Siblings Together and Apart.* This show would encompass the lives of William Wordsworth and his sister, Dorothy; and Charlotte, Emily, Anne, and Branwell Brontë. An up-and-coming curator in the literature department had dreamed this up.

What about a Felix Mendelssohn and Fanny Hensel exhibition?

Yes, absolutely: the Mendelssohn siblings deserved an exhibition—as he would explain to his fellow curators at the meeting on Thursday. The MacLean housed extensive archives centered on them, including a large number of letters written by Fanny and Felix, an array of Felix's terrific watercolors and drawings, and sixteen Mendelssohn and four Hensel music autographs. Because Fanny and

Felix were composers, such an exhibit would provide a unique opportunity to explore technological advances in museum presentations. Technology now allowed visitors to study the original manuscripts while hearing the linked music at individual listening stations.

In addition, the New York Public Library, which owned a trove of Mendelssohn material, might be willing to make some loans to the exhibit. Alternately, Scott could try to convince the Public Library to mount its own show. Two Mendelssohn/Hensel exhibitions simultaneously in New York City would garner a good deal of international publicity. He could secure loans from other institutions, as well. Masses of material had survived, even amid the wreckage of World War II in Germany. He seemed to recall a particularly touching item of Mendelssohn-family biographical interest . . . After a few moments online, he was examining the first issue of the *Gartenzeitung*, prepared in the mid-1820s by Felix, Fanny, and their friends and family. Several issues of the mock newspaper had survived, now scanned and displayed on the website of the Staatsbibliothek in Berlin. Remarkable. If he could convince the curators of the Staatsbibliothek to loan one of these, what a coup that would be.

Cultural issues were at stake in any examination of the Mendelssohn siblings, making the exhibition even more compelling. As the ideas poured into his mind, he began jotting down notes. He would write up his proposal as soon as possible and circulate it before the meeting. Fanny and Felix were Jews who'd converted to Christianity. They'd seemingly led lives of complete assimilation. Or had they? This was worth exploring. It wasn't an issue Scott had ever focused on.

Furthermore, the dictates of nineteenth-century society (enforced by her father and her brother Felix) had prevented Fanny from performing in public and publishing her compositions. Only shortly before her death at age forty-one—and with the support of her husband, the gifted artist Wilhelm Hensel—did she gain the confidence to force this issue and move ahead with publication. Much of her solo piano music was excellent. Lieder were her specialty. Her songs were dreamlike and filled with emotion.

Felix had published some of Fanny's songs under his name. Feminist critics got into a tizzy about him supposedly obliterating Fanny's identity, but Scott was willing to view this in context: a properly raised woman from the upper echelons of society did not ordinarily, during that era, publish under her own name. At least Felix had thought his sister's work worthy of publication. Scott could hear the critics coming down on him: Who was Felix to decide whether his older sister's work was good enough to be published, and, worse, to publish it as his own?

The issue was complicated, however. Evidence showed that Fanny had participated in the technical preparation of the song sets for publication. This implied that she didn't simply allow the subterfuge but was an active collaborator in it. During one of Felix's visits with Queen Victoria, the queen especially admired a song that had been written by Fanny. Felix had confessed to the queen immediately, to his credit. In addition, proving that the problem wasn't entirely gender-based, Felix had in fact supported the work of a female pianist and composer, Clara Wieck Schumann, the wife of Robert Schumann. Clara was middle class; not upper class, like Fanny. Scott seemed to recall reading anti-Jewish comments that Clara and Robert Schumann had made regarding Felix.

These complexities proved Scott's point: the exhibition was a terrific idea and would stir up lots of controversy and fill the galleries with visitors.

Scott hadn't reviewed the Felix and Fanny correspondence in years. His schedule this afternoon was free, so he could look into it now. If some of the letters discussed specific pieces of music, and if by some miracle the MacLean collection included autographs of those pieces—the possibilities filled him with excitement. He checked the archive's computerized index of holdings and wrote down the call numbers of the items he needed.

"I'm going to the vault," he said to his assistant.

After he passed his ID card over a series of security monitors, the staff elevator took him several stories beneath ground level. He could have asked the archivists to bring the letters to his office, but he had the privilege of going into the vault, and he liked to take advantage of it. *The vault* sounded mysterious, ominous, and altogether terrific. Simply using the word made him feel like one of the superheroes admired by his younger nephews.

"Scott!" said Edith Corbin, his favorite librarian-archivist. Edith was petite and slightly stooped. She looked like someone who might be obliged to buy clothes in the children's department. The sleeves of her sweater hung loose at her wrists despite being rolled up. "So very nice to see you."

"Good to see you, too, Edith. I should come down to visit you more often. I always love being here."

"I'm not surprised." Her eyes shone. "What can we do for you today?"

Edith often used the pronoun *we*, as if the materials of the vault were alive and conversed with her.

"I'm researching an idea for an exhibition. Fanny Hensel and Felix Mendelssohn."

"Fanny and Felix! They've been waiting for decades for someone to take proper notice of them."

"I can well imagine." He wasn't certain how seriously to take her personal identification with the holdings. He didn't think she was crazy. Maybe she spent too much time alone in the vault, and she took pleasure in conjuring up some activity around her. "I'm looking for—" He checked his note.

"146A to 398B," said Edith.

"Exactly."

"This way."

Edith guided him down the rows of stacks. Despite its evocative name, the vault was simply a modern version of an old-fashioned library, different from other libraries only in that many of its shelves held legal-size boxes stacked horizontally. One of the vault's few distinguishing features was that its air was filtered and controlled for temperature and humidity. It was maintained at a steady 65 degrees Fahrenheit, 42 percent humidity. The air quality was marked by an extreme purity that could be achieved only at great expense and by continual computerized monitoring. Scott already felt a bit light-headed from it. This atmosphere must have wielded its powerful influence on Edith, too.

"Here we are," she said. "I'll leave you to it, then."

"Thank you."

Edith never hovered, which Scott appreciated. Possibly she was watching on security cameras, so she didn't need to hover.

Among the many boxes of letters written by Felix or Fanny, he chose one at random, from the 1840s. He took it to a nearby table, which was equipped with a computer terminal, excellent lighting, and a series of recharging outlets. He sat down and opened the box. Taking out the first file, he began reading. Felix's handwriting was graceful, clear, and consistent, as if he'd taken very seriously his boyhood instruction in penmanship. In fact, Felix's writing was rather beautiful, for example in the way he crossed the *p* and *z* in *Leipzig* to create a decorative flourish.

Fanny's writing was less studied, faster, tossed off. At times it approached a scratchy scrawl. Nonetheless he was able to follow it.

The letters were addressed to friends and family members. The letters between the siblings were the ones he liked best. Fanny's letters to Felix revealed both a special warmth and a rather sardonic humor:

Da man noch immer das Volk ist, das im Dunkeln wandelt . . . *If one is a member of the people walking in darkness who don't know when they will see you, the Great Light, in person, then one probably had best proceed with the help of quill, ink, and paper. . .*

Mein lieber Felix, sey einmal recht barmherzig . . . *My dear Felix, be kind and merciful toward me sometime, and after you will have delighted Europe and neighboring countries, delight and gladden your own family once again. Either come here for a few days incognito . . .*

The siblings shared such a deep affection. Such mutual sympathy. They used pet names for each other. They exchanged musical sketches, and highlights of the places they visited and the people they met. He could imagine them at their desks, writing down the details that each knew would make the other smile.

He wished he felt such empathy with his own siblings. And yet . . . was there an undercurrent of anger in Fanny's tone? Of fighting to maintain a pretense of good relations with her brother? She had every right to be seething with resentment toward him, for his control over her life—if one listened to the feminist critiques, that is.

No one could ever know her mind for certain, however, and he wasn't about to start psychoanalyzing her.

Lieber Felix! Wozu sind die dummen Streiche in der Welt . . . *Dear Felix! Why do blunders exist in this world if not to be committed? I've made a truly stupid one, for I rejected the arrangement concerning the piano that you offered me . . .*

As he studied the letters, he realized that Fanny's handwriting looked familiar. He felt as if he were reading messages from an old friend.

And then he knew.

He turned to the computer terminal on the table and opened one of his password-protected files, to double-check.

It was Fanny Mendelssohn Hensel who had written upon Susanna Kessler's cantata manuscript, *Im Privat-Kabinett halten*. Keep in the private cabinet.

## Chapter 37

Dan was in Berlin, staring at love. He sat at a worktable at the Staats-bibliothek on Unter den Linden, boxes of music manuscripts once owned by the Berlin Sing-Akademie arrayed around him. Sara Levy had left much of her music collection to the Sing-Akademie.

Sara Itzig Levy and Samuel Salomon Levy. He studied their library stamp, symbol of their unity, typically placed on the music in their collection . . . the graceful sweep of the *S* of *Sara* and the *S* of *Samuel*, intermingled with the flourishes of the *L* of *Levy*.

This stamp was not, however, on a cantata that they'd safeguarded but most likely didn't want.

What were their lives like? Before arriving in Berlin, Dan had learned a good deal about them. A long-lost world had come alive before him, of salon afternoons and private concerts. He imagined Sara's loneliness after her husband died, and the forty-eight years she lived without him. Dan sympathized with the pain she must have experienced, being without children during an era when having children was the primary purpose of a woman's life. He had read her will, a copy of which was kept here at the Staatsbibliothek: she'd left a large part of her fortune to Berlin's Jewish orphanage. So far, he hadn't found any more evidence to show her possible interactions with the orphanage, but the link made sense: a woman without children, and children without mothers, brought together.

Dan had been working at the Staatsbibliothek for three days. The massive library, which dated from the early twentieth century, had been heavily damaged during World War II, both from aerial bombardment and from street fighting. It was only partially rebuilt. During the war, the librarians had taken their treasures, including those he was examining today, to monasteries, salt mines, and caves, to keep them safe. At the end of the war, the Russians took whatever they stumbled upon in the chaos of Germany's defeat. More than twenty years after the fall of communism, German musical archives were still coming to light in the libraries of the former Soviet Union.

Turning to the next Sing-Akademie box, he began to review its contents page by page, skipping nothing. He found before him W. F. Bach's Flute Concerto in D Major.

Dan examined the flute concerto with care. He was struck with near certainty that the title page included the handwriting of Samuel Salomon Levy. For confirmation, he compared it to the *Stammbuch* entry that he'd photographed with his phone. The similarities here, as well as with the notation on Susanna's cantata wrapper, were unmistakable. He'd order a reproduction of the flute concerto's title page so that eventually he could include it as an illustration in the article or book that he and Scott would write about Susanna's manuscript.

Dan noticed that the Levy collection included a lot of flute music.

Was Samuel Levy a flutist? Was the W. F. Bach concerto a piece that Samuel and Sara had performed together?

Sunlight filled the long windows of the music division's reading room. The room had been renovated recently and was filled with such modern amenities as good lighting, well-placed electrical outlets, and moderately comfortable chairs. The paint was no longer peeling. Dan found himself wishing for the old, albeit shabby, stateliness that he'd experienced during his first visit here years before.

Dan looked at his watch. In ten minutes, he'd see Susanna. She was meeting him downstairs, at the library entrance. He checked his phone for texts and voice mail. While Dan was in Germany, Becky was staying with Dan's sister and her family, and they were in touch frequently.

Susanna had arrived in Berlin from New York this morning. She'd done something that seemed to Dan, with his parsimonious upbringing, to be almost shockingly radical: she'd booked her hotel room from the night before, so that she'd have a place to go in the early hours after her plane landed. On more than a few occasions, Dan had wandered around German cities in a daze before conferences while waiting for his hotel room to become available in the afternoon.

With his fingertip, he followed the intertwined initials of Sara and Samuel's library stamp. What record would he leave, of the love he'd experienced?

He checked his watch again. Nine minutes.

He touched his chin. Still smooth. This morning he'd shaved carefully. He'd donned a relatively new oxford shirt, as if this would make a difference. He had enough distance from himself to be amused by his focus on these small gestures that no one else would notice, by his hopes half-hidden from himself, and by his hesitations as he contemplated the risks he might be about to undertake. Despite his graphic imaginings, he didn't know what risks he was actually prepared to take in reality—if in fact she gave him the opportunity to take any risks at all.

He focused on the music manuscripts.

He checked his watch. Six minutes.

More manuscripts.

Two minutes.

He didn't want to be waiting downstairs when she arrived, creating the impression that she was late. Nor did he want her to wait and possibly worry. With both those considerations in mind, he needed to organize himself and get downstairs *now*. He gathered up the materials and returned them to the librarian at the desk. He filled out a form to order a reproduction of the title page of the flute concerto.

"*Vielen Dank für Ihre Hilfe,*" he said to the librarian. *Thank you for your help.*

"*Schon gut.*" *Very good.*

He walked down the passage to the central hall. The formal entry doors to the original, domed reading room were before him. These doors were kept always locked. He'd seen photographs of what lay beyond them: a huge, round ruin. A deformed steel skeleton. During the Allied bombing, the reading room's massive glass-and-steel dome had collapsed upon itself. The library's stones were still black from firestorms and riddled with holes from the shelling.

He approached the grand staircase.

He began to walk down.

She entered the vestibule. She wore a sleeveless dress and sandals. Her arms, bare. Her legs, bare. She reached the bottom of the stairs. Looking up, she spotted him. She smiled with excitement and happiness. Happiness, he dared to believe, to see him.

She began walking up, until they embraced.

"How are you? You look wonderful," he said, and she seemed to be saying the same to him, their words blending together, as she kept her hand against his back, while his hand was around her shoulder. Arm in arm, they walked down the stairs and left the library.

═══════

He took her to the outdoor café in the park between the Staatsoper, the State Opera House, and the Opernpalais. The café was about a block from the library, past the square that had been a book-burning site for the Nazis. Dan refrained from pointing out how convenient it was, to burn books near a library. Susanna could make that dismal connection herself.

The café was crowded, but they found a shaded table at the end of a row, giving them a measure of privacy.

"How lovely," she said, slipping into the chair opposite him.

In the gentle breeze, seeds from the sycamore trees fell upon her hair. He brushed them off.

"I thought you'd enjoy it."

Here in the shade beneath the trees, away from the noise and exhaust of the street traffic, a scent of the countryside seemed to fill the air.

Menus were already on the table. Susanna opened hers.

"This is a little daunting," she said.

And it was, with dozens of varieties of cake . . . cheesecake with *Quark* and without, raspberry Linzer torte, apricot Linzer torte, Black Forest cake, on and on the listing went. Starlings dive-bombed the leftovers at other tables.

"How about the Sacher torte?" she said. "Would you like to split it?"

"Sounds good." When the server arrived, Dan ordered for them in German. Then: "How was your trip?"

"Long but smooth."

"And your hotel?"

"It's perfect."

Although people were all around them—young couples leaning close, distracted parents attempting to rein in rambunctious children, old men reading newspapers, chic older women drinking tea—he felt alone with Susanna. They inhabited a kind of heightened reality where two conversations were taking place simultaneously: the one on the surface concerned the merits of various types of cake as well as the details of her journey and his stay in Berlin, while the other, within them, was about what would happen next, and where they would go when they left here.

Their cake arrived, the chocolate flavorful, the accompanying coffee acidic, exactly the way he liked it. Say what you will about Germans, they were masters of coffee and cake. Dan noticed a few of the men and women at other tables glancing at Susanna, and he was pleased and proud.

"How has your work been going?" she asked.

"Our work, isn't it?"

"Yes. Thank you for putting it that way."

"It's going well. I want to tell you a story." The story began long ago, with an adolescent girl who was the sole Berlin student of the son of Johann Sebastian Bach. Susanna looked into the distance as she listened, and he knew by her concentration that she was imagining the lives and the history that he was laying out before her.

"We have a few things left to figure out," he said. "Like where the cantata manuscript was in the years between the death of Fanny Hensel and World War Two. Also, who originally gave the cantata to Sara Levy or to her husband."

"It's a remarkable story."

"Yes."

Soon the check arrived, and with it, the moment of decision on where to go next. As he looked at her across the table, she was again staring away from him, toward the architectural confection of the opera house.

She turned to him. "Oddly enough, my hotel has a historical exhibition in the lobby about a German civilian uprising against the Nazis during the war. The uprising took place on or near that site. It was among the very few instances of civil disobedience during the Nazi years."

A starling accosted the table next to them and flew off with the stem of a strawberry.

"Maybe you'd like to see the exhibit."

She seemed to relax in acknowledgment of this variant of *would you like to come up to my place for a drink?*, a phrase he knew only from old movies.

"The exhibit sounds interesting. I'd like to see it. Really," he added, residual anxiety compelling him to pretend this was the primary reason he wanted to go to her hotel.

She let him pay the check, and he was pleased to treat her. They walked across the bridge onto Museum Island. They passed the Dom, Berlin's cathedral, its walls black from the fires of war. In the near distance, the museums of Berlin were packed together.

They crossed the next bridge, and they turned to walk along the Spree. He tried to see the city as if for the first time, through her eyes . . . The monumental and war-damaged older buildings. The stark apartment blocks from the Communist era. The new towers with their gleaming glass. The massive construction sites as the former East Berlin continued to be modernized and integrated with West Berlin. The swaths of emptiness still remaining from the bombing raids. So much history, so many centuries, alive together. He sensed in her a disquiet that he couldn't penetrate.

He already knew the name and location of her hotel. She'd e-mailed it to him last week, and he'd looked it up. He'd plotted their route from the café to the hotel in advance, just in case. "I want to show you something."

They passed the Museum of the DDR, as the former East Germany was called. Tourist boats were moored along the river bank.

Outdoor cafés crowded the quay. He led her to the corner of Burg-strasse.

"The story I was telling you . . . as far as I can work out, this is where Daniel Itzig's mansion was. Where Sara Levy grew up."

All around them were modern structures, some from the Communist era, some newly constructed.

"In those days, this area was outside the traditional Jewish quarter. The wealthy built their palaces here."

In his mind he saw the old city. He heard the carriages rattling on the cobblestones. Behind the tall windows of the palace of Daniel Itzig, the King's Jew, a girl practiced the harpsichord.

"And over there," he said, as they continued along the river, "on what's now called Museum Island, that's where the home of Sara Itzig Levy was, the mansion where she lived after her marriage. Her home was surrounded by gardens and was famous for its trees. When she was very old, she even stood up to the king, when he wanted to destroy her garden as well as a wing of her home to build the Neues Museum. She wouldn't budge. So the museum's design had to be adjusted."

The centuries existed simultaneously around them, the era of Sara Levy as close as the Nazis, the Communists, the present.

A child, about three years old, with white-blond hair, ran before them.

*"Halt!"* a man shouted behind them.

Susanna gripped Dan's arm and turned. The man, the boy's father by the look of him, ran to catch up with the child. He passed Dan and Susanna. The unheeding child was now approaching the steps leading down to the river.

*"Halt!"* At last the father caught up with his son and scolded him.

Running off—a common predicament with kids that age, Dan knew from raising Becky. But Susanna clutched his arm with both her hands, and Dan knew that she hadn't heard it that way. She'd heard something else. She'd heard a memory of war, of films, books, and historical accounts. *Halt* meant that you were as good as dead. After the war, the writers who called themselves Group 47 tried to purge the German language of its Nazi overtones, but how could you purge the word for "stop"?

In silence they turned away from the riverbank and walked along Burgstrasse. She continued to hold his arm, now more for pleasure than protection. He felt a tranquillity envelop him, both because he was far from the constraints of home and because she seemed to feel that he could give her what she needed.

They reached Rosenstrasse, the location of the hotel. The small street was abruptly quiet after the bustle of the main thoroughfare. Entering the hotel, they were greeted by a museum display, with large-format photos and explanatory placards. Dan stopped to examine the exhibit. He learned that the hotel was near the site of a factory where in 1943, German Jewish men married to German Christian women had been imprisoned. A rumor spread that the husbands were about to be deported. Their wives protested on the street each day until the men were freed. Dan hadn't known anything about it. He translated the German documents for Susanna.

When he was halfway through, Susanna said, "You can look at the rest of the exhibit later." She glided her hand down Dan's arm and took his hand. She led him to the elevator.

Her decision was fine with him.

※※※※

Now they were upstairs in her room, sleek, modern, sunlit, windows open. The gauzy curtains billowed on the breeze.

Susanna turned to Dan and reassured herself, everything will be okay, and she reached up to embrace him, her hands pressing into his shoulders, his neck, his hair, caressing his cheeks, outlining his eyes with her fingertips, bringing her face to his.

Even as Dan felt himself present in this moment, Susanna unbuttoning his shirt, stroking his chest, his back, he sensed Julie doing the same in a flash within his mind. Julie at nineteen, lithe and strong, the first time they were together. Julie later, her body misshapen by disease yet still the person he'd loved so long. He wanted to stay in the present, but he couldn't bear to push Julie away and he wouldn't. Julie, Susanna. He unzipped Susanna's dress. And then something inside himself eased and he understood he could have both, this and the other, the memories and the present. The two didn't cancel each other out. Susanna stepped out of her dress. She pulled off his shirt. He drew her close, feeling her skin upon his, letting her envelop him.

Susanna, lying on the concrete beside the garbage cans . . . the other man, not her husband, the man who was in prison now, entered her mind, and she tried to force him out but he kept returning in flashes that were like still photographs—*flash*, his hand over her mouth, *flash*, his struggle to get inside her, *flash*, the press of her head against the concrete, the taste of his blood as she bit the hand he pressed over her mouth and nose, as she struggled to breathe. And then she saw Alan, *I can't, I can't, I can't* . . . the film stuck in the most awful spot, repeating itself even as Dan ran his hands over her shoulders and down her back and they discarded the last of their clothes and he pulled her close and she felt him all around her. Now they were on the bed, Dan's hands in her hair, and she tried to push him away to protect herself even as she lost track of which was the past and which the present—until she opened her eyes to see, to create new, different footage to play within her mind.

As she massaged her hands into his legs, his back, she felt free, no more ghosts, only Dan, and now he was inside her and she rose toward him and held him tight within her.

## Chapter 38

A week later, in the evening, Susanna stood in the arched entry tunnel leading into a courtyard off Sophienstrasse. Dan was beside her. In this part of the former East Berlin, called the Mitte, many buildings were designed in a series of connecting courtyards, with shops, galleries, and cafés hidden from the street. The dank smell of the tunnel mixed with the scents of nature from the overgrown churchyard across the street.

Dan and Susanna stared at a memorial plaque on the wall before them.

RACHELE SIMMERMAN, 1914–1941. MAX SIMMERMAN, 1909–1941.

These were the names of Berlin Jews who'd lived in this building.

A group of tourists, three men and two women, their clothes stylish, entered the tunnel. Because of their offhand elegance, Susanna guessed they were French even before she heard them speaking. One of the men led the others into the courtyard, which was filled with outdoor tables served by the café on the far side.

The French tourists didn't stop to read the plaque.

Two young men in tight black T-shirts, speaking German, came into the tunnel. They also headed toward the café without glancing at the plaque. According to Susanna's guidebook, Berlin was the coolest city in the world. A cutting-edge contemporary ethos swirled around her, while she focused on the past.

CHANA SIMMERMAN, 1936–1941.

Dan examined a poster taped to the wall. "Apparently there's an art opening in the second courtyard. Shall we take a look?"

DEVORAH SIMMERMAN, 1883–1941.

"You go ahead." She felt she owed the dead more than glancing attention. "I'll catch up."

He squeezed her hand and released it. She watched him walk across the first courtyard, past the café tables, through another tunnel, and into the second courtyard. How attractive he was. He seemed unaware of this aspect of himself and bewildered when first she'd pointed it out. She'd seen women turning to stare at him on the street. Most of these women were gray-haired and closer to elderly than middle-aged, but nonetheless, he deserved their admiration. She could still feel the imprint of his hands upon her, from their lovemaking this afternoon, before dinner. She could still sense the smell of him, despite the shower she took afterward.

This evening they'd followed the routine of each evening of their week. Dinner in one of the courtyards of the Mitte, followed by a walk. The sun set after 9:30. The long days extended their explorations. He'd moved out of the home of his friends and into her hotel room. These past days, as they visited museums, tourist sites, and cafés, they'd created a kind of circle around themselves. She was dependent on him, on a surface level because he was fluent in German (although she was picking up phrases), and more deeply because each day she'd allowed herself to become more vulnerable to him, to care for him and to trust him more.

JOSEF NAUMANN, 1912–1941.

JOSEPHINA NAUMANN, 1938–1941.

Josephina was only three years old. Who took her and the others away? Young men, Susanna imagined. Eighteen or nineteen years old, barking orders, carrying rifles, trying to act grown-up. What was going through their minds as they marched the families—the grandmother stumbling, the father clinging to his dignity, the child clutching her mother's skirt—into the waiting trucks? She felt the fear of the families. She smelled the scents of cooking wafting down from other apartments, as life continued all around, neighbors going about their business, not daring to watch.

Enough. She turned away from the names and their stark evocation of the past. She willed herself back to the present. She walked into the first courtyard, crowded with the glamorous standing in line for the café's outdoor tables. She continued on, into the second courtyard.

The gallery, with its factory-style windows and track lighting, was on the right side. Visitors filled the loftlike space. From the courtyard, she could observe the comings and goings inside, people holding wineglasses and circulating from one painting to the next, the short-haired woman at the desk reviewing paperwork with a couple who wore matching leather jackets despite the summer heat. The paintings, at least as much of them as she could see through the crowd, projected a brutality: faces rendered so large and close, the features were distorted.

She didn't see Dan. She closed her eyes, as if pressing a reset button. She looked again. Where was he?

She spotted the man who'd raped her, laughing at a comment from his companion. He glanced out at the courtyard, saw her, and smiled.

The world shifted away from her. She felt light-headed from the shock.

It couldn't be, the rational side of herself insisted: the man who attacked her was in prison, across the ocean.

But that was him, the pudgy cheeks, the black polo shirt, this evening draped with a dark blazer.

Her sense that she had control over her life—it was false. She was at the mercy of others.

No, her rational side said as she continued to stare into the gallery: the man who'd attacked her was nothing like the guy chatting near the front desk.

But Dan had left her. That part was true. She was alone, even though she still felt the imprint of his hands upon her body. She was in Germany, a country where she wasn't wanted. Where men shouted *halt* on the street. Where people like her were murdered. She would be taken away, like Rachele Simmerman. Fear twisted at her insides. She felt faint. She made her way to the gallery steps. She sat down. The brick walls of the courtyard were covered with holes . . . from bullets sprayed by a machine gun. What should she do, where should she go, now that these past days of companionship had turned to nothing? She should have foreseen how quickly Dan would disappear.

"Decided you didn't want to see the exhibit?" Dan sat down on the steps beside her.

Him? Really? She felt disconnected from her perceptions.

He pushed her hair over her shoulder as if nothing were wrong. Then he must have realized. "You okay?"

"Yes." What could she say—*I looked for you, and you were gone. I saw the man who attacked me.* "I'm tired." She couldn't say, *I panicked when I didn't see you. I thought you'd left me.* She would sound like a child. Her phone was in her handbag, she could have called or texted him, but fear had overtaken her.

"It's an interesting show, I suppose. The crowd seemed excited about it. Not my kind of thing, though. Another room beyond this one, filled with more of the same. What you see through the windows gives a pretty fair idea of everything." He cupped his hand over her knee.

"It's not my kind of thing, either." She tried to sound normal.

"Nine forty-five, and still light."

The long June days of northern Europe, the sky clear, a sliver of moon above them.

"Yes." She felt pivoted between past and present, bullet holes and art galleries, the cries of those pushed into trucks mingling with laughter and clinking wineglasses.

"We'll get you back to the hotel." He shifted his hand and rubbed her calf as if to put strength into it for the walk. "Get you to bed early." Taking her hands, he stood and drew her up toward him, embracing her. "We've seen a lot today, don't you think? We deserve to go to bed early."

He pulled her close, and she pressed her face against his shoulder.

## Chapter 39

Paul Mendelssohn-Bartholdy, age thirty-nine, stood beside the closed piano in his sister Fanny's study. On dozens of occasions, he'd stood here and listened to her play.

Not today. Today the room was musty, the windows shuttered. He turned and contemplated the job he faced: taking the room apart and disposing of the contents . . . the piano, the desk. The bookcases, with their well-read volumes. Fanny's music library, the scores organized with her idiosyncratic precision. The watercolors by their brother, Felix. Hensel's paintings and drawings. Paul opened a window to bring fresh air into the room.

Fanny was four years dead. She'd died six months short of her forty-second birthday. Like their mother, she'd succumbed to a stroke. Felix died roughly five and a half months later. He was thirty-eight. He'd never recovered from Fanny's passing.

They'd both died at the apex of their lives. So much more, they might have accomplished. Fanny especially. At least she'd lived to see some of her compositions published.

Paul felt as if he were committing a sacrilege by dismantling this room. For twenty-six years, Leipzigerstrasse 3 had been his family's home. Now his parents were dead. Fanny and Felix were dead. And he, Paul Mendelssohn-Bartholdy, the perpetual younger brother—he was alive, to deal with what remained of better days.

In a perfect world, the house would have stayed intact until Hensel died, or longer, someday providing a home for Sebastian and *his* family. But this was not a perfect world. Hensel no longer had the ability to maintain the house. Or himself. In the years since Fanny's death, grief had overpowered Hensel. He'd stopped painting. Unfinished commissions filled his studio. His drinking was uncontrolled. His gambling debts mounted. Hensel wasn't capable even of maintaining a household suitable for his son. Sebastian lived now with his aunt, Paul's sister Rebecka, and her family.

Paul had delayed as long as he could. Now the house and its beloved garden must be sold. The Prussian government had approached Paul with an offer. After recent political upheavals, the government was looking for a suitable building to use as the upper house of the newly formed parliament. Much to Paul's surprise, his family home, center of memory, had been deemed suitable to serve as the nation's parliament.

The glittering Mendelssohn-Bartholdys. Here was what their musical studies and achievements and childhood games in the enchanted garden had come to: brother Paul, the banker, cleaning up after the dead.

The door opened.

"Brother-in-law, you're early." Wilhelm Hensel shambled into the room. Eleven in the morning wasn't early, by Paul's standards. Hensel still wore his dressing gown. Clearly he hadn't shaved or bathed in many days. "It's bright, eh?" Hensel looked out the window and squinted. The sky was gray. Hensel reeked of whiskey. He sat down heavily on a delicate, ornate chair. He was red-faced. Bloated. "Take anything you like. Take everything. What am I going to do with any of it?"

Inwardly, Paul grimaced at his brother-in-law's condition. He remembered Hensel filled with good humor and high spirits. "We'll donate the music manuscripts to the Sing-Akademie, or to the Royal Library," Paul said, wanting confirmation.

"Whatever you believe is best." Hensel's voice caught. He turned away and covered his face.

Was he weeping? Paul approached him. Put a hand on his shoulder. Hensel waved him off.

"Leave me be."

"As you wish." Paul stepped away. He wanted Hensel to say, I'll help, we'll do this together. Paul wanted a conversation, an acknowledgment of their shared memories, and their grief. Hensel had been a loyal husband to Fanny. Paul respected Hensel's talents as an artist. Because of Hensel's dazzling portraits, the Mendelssohn-Bartholdy family was forever spritely and charming; Fanny was a glorious muse, Lea was lovely and welcoming, Abraham was handsome, learned, supportive.

"I'll begin now," Paul said.

"As you wish." Hensel sighed and slouched. "I'm happy to assist." Hensel did not rise from his chair.

I mustn't leave jewelry here, Paul realized. Most likely Hensel was already selling off Fanny's jewelry piece by piece to pay for his drinking and gambling. Paul had an obligation to Sebastian, to preserve what was left of his inheritance.

Taking apart the house was a grave duty. Organizing this room alone would take weeks. After he'd gone through the desk to find any financial records, after he removed the most important music manuscripts, and found his sister's jewelry in her dressing room, he'd turn the task over to Albertine, his wife. She could deal with the rest of the house, the silver and the china, the books, furniture, and musical instruments. She could hire a suitable firm to help her.

And Albertine would have to deal with Hensel, and with the drawings and paintings stacked in his *atelier*. She'd help him find a new home. Obviously the man had lost all initiative.

Paul had no patience with lost initiative. Paul had never had a moment in his adult life when he could allow himself to be lost, in this or any other way.

Recently, Paul had noticed a shift within himself. He was barely thirty-nine years old, but already he felt his shoulders rounding despite his efforts to stand straight, and his eyes losing their sharp focus when he tried to read. Fanny, dead before her forty-second birthday. Felix, dead at thirty-eight. How long did Paul have left?

On the desk was Fanny's inventory of her family's collection of music. It was extensive. Someone, he or Albertine or a solicitor, would have to go through and check if the listing bore any relationship to the materials that were, in fact, here.

Paul opened the desk drawer. The smell of his sister surrounded him, powdery and soft. Her letter opener. Her pens. Her fine stationery. How many times she'd written to him on that stationery. Invitations. Requests for funds.

Paul thought, I was the steady brother, the designated bearer of responsibility, the one required to join the family bank to keep the family fortune going. To provide the money so that everyone else could do as they wished. I was the one who had to be at work in the morning, so that Fanny could have a silver-handled letter opener. So that Felix could travel Europe in style as a composer and conductor.

And I'm the one who's here to clean up after the others. He was younger than Felix and Fanny, but now he felt far older.

He'd experienced some accomplishments as a banker, that was true. He'd made commercial contacts with Russia and thereby expanded the bank's reach and success, contributing to the prosperity of Prussia itself as trade routes opened to the east. He'd even learned Russian. He traveled frequently to St. Petersburg.

Alas, their father would not have viewed these activities favorably. Not compared with being hailed as the greatest composer of the age, the equal of (if not greater even than) Mozart—or so said Goethe about young Felix. Their father had determined that he, Paul, the younger son, would be the one to work for the family bank. And then their father had denigrated him for being a banker. *Procurator Paul,* Abraham had called him, after the financial officers of the Roman Empire. The apparent jest had certainly never sounded like a compliment.

Paul closed the desk drawer. He couldn't take up his time with ladies' stationery. Albertine would know what to do with it.

Paul opened the first cabinet. He found the instrumental and vocal materials for the family's Sunday concerts, all well-organized and labeled . . . the music of J. S. Bach, C. P. E. Bach, of Haydn, Beethoven, Felix Mendelssohn, and many others. He found Lea's copy of Bach's *Well-Tempered Clavier I,* a treasured gift, Lea had once told him, from his now-ancient great-aunt, Sara Levy.

He went to the next cabinet. Here he found autographs of his sister's compositions—dozens and dozens of them, in clean copies. In the next cabinet, he found musical sketches in his sister's writing, along with her composing scores, many unfinished or in the process of being revised. Among these, he saw a manuscript on which Fanny had written, *Keep in the private cabinet,* although it wasn't especially concealed. Was *this* the private cabinet, even though it appeared identical to the others? Paul didn't know and he wouldn't call attention to the question by rousing Hensel to ask him.

Fanny had never shared with Paul her personal thoughts or feelings. She'd reserved those for Felix.

Paul looked through the manuscript marked *Keep in the private cab-*

*inet*. He saw the signature. Old Bach himself. Paul still played the cello, when he wasn't occupied with running the bank and making certain everyone in his extended family had a rainproof roof to live beneath and an advanced education provided by private tutors. Paul could read music, hear it, even, in his mind. He could have been a professional musician, if he'd been the eldest instead of the youngest.

Paul made out the manuscript's words, horrendous by any standard. Where had Fanny found this? Who could he ask?

He glanced at the copy of *The Well-Tempered Clavier I*. He hadn't visited Tante Levy in years. Paul felt a pang. He'd been remiss in his familial duty. Lea would have expected more from him.

Hensel had slipped into a stupor.

Paul added the Bach cantata to the collection of items he was taking away with him, the family heirlooms that had to be protected from the grieving man slumped before him.

———

A few days later, Paul Mendelssohn-Bartholdy knocked upon the door of the Baroque palace at Hinter dem Neuen Packhof 3. What a shock this neighborhood was. A steam engine pounded pilings into the swampy ground. A rail line carried building materials to the site and took away refuse. The noise was deafening. Mud, smoke, sawdust . . . not the green serenity Paul had been expecting. The king had determined that museums and public grounds should cover this island in the Spree, not the palaces of the wealthy. Tante Levy's home and garden were the last vestiges of a lost era. Paul recalled a story that had made the rounds: Sara had stood up to the king himself to protect her property, when Frederick William wanted her land and part of her house for a new museum. Frederick William IV might think he owned Prussia, but he didn't own *her*, was the rumor of what she'd said. She'd forced the king to change his plans. Such was his great-aunt Sara.

After a moment, an elderly, stooped servant opened the door. The servant wore an embroidered waistcoat and a swallowtail jacket. At first Paul thought the man was dressed for a costume party, and then he realized: this was the uniform of servants fifty, sixty years past, unchanged. The man could easily be eighty, or even older.

"Paul Mendelssohn-Bartholdy to see Frau Levy," he said.

"You are expected, sir. You will please enter."

Paul followed along with the pantomime. The servant closed the heavy door. The construction noise was muted. Paul gave his topcoat and hat to the servant. He was ushered into a receiving room. He heard a piano being played. As the servant ushered him forward, the music became louder. The servant opened a door, into an oval music room, the walls painted with country scenes. The furniture was from the late eighteenth century, although none of it appeared worn. All was up-to-date, for the year 1790.

A harpsichord and a fortepiano graced the room. Sara sat at the fortepiano and played from memory what Paul recognized as one of old Bach's Two-Part Inventions. She wore the black clothing of a widow.

The servant watched her play. When she finished, raising her hands from the keyboard and holding them still, he said, "Herr Mendelssohn-Bartholdy, madame."

She turned. "Paul! How good to see you!" Her skin was wrinkled, but her expression was animated and filled with life. She was ninety-one. "Thank you," she said, indicating to the servant that he could leave. "Come into the light, Paul, let me look at you."

She took his hands and led him to the French doors.

"I see your parents and your grandparents in you."

"Thank you." He felt moved for reasons he couldn't have explained.

"We'll walk in the garden."

She rang the bell and the butler reappeared. Instructions were given. Paul's coat and hat were returned to him. A lady's maid entered, bearing walking shoes, a cape, and a bonnet. Sara sat, and the maid helped her to change her shoes. The bonnet and cape were secured. A walking stick was provided for Madame.

At last Sara was prepared to go outside.

The butler opened the door onto the veranda. "Take care, Madame Levy. The lawn may be damp. Shall I accompany you at a distance?"

"Paul will look after me, won't you?" she said, patting his arm.

"She is safe with me, I assure you," Paul told the butler, who shook his head in disapproval.

Sara smiled wanly. She held Paul's arm as they went down the veranda steps. She used her walking stick as they crossed the lawn and reached the path along the river. She displayed an inner determination that overcame her outward frailty.

"I'm very pleased that you've come to see me, Paul."

The construction noise was in the distance, the booms and screeches of machinery providing a startling contrast to the peace of the garden. She appeared not to notice the noise. He, in turn, didn't mention it. The breeze touched his face. The sunlight filtered through the weeping willow trees, the branches touching the surface of the water.

"I remember you when you were a boy. You were delightful. And handsome, even as a boy."

He felt himself blush. "Thank you."

"Do you remember coming here for concerts when you were young?"

"Truthfully, I don't. Not the concerts, I mean. I do remember skimming stones into the river."

"That's what a boy *should* remember. How the years pass . . . here I am, ninety-one and still not dead. I'm a living miracle."

"Didn't I hear a rumor about you dancing in the street?" The story came back to him.

The look she bestowed on him showed how pleased she was. "Sometimes the weather is so glorious, what choice does an old lady have, but to dance in the street?"

What a wonderful woman she was. A pity she'd never had children. Nowadays this was the first thing people remembered about her. At breakfast, when he'd told Albertine where he was going, she'd said: *Tante Levy, isn't she the one without children?* A grief that never lessened. Or so he imagined. He knew of her work for the orphanage, and he hoped it consoled her.

"At my age, Paul, I'm allowed to speak frankly, and so I will confess to you: *everyone* comes to visit me. Poets, dramatists, writers, musicians, artists. The famous and accomplished from across Europe. You should attend my gatherings, too. Bring Albertine. And your cello. I remember you as a brilliant cellist. Do you still play?"

"When I can. When business allows. You're kind to ask."

"My husband was a banker who played the flute, and very well, too, I must say. I understand the demands of business."

"I wish I could have heard him play. I wish I could have met him. I was born too late."

"And he died far too young. I miss him every day. He would have liked you. And you would have liked him."

Paul stopped walking and turned to her. Her eyes were watery from age yet filled with encouragement and affection—for him.

Paul said, "I must ask your advice on a difficult question."

"Yes?"

"Leipzigerstrasse Three must be sold."

"So I've heard. And I've heard that your unfortunate brother-in-law is suffering. Is there anything I can do to help him? Or to help you, as you try to help him?"

"Thank you. If there is, I will let you know."

"And what about Fanny's compositions? Can anything more be published?"

"I don't know. Organizing a publication—I just don't know. There's so much to be done, taking apart the house. I—I . . ." He stumbled over his words, unable to continue, tears smarting in his eyes . . . now, here, with his great-aunt, would he weep at last?

She placed her hand upon his arm.

"Time will pass, Paul, and the pain will lessen, although it will never cease completely. Alas, I have enough experience of grief to have learned this. Months from now, your torment will ease. One morning you'll wake up and you'll see a way to resolve these questions that now seem impenetrable. Try to wait until that moment, before pressing forward."

"Thank you, Tante." He regathered his strength. Gradually he resumed his habitual, concealing cloak of stalwart, steady banker. *Procurator Paul.* "I must discuss something else with you."

"Yes, my dear?"

"The fact is, I discovered something. Something surprising, when I went through my sister's music manuscripts. A cantata by the old master himself."

"Ah."

She didn't seem curious about it. All at once Paul perceived that she already knew what he was going to say. Nonetheless he continued with his prepared speech.

"The text is repugnant. I don't know where the manuscript came from. I don't know what to do with it. The music is magnificent. I'm hoping you can guide me."

Sara stared out at the boats and barges, at the busy commerce on the river. He thought of all his great-aunt had seen during her lifetime: the French occupation of Berlin during the Napoleonic Wars; the coming of the railroads; the development of gas lighting; the invention of the telegraph. The changes of four generations. What was she seeing now? The city as it was from this spot sixty or more years ago, when she first lived here? Was she remembering the incident with Count von Arnim, who'd shown himself to be a nobleman in name only? The events of that afternoon were still debated, still written about. Of the many guests who'd been here, each seemed to have a different memory of what had occurred—yet everyone agreed that *she*, Sara Levy *geborene* Itzig, had proven herself to be the proper aristocrat.

"Do you ever consider returning to the old faith, Paul? Your parents are gone now. You could go back, without them pressuring you in one direction or another."

"No, I don't think about it. Faith has never played much of a role in my life."

"I expect not."

He didn't know how to interpret this.

"I have read Richard Wagner's screed in the *Neue Zeitschrift für Musik*, 'Das Judenthum in der Musik,'" she said.

"Richard Wagner is jealous of my brother."

The article had enraged Paul. Coward that he was, Wagner published it under the pseudonym of *K. Freigedank, Free Thinker*, but his identity as author quickly became an open secret. In his long harangue, Wagner had condemned Felix's music as lacking in passion and profundity—because Felix was born a Jew.

"Wagner wanted my brother's approval, and when he didn't get it, he plotted this revenge. And a craven revenge, too, since my brother is dead and can't defend himself."

Sara waited before replying. Paul felt her giving him time to regain his composure.

"Does Wagner represent the future of Europe?" she asked. "I suspect that he does."

"I hope not."

"I'm the one who gave the cantata to Fanny. My teacher, the master's son, gave it to me."

Paul reflected with awe that he was walking beside a person who had a direct link to the Bach family.

"I've been intending to speak to Hensel about it. But given his sad hardships, I hesitated. I'm relieved that I may now speak of it with you. I thought Fanny would outlive me. Sebastian is too young to entrust with this cantata. You must have it now, Paul. And you must outlive me. In fact, I'm relying upon you to do so." Her eyes glistened. With tears?

"I'll try my best."

"I trust you to do what's right with it. You're only thirty-nine. From my perspective at the elevated age of ninety-one, you're very young. You're a brilliant man. You think that here in my isolated *palais* I don't hear about your work in Russia? About the prosperity you've brought to the Mendelssohn bank and to the nation? Of the sacrifices you've made, to devote yourself to business? You'll survive for a while more. Decades from today, you can decide what to do with my cantata."

"Thank you, Tante." He felt an outpouring of love toward her. She'd given him a profound gift today, one he couldn't quite define.

The gift, he realized as she turned and they continued their walk along the Spree, was that she'd seen him for himself, as he truly was, and she respected him for it. "I won't disappoint you."

"I know." She took his arm for support.

## *Chapter 40*

Frederic Fournier felt a frisson of excitement. Right here in the standardized, excessively air-conditioned, air-freshener-saturated reception room of the Westin, a convention hotel that could be anywhere in the world but in this case was in Leipzig, Germany; right here at the opening cocktail party for the *Wissenschaftliche Konferenz* of the Neue Bachgesellschaft—who could have predicted? Susanna Kessler, waiting for him across a crowded room (to paraphrase Rodgers and Hammerstein's *South Pacific*, a musical that he publicly hated and secretly adored). She didn't yet know that *he* was here, but he'd enlighten her soon enough. He found an extra measure of pleasure in the realization that he possessed information not yet known to others in the crowd. Yes, she was here, the woman who could—who would, if he had anything to do with it—galvanize their field.

"Excuse me, Herr Professor Doktor Doktor Honoris Causa Fournier," said a man wearing dark-framed glasses and an unpressed suit, press credentials hanging on a chain around his neck.

Frederic had an honorary degree from Humboldt University in Berlin in addition to his PhD from Harvard, which accounted for the somewhat complex title. He appreciated that Germans showed proper respect for academic degrees.

"I'm Joachim Schmidt, representing the *Frankfurter Allgemeine Zeitung*," explained the man. "I wonder if you might honor me with a few minutes of your time."

Always accommodate the press, that was one of Frederic's rules. He was pleased to admit that in Europe, the press hounded him. Classical music remained a vital part of European culture. In Germany every town had its always-packed opera house, its oversubscribed summer music festival. The opinions of conductors and musicians counted even in politics, especially in the former Communist bloc. If the press needed him, Susanna Kessler would have to wait.

"Yes, of course. How may I help you?"

"I'd like to get your opinion on the arrest of Herr Professor Doktor Doktor Honoris Causa Doktor Honoris Causa Pfarrer Dietrich Bauer."

Frederic had already foreseen and planned his response to this question, and he jumped into it: "Pardon, who?"

"Professor Dietrich Bauer, arrested for mass murder and crimes against humanity during the war."

"Ah, yes . . . I believe I saw something about that in the newspaper. I can't recall ever meeting him."

Frederic knew that photos might surface showing them together in a group, so he'd given himself the out of saying he couldn't *recall* ever meeting Bauer rather than categorically denying it. His memory could be refreshed, and he'd thank whichever member of the press kindly did him the service.

"I wish I could help you. But look here, if you need information about anything else, don't hesitate to be in touch." Frederic gave the journalist his card. "We've got a terrific group of scholars gathered for the conference. I hope you'll be able to attend some of the sessions."

"In regard to Professor Bauer, my editors . . ."

Frederic looked around to find someone to relieve him of Herr Schmidt. He spotted the Bach-loving minister—what was his name?—ah, yes, Reverend Frank Mueller, in full-collared religious uniform. Frederic called to him, "Reverend Mueller, do you by any chance know Joachim Schmidt from the *Frankfurter Allgemeine Zeitung*?"

Mueller joined them with alacrity. "No, we haven't met." In a hearty fashion, Reverend Mueller put out his hand. "I'd love to get your advice, Herr Schmidt, on any concerts or plays I should attend while I'm in Leipzig, and also your advice on the best beer gardens . . ."

Ministers could always be counted on for small talk, so with God's help, Frederic was free to return to his previous pursuit: Susanna Kessler. Oh, damnation—while Frederic was doing his journalistic duties, Daniel Erhardt had found her and now seemed glued beside her. Nothing to be done but face down the challenge.

"Dan, how are you?" Frederic greeted Dan as if they were long-lost friends unexpectedly reunited. "And Susanna Kessler, am I right? I believe we met at the home of my Harvard friend Robertson Barstow."

*Yes, yes, good to see you.* Handshakes ensued, Frederic all the while planning his next move. *Look ahead*, his childhood piano teacher had always instructed him, advice he'd found useful throughout his life.

"What brings you to Leipzig, Ms. Kessler?"

"A short summer holiday."

She was smooth. He had to admire her.

"Beautiful time of year for a holiday," he said.

"Yes."

"And where do you plan to travel from here?"

"I haven't made any definite plans. I'll go wherever the spirit moves me."

"The perfect way to travel! You know," Frederic leaned toward her and feigned speaking to her in confidence, "Dan here was one of my most prized students. He's gone far in his career, if I do say so myself."

Susanna smiled, but Dan had the effrontery to look annoyed. He, Herr Professor Doktor etc., etc., Frederic Augustus Fournier, was the one who had every right to be annoyed, what with his former students attempting to surpass him.

"Professor Fournier! Good to see you!"

It was Scott Schiffman. What in God's name was *he* doing here? Okay, of course he was here, this was an international Bach conference.

"How are you, Professor?" Schiffman asked, with a tone that told Frederic that Schiffman had no interest whatever in how he was.

Were all of his former students so irritating? Frederic regretted every recommendation he'd ever written for these two, every research paper he'd vetted for them before publication. To make matters worse, as far as he could ascertain these two hadn't yet completed their research on the newly discovered cantata. What on earth had they been doing these past months when he was relying on them to pave the way?

"Susanna Kessler is our emissary from the outside world," Schiffman said.

"Yes," Frederic agreed, "we're fortunate to have you here, Ms. Kessler. Bringing in some fresh air. How did you become interested in Bach?"

She paused an instant, and Frederic thought, now, at last, she'll reveal the secret.

"I would have to say that Bach's music made me interested in Bach."

What an impossible young woman.

"Excuse me, Herr Professor Fournier." A black-haired, black-clad youth joined them. "So sorry to interrupt."

What now? Who was this? Right—the German twit who'd organized the logistics for the conference.

"Would this be a convenient moment," he stammered.

The time had arrived for a few words of welcome from Frederic, as the senior scholar in attendance. Frederic was pleased that Susanna would see this public recognition of precisely who he was: the leader of the group.

"Forgive me, Ms. Kessler," he said with a slight bow to her. "I must do my duty. Dan, Scott," he acknowledged them.

He followed the young man to the lectern and called the gathering to attention. "Welcome, my friends," Frederic said, "to this conference of the Neue Bachgesellschaft. I could say *welcome* in eight or nine languages and be understood, because I look around the room and see colleagues from Japan, France, Portugal, Italy, Sweden, Russia . . ."

And so on. When Frederic completed his remarks—by urging the attendees to enjoy the conference and eat and drink their fill of the fine German food and excellent German beer and wine—a receiving line formed. Ever the good sport, Frederic shook hands and exchanged a few words with everyone who wished to shake his hand and exchange a few words.

When he finished this task, he was abruptly, and improbably, alone. He looked around, hoping to find another opportunity to catch Susanna Kessler. She couldn't possibly spend every single second with those irredeemable former students of his.

"*Bonjour*, Professor Fournier."

Why, Natalie, and her Sorbonne colleagues. How chic they were. How respectful. He loved the French.

"We require your opinion regarding a piece by Lully that Bach may have known."

"*Enchanté*." What a nice surprise. He allowed himself to be drawn into their group. But even as he answered their questions, he looked over their shoulders, hoping to spot Susanna.

His search yielded a scene that he regretted witnessing. Susanna Kessler, laughing about something or other, turned to Daniel Erhardt and reached up and placed her hand upon his cheek. Frederic had a direct view of their profiles. Susanna looked at Dan with . . . what was the word for such a look? Dan gave her that same look. More than happiness. Trust. Tenderness. A kind of grace, unexpected and shocking. Susanna put her arm around Dan, under his jacket, pulling him close. They slipped away.

"Would you say then, Professor, that French dance forms were salient in the development of Bach's concerto structure?" Natalie asked.

"This is an important and complex issue . . ." As he answered the question, Frederic felt a twisting sensation inside himself. He hadn't felt such an ache in . . . decades. He'd felt it briefly forty-one years ago with the woman who became his wife. He hadn't given their marriage much attention since then.

A sad regret filled him.

———

Scott, too, watched Dan and Susanna leave. He'd accepted their feelings for each other, even though he didn't quite understand them. Luckily, work commitments at the MacLean required that he return to New York after the conference; he wouldn't have to face going to Weimar with the two of them.

He contemplated what to do with the evening ahead. He'd been invited to dinner with friends, the usual type of conference dinner that was followed by a visit to a bar and drinking into the night, professional gossip becoming more and more revealing as the hours passed. Several attractive women were included in the group, too.

Somehow the fun of it was gone. As he looked around the room, this conference merged with all the others he'd attended, all over the world, and began to seem empty, almost preposterous. Was this how he wanted to spend the next twenty or thirty years of his life? Engaging in pedantic discussions, drinking, gossiping, getting laid? He flinched at his own crudeness. He still loved the music and the research, but because of the cantata, and because of the arrest of Dietrich Bauer, the many intrigues surrounding scholarship had become less compelling to him.

So here he was, alone in the former East Germany on a Friday night. He recalled from previous visits that, remarkably, Leipzig had a small Jewish community and a functioning synagogue, on Keil-strasse. There'd be services on a Friday evening. His nieces and nephews always seemed to be in the process of studying for, doing, or recovering from their bar and bat mitzvahs. His experiences in a synagogue in Germany, the former East Germany no less, would be something he could discuss with them. Something they might even be able to use in their bar and bat mitzvah speeches.

He checked his watch. He had plenty of time to get there.

## Chapter 41

A memorial constructed of chairs alone.

Susanna stood at the corner of Gottschedstrasse and Zentralstrasse, in a neighborhood of both gracious nineteenth-century apartment buildings and the utilitarian structures of the Communist era. She faced a raised platform covered with rows of immovable steel chairs. Until 1938, the main synagogue of Leipzig had stood on this spot. It was destroyed on Kristallnacht.

During the past few days, while Dan attended lectures on topics that didn't interest her, Susanna had been on her own, touring the city, reading in cafés, meeting him at the hotel before dinner. She felt more at ease now, finding a way to navigate this country. She'd learned to shift smoothly between past and present, mass murder and marzipan, Hitler and Mozart.

Amid the empty chairs on the platform, three youngsters chased one another. Three nannies, university students by the look of them, sunned themselves and chatted on a bench a few dozen feet away. Nearby, a man sat on a bench in the shade. As she walked closer to the memorial's explanatory plaque, Susanna saw that the man on the bench was Reverend Mueller. She'd spoken with him briefly at the cocktail party. He was coughing.

Susanna approached him. "Reverend Mueller?"

"Ah!" He frowned and smiled simultaneously. "Good to see you. I wish I could be more polite." He struggled to catch his breath as he coughed. "The heat, it does me in."

To Susanna, this was a pleasant summer's day.

"Do you need anything? Can I help you in any way?"

"No," he said in a gasp. "I'll be fine." Soon his breathing calmed. He cleared his throat. "You see? Back to normal. It's allergies. Asthma. Please, join me."

Susanna sat beside him.

"The hotel is air-conditioned, of course, and I do better there. But I can't lock myself in the Westin every minute of the day. I have an inhaler, but naturally I left it in the room. God is testing me. For what, I'm not certain."

He laughed, which brought on another bout of coughing. Afterward he said, "Notice I've refrained from smoking. *That* would be a sacrilege. One doesn't smoke in a church, as this once was." He caught himself. "I mean, a house of worship. That is, a synagogue."

"I understood what you meant. You're not attending the conference today?"

"Today is 'Authenticity and Chronology of Bach's Early Keyboard Works.' That's not for me, even though I'm sure sparks are flying among those who obsess over such things."

"I'm sure you're right."

"Is Dan an obsessive?"

"Not about that."

"Dan obsesses over more important matters. By which I mean

matters that are more important to *me*. The truth is," he leaned toward her, as if he felt a need to speak confidentially, "I've been having some trouble at the conference. I've been concerned about our esteemed colleague who was arrested for war crimes. Dietrich Bauer. Most people are pretending they don't know him. Never even heard of him."

"Dan isn't pretending that."

"No, not Dan. But plenty of others. *Durch Abwesenheit glänzen,* as the Germans say. To be conspicuous by absence. The phrase could be applied to a good deal about this country. I know that pretending to forget is easier than admitting to remember, but come on."

Susanna understood this from her own family. "I know what you mean."

The children continued their romping among the chairs.

"This memorial is moving, don't you think?" he said.

"I'm not sure."

"Oh?" He sounded surprised. "Why?"

Susanna thought but didn't say: How many years until no one recalled the purpose or the meaning of these chairs? Until the explanatory plaque was worn down by the weather, or overgrown by ivy, or simply ignored? How soon until the memorial became nothing but a peculiar playground?

"I don't like the kids playing on it," she said.

"I agree with you. But I suppose the city authorities don't want to put a barbed-wire fence around it. That would be worse."

"Yes." She knew he was right, but she still felt disquieted.

"Where do you travel next?"

"After the conference, Dan and I are going to Weimar. We're going to visit Buchenwald. My uncle was there, at the end of the war. With the American army."

"And you want to feel closer to your uncle?"

"I want to try to understand him better."

After a moment's pause, Mueller said, "I'm curious, and forgive me for prying, it's a professional fault. Of course I remember meeting you at Vespers a while back. I can't deny I was surprised to see you and Dan together at the opening reception for the conference—although I'm absolutely not prying into *that*." He lifted his hands palms outward as if to ward off the prospect. "I'm just wondering what brought you into church that day."

"I was walking by."

"You'd probably walked by a dozen times without coming inside. What drew you in on that particular day?"

"I saw the sign, for a lecture about Bach."

"Did you have a special interest in Bach's music?"

She studied him. He was a man of God. Granted, not precisely the God of her family—and she didn't even believe in God—but a man of God nonetheless. In theory at least, his actions were governed by a high standard of morality. She'd like to have his counsel about the cantata, and gain his insights about what to do with it, even though she knew to be wary. "I inherited something from my uncle. Something disturbing. I saw the sign outside the church, and I went in. I thought Dan might be able to help me."

"And has he?"

"Yes. In several ways."

"I'm glad to hear it."

He did seem genuinely pleased for them.

"What did it turn out to be?" he said. "The item you inherited from your uncle?"

He regarded her intently. Mueller's keen expectation was like a warning to her, to stay silent.

After a moment, he added, "I'm here, Susanna, for anything you might want to discuss. At any time."

"Thank you." She said nothing more.

I could kick myself, Mueller thought. I *should* kick myself. I've scared her off.

He watched Susanna staring at the rows of empty chairs. A gentle touch, that was the best way to elicit confessions. Not coming right out and asking.

Nonetheless, putting together the little Susanna had told him with the cryptic hints Dan had given him in Princeton, Mueller suspected that Susanna had found something that might taint the religion to which he'd devoted his life. He would strive to be more measured the next time he spoke with Dan and Susanna, so that they would confide in him, and he could advise them properly. Properly in terms of how he saw the world, admittedly.

He, too, was going to Weimar after the conference. And to Buchenwald. To him, the camp was a lesson from God about the depths of human sin; about the nature of evil and the nature of goodness both: individual Christians can be good or evil, while Christianity itself is pure and eternal.

Before coming to Leipzig, he'd visited his elderly relatives in Lutherstadt-Wittenberg. They had been Nazis. Small-time party members, his uncle an accountant, his aunt a bookkeeper. Aunt Elsa prepared a sensational meal for him of sausage, thick mustard, and flavorful dark bread, topped off with a terrific Pils.

And he'd said nothing about the past. Asked nothing, even though he wanted to understand the choices they'd made years ago and how they viewed those choices today. He was a coward. Or maybe he was merciful. He didn't challenge the protective masks they'd made for themselves. They were in their late eighties and unless they were out-and-out murderers, what could it matter now, what had happened long ago? Three generations had passed since they'd done whatever they'd done. After the Nazis, they'd lived under communism. For all Mueller knew, they'd reported on their neighbors to the Stasi. He wasn't going to ask about that, either, although he wondered.

When an entire society has committed a crime, who is responsible?

He didn't share his travel plans with Susanna. He didn't want her, kindhearted as she seemed to be, to say to Dan, *We should ask Reverend Mueller to have dinner with us in Weimar,* or, God forbid, *We ought to ask Reverend Mueller to tour the concentration camp with us, so he won't be alone. No one should have to go there alone.*

In fact, he *was* apprehensive about touring the camp alone, and confronting such evil, alone.

Although he wouldn't be entirely alone, he reassured himself: he'd have the music of Johann Sebastian Bach with him on his iPod. And through the music of Bach, the Lord Himself would be with him. Every step.

Wouldn't He?

## Chapter 42

"You're a lucky man," said Dr. Joseph Werner, finishing his examination.

The doctor was average in appearance: average height, average hair color, average weight. Paul had it on good authority, however, that the doctor was above average in medical ability, so Paul had decided to trust him. Therefore, for the purposes of this particular conversation, Paul Mendelssohn-Bartholdy would accept that he was, in fact, a lucky man.

"You may get dressed," Dr. Werner said.

Paul didn't like taking orders from those younger than he, especially in his own home. They were in the library, supposedly engaged in erudite conversation over coffee. The coffee service placed on the side table supported this ruse.

"After you're dressed, we'll talk."

Decorously, Dr. Werner turned away and looked out the window, thus giving Paul a measure of privacy as he put on his shirt, tied his cravat, donned his jacket. If Paul had rung for his valet to assist him, the cause of such a disrobing and rerobing in the middle of the day would be known throughout the house, upsetting one and all.

When his brother lay dying, Paul had patted Felix's forehead with a cloth soaked in vinegar. This was supposed to help him. Felix, that is. So much for medicine.

Nonetheless, one sought the opinion of medical doctors when symptoms occurred.

"Herr Mendelssohn-Bartholdy?" Dr. Werner said, a trace of impatience in his tone.

"Almost ready."

Paul felt a boyish glee in making the doctor wait. He could well imagine what the doctor was going to say. Paul would be sixty-one in a few weeks. He had lived longer than his siblings, but, given the ache that cut through him now, part of him believed it still wasn't long enough.

Above the mantelpiece was a portrait of his eldest daughter, Pauline. Dead at nineteen, suddenly, and no one was able to tell him how or why. In the portrait, she never grew old.

He would have been glad to die before her.

"May I assist you in any way?"

Poor Dr. Werner.

"No, thank you, Doctor. Just about finished."

After they were properly resituated, Paul behind his massive desk, Dr. Werner in a low, hard-backed chair in front of it, Dr. Werner began his learned disquisition, proving that Paul wasn't lucky at all, except in that his condition might have been worse than it was.

---

And so it began: the journey to the end. But first, an afternoon *musicale*, continuing the family tradition.

Paul left the study, Dr. Werner following, and went to the reception room. Albertine joined them. Guests arrived. Paul greeted each of them, considerate host that he strove to be. At a time determined by Albertine, he entered the adjoining music room. The guests took their seats.

Paul adjusted the tuning of his cello. He nodded to the pianist. He began to play: the *Variations concertantes* in D major, op. 17 (originally entitled the *Andante con variazioni*), by Felix Mendelssohn Bartholdy.

Paul had been performing this piece for more than forty years. The piece had grown older as he did, and he'd found within it ever more subtlety and depth. Its twists and turns, its balanced interchange between cello and piano, these were part of him, part of the sweep of his life. A living link to his siblings, and to his parents. He could weep, from his love for them.

When he finished, the applause was more extended than Paul expected. Had he performed the piece with more emotion than usual, in light of the news he'd just received?

After taking a second bow, Paul retreated to the back of the room. Dr. Werner, a talented violist, joined three friends to perform Schubert's Quartet in A Minor. Usually this piece affected Paul deeply, but today he couldn't fully hear it. Dr. Werner's diagnosis kept circling through his mind, all but shutting out Schubert's transcendent music.

He needed to begin to put his affairs in order. Albertine's future welfare, his children, leadership at the bank, the disposition of the many charitable organizations he supported . . . there was much to be done. And he had to decide what to do with Tante Levy's cantata. Sara had died when she was ninety-three, almost twenty years ago. When he sat down to practice the cello, he often remembered her, and her encouragement.

His surviving children were too young to entrust with the cantata manuscript. They were adults, in their twenties, true enough, but possibly they'd always seem too young to him. Oh, they were fine-enough children, all four of them (they'd been five, with Pauline), even though they weren't everything he might have wished. They weren't musical. They weren't literary. They weren't scientific. Ernst was already at the bank and proving himself competent. Gotthold was giving every sign of planning to live off his inheritance for the next fifty or sixty years, but at least he was a gentleman. The girls would marry and take up their proper roles in society.

Such were his children. He wouldn't trouble them with Sara's artifact. What about Fanny's son, Sebastian? Or Felix's children, or Rebecka's? They were all fine and upstanding, but none seemed suitable.

He needed to ponder this question.

The Schubert concluded. Soon their afternoon gathering was complete. Albertine gracefully organized the departures of their guests. Dr. Werner delayed his goodbyes. Paul sensed the doctor wanted a moment alone with him. Perhaps the doctor was feeling guilty.

"Dr. Werner," Paul offered with as much exuberance as he could muster, as if to say, no hard feelings, we are both professionals, we give our opinions forthrightly: death, bankruptcy, whatever our professional experience has empowered us to determine. "You must visit us again soon."

Paul walked with Dr. Werner along the balcony overlooking the central hall. What a beautiful house this was, the central hall with its paintings and tapestries, rendered brilliant from the sunlight pouring through the skylight . . . Paul saw his home with an abrupt clarity.

At the top of the stairs, they paused. They were alone. "I believe my wife is planning another gathering on Saturday afternoon. I hope you'll be able to join us."

"Thank you, Herr Mendelssohn-Bartholdy. But I keep the Sabbath. I could join you on Saturday in the evening. If the party will continue into the evening."

"You keep the Sabbath?"

Paul was surprised. He'd assumed the doctor was a nominal convert to Christianity, like himself. Paul had experienced a fraught entanglement with the two religions he didn't practice: because of the anti-Jewish tirades of Richard Wagner and his followers, Felix had been denigrated in public perceptions. Although Felix was a baptized Christian, the Jew-haters had destroyed his legacy. *Our Mozart* had become *the Jew Mendelssohn*.

"This has never been mentioned, that you practice Judaism." Paul hoped he didn't sound hostile to the idea.

The doctor appeared to take no affront. "All your previous invitations have been for Sundays," he replied.

"Have you always?"

"Always?"

"Kept the Sabbath?"

"Yes. Since childhood." The doctor seemed confused. "Being Jewish."

Paul wasn't certain if something else was being implied here, about the Jewish background of the Mendelssohn-Bartholdy family.

"It's become a habit, I'm afraid," Dr. Werner said humorously, with no trace of either the defensive or the boastful. "I no longer live in my father's house, but I still observe the Sabbath."

"We meet next Saturday for music because of a family obligation on Sunday." Paul was surprised to find himself giving an explanation. As host, he had no need to explain himself. "Come to us two Sundays hence, if you are free. And do bring your viola."

"Thank you. I would be delighted."

The notion came to Paul in a flash: as an observant Jew and dedicated musician, Dr. Werner might feel compelling reasons to safeguard Sara's artifact. Paul had no obligation, legal or moral, to keep the manuscript within the family. No document listed it, and he was the only family member who was even aware of its existence.

Paul realized he was being impetuous, which heretofore he'd never permitted himself to be, dependable banker that he was. And yet as he considered the idea, he felt increasingly confident in the choice. He wished he could settle the matter by giving the manuscript to the doctor today. Alas, he needed to retrieve it from the safe in his office.

"In two weeks, Doctor, kindly arrive early, so that we may again speak privately."

"Herr Mendelssohn-Bartholdy, I must lay emphasis on a particular issue: if your symptoms change, if your pain becomes worse, please contact me."

The doctor spoke with a sympathy that sounded genuine. Paul was touched.

"Regarding the pain—"

"I don't imagine I'll be needing another medical examination. Not so soon, that is."

"But the pain—"

"I've been living with the pain for some time. That's the reason I requested our consultation."

Paul had hoped to garner a smile from the doctor for this admittedly weak witticism, but the man's only response was increased concern.

"Truly, Herr Mendelssohn-Bartholdy—"

"I have something I want to give you, when next you visit. A gift, to thank you for your astute diagnosis."

"That's kind of you, but a gift would embarrass me. I can't treat you for anything more than the pain. Only charlatans would recommend more treatment than that, subjecting the patient—you, in this case—to needless suffering."

Paul would have been happy to have such a son as this. "Thank you for your consideration, which I appreciate."

"I can't save you. Therefore, please, no gifts are necessary."

"This is a gift I must ask you to conceal. You may very well come to regard it as an affliction. So we'll consider ourselves equal."

Paul walked the good doctor down the curving staircase.

# Chapter 43

Say what you will about Germans, Dan thought, and not for the first time, they put on a fantastic breakfast buffet. As the maître d' led them through the dining room, Dan couldn't help but feel lucky. He wasn't accustomed to opulent surroundings, and in his opinion the Hotel Elephant in Weimar was opulence itself. As for the style of the place, this could best be described as Art Deco Fascist. Roughly seventy years ago, Hitler had exhorted the masses from the hotel's front balcony overlooking Weimar's market square. Three hundred years ago, what was now the hotel parking lot had been the site of the home where Johann Sebastian Bach and his family lived, when Bach worked for the ducal court of Weimar. His sons Wilhelm Friedemann and Carl Philipp Emanuel were both born in Weimar, presumably in the house on the site of the hotel parking lot, mere yards away from this very dining room.

Dan could never have afforded this hotel. Susanna, who was

paying for it, must be earning an excellent salary indeed in her job of advising a family on how to give its money away. She was introducing him to a way of life he'd never known. Their fellow guests were German *haute bourgeois*, evidenced by their tweeds and sensible shoes. Dan observed them while the server poured exceptionally strong coffee for him, and Susanna ordered East Frisian tea, which in due course she reported was also exceptionally strong and delicious.

Once the tea and coffee had woken them up, they went to the buffet, which occupied a room of its own. The aromas of bacon and sausage filled the air. Trays of cold breakfast meats and cheeses covered a side table. Platters of brown bread, three varieties. Eggs in four types of preparation, arrayed on hot plates. Cinnamon pastry and cherry strudel, just baked. A chef creating omelets to order. Dan stood in the middle of the room and breathed deeply. He felt a kind of bliss, a memory of being four years old . . . it was Christmas morning, and his grandmother was making an old-fashioned German breakfast.

At the Hotel Elephant, every morning was Christmas morning.

As he filled his plate with eggs and sausage, he looked for Susanna. She was waiting in line for oatmeal, presented from a large silver tureen. She held a side plate heaped with bacon. To his ever-lasting confusion, she refused to eat pork, saying it wasn't kosher (even though she didn't keep kosher), but she loved bacon and claimed that, in some inscrutable philosophical sense, it didn't count as pork.

An older woman, dressed in a sweater set with a plaid skirt, slate gray hair pulled into a bun, representing the German *haute bourgeois* to perfection, stood behind Susanna, staring at her with a frown, no doubt disapproving of Susanna's extravagant portion of bacon. The German *haute bourgeois* were notoriously supercilious. Dan joined the omelet line.

Again he glanced toward Susanna. The woman still stared at her, stared frankly at his Susanna, even at 8 a.m. dressed with flair, her hair curling in ringlets. Now that he shared her day, waking up with her, going to sleep with her, he knew that she didn't work to look this way. She simply did. She couldn't help it.

When they were seated at their table, he looked around and saw others glancing in their direction. He said, "People are staring at you."

"Pardon?"

"They're staring at you."

"Who is?" She glanced around. "No one's staring at me."

"Look again, more slowly."

Dan followed her gaze. The woman directly opposite was looking intently at her. The woman leaned toward her husband to whisper. The husband in turn peered over his shoulder at them. On the other side, a husband gestured to his wife, to look around at Susanna.

"I'm not properly dressed, that's the problem," Susanna said. "To stay at hotels like this, I need to adjust my wardrobe. The hotter the day, the heavier the tweeds. Plus clunky shoes. Those are de rigueur."

The staring women, all decades older than Dan and Susanna, wore stockings and proper shoes. Susanna, by contrast, wore a dark skirt with a sweater, sleeves pushed up, buttoned over a V-neck tee. She wore sandals and no stockings. Today's forecast predicted temperatures in the mid-'80s. By American standards, she was conservatively dressed for a hot summer's day of touring.

"On the other hand, they may suspect we're too young to afford this place," she continued. "They're expecting the manager to toss us out any second."

He resisted her urge to make light of the situation. "Possibly, but the family over there," he indicated them, "the couple with the infant, they look younger than we are, and no one's bothering them."

"No one's bothering us."

"I know why they're staring," he said, abruptly convinced. "The good German with the dirty Jew. They have a sixth sense for it. What's she doing here, they're thinking. They'd assumed your family would have been rounded up and taken away for good."

"Which—just for the record—is probably exactly what happened to most of my family."

"And these people reserve a special hatred for Aryan men like me, who consort with women like you."

"Dan, you're imagining this."

He motioned with his chin, indicating a table on the side. "The woman over there has evidently told her husband to look at you. Now they're both staring at you. And they're not even polite about it. They just gaze openmouthed. Like you're a giraffe or a zebra."

Susanna did stand out, Dan knew. She was exotic. He'd grown accustomed to her, in a good sense. He'd forgotten how different she was. In Germany she would especially stand out. This was a homogeneous culture, where every difference was noticed. Turks, North Africans, Roma, Jews: each received a different gradation of judgment. None belonged at the Hotel Elephant. Yet here she was, a Jew, sitting at breakfast among the *Herrenvolk*. To his shame, Dan knew he looked the part of an SS officer. He appeared more Aryan than most of the bourgeois German men around him, who'd aged into baldness and wide waists, shirt buttons straining over their middles. Dan represented the Aryan ideal.

"That woman won't stop whispering," Dan said. "This can't be happening."

"You're right. It isn't happening. Whatever you think you're seeing, you have to ignore it. I want to enjoy this bacon in peace."

"What is it with them—pure hatred? Guilt? Curiosity? A fear that Jews will take revenge on them?"

"Look, I admit it: I see what you're talking about. But I'm not sure you're right about the reasons. They might be happy that I'm here. They may be trying to welcome me. To ask for my forgiveness. Get my autograph. Touch my curly hair. Weimar isn't Berlin. It's a small town. They're probably not accustomed to visitors like us."

"This is a hotel. The people staying here are tourists, from all over, like us."

"Point taken. But more important, who cares what they think? They're just a bunch of old Germans."

"I've had enough." He stood up even as Susanna wrapped both her hands around his arm to make him stop. Her hands slid down his arm, she gripped his hand, but he shook her off. As if heading to the buffet, he passed the nearest woman's table and said loudly, for the benefit of all, *"Wollten Sie denn ein Photo knipsen?" Would you like to snap a photo?* He walked on without waiting to see their reaction.

Instead of going to the buffet, he headed outside to the garden, adjacent to the dining room. The grass was damp from an early morning rain. He was shaken, both at the response Susanna's presence had provoked and at his reaction.

Then she was beside him.

"Are you feeling okay? You don't seem yourself today."

"Your being here reminds them of what they did."

"But that's our victory, isn't it?" Susanna took his hand. "I'm eating breakfast in their midst. Sitting at the next table. They can't order me to leave. Or call the police to take me away. And that says everything." She opened his hand and kissed his palm, then pressed his fingers into a loose fist, so he wouldn't lose her kiss.

"Well, then," she said, as if beginning a new chapter of their day, "I'm ready for dessert. I want to try the *Kirschstrudel.* I wonder how it would taste with bacon on the side."

⸻

The concierge, a slender blonde in her early twenties who looked pert in her hotel uniform, was confident of her knowledge. She only wanted to help, by correcting Susanna's misconception: "No, madam, we have no such place in Weimar. No 'Buchenwald,' as you call it."

"It isn't *in* Weimar, it's *near* Weimar." Susanna kept her voice measured. Her pronunciation might be incorrect. *W* was pronounced *v* in German, she should have remembered. *"Buchenvald.* It's just outside town. I'm only trying to find out the location of the nearest bus stop, to go there." She'd read in the guidebook that a public bus route went to the camp and the trip took about fifteen minutes from central Weimar.

Although the concierge gazed at her with an unbroken smile, her tone conveyed a suspicion that Susanna might just be a little crazy. "Forgive me, madam, but we cannot have a bus line to a place that does not exist." The woman's English was good, her accent American.

"Please," Susanna said, "let's accept between us that the camp does in fact exist, and then you can give me the bus information."

"I'm sorry, madam, I must say again that you are mistaken. There is no 'Buchenwald' near Weimar."

Had the concierge actually never heard of the camp? Was she embarrassed? Ashamed?

"I can go to my room and get the guidebook to show you."

"Excuse me a moment, madam." She went into the back office.

Susanna waited. Dan was glancing through the German news-papers displayed on the table at the far side of the hotel lobby. She didn't want to call him over for German-language assistance, when English did not seem to be a problem for the concierge. How strange, the reactions she was eliciting.

After a few minutes, a different concierge appeared, equally blond, lovely, and fastidiously uniformed, as if the concierges were mass-produced. This young woman held several photocopied sheets of paper.

"Here we are, madam," she said, as if there'd been no problem. "This is the public bus schedule from Wielandplatz, the closest bus stop to the hotel, plus the return schedule. The bus destination you want is Buchenwald/Gedenkstätte. And here is a map. I've marked the way to walk to Wielandplatz from the hotel. The fare is one euro sixty each way. Have a good day," she added. Pushing the papers across the counter to Susanna, she turned her attention to the next person on line, an elderly man dressed in the requisite tweeds and leaning on a cane.

*"Guten Morgen, mein Herr,"* the concierge said to him. *"Wie kann ich Ihnen helfen?"*

Susanna took two steps away from the counter, close enough to hear the man's inquiry about the visiting hours at the Goethe Museum. She examined the photocopies. The buses ran frequently.

## *Chapter 44*

WEIMAR, GERMANY

*June 1942*

In the early evening, Dr. Gertrude Gensler, *geborene* Werner, sat on the terrace of her home on Tiefurter Allee, overlooking the valley. Everything around her glowed . . . the lawn, the valley, the hills on the opposite side.

The problem she faced, or so she reflected, was that her husband was an optimist. Throughout the time she'd known him, more than forty-five years, no matter what misfortune the world had tossed him, he'd seen hope and potential.

She was not an optimist. She was the worrier in their household. Lightning striking the roof, storms flooding the basement, gas leaks in the kitchen, such potentialities were a constant concern for her. Odd for a physician, a scientist, after all. She was a pediatrician, however, so maybe her anxieties weren't so unusual: mothers worried. But worrying wasn't able to save her own child, dead when he was six years old from scarlet fever.

How dispassionate she could sound, all these years later. He would be grown up now, her little Gustav. Married, with children of his own. She'd be a grandmother several times over. She'd have something to live for, besides her husband.

At any rate, Ernst joked that he didn't have to worry about anything, because she worried about everything.

This morning a nagging fear had become reality: they'd received a deportation notice. Although Gertrude didn't tell Ernst *I told you so*, the news did provide a grim private satisfaction. She'd predicted this, and it had come to pass.

The surprise was that their deportation notice hadn't been sent sooner. Even so, Ernst was at the Rathaus, begging for a reprieve from his dear friend Stefan, who had, alas, joined the Nazis. She doubted Ernst could secure a delay, now that the official notice had arrived. This friend, Stefan Rukeyser—they were close, he and Ernst. Or at least they had once been. They'd come up through the ranks of young attorneys together.

After the Nazis came to power in the 1930s, and before the war began, she and Ernst might have left the country. Several offers of help, two from Great Britain, came their way. Ernst was well-known in his field, the author of several books on international law. Ernst refused the offers, even after he, as a Jew, was forbidden in Germany to practice law, or teach, or publish the books and articles he wrote. Even after more and more shops were closed to them, and food became harder and harder for them to find. Even after they were forced to sell their prized possessions one by one, for a pittance of their value, in order to survive. Leave the nation of Beethoven, Schumann, Mendelssohn, and Goethe? Of Schiller? Never. So said Ernst. Someone must remain to bring the country back to itself when this madness ends and the nation returns to normal.

Optimists didn't slip away in the dead of night. On the other hand, perhaps optimists *did* slip out in the dead of night. Maybe Ernst wasn't really an optimist. Maybe he was a naïve coward.

No—Gertrude caught herself. She might be a cynic, but she loved him. She'd loved him from the first moment she saw him, over cocktails here in the home of her parents. Her brother had invited him. The two young men were at university together. Her brother had died of pneumonia before that year was out, but as if in his honor, Gertrude and Ernst had had a good life together. Although their son, Gustav, hadn't lived to share it.

Some months ago, Gertrude had heard the phrase *pet Jew* whispered behind her back, literally behind her back, on the street. That's exactly what Ernst was to his dear friend Stefan Rukeyser. Most likely Stefan *had* protected them, while he could. She would credit him with that. Here they were, still living in this large house, undisturbed from day to day. Gertrude remembered summer dinners on the terrace with Stefan and his wife, Monika . . . dinners long ago, when pets were dogs or songbirds, not Jews. The last time Gertrude saw Monika, who happened to pass her in the market square (when Jews were still allowed to shop in the market square), Monika had looked through her as if they'd never met.

This afternoon, after Ernst left for the long walk to the Rathaus, Gertrude, cynic that she was, had decided to prepare for the worst. She'd packed some personal items . . . extra pairs of eyeglasses, good walking shoes, double-knit sweaters. She felt certain that where she and Ernst would be going, these would prove to be more valuable than, say, books that had once belonged to Goethe (several were still on the shelves). Gertrude had always heard that diamonds were the currency of last resort, so on the principle of hiding in plain sight, she'd taken her diamond necklace, earrings, and brooch out of the safe, and these she would wear tomorrow. She'd practiced the lines, *These old things, real diamonds? Take them, if you think so.* The thought of saying this to an SS officer was strangely satisfying, whether he fell for the trick or not.

As to the other items in the safe—stock certificates, deeds, testaments—what did any of it matter now? She'd left it all. Except for one item, precious to her father.

Thinking of him, wondering if she'd done right, Gertrude felt moved to reminisce. She'd grown up in this house. She and Ernst had returned after Gertrude's mother died, to give companionship to her father in his final years. He had been a wonderful man, an amateur violist as well as a physician. In his twenties, he'd spent time in Berlin pursuing advanced medical studies. He'd had many adventures there, before marriage to Gertrude's mother, his childhood sweetheart, brought him back to Weimar. He enjoyed sharing his memories with Gertrude when they relaxed together during long summer evenings on the terrace. He'd even played the viola at the home of Paul Mendelssohn-Bartholdy, brother of Felix.

Herr Mendelssohn-Bartholdy had given to her father what became his most valued possession, an original manuscript of choir music by Johann Sebastian Bach. This was kept in the safe because of something disturbing about it that her father for some reason refused to discuss. Gertrude had looked through it several times over the years. Truth be told, she had no interest in J. S. Bach or in classical music, despite her parents' efforts to force her to play the piano when she was a girl. The text of this old manuscript had always appeared, to her, to be mostly illegible gibberish.

Now, however, she wished she'd had the foresight to sell the manuscript when doing so would still have been workable for her. Her father had made her promise never to sell it, and she had kept her promise. She'd fallen victim to pointless sentimentality. The manuscript might be worth a fortune. Enough to buy their way out of the country even now. If Ernst could be convinced to leave the country, which he couldn't be.

Continuing with the principle of *hide in plain sight*, she'd put the manuscript into the piano bench along with her father's viola music and the sorry-looking volumes her piano teacher had used when attempting to instruct her. Sharps and flats, scales and arpeggios, legato and staccato—what did she care? Her parents had despaired of her . . . until one day at school a microscope was placed in front of her, and she'd discovered an endeavor she cared about very much indeed. Her father had encouraged her to study medicine, and he'd never wavered in his confidence in her.

Yes, stashing a valuable music manuscript in a piano bench was the right and proper course.

While they were away (even she succumbed to reassuring euphemisms on occasion), she would turn the house over to Lena, their housekeeper. She'd already given Lena what money remained in the safe. Lena had been with Gertrude ever since she and Ernst married. Lena would care for everything, with her granddaughter Eva to keep her company and assist her.

"Gertrude?" Ernst was calling to her. "Darling?"

"Out here," she replied. "On the terrace. Make yourself a drink and join me."

They had only water, but they followed their usual routines.

---

Twelve-year-old Eva Reinhardt sat down on the edge of the terrace and reached for a stick. With her back to the Genslers, she peeled off the bark. She always tried to be on the terrace in the evening, when the clouds turned lavender over the valley. *Grossmutter* Lena said Eva wasted too much time studying clouds, but she said it with a smile, which told Eva that she could do it so long as she didn't call attention to herself. Lena had two rules that had to be obeyed absolutely: washing hands before meals and not talking to strangers, especially Jews and gypsies. The Genslers were Jews, but they weren't strangers, and they were also *gemütlich*, so they were an exception.

Lena also had a rule of not talking about the fact that she worked for a Jewish family, or that she and Eva lived in rooms in the Jewish family's attic. Lena was old, and had worked for the Gensler family for so many years, she had very special permission from the town to continue working for them.

"I spoke to Stefan," Eva heard Herr Gensler say. "He told me everything will be fine. We'll be sent to a simple but comfortable place. Many of our friends will be with us. We have nothing to fear. He's given me his personal guarantee."

"And you believed him?" Frau Gensler asked.

"Of course I believed him." Herr Gensler sounded surprised by the question. Shocked, even. "Stefan has never lied to me. Not in forty years has he lied to me."

"I don't suppose he offered to hide us in his cellar."

"Don't be absurd. Why would he do that, when he knows we're going to an agreeable refuge? He's offering us better protection. Bohemia. Theresienstadt. He's heard from colleagues who've been there that it's like a spa town. You know how lovely Bohemia is, especially at this time of year, and the spa towns are especially beautiful. Karlsbad, Marienbad. Theresienstadt isn't all that far from Prague. Who knows, maybe we'll be able to go on sightseeing excursions. I thanked Stefan."

Eva liked Herr Gensler because he taught her to play chess in the evenings after dinner. A half-hour lesson, followed by an hour of play. Twenty-three days ago, she'd played him to a draw. This was her best score so far. She'd never beaten him. I won't let you win, Fräulein Eva, simply to make you happy, he'd told her at the beginning of their lessons. So when she played him to a draw, she knew she'd really done it.

A long time ago, when Eva was younger, Herr and Frau Gensler used to go out in the evenings. But not anymore. Frau Gensler said there wasn't anywhere they were allowed to go. Herr Gensler filled the evening hours by teaching Eva chess, while Frau Gensler read books. He was a nice man, even though his clothes smelled of mothballs.

"No, no need to hide," said Frau Gensler. "And Stefan has never told a lie."

Every two weeks, Eva and Lena went to the Rathaus and reported to a man there everything that happened at the Gensler house . . . who came to visit, where the Herr and Frau said they were going when they did go out, and interesting conversations, like this one. Each time, the man gave Eva half a bar of Milka chocolate and Lena an envelope filled with money. Lena was happy to help, and so was Eva. It gave Eva something to do when she wasn't in school, and she loved chocolate.

"These are honorable men that we're dealing with. Not the Nazi riffraff. Stefan has given his *guarantee*."

"Stefan is a party member."

"Because he's working for justice from within."

The clouds on the far side of the valley were pink now.

"Was he wearing a uniform?"

"Of course he was. He serves his country. Our nation is at war—as you well know. But that doesn't mean he agrees with the riffraff."

Herr Gensler was an important man. Books he'd written, lined up in order of size, filled a special shelf in his study. Frau Gensler didn't permit anyone else to dust them. Only herself. He'd served in the war before Lena was born, and he'd been given two medals that he kept in a display box on his desk.

"If all the good people leave, who will be left to rebuild?"

The sunset breeze picked up, and Eva felt a chill on her arms. She spread her arms wide, to feel it all over.

Frau Gensler said, "You're such an idealist."

"If idealism means working toward a better future, then yes, I'm an idealist and I hope I never stop being one."

"Ernst, why don't we leave right now? This moment. We'll start walking toward Switzerland. How far can it be? If we're arrested along the way, we'll probably end up in the same place they'll be sending us tomorrow anyway."

This was a conversation the man at the Rathaus would especially like to know about.

"Dearest." Herr Gensler sounded amused. "All these years, and I still love you. Do you realize that?"

Frau Gensler waited before answering. "Yes." She sounded sad. "I do."

"Eva, come into the kitchen," Lena whispered behind her, startling her. Lena never shouted across the terrace. *Never disturb the Frau and Herr,* that was another rule. "Wash your hands. Set the table."

Eva rose. *Don't dawdle.* Every evening, Eva set the table for the Frau and Herr's dinner whether Lena had found food for them or not. *As long as we can boil water, we can pretend to have soup*—Frau Gensler had said that once, and the man at the Rathaus had laughed when Eva told him. Lena always found food for Eva.

When Eva had first come here to live, there'd been three servants plus two girls who visited each week to wash the clothes, towels, and bed linens. Lena did everything in the house now: shopping, cooking, serving, cleaning, sewing, laundry.

And she, Eva, was busy, too, helping with chores, playing chess, going to school, and listening to other people's conversations.

―――――

As Eva obediently rose and went into the house, Frau Gensler turned to watch her. Such an unusual girl. Gertrude recognized that something was not quite right about Eva, but the girl did well in school, and hopefully she would grow out of the obscure lack of connection that Gertrude sensed in her. Gertrude didn't dare perform a physical examination of the girl, in case Eva mentioned it at school. A Jewish doctor and an Aryan patient—not permitted in the nation of Beethoven, in the town of Goethe.

Ernst went inside to change for dinner. Gertrude, who'd changed earlier, stayed on the terrace. They maintained their standards, no matter what Lena had or hadn't scrounged for their dinner. Gertrude knew that Lena concealed food for Eva, but it was proper that the young should thrive at the expense of the old.

How calm she felt, when tonight she should feel anything but calm. She would have expected herself to feel desperate, panicked, anxious. Instead she felt serene.

Her last evening in her beloved home. No doubt by tomorrow evening some Nazi grandee would be ensconced here with his wife and children and food and drink in abundance. So long as they took care of the house, and kept Lena on, Gertrude would be grateful.

She promised herself that when she reached her end, she'd fill her mind with the view across this green and shimmering valley.

## Chapter 45

In the distance, the Harz Mountains glowed in the summer sunlight. Wildflowers grew along the barbed-wire fencing. Dan heard the roar of the wind in the trees and the sound of birds, singing.

He and Susanna had passed through the gates into Buchenwald.

The plateau before them held several stone structures and dozens of gravel rectangles, commemorating the barracks that once had stood upon them. The camp had held 250,000 prisoners during the war years. Communists and other political prisoners, Jews, homosexuals, gypsies, Jehovah's Witnesses, Russian prisoners of war, American prisoners of war who happened to be Jewish . . . forced to be slave laborers in nearby armaments factories. More than 50,000 had died here, from starvation, disease, execution, and other causes.

*Birdsong must have filled the air in those days, too,* Dan thought.

Ever practical, Susanna studied a map of the camp. "I think we should visit the crematorium first. It's over there."

She led the way.

Too soon, they stood before the six ovens of the crematorium. The guidebook explained that the ovens were made by Topf & Sons, a company based in the nearby town of Erfurt. This firm also supplied the ovens for the crematoria at Auschwitz-Birkenau. During the war, repairmen were called in regularly. Unlike Auschwitz-Birkenau, Buchenwald had no gas chambers for mass murder. Nonetheless, dead bodies had piled up, more than the ovens could easily accommodate.

Fresh white roses were strewn at the base of each oven. Dan knew that white lilies at Easter symbolized the resurrection of Jesus, but he didn't know what the white roses meant. They could be a symbolic link to the White Rose group, the students in Munich who had distributed anti-Nazi leaflets and were captured in 1943 and murdered for their courage. White roses, a symbol of resistance. Who had brought the roses and left them here?

Now Dan and Susanna stood in the cellar, where corpses had been stored at busy times. The corpses were put onto a makeshift elevator for transfer upstairs to the crematorium. Although the cellar was empty now, Dan had seen photographs and could imagine the stacks of corpses, bones protruding, the living turned into skeletons long before death. He felt sick from the horror of it.

Now they were in a room filled with meat hooks. Thirty-one meat hooks, for torture and murder. Roughly one thousand prisoners had been killed on the meat hooks, according to the placard on the wall.

Again, fresh white roses, strewn across the floor. Dan looked at Susanna, as she looked at this. She seemed to have become a mask of herself, and he couldn't read her.

Now they stood outside a room that looked like a standard doctor's examining room, with a table for the patient to lie down, and glass-fronted cabinets holding bandages and other implements of healing, circa the 1940s. On the explanatory placard, Dan read that this was a reconstruction of an actual room that had existed in a different part of the camp complex.

A yardstick for taking the patient's height was painted onto one wall of the room. This measuring device, however, was hollow in the middle, with a slit big enough for a pistol butt. Around the back of the doctor's examining room was a kind of closet. In this closet, during those years, a soldier stood and shot the patients through the slit as they were being measured. Blood must have been everywhere. Maintaining the charade that this was an actual medical examining room would have been impossible. The setup must have been an SS officer's idea of a joke.

Here, too, in this sad closet, was a rose. A single white rose in pity or forgiveness for the man who stood in this booth and pulled the trigger, killing other men, some who might even have believed that their height was being measured. As many as four hundred men a night were murdered this way, according to the placard. Dan wondered if the gunman received special rations for doing this job, or if he was drunk when he did it. Dan wondered, too, if the gunman saw his victims' faces through the slit. Maybe he was only a teenager, like Dan's student Derrick.

As Dan looked at the single rose on the floor, he remembered reading that German troops were permitted *not* to take part in mass murder. The idea that they had no choice, that they'd be killed if they refused, was a myth, a piece of postwar propaganda. Dan had read that SS commanders urged their subordinates to rely upon their reason to overcome any involuntary emotional revulsion to such killing, and to focus on the fact that they were helping the German nation. Those who still couldn't bring themselves to do it, because of their too-sensitive natures . . . their decision was regrettable but tolerated.

And the roses . . . maybe the roses indicated a quest for God's

grace. Hans and Sophie Scholl, the leaders of the White Rose movement, were devout Lutherans.

*Mache dich, mein Herze rein* . . . The strains of this most profound
and consoling aria from the *St. Matthew Passion* by Johann Sebastian
Bach came into Dan's mind, as he stared at the white rose upon the
floor and thought of Hans Scholl and Sophie Scholl, offering their
lives to resist tyranny—as if good could, in fact, triumph over evil
because good people wished it so.

Nonsense. Tanks defeated evil, not white roses.

How could anyone believe in an all-loving, all-powerful God after
seeing Buchenwald?

Bach was convinced of the presence of God. Or at least his music
was. Bach, however, had not known Buchenwald.

The music continued within him, filling the emptiness and posing
a spiritual conundrum Dan couldn't resolve.

They were outside again, gazing toward the valley, ravishing in its
beauty. The day was cool and clear, the breeze refreshing. The music
playing in Dan's mind had ceased. He heard only the wind and the
birdsong.

He watched Susanna as she studied the long gravel rectangles
where the barracks had once stood. This was a sanitized version of
reality, deserted, lonely, windswept. Her uncle, Henry Sachs, had witnessed the aftermath of the actual crime, the camp teeming, looking
like a multistoried town, the prisoners starving, many naked or wearing only tattered clothing, a community of beings clutching at life.

Next: the art exhibit in the former "delousing" building. This was
a collection of drawings created at the camp. In exchange for food
or a bit of money, the guards hired artistically talented inmates to
draw portraits to send to their families. In these portraits, the young

SS recruits were handsome, innocent, and eager-looking, reminding Dan of himself when he was eighteen. Mothers, wives, and girlfriends must have received the portraits with gratitude. The gulf between the ordinary-looking youths in the drawings and what they'd done here was incomprehensible.

Dan and Susanna entered the museum, organized in the former warehouse used for sorting the stolen possessions of the prisoners. The exhibition began by presenting the context of fascism. Posters bore the Nazi slogan *"Deutschland erwache, Juda verrecke!"* This meant, "Wake up, Germans, die, Jews!"—awful enough, but Dan knew, further, that *Verrecken* was the verb for the death of animals, while *Sterben* was used for the death of humans. So the posters proclaimed that Jews were *animals* who should die. He glanced at Susanna, also studying the posters. He didn't enlighten her by explaining the linguistic distinction. Susanna, slaughtered like an animal.

The English captions on the displays were brief and gave overviews, not specifics. Dan had the curse of being able to read German, so he knew fully what the original documents said. Innumerable, mundane regulations governed life in the camp, for prisoners and guards both. The documents revealed an excruciating attention to detail. Some documents he translated for Susanna. Most, he spared her.

As they left the museum, they saw Reverend Mueller standing at Exhibit 3.1, Barrack Life. As they approached him, he must have heard their footsteps. He turned to look at them. Dan thought Mueller looked devastated. A big man, collapsed in on himself. Bereft. As they came closer, Mueller waved a hand before him, not a welcoming wave, but a rebuff. He shook his head sharply *no*. His earbuds were hanging loose from his jacket pocket, where his iPod must be stored. He turned away.

Dan and Susanna said nothing and left.

What was there to say?

Dan and Susanna got off the bus at Goetheplatz in central Weimar. They walked along the curving cobblestone streets with their eighteenth-century buildings meticulously, lovingly restored after the Allied bombing, the fires, and the battle for the town. Today Weimar was as captivating as it must have been long ago.

Dan felt numb. Drained. "What should we do now?" The question was both global and particular: how to integrate what he'd seen at the camp into his thoughts and feelings, into his life, as well as how to fill the next hour.

"Let's go to a café and have coffee and cake," Susanna said. "To celebrate the fact that we're alive."

"That *you're* alive."

"Both of us. Walking these streets together."

They found a café off the main square, in a shaded garden. He enjoyed the tart-sweet flavor of the apricot *Kuchen* they shared. He drank the marvelously bitter coffee. He greeted several colleagues from the Leipzig conference who were also visiting Weimar and strolling through the town. Jeremy Meyers offered him two extra tickets to tomorrow evening's harpsichord recital by Bob van Asperen at the Weimar Conservatory, which Dan readily accepted.

The older men and women stared frankly at Susanna, but by now Dan was accustomed to this. He and Susanna laughed about it and stared back until their fellow coffee drinkers looked away.

Tomorrow, they'd search for the house where Henry found the cantata. Depending on what they found—and Dan was prepared for them to find anything from a vacant lot to an apartment complex— they'd go to the municipal archives to trace ownership deeds. They'd review online records. Might they find someone to whom they were obligated to return the cantata? Might they uncover other such artifacts that had survived? He was impatient to learn the answers.

In three days, they'd return to Berlin. From Berlin, they'd fly back to the States, Susanna to New York and Dan to Chicago. In Chicago he'd change planes and travel to St. Paul, Minnesota, to his sister's home, where Becky was waiting.

Without conscious intention, he slipped into an alternate sphere, travel mode: determining what to take into the airplane cabin and what to check in his bag; figuring out how much time he'd have between flights. He saw himself renting a car, reuniting with Becky, and joining Julie's family, as they did every summer, for a week of camping on the shores of one of Minnesota's glistening lakes. Logistics pressed upon him.

He was taken aback by how fast all this swarmed into his mind. In the past weeks, he'd been living in the moment, out of time.

He looked at Susanna. They had decisions to make.

Or perhaps not. When they returned home and resumed their old lives, they would know how things stood between them. Nothing needed to be said now. No promises could be made, today, that would mean anything afterward. He studied her. She sipped her coffee. She stared into the distance. He didn't want to leave her. The ache of missing her filled him already.

Tonight they had tickets for a Vivaldi concert, with the brilliant Amandine Beyer playing the violin. A summer music festival was in progress. Weimar was a UNESCO World Heritage site, teeming with culture.

And yet not so long ago the ashes from the crematorium at Buchenwald had blown across the central square on windy days, dusting the windowsills and sidewalks, the trees and gardens, and the tables at the outdoor cafés of the town's supposedly unaware citizens.

---

Hours later, in her robe after a bath, Susanna sat on the window seat in their hotel room. The casement window was open to the cool night air.

Dan, catching up on e-mail, sat at the desk with his laptop. The Chopin nocturnes played on his iPod, through portable speakers. The music was filled with melancholy.

She understood Uncle Henry better now . . . trying to live on, after confronting the worst that humanity can do.

"Almost finished," Dan said. "Just one more e-mail: Becky's cat keeps sneezing—okay, it's my cat, too—and the house sitter wants my approval to take him to the vet."

Studying Dan, Susanna saw herself in New York, returning to her apartment, resuming work, seeing friends. She couldn't imagine herself as a suburban wife in Granville, Pennsylvania. And yet, she loved him. For nearly three weeks, she and Dan had been living outside their normal lives. Soon the reckoning would begin.

"Ready for bed?" he asked.

"Yes."

He closed the computer. She watched him as he undressed, unbuttoning his shirt, placing it on the back of a chair. Undoing his belt. Removing his trousers, socks, underwear, until he was naked before her. Desire cut through her.

Susanna turned out the lights. The Chopin nocturnes serenaded them. She opened the curtains at each window, and opened each casement, so that they'd wake in the morning surrounded by fresh air and sunshine. She joined Dan in bed. They made love slowly, gently, filled with gratitude for each other. Afterward, still linked, he eased her to her side so they lay enwrapped.

Susanna felt him pull her closer even as she pushed herself more tightly against him. Sorrow filled her, as she anticipated what the coming days would bring.

## Chapter 46

### Weimar, American-Occupied Germany

*May 1945*

*Grossmutter* Lena was dead. She lay in the big bed in the room that Herr and Frau Gensler had shared. Her vacant eyes stared at the ceiling.

Eva pressed Lena's eyelids closed. When she took her hand away, Lena's eyes opened again. Two pennies—that's what Eva was supposed to use, to keep Lena's eyelids closed. But wasting two pennies that Eva might need later . . . Lena wouldn't want her to do that. Eva pulled up the sheet to cover Lena's face, unveiling Lena's bluish feet. That wasn't good, either, but it was the best Eva could do.

For weeks, Lena had been experiencing pain in her chest and trouble catching her breath on the stairs. Her ankles had been swollen. No doctor could help with everyday complaints like that, especially in an old person. Doctors had more important problems to deal with, like amputating arms and legs that had been blown up or mangled.

Eva had stayed with Lena throughout the night, sitting in this very chair beside the bed, holding Lena's hand as she moved in and out of sleep. Lena had called Eva's name and told her things that Eva couldn't understand. Eva didn't want to interrupt Lena and ask her to repeat herself. The electricity was off and they'd already burned all the candles, so Eva had made her vigil in darkness.

This afternoon, when Lena was sleeping peacefully, Eva had gone downstairs. She'd boiled water in the kettle in the fireplace and pretended it was tea. She was lucky to have the water. She'd filled a bucket from a neighbor's well the day before.

With her tea, she'd gone outside to sit in the sun. Lena had used the time to die, as if she wanted to spare Eva the moment of her passing. Or maybe Lena simply needed to be alone, to let go of earth's bonds.

What now? Eva knew she should venture out to try to find someone to take Lena's body away, or to help Eva bury her in the garden. Eva had seen enough of death in the past few months to know that you couldn't leave a dead body on a bed for more than a few hours without gruesome results.

Yes, Eva reflected, she was practical now. She was fifteen, almost a grown-up, and she was past crying. Lena was in a better place. On her way to Heaven. Eva would miss her grandmother, but didn't begrudge Lena her good luck.

For a time they'd both had good luck. After the Genslers went away, their friend Colonel Stefan Rukeyser took over the house. He brought his wife and his wife's younger sister whose husband had died in the war, plus the wife of their son who was in the Luftwaffe, and their three grandchildren. The house was big enough for all of them.

Colonel Rukeyser's wife, whose name was Monika, kept Lena on. Lena was indispensible, that's what Frau Rukeyser told her friends who visited. Lena knew the house, she was an excellent cook when food was available (the Rukeysers had access to special shopping), and even when food became scarce, Lena knew how to improvise.

When the Rukeysers ate well, Lena and Eva ate well, too, feasting on leftovers. Eva attended school as usual, and she grew to become a star at math. Lena was proud of her—not that doing mathematics was good for anything, Lena also said. Eva would have to work for a living like everybody else, and she'd best get started on the laundry. At school, Eva met several boys she liked, but one by one they went away to fight.

A month ago, Eva and Lena woke up one morning and the Rukeysers were gone. They didn't even leave Lena's final wages. For weeks, Lena had been working for nothing. Gradually the entire street became deserted, except for servants.

After this, Lena and Eva decided that if the war was almost over, they might as well live in luxury until the Russians or the Americans arrived. Lena took over the master suite, with its silken sheets. Eva took the second bedroom, overlooking the garden. She enjoyed a bath every night while they had running water. She wrapped herself in thick towels. She dressed in the clothes left behind by the women of the house.

When the electricity went off, Lena and Eva sat in the dining room with candlelight, whether they had food or not, until the candles were used up. Afterward a fire in the solarium fireplace took the chill off the evening air, or so Lena said, even if they had to burn books. They didn't have firewood, and no one was going to be delivering any. Luckily, Lena had collected a large supply of matches, enough to last for years if they kept them dry and used them wisely.

Eva didn't go out to meet her friends. The streets weren't safe. She couldn't leave Lena alone, that's what she told friends who visited, so they wouldn't tease her about being afraid.

And she *was* afraid, of this street with its big, dark houses. Of the thieves who might be peering into the windows, searching for food. She was afraid of the town down the hill, pocked by bombs. She'd seen dead bodies on the streets. She'd heard whispers about the camp called Buchenwald. Eva had gone on school outings to the forests near there, hiking and picnicking. Now the whispers said that if the Jews got free, they'd take vicious revenge. That's the kind of people they were. Despicable criminals and Communists, the whole lot of them. They'd murder and steal from any German they could find. As everyone knew, that was the nature of Jews. Except for Frau and Herr Gensler, Eva always said to herself when she heard such talk: the Genslers were different. They weren't like other Jews.

A sound, from downstairs. Footsteps. Muffled conversation.

Friends? Thieves?

Eva took her pistol from the bedside table. It wasn't really *her* pistol. It had belonged to Frau Rukeyser. She'd left it behind in its hiding place, pushed to the back of the top shelf of the bedroom closet, where her grandchildren couldn't reach it. No doubt she'd regretted her forgetfulness later.

Eva went to the top of the stairs. Men were talking below, in a language she didn't understand. Whoever they were, they must be stealing. She wouldn't allow it—not from her house. Now that everyone else was gone, it *was* her house. Her home.

She had to protect it from the enemy.

## *Chapter 47*

Dan parked their rental car across the street, and they peered at the house.

"This has to be it," Susanna said, again checking the map and directions Henry had given her. She'd expected the house to be a ruin, or at least shabby and decrepit, if it existed at all. Instead it was resplendent, with a mansard roof, modern windows, and luxuriant landscaping. It was a well-maintained mansion, surrounded by other mansions. The scent of pine trees filled the air.

They got out of the car. Two BMWs were parked at the curb in front of the house, so presumably someone was home.

Susanna felt paralyzed, here at the final stop. Her practicality deserted her.

"Come on," Dan said, squeezing her shoulder. "Whatever we find out or don't find out, everything will be all right. In a half hour, it will be over."

He took her hand. With Dan leading the way, they walked to the front door. Dan pushed the doorbell. Susanna heard it ringing inside. No response. He tried again. Still no response.

"They might be in the garden," he said.

They opened the gate in the low fence and walked around the house. They heard the voices of children playing. When they reached the back lawn, Susanna saw six children, two uniformed nannies, and one mother (or so Susanna concluded, because the third woman wasn't wearing a uniform).

Seeing them, the mother called, a question in her voice, *"Guten Tag."*

"Let's stay here," Dan whispered, "so we don't scare her."

The woman was hurrying over to them. *"Darf ich Ihnen helfen?"* She was about thirty or thirty-five—my age, Susanna realized, although she was different from Susanna: she was blond, tanned, her hair pulled back into a ponytail. She wore a white short-sleeved blouse and tan Capri pants.

*"Wir sind Amerikaner,"* Dan said.

Susanna imagined how they must look to the woman: Dan in an oxford shirt and chinos, Susanna in her traveling outfit of black skirt and blue tee, sweater around her shoulders, both of them looking like staid middle-class Americans.

"Ah, welcome to Weimar," the woman said, switching to English. "How may I help you?" She spoke American English with only a trace of a German accent.

"Forgive us for disturbing you. We're on a voyage of discovery, is the best way to describe it," Dan said.

"Yes?"

"My name is Daniel Erhardt." Instead of reaching to shake her hand, he took out his wallet and gave her his card. "I'm a professor in America."

The woman read the card. "Professor Daniel Erhardt."

"Indeed."

"Welcome. I'm Inge Oberweger." They shook hands.

Dan had told Susanna that the title *Professor* opened doors in Germany, but she was surprised to see how true this was.

"And you're a professor of music—that sounds like fun."

"I've been lucky."

"I spent a year at Bryn Mawr College as an exchange student. I visited Granville once or twice. It's beautiful."

"Yes, it is beautiful. Thank you for saying. Bryn Mawr is beautiful, too."

"Yes. Thank you."

"This is my companion, Susanna Kessler."

The woman hesitated for a fraction of a second—or was this Susanna's imagination?—before reaching out to shake her hand.

"What brings you here?"

"Susanna is trying to trace something that happened in the war. To her family."

Susanna heard Dan choosing his words with care.

"Your family was here?" Inge said to Susanna.

Was Susanna imagining things, or was Inge caught off guard? Parsing this, Susanna said nothing.

"Yes," Dan said for her.

"My husband and I knew when we bought this home that Jews had once owned it, but we followed the proper procedures. We did all the required investigations related to restitution."

Of course: as in the breakfast room of the Hotel Elephant, Susanna didn't have to identify herself as Jewish, for Inge to know. Germany wasn't like America, the supposed melting pot (except if you were black or Muslim). Germany was a homogeneous society and *others* stuck out.

"The process was very thorough," Inge was saying, as if defending herself. "We hired a researcher to help us. We discovered that a married couple had owned the house before and during the war. The husband was a jurist here in Weimar, quite prominent. Ernst Gensler was his name. His wife was a pediatrician. Dr. Gertrude Gensler."

Now Susanna had their names. She could almost imagine them, sitting here on the terrace.

"They'd inherited the house from her father, who was also a physician. Dr. Joseph Werner. The husband and wife disappeared during the war."

As Inge went on to explain the specifics of her search for the Genslers, Susanna thought, *disappeared* was such a neutral term, compared with *rounded up* or *murdered. Disappeared* implied that the family might even have vanished of its own free will, to avoid paying taxes, for example, or to escape responsibility for an armed robbery.

"We do know they went to Theresienstadt. From there they went to Auschwitz."

Inge's tone and language implied, at least to Susanna, that the Genslers had enjoyed some choice in the matter.

"After Auschwitz, the record ends," Inge said. "From what we've learned, we know it was a small family. The Genslers had one child, a son, but he died when he was a boy. We searched for their cousins, and more distant relatives, but everyone was gone."

Gone where, exactly? Inge wasn't saying.

"So we felt confident . . ."

An inclination to mourn the Genslers overcame Susanna, as if they'd been members of her own family.

"But if you believe your family has some link, and that you might be entitled to restitution . . . well, we would never want to—"

"We didn't own the house," Susanna broke in. "Far from it." She tried to sound upbeat. "My uncle was an American soldier, and he was stationed in Weimar at the end of the war. He visited this house."

"Ah." Inge looked relieved.

"When my uncle was here, he found some . . ." Susanna was at a loss to describe what he'd found, but plunged on. "Curiosities, relating to Jews. We were wondering who owned these items, and whether we could find any family members to return them to. We were also wondering if anything else survived. I know it sounds foolish, to think anything would have survived, but my uncle died recently, and we were close. I'm trying to do what I can to remember him. To visit the places he visited." Such as Buchenwald, on its high plateau.

"I'm sorry for your loss," Inge said.

"Thank you."

"When we bought the house after reunification," said Inge, "it was in terrible shape. We learned that after the war, four families moved in. Then a Communist Party grandee took it over. Communism was hard on people, I understand that, but honestly. We're from western Germany originally. From Dortmund. My husband was transferred here for his work. We never found any Jewish valuables, but the renovation uncovered such awful things, you can't imagine. Bullet holes in the solarium floor and walls. Bloodstains."

Susanna began to piece together what had happened to Henry here.

"We had to replace the floorboards, because even sanding wasn't good enough. However," Inge added, "a piano survived, in the solarium. A Bechstein, over a hundred years old. Too big to move easily, out of that room. I assume that's why it was never sold, or appropriated by the Communists. It created quite a scene here, when we were replacing the floorboards, trying to maneuver around that giant piano."

"I'd love to see it," Dan said. "Although I don't want to impose on your hospitality."

Evaluating her options, Inge looked into the distance. "All right. The children can spare me for a couple of minutes."

Susanna and Dan followed Inge across the lawn. Inge exchanged a few sentences with the nannies, who paid little attention. She walked up the three steps to the terrace, Susanna and Dan behind her. The glass-and-wrought-iron table held the remnants of the children's snack.

"Your children are adorable," Susanna said, trying to find a way to connect with Inge.

"Thank you. Two are mine. The others are their friends."

They entered the oval-shaped room off the terrace, with its skylight, glassed bookcases, and intricately carved mantel. The view across the valley was painted onto the far wall.

"We restored the fresco. Enough of it had survived that the artist we hired could match the style."

In the middle of the room was the massive Bechstein.

"How fantastic!" Dan said.

"Yes." Inge was clearly pleased. "I'm afraid only my seven-year-old plays it. Do you play? Would you like to try it?"

"I don't really play. Only enough to teach my classes."

"I believe he's being modest," Susanna said.

"Please," Inge said. "My husband and I don't play at all. You can't imagine how tedious it is, hearing a seven-year-old run through scales day after day, followed by nursery songs like 'Twinkle, Twinkle Little Star.'"

"Let's not forget that Mozart wrote variations on that same melody," Dan said. "It's quite a delightful tune."

"I'm glad you think so. Hearing the piano played properly would make me happy."

"In that case, okay." Dan pulled out the shiny modern piano bench and removed the pillows that the seven-year-old sat upon to reach the keys. He opened the keyboard cover. He played a series of scales. "Don't worry, I'm just loosening up."

In the solarium, the tone of the piano was full and resonant.

"In honor of your seven-year-old, I'll continue with Mozart. Especially because the first movement from the Piano Sonata in A Major, K. 331, is among the few pieces I can play without the sheet music."

He began. With the soft iteration of the notes, the melody sequencing down the keyboard, Susanna felt a weightlessness fill her spirit.

## Chapter 48

On a Saturday morning in September, the day of Helen Krieger's bat mitzvah, Susanna made her way to the front of the sanctuary of the Rodeph Sholom synagogue on West Eighty-third Street. With its long windows and Romanesque arches, the sanctuary was soaring, airy, and expansive. A good-sized crowd was in attendance despite the 10:00 start time, and teenage girls, Helen's friends, filled several pews. Susanna felt touched by an atmosphere of affection that had surrounded her from the moment she arrived.

"Congratulations," Susanna said to Miriam, giving her a quick hug.

"Thank you for being here." Miriam's smile looked pasted on.

A line of friends waited to greet Miriam and Ben, so Susanna didn't linger. Looking for a seat, she spotted Sofia, Miriam's grandmother, sitting at the end of a pew and talking with friends. Even in her evident happiness at this occasion, her expression was defiant.

The lights dimmed and brightened, signaling everyone to take their seats. Helen was seated on the front platform, or stage, or altar—Susanna was disappointed with herself, to realize that she didn't know the correct word for this part of the synagogue. Surreptitiously, she used her phone to look it up. It was called the bimah. Helen, with her long dark hair and simple white dress, looked innocent and apprehensive, not the feisty girl that Susanna was accustomed to.

As the service began, Susanna followed along in the prayer book. She was surprised by how the service drew her in, especially the singing. The cantor was a woman, her operatic voice impassioned.

Susanna had returned from Europe weeks ago. Through further research before they left Weimar, she and Dan had confirmed what Inge had told them about the Gensler family. Knowing the family's fate, Susanna felt free to consider all options for the cantata, even including destroying it. But the centuries of protection it had received, from Sara Levy through Henry Sachs, stopped her from taking that irrevocable step. Before she did anything, she needed to consult an attorney to confirm that she actually owned it. She hadn't wanted to deal with an attorney right now. Resuming her daily life of work and friends in New York, she'd put the manuscript's fate aside.

As to Dan . . . they'd exchanged texts when their flights landed, assuring each other of safe arrival, and since then they'd corresponded about superficialities. They'd spoken on the phone a few times, but the conversations had been so awkward that e-mails and texts seemed better. She knew this was odd, even strange, but she didn't know what to do to resolve the situation. She didn't know if she wanted to resolve it. They'd parted as friends, as lovers. Would they be able to build a future together? Could they commute back and forth long term, with a child's schedule to balance? Could Dan secure a job in New York, assuming he even wished to? She hoped for children, but the difference in religion might be an obstacle for them, especially with Becky to consider. Susanna didn't want them to end up with an awful confrontation that would forever color their memories of the happiness they'd shared. Judging from the evidence, Dan felt the same. And yet, she missed him, thought about him, wondered what he was doing each day. She imagined his voice, his body, his being.

The rabbi, a bear of a man, and the cantor accompanied Helen to the Ark. The Ark was opened, and the cantor took out a Torah scroll and positioned it in Helen's arms. The rabbi told Helen to carry the Torah in her heart for the rest of her life, and to work to make the world a better place.

With the cantor's help, Helen made her way down the stairs from the bimah. The Torah was large, Helen was petite, and the scroll concealed much of her body. It didn't conceal her face. Her happiness was open and pure. As she carried the Torah through the sanctuary, the onlookers touched their prayer books to the Torah scroll and kissed the books. Susanna felt profoundly moved. She sensed herself part of a continuum, past, present, and future. She didn't have to believe in God to be joined to thousands of years of history.

Helen returned to the bimah. The service continued. Helen chanted her Torah portion. Her voice was confident as she stood at the pulpit and recited the ancient language.

She began her speech: "First I want to thank my parents and my sister for all they've given me. I also want to thank . . ." As Helen went through a list of friends and family, she told funny stories that made each person come alive.

Turning serious, she said, "Today I decided to talk about my Haftarah portion, which I'll recite after my speech. For visitors who don't know, the Haftarah is a reading from the Prophetic books of the Bible. My Haftarah portion, Isaiah 54:1 to 10, is very meaningful for me. This passage was meant to encourage people after the destruction of the First Temple in 586 B.C.E. It says that even though things seem bad, the Lord will return and make everything better. Most people think this message is hopeful. I disagree. In verse eight of the passage, the Lord says, *I hid My face from you.* When I think about that line, I know for certain that I can't believe in God. If there really was a God, he, or she, wouldn't turn away and let bad things happen in the first place."

Helen's tone was matter-of-fact. She didn't sound rebellious, angry, or teenage sulky.

"My family, like all the Jewish families I know, suffered during the Holocaust. To prepare for my bat mitzvah, I asked my great-granny about her experiences during the war. She never talked about this with anyone, but she decided to tell me because of my bat mitzvah. During the Holocaust, my great-granny lost her first husband, Josef. He was murdered right in front of her. She loved him very much. He was a fine man, very serious. I know this because she told me. He had brown eyes. He had a beard that was soft to touch. He worked as an apprentice to a shoemaker, and he worked hard. She was training to be a seamstress. This is what they were doing when the war began, building their futures and hoping to have children before too long . . ."

The childlike simplicity of Helen's presentation made the story even more powerful.

" . . . and then great-granny and her husband went into hiding, in a hole in the floor of a barn. A family that wasn't Jewish helped them. The day came when they were discovered. Great-granny told me exactly what happened next, but she asked me not to tell the congregation, because this part is so awful it's for only our own family to know about. She did tell me I could say that the Christian family who helped them was murdered, too."

Helen stopped, biting her lip to keep herself from crying. Susanna felt her own eyes smarting with tears.

"When I was young and I first learned about the Holocaust here in Sunday school at Rodeph Sholom, that's when I first started wondering if there was a God. This made a problem for me, because I'm still Jewish and I always will be. For me, Judaism is about my family, my family's history, and our holiday parties and the special food that great-granny teaches me to cook from the recipes she remembers from when *she* was a girl. I also believe that the most important part about being Jewish, and about being alive in general, is helping others. I don't need to believe in God to share the value of trying to make the world a better place. This year, I've been volunteering at an after-school program in Washington Heights and helping to teach first graders to read." Helen spoke about the individual children she worked with, and about their progress.

"In conclusion, my great-granny wanted me to tell you that in spite of the tragic story I told today, we should enjoy ourselves and not be downhearted. We shouldn't forget the past, but we should still have fun now, because that's what it means to be alive. So says my great-granny, and she should know."

Helen turned to the cantor, who hugged her. The service continued along its required steps. Helen recited the Haftarah portion she'd just spoken about. The Torah was returned to the Ark. In his sermon, the rabbi praised Helen for grappling with the most important issues anyone can face, and also for understanding the crucial role of morality and ethics in all our lives. As the service ended, Helen's family joined her on the bimah. Sofia pushed off assistance and made her way across the bimah. She embraced Helen tightly. Miriam wrapped her arms around them both.

As Helen and her family filed out of the sanctuary, Susanna saw Scott Schiffman standing in a pew toward the back. She caught up with him as he made his way out.

"Scott."

"Susanna." He regarded her with surprise. "Good to see you."

Part of the crowd lingered for a reception in the lobby. Scott and Susanna went outside and found a quiet spot to talk.

"How do you know Miriam and Ben?" she asked.

"I don't. Do you?"

"Yes. Miriam and I were at college together."

"Helen's speech was shocking, it was so good. I never thought I'd hear something like that this morning, from a thirteen-year-old."

"It's no surprise to those who know her." Susanna wanted to ask, but didn't, *What are you doing here, if you don't know Miriam and Ben?*

As if he'd heard her silent question, or independently felt a need to explain himself, Scott said, "I'm here with my nephew David. He's studying for his bar mitzvah next year, and he heard a rumor about today's speech. With his parents busy escorting his siblings to soccer games, he asked if I would bring him. I suspect he also wanted to attend for the cookies at the reception. He left the sanctuary in a flash at the end, saying, 'They always run out of the black and white.' He didn't need to clarify, for me to know. Look," he said, making a quick shift, "you and I have a lot to talk about. Why don't we have dinner together sometime? Absolutely simply dinner, nothing else intended."

Despite his disclaimer, dinner sounded too potentially romantic.

"How about lunch?" she countered.

"Good. Lunch. When?"

"E-mail me and we'll set a date." She wasn't in any rush to accommodate him.

"No, wait," he said. "The upcoming week is crazy for me—wining and dining visiting Mendelssohn scholars, for an exhibition we're planning. How about brunch next Sunday? One week from tomorrow?"

"I'm going to Buffalo next weekend."

Diane and Jenna, who'd bought Uncle Henry's house, had e-mailed her. They'd found something that belonged to her, they'd said obliquely, and they didn't want to entrust it to the mail. They'd always been kind to her and her family, so Susanna had decided to give them the benefit of the doubt and make the trip.

"How about during the week after? How about that Monday?"

Susanna was caught. She didn't want to be rude. She checked her calendar on her phone.

"Okay."

"I'll make a reservation and let you know where and when," Scott said.

"Sounds good."

In her peripheral vision, she saw Miriam and Ben's friends gathering to leave for the luncheon.

"I need to join everyone."

"And I need to remove David from his post at the cookie table. I'll see you soon, then."

"Yes, see you soon."

# Chapter 49

In the playground, Dan sat on the bench and watched Becky and Lizzie on the swings. Katarina sat beside him. Katarina had been away all summer, doing Smetana research in Sweden, where the Czech composer had spent part of his career. This was their first opportunity to catch up.

"Becky looks like she grew about a foot over the summer," Katarina said.

"One inch and one quarter, according to the doctor. That's what comes from breathing the pure air of Minnesota."

"Or it's genetics. She's catching up with you and Julie."

Julie was five feet nine. "Maybe so."

"How was your trip to Germany?"

He didn't want to discuss the details. "It was good. The usual conference politics. The usual great food and terrific beer."

That much was true. For the rest, he didn't know. Maybe he was a coward, not arranging to meet Susanna. Somehow he couldn't, not after seeing how happy Becky was during the camping trip with Julie's family, and sensing himself welcomed, in fact loved as a son, by his in-laws. He'd even attended church, keeping his apostasy to himself. He recognized the importance of continuity for Becky, who'd been through so much. He supposed he wasn't the only parishioner who'd made a similar compromise.

He couldn't imagine Susanna sitting in that church with him. Nor could he imagine her at this playground, day after day. And New York was two hours away. These hurdles seemed insurmountable, even though he loved her.

She must feel something similar, he decided, or she would have insisted on a frank discussion. She wasn't the type to sit around and wait.

As far as Dan could tell, Katarina was unaware of Susanna. On the other hand, Dan wouldn't be surprised if Katarina had heard about her from one of their colleagues at the conference.

"Let's discuss how we proceed from here," Katarina said.

"How we proceed?" He knew exactly where her thoughts were headed.

"With the line of women waiting to meet you. I won't let you mope."

"I'm not moping."

"Moping is in the eye of the beholder. It's September, it's a new school year, it's time for a fresh start."

"Who says I want a fresh start?"

"It can't be helped, you have to start afresh at the beginning of the school year whether you want to or not. So," she said, seeming to read off an invisible list, "how about a divorced woman with a daughter younger than Becky?"

"Katarina—"

"Look," she interrupted, "I wish I could offer you a *widow* with a child, but this is the best I can do at the moment."

He didn't know how to stop her. He didn't want to talk about Susanna at the playground.

"This particular woman teaches at Haverford College and lives near there, so geographically she's close but not too close, in case things don't work out. You wouldn't be running into each other at the supermarket. She teaches art history, with a specialty in Gothic architecture. Doesn't she sound perfect?"

"Aren't you being a little too . . . practical? It's not very romantic. You make it more like a business exchange."

"No, no, you're wrong. This is the way of the world. You *want* too practical, you want business exchange, you can go online."

"I would never go online."

"And why should you? You have me."

"From that perspective, I see your point."

"How about if I give a dinner party to introduce you."

"Please don't go to any trouble on my account."

"Then don't put me through any trouble. Arrange to have coffee with her at Starbucks."

"Katarina, the truth is . . ." he stopped, feeling unsure of himself. "I met someone."

She sat up and turned to him. "Finally, you're telling me this? It's been the talk of musicologists around the world. Since you didn't mention it, I assumed you'd broken up. That it was just a summer fling."

"It wasn't."

"Good. You don't seem like the type for a summer fling."

"It doesn't seem workable, though. She lives in New York."

"Not workable?" Katarina was incredulous. "As you probably know, there's a guy in the history department who commutes three times a week from New York."

He did know. "There's Becky."

"Who wouldn't love Becky?"

"And there's religion. She's Jewish."

"You think I don't know she's Jewish? Who doesn't know that?"

"Really?" He was astonished.

"I agree, we're a pretty dull crowd, with nothing to talk about but you. As to the religious difference, all I can say is, so what? At least give things a chance before you put up roadblocks. I'd be happy to host Becky some weekend so you can go to New York and see what happens."

"Thank you," he said, all at once delighted. "I'll make a plan."

## Chapter 50

Susanna stood at the entryway to Diane and Jenna's renovated kitchen. The pantry was gone, and light entered the room from both sides. Green granite countertops and white cabinets created an airy, tranquil impression, as if the house were near the ocean. A sprig of fresh mint was in a vase on the counter.

"This is gorgeous," Susanna said.

"Thank you," Jenna said. She taught studio art at a private school in the suburbs. With her long hair pulled into a loose bun, Jenna had a nineteenth-century aura about her, as if she could have modeled for Whistler or Sargent. "We were hoping you'd like it."

Diane said, "We were a little nervous about your reaction, too." Diane looked professional even in her casual weekend clothes, but she had a diffidence that was surprising to Susanna, given her work as a corporate litigator.

"I more than like it. It's fantastic. You've made it your own."

As they toured the house, Susanna felt disoriented. On the second floor, the hallway had been reconfigured. Two small rooms had been merged into one. Susanna couldn't precisely delineate her childhood bedroom. They returned downstairs. Diane and Jenna had made Greta and Henry's bedroom, with its bay windows overlooking the backyard, into a den.

And this was where they'd set up a card table, covered it with an old tablecloth, and placed upon it the box they'd found in the basement.

"We wanted to give you some privacy," Diane said.

"We never would have found this," Jenna said, "except the contractor was looking around with a flashlight because he wants to replace the boiler."

"I don't understand why anyone would hide a cardboard box behind a gas boiler with a pilot light," Diane said.

"It's like you're asking for it all to go up in smoke," Jenna said.

*Maybe that was exactly what Evelyn and Henry had been hoping for,* Susanna thought.

"Anyway, we'll leave you to it," Jenna said. "We'll be sitting on the front porch, if you need anything. Help yourself to whatever you like in the refrigerator."

"Thank you."

Then Susanna was alone. The room now featured pale gray paint and a wall of floor-to-ceiling bookcases. She couldn't recall where the bed had been, or the bureaus. Uncle Henry had died in this room, but she didn't feel haunted by his presence. She was in a stranger's home, with no pull of nostalgia or regret.

The box was bigger than a shoe box, more like a box for winter boots. The top of the box was streaked with embedded dirt. Diane and Jenna must have tried to clean it, and this was the best they could do. Faded lettering covered the box, too faint for Susanna to make out.

Susanna took off the top and put it aside. The box was filled with envelopes and folders, each one labeled.

She opened the first folder.

It held dozens of photographs. Names were written on the backs. The handwriting was spidery, as if the person doing the writing were infirm, or upset. Susanna's grandmother, who'd known these people, must have written their names. The pictures were in black and white. Some were snapshots. Others bore the stamp of photographers' studios.

Here was a stolid man posing in front of a shop. Max, said the note on the back. Next, a serious little boy wearing a Tyrolean jacket, accompanied by an elderly man who stood beside him, a protective hand on the boy's shoulder: Abraham and Franz. Susanna didn't know which name was for the boy, which for the man. A woman wearing a fur-collared coat stood in a garden: Chana. A couple, holding hands, sat on a porch: Sophie and Leo. Sophie looked away from the camera, as if she were shy. Next, a young woman, her hair pulled back, the turn of her shoulders revealing a sense of style: Shoshanna. A young man, reading a book: Jakob.

A studio portrait labeled *my mother* showed a white-haired woman wearing a long, dark dress. The woman smiled down at a baby cradled in her arms. Perhaps *my mother* was actually the baby. Susanna had no way of knowing.

This was only the beginning of the collection of pictures. Susanna put the photos aside for now.

The next folder held letters. These were addressed to Susanna's grandmother in Brooklyn. The family name on the return address was Alshue, as Evelyn had said. Alshue, in the town of Eger—one of the towns Susanna had checked, without finding a reference to her family. The letters were written in German. Susanna couldn't read them. Also included in the folder were receipts for money orders sent to the family in Eger.

The following folder held carbon copies of correspondence with attorneys and government officials in America and in Germany.

As Susanna read through the correspondence, she realized that her grandparents had promised to sponsor family members so that they could enter the United States. They'd sent $4,000, which must have been a fortune at that time, to help the family secure visas and other documentation. More letters were sent. More replies were received, family letters interspersed now with official communications.

And then the letters from Eger stopped.

The next folder was devoted to materials from after the war. Carbon copies of inquires to the Red Cross, the International Tracing Service, the Joint Distribution Committee. Clippings of advertisements placed in newspapers. These reminded Susanna of the heartbreaking pleas for news about the missing after 9/11. Judging from the stack of materials, Susanna's grandmother had devoted years to trying to discover what had happened to the family. She'd found nothing.

Susanna returned to the photographs. Two men, Isaak and Samuel, in World War I uniforms. A girl, Ruth, about fifteen, holding school books and standing at a garden fence. Susanna's great-aunts and -uncles. Her cousins. Her great-grandparents. Young women who seemed eerily familiar. Susanna could almost hear their voices. See them sitting down to dinner together. She could attend their engagement parties and weddings, and celebrate the births of their children. She could share the walks they took on summer evenings in the twilight.

Her family. Susanna didn't need to continue her search for details about their terrible deaths. Their lives had been restored to her.

*Chapter 51*

Late on Sunday afternoon, Susanna stood amid a crowd of families in the gym of an intermediate school in the Bronx. She'd taken an early flight back to New York from Buffalo, bringing with her the photos, letters, and documents, packed in one of Diane and Jenna's carryalls. After dropping her bags at home, she'd come here to watch a chess tournament. The pungent smell of years of sweat filled the air. Chain-link fencing covered the gym's windows. The low-wattage overhead lights left the gym dim. Yet the family area teemed with excitement—a near-silent excitement, because no one wanted to distract the players in their cordoned-off area.

Susanna kept her eye on Dexter Vega, a thin boy with short hair who was dressed in chinos and a plaid shirt. He studied the chessboard with frowning concentration.

This tournament was sponsored by the Chess in the Schools program, supported in part by the Barstow Foundation. Hundreds of kids were competing. The organization sent detailed metrics to Susanna, outlining the school achievements of kids who played chess. The game developed problem-solving abilities. It cultivated patience, and thought before action. Granted, the majority of the kids wouldn't go on to be chess masters, but that wasn't the point. The program gave them a supportive community, and it helped them to develop the mental tools to succeed. Susanna included the statistics in her reports to the foundation board, but what made the program worthwhile for her were the individual kids, like Dexter, whom she'd been following for several years.

"You go, girl," whispered the woman standing next to her. She wore white sneakers and a green medical uniform. *RN*, in big letters, was printed on the identification tag around her neck.

Dexter wasn't playing against a girl, so Susanna didn't feel disloyal in asking, keeping her voice low, "Your daughter is out there? Winning her match?"

"My niece. Third from the right," the woman said, indicating a graceful girl who looked like a gymnast or a ballet dancer. "What about you?"

"I'm following the boy here, with the plaid shirt. He's a friend."

Dexter Vega easily triumphed.

"He's looking good," the woman said.

"He loves the game."

Rather than raising a fist or otherwise celebrating, Dexter held on to his steady focus, shifted to a new seat, and began his next match. Dexter was in sixth grade. He'd matured since Susanna had first met him, developing from a vulnerable youngster struggling to learn to read into a confident boy who was a good student, regularly receiving A's and B's. Was his transformation caused by his passion for chess? Or did his innate abilities lead to his passion for chess?

Susanna didn't know and didn't care. Results were what mattered, and clearly the Barstow Foundation had helped Dexter. That meant she had helped him, too.

"I hope your niece does well," Susanna said.

"Thank you."

Taking a break, Susanna went to the canteen on the other side of the gym and got a cup of coffee. She returned to the area where Dexter was playing and looked for a free chair. She spotted one in the middle of a row and sat down. Two boys, about six or seven years old, were next to her. They'd set up a small chessboard across the space between their folding chairs, and in silence they played a match of great drama, expressed through their pantomimed gestures. With any luck, in a few years the Barstow Foundation would be helping them, too.

A question came into Susanna's mind: What was Uncle Henry's cantata worth? Dan had once called it priceless. She could auction it and give the money to charity.

Now that she'd thought of it, the idea seemed obvious. What was the point of donating the cantata to a museum, or keeping it hidden or even destroying it, when it could be put to good use and change individual lives for the better?

A negative voice inside her said, what if a white supremacist tried to buy it and exploit it?

Such a person would be unlikely to have the money, or to get involved with high art music.

Would reputable charities even accept money gained from such an artifact?

Some, maybe even many groups would surely see the justice of her plan.

From a legal perspective, could she do this? Did she in fact own the cantata or have the right to sell it for charity?

She needed to do research on these issues. The time had come to consult an attorney, as soon as possible.

An array of positive outcomes jostled for her attention. Bringing the cantata into public scrutiny would encourage discussion of its unsettling messages. It would force people who didn't normally want to talk about such issues to at least think about them. Furthermore, Susanna would break the web of secrecy in her own family. Auctioning the cantata for charity felt like a way to take power over it and over what it meant, in history and in her family.

The idea filled her with energy. She wanted to start working on it right away. She was having lunch with Scott tomorrow; he might have some suggestions.

Dexter Vega kept winning, so she didn't have a chance to say hi to him. She'd seek him out and congratulate him the next time she observed the program.

## Chapter 52

For lunch, Scott chose the restaurant Robert, on the top floor of the Museum of Art and Design at Columbus Circle. Susanna had thought Robert was too grand, too expensive, too delicious, and that it implied too much in its beauty and its view, for this lunch. She'd suggested an informal café across the street.

*Oh, come on, let me do my part to help the economy,* Scott had replied.

And so here they were, being led to a window table with a view that stretched for miles across the city, Central Park deep green, office and apartment towers glinting in the sunlight.

When they were settled, Scott said, "I spoke to Dan over the weekend."

Susanna felt wary.

"We're completing our research into the cantata. He asked how you are."

"Why did he think you'd know?"

"Okay, I confess: I e-mailed him that I'd seen you. What's going on between you two?"

"I'm not certain. What did he say?"

"He wasn't certain either."

"So he and I agree."

"Does this mean I wouldn't be considered aggressive if I—"

Intuiting where this was going, Susanna said, "You're impossible." But she laughed as she said it. "However," she added, "I did write to him last night. Requesting German translation services for some family letters I found in Buffalo."

"Translations—good ploy."

"I thought so. He wrote back that he really needs to see the letters to translate them. Photocopies or scans just aren't good enough. So he's coming to New York next weekend, to take a look."

"I'm a good translator from German. Just FYI. In case he has trouble."

"I'll keep your talents in mind."

"Thank you. I've been thinking about you, because I've been following in your footsteps."

"How so?"

"I've become a volunteer at the Third Street Music School. I felt I had to start doing something socially worthwhile. I'm teaching a rock-band class for twelve-year-olds from needy families. In high school I played keyboards in a heavy metal group, and that, along with my other musical training, prompted the school to approve me."

"This is terrific news, Scott." She was surprised to hear it from him. "I know the school. The Barstow Foundation supports it."

"I saw the name on the plaque in the reception area."

"The plaque is there to encourage others to give."

"It's certainly encouraging me," he said provocatively.

"Enough."

The server was at the table. Susanna ordered a salad, Scott the salmon.

"Look, Scott, I need your advice."

"Now, there's music to my ears."

She ignored this. "I'm making a plan for what to do with the cantata manuscript."

"I have to confess, one of the reasons—just one of the reasons—I asked to have dinner with you, a dinner you so deftly turned into lunch, was to make a plea that you consider an offer for it from the MacLean. We'd take good care of it."

"I'm sure you would. However, first I do have to find out if I actually own it. Although the family in Weimar didn't survive, that doesn't necessarily mean I'm the owner. I'm looking for an attorney with expertise in this area. If in fact I do own it, I've decided to sell it at auction and give the money to charity."

"You could accept the MacLean's offer and give that money to charity."

She paused, thinking this through. "I'd like to keep the process objective. I'd also like to find out how much the cantata is really worth. An auction is the best way to do that."

He said nothing, so she continued, "If the attorney tells me I can proceed, my plan would be for three categories of charitable donations, touching on the past, present, and future."

Last night she'd stayed up late doing Internet research into the possibilities, and the formulation had come to her this morning: one third to groups that were restoring Jewish cultural monuments in Eastern Europe; a third to organizations creating libraries around the world; and a third to environmental groups, to help the earth, and the human race, to survive.

She shared this with Scott.

"You'd set up a foundation?"

"No. I wouldn't want to be involved in administration. I'd make onetime gifts, outright, to established charities. I realize my plan goes against your preferences, but I'd appreciate your help. If only as a sounding board." She suspected this area was outside Scott's expertise, but she wanted his reaction.

"You should talk to Freddy Fournier."

"I'm reluctant to consult with him. I know how you and Dan feel about him."

"Susanna, in this undertaking, I insist upon your having the best. That's how much I care for you, if you don't mind my saying and even if you do mind. He's the best. I'll arrange a meeting for you. My prediction is that after he's found you a lawyer who'll fight for your rights, and after he's made a plea for you to sell the cantata to Yale, he'll advise you to consign it to Sotheby's in London. I can virtually guarantee that he'll become the front man for whatever happens next."

"That would be fine," Susanna said. "I like the idea of having a front man. I want to stay in the background. Do you think Dan would be okay with this? He has a stake here, too."

"I can't speak for him. My guess is that he'd want you to do what you think is right."

That was most likely true. "I'll talk to him about it."

"After you discuss the German translations."

"Exactly."

"You do realize that Freddy will want to look at the entire manuscript, not just a few photos. And if you're going to auction it, you'll have to turn it over to Sotheby's. That means you'll have to take it out of the bank vault and place it into Sotheby's guardianship."

"I'm ready to turn it over," Susanna said. "I wasn't ready before, but I am ready now."

## Chapter 53

In the early morning, Reverend Frank Mueller sat on his rooftop. The weather was bizarre. It was late January, but temperatures were expected to reach 60 today. Normally he never sat on the roof in January. No complaints, however. He was exceedingly happy to be here, coffee in hand. Today on his iPod he was listening to the Bach Trio Sonatas for organ, transcribed for strings and splendidly performed by the group London Baroque. The music was suffused with verve and filled him with the same.

Until he examined his newspaper.

*Previously unknown Bach cantata with anti-Semitic content discovered in Buffalo,* he read in a box at the bottom of the front page of the newspaper. *Taken from Weimar by an American soldier at the end of World War II; authenticated by scholars,* said the subheading. *See page C1.*

The story took up most of the front page of the Arts section, complete with several photographs. It continued inside the section.

Excerpts from the cantata's libretto were singled out, including horrifying passages drawn, alas, word for word from the works of Martin Luther.

Too late for him to intervene, Mueller finally understood what Dan and Susanna had been struggling with.

He could have stopped this. He could have convinced Dan and Susanna to destroy the cantata, or at least to keep it hidden. He could have spared himself, and his faith, this embarrassment. If only he'd seen and understood.

> "The family involved wishes to remain anonymous," said Frederic Augustus Fournier, Centennial Professor at Yale University, who was empowered to speak for the family. "The artifact was stumbled upon while family members were clearing the home of deceased relations. It was discovered in a piano bench . . ."

On and on the story went, sparing no detail.

> "At my suggestion, the family has decided to bring the artifact into the light of day, auction it at Sotheby's, and donate the proceeds to charity. By this means, the artifact, despite its dismaying polemical overtones, can itself be put to good use."

Who was Frederic Fournier, to determine what constituted *good use*?

> "My colleagues and I have completed an extensive research process to authenticate the artifact. Sotheby's has examined this research and also independently confirmed the artifact's authenticity."

Mueller was confident that Dan's research, and that of his colleagues, was thorough and reliable. The *artifact*, as both the reporter and Fournier persisted in calling it, would be auctioned in London in the spring. The artifact's value at auction was difficult to determine, Fournier noted, because nothing like this had ever been auctioned before. Nonetheless there was already tremendous interest from around the world, et cetera, et cetera.

The news story was accompanied by an opinion piece by one of the newspaper's music critics. The purpose of this essay was to inform readers that the unenlightened beliefs of long ago weren't pertinent to our appreciation of masterpieces of art from the past. We listeners and viewers of today should simply enjoy the beauty of any music, of any art form, and ignore the now-irrelevant context of its creation.

What claptrap. No Bach cantata was an *artifact*.

Mueller felt as if the blood had drained out of him. How was he to reconcile himself to this appalling work? It forced him to confront again a question he'd spent tremendous energy, over many years, attempting to suppress: How much had his church, his heritage, his faith, contributed to what happened in the war?

Because he kept up on all things German, he knew that current research demonstrated overwhelmingly that, contrary to the common postwar myth, the vast majority of Nazis and their followers were *not* in fact anti-Christian. A great many Christian parishioners were members of the Nazi party, and the party's long-term plans for the Reich included a restructured Christianity.

Hardly anyone ever talked about this. Rarely even raised the issue. Were they ashamed?

Shame was a strong motivator, he knew from his years of providing pastoral care.

Mueller also knew that church leaders, Protestant and Catholic both, had spoken out against the Nazis' so-called euthanasia program, the widespread murder of the disabled. As a result, the program had been curtailed.

The overwhelming majority of church leaders had said nothing, however, to help their Jewish neighbors.

This past summer, Mueller had been devastated by his visit to Buchenwald. He hadn't been able to put what he saw into any kind of perspective or understanding.

After his time in Weimar, he'd returned to Leipzig to visit a colleague at the theological school of the university. Together they'd gone on a day trip to Dresden, to see the Frauenkirche, destroyed during the war and now spectacularly restored. Mueller wasn't moved by the church. With its overly brilliant colors, it seemed fake, more like a Disneyland attraction than a historic house of worship.

Afterward he and his friend had walked to the nearby Kreuzkirche, on the Old Market Square. Outside, a plaque on the wall of the church caught his attention. He'd been so touched by the words that he'd taken a photo of the plaque with his phone. He still remembered much of it:

---

IN SHAME AND SORROW CHRISTIANS KEEP IN MEMORY
THE JEWISH CITIZENS OF THIS CITY.
IN 1933, 4675 JEWS LIVED IN DRESDEN. IN 1945 IT WAS 70.
WE WERE SILENT AS THEIR HOUSES OF WORSHIP BLAZED . . .
WE DID NOT RECOGNIZE THEM AS OUR BROTHERS AND SISTERS.
WE ASK FOR FORGIVENESS.

---

Maybe he was wrong, in his wish that the cantata had remained concealed. From his work with parishioners, he knew that bringing painful facts into the light could heal the soul.

Susanna Kessler had found the cantata—where? He checked the article. In a piano bench. Mueller's family secrets were in a shoe box under the bed. He could bring them out, too.

Yes, he decided as he mulled this over, the time had come for show-and-tell. He'd display his family photos on the bulletin board in the church basement. He would discuss them, as well as the newly discovered Bach cantata, in his sermon this Sunday. He'd encourage others to put similar family photos on the bulletin board.

His parishioners wouldn't be pleased about it. Too often recently, his role as a pastor seemed to have devolved into being upbeat, reassuring, and always ready with a smile.

But in truth it wasn't his job—or at least it wasn't his only job—to make his parishioners happy.

# Chapter 54

The auctioneer banged his gavel on Lot 186, a letter from Ludwig van Beethoven to the manager of the Court Opera Houses in Vienna. "Sold, to the online bidder, for one hundred and sixty thousand pounds."

Keeping herself occupied, Susanna made a note of the price in her catalog. The auction continued. Eighteen more lots to go, before *her* lot. She sat in the sales room of Sotheby's on New Bond Street in London. Concealed behind the building's historic façade, the room was sleek and high-tech. Echoes of tradition and stateliness were provided by architectural ornaments, such as the moldings on the ceiling and the doorways. Along the front of the room and down one side, on desklike raised platforms, Sotheby's officials were positioned at landline telephones, covering their mouths as they talked.

The following lots sold in brisk order.

"And so, ladies and gentlemen," said the auctioneer, "we reach the end of today's sale of fine musical manuscripts." He was about forty, dark hair brushed back, lithe body relaxed. He wore a dark suit, white shirt, and gray tie. He was alert, animated, and responsive to every detail around him. He was also supremely confident, a benign ruler surveying his kingdom.

His realm was surprisingly varied: an older man in a plaid jacket obsessively studied the catalog, holding it close to his face. A dashing, bearded man stood at the side as if showing off his striped fisherman's shirt. A sprinkling of women who could pass for fashion models sat at the edge of their chairs. A clique of gentlemen in baggy suits exuded a weary sense that this auction was all in a day's work for them; Susanna concluded they were professional art and manuscript dealers. A teenage girl with a nose ring, arms tightly crossed, clothing skimpy, focused a hostile glare at the innocent-looking middle-aged couple beside her. People entered the room, others left.

"We'll proceed directly to our final event of the day. This, of course, is the lot we've all been waiting for." Sotheby's had printed a special booklet about the cantata, providing illustrations of several pages from the manuscript and featuring brief scholarly essays about its authenticity and provenance. "A flagship lot, as we say in the business," the auctioneer added.

He was having fun, and why not? On any given day a river of life flowed through his hands, the creations of humanity—paintings, sculpture, furniture, pottery, stained glass, books, manuscripts. Items that represented heartbreak or happiness, dreams fulfilled or defeated, and hard cash. Susanna had brought her contribution, too.

"And here we have it."

The first page of the cantata appeared on the large screen to his right.

"This artifact is the full-length, complete autograph composing score of a previously unknown Leipzig church cantata by Johann Sebastian Bach . . ." The auctioneer gave a description of the autograph and its condition. He used the word *artifact* as if it provided a shield against the cantata's horrific text.

When Sotheby's first announced the pending sale several months earlier, an uproar had ensued. The German government had protested, demanding the return of stolen German property. The descendants of the Mendelssohn family had made inquiries because of Fanny Mendelssohn Hensel's handwriting on the wrapper, indicating her, and their, previous ownership. How had the manuscript ended up being owned by the Genslers in Weimar, they wondered. This was a question that couldn't be answered.

Frederic Fournier had handled the German government adroitly, through a highly publicized accusation: first you murder the owners, then you claim possession of their property. The German government dropped its demand.

Fournier went to Berlin and met with a representative of the Mendelssohn family, and he persuaded the family to take the same approach to the cantata as Susanna did: she wasn't going to profit from it personally, and neither should they. The family's endorsement of the auction was specified in the catalog. The issue of whether the family actually had any legal claim to the manuscript was ignored (and had in any event, through their endorsement of the sale, become moot).

Occupied as she was with her own work, Susanna had followed the developments from afar. For the ability to do this, she was grateful to Frederic Augustus Fournier, seated near the front of the room. At Sotheby's, only Ian McCloud, director of the department of books and manuscripts, knew her identity, and he would preserve her anonymity, as was customary in the auction business.

Fournier never referred to Susanna as the *owner* of the artifact. She was *the anonymous consignor*. Who did own the artifact? Apparently no one. It was something called *an orphan work*, according to Fournier and his attorney. They'd somehow convinced the IRS that Susanna certainly didn't own it, and her uncle hadn't owned it, and besides, the funds realized from its sale were to be given to tax-exempt charities.

Because the sale was to benefit charity, Sotheby's had agreed to waive the usual seller's premium, or commission. Sotheby's would, however, receive its customary commission from the buyer, so the company's work wasn't without remuneration.

The catalog gave the estimate for the artifact as between £7 million and £8 million.

"We'll begin at six million, five hundred thousand pounds."

A near-silent pandemonium broke out, paddles raised here, there, Susanna unable to track them. But the auctioneer found them effortlessly, the numbers going up and up, seven million six, seven, eight—*in the room, from the telephone,* and *in the room* once more. Eight million one, two . . . the monetary figures became a kind of code. Eight million eight, nine, nine million, nine million one, a barrage of numbers spinning around her.

She focused on the small overhead screens. Whoever was operating them fell behind, and abruptly the number was twelve million and rising, fifteen million, a swirl of numbers. "Sixteen million six online," the auctioneer said, ever affable and calm, as if he were at a garden party. "Sixteen million seven, eight . . ."

At the Sotheby's telephone bank in front, an older woman raised her hand. She was demure, wearing pearls and a sweater set.

"With Lily on the telephone," the auctioneer said, acknowledging her, "eighteen million. Thank you, Lily."

At the end of Susanna's row, a woman on a cell phone, taking directions from whoever was on the phone with her, began bidding. She had short dark hair, and wore a plain black blouse and skirt. Her entire body looked tense, as if she'd been entrusted with responsibilities she wasn't certain she could handle, now that the moment to exercise them had arrived. She gripped the phone like a lifeline, pressing it hard against her ear.

"Eighteen million one, to the lady on the cell phone at the end of the row," the auctioneer said. Others bid against her: "Eighteen million two online . . . three, four . . . nineteen million—"

The woman on the cell phone raised her hand again and again.

Susanna glanced at Fournier on the far side of the room. From the way he positioned himself, turned aside from the woman with the cell phone instead of eyeing her as the others did, Susanna guessed that she represented his interests. From hints he'd given, Susanna suspected that Fournier had put together a consortium of wealthy supporters of Yale who would purchase the manuscript as a group and donate it, in his honor, to the Beinecke Library. *Be prepared*, his motto, had been mentioned somewhat frequently by him during the dinner they'd shared last evening.

"Twenty-one million with Owen on the telephone . . ."

Attention shifted to the phone banks, to find Owen. He sat two places down from Lily. He was in his twenties, and he looked as if his tie was too tight. Susanna again glanced at Fournier, who—as the auctioneer said, "Twenty-two million, six hundred thousand, for Lily on the telephone"—appeared confused.

Within seconds the auctioneer said, "Twenty-four million pounds, do I have . . . twenty-four and a half, thank you, Lily . . . I have twenty-five million online . . ."

Audience members pointed to the phone bank, where Owen was calling for attention. "Twenty-six million from Owen. Thank you, my dear audience members, for the prompt." The auctioneer was having so much fun, he looked as if he were performing the role of an auctioneer in a play.

As the number went over twenty-six million, five hundred thousand, the woman with the cell phone put her phone in her lap. Fournier looked incredulous. The numbers had spun away from his control.

The ever-cool and concise Lily at the phone bank raised her pencil and kept it raised. Bidding for the cantata had become a contest between Owen and Lily, with numbers that shocked and shocked again, through the required increments, in a battle of raised pencils and hand waves—twenty-eight million, twenty-nine million, thirty-two million.

And then, stillness.

The auctioneer gazed around the room. He studied Owen and Lily. His serenity appeared boundless. After some time passed, he said, ever so gently, "Fair warning, Owen."

Owen was talking intently on the telephone, his body arched around, concealing the phone and hiding his conversation. At last he straightened, his dark hair disheveled, a look of exhaustion on his face. He shook his head no.

"Sold, ladies and gentlemen, for thirty-two million pounds, to Lily's telephone bidder." The auctioneer banged the gavel. "Lily?"

Lily gave the bidder's registration number.

"Thank you very much, Lily. And thank *you* very much, ladies and gentlemen. That concludes our business for this afternoon."

Applause filled the room.

The overhead screens provided monetary conversions into several currencies. At £32 million, the cantata had sold for more than $49 million.

Susanna felt dazed.

Fournier rose. A crowd gathered around him. He bowed, one hand across his chest, signaling his modesty and gratitude. Susanna saw that his smile was false. He was putting on a show of happiness at the extraordinary amount of money the cantata had yielded.

People organized themselves to leave. Fournier moved from

one area of the room to another, speaking with acquaintances. He nodded, he frowned . . . he was gathering facts, evaluating clues from gossiping dealers and other experts in the room. Bound by standard confidentiality agreements, Sotheby's wouldn't reveal who had purchased the cantata.

Now Fournier and Ian McCloud were leaving the room, surrounded by a flow of conversation. Fournier gave Susanna a sharp nod, as if he himself were making an auction bid: their signal that she should make her way upstairs, where McCloud was hosting a private reception.

She didn't share the elevator with them.

Upstairs, Fournier was waiting for her.

"My dear, my dear." He looked shaken. "I don't know what happened. And old Ian can't and won't, even for a friend like me, reveal a thing. Very smug he's looking, too. He certainly turned a tidy profit for his company today."

Susanna followed his gaze. McCloud was in the center of a crowd of company executives, accepting congratulations. In his late fifties, going a little soft in the middle, hair thinning, McCloud radiated an aura of trustworthiness. The Sotheby's sales commission on the cantata would come to almost £4 million, more than $6 million, added to the so-called hammer price.

"All I know so far is Owen was on the telephone with a Japanese individual. Owen covered his mouth with his hand, but my source was sitting nearby and definitely heard him speaking Japanese. I'm assuming Owen was on the phone with a certain hedge-fund fellow, well known to me, a secretive collector. Someone I could have worked with, even though he was outside my original plans. Why did he, too, drop out?" Fournier asked, exasperated. "What's a few million either way to a person like that? Idiot. Now I've ended up in a situation where I've got not one single clue to the identity of the person who acquired the manuscript."

It could be anyone, Susanna realized. Maybe even a neo-Nazi, after all.

"I need a drink," Fournier said.

They walked to the drinks table, and Susanna asked for tonic and lime. She wasn't in the mood for alcohol. Her sense of remorse grew. Had she made the right decision, bringing the cantata here?

Hors d'oeuvres were served by the black-clad wait staff. Gradually other guests arrived, mostly dealers and journalists. Susanna, reluctant to have herself identified even in an introduction, stayed a bit apart from the crowd, and for now at least, Fournier kept her company, as if they were simply companions for the afternoon. He related to her the names and occupations of the people he recognized.

A woman with dark blond hair cut into a pageboy style, and wearing a loose, flowing jacket, approached them. "Frederick Fournier, am I right?" Her manner was exuberant. Her accent, American. "I'm Amy Cowden, from *The Washington Post.*"

Greetings were exchanged, and Frederic glided over Susanna's name.

"I'm wondering what you think about the artifact going to the Holocaust Museum in Washington."

Fournier paused. "Sorry?"

"Forgive me, I thought you knew."

"We've been rather on our own up here—escaping the vultures of the press, if you don't mind my putting it that way," he said, teasing her but also buying time to think this through, Susanna understood. "So what's this rumor you've heard, Ms. Cowden?"

"No rumor. My information is from a direct source. I'm told the artifact will be sent to the Holocaust Museum on permanent loan."

Fournier said nothing. Then he exclaimed: "The perfect place for it!"

"The donor, if that's the correct word for him—or her—" Ms. Cowden said, "will be making it available to approved scholars only. No publication, no performances, no recordings."

Susanna almost took Fournier's arm to steady herself, she felt so buoyed by her good luck. The cantata had found another guardian, someone with the financial means to protect it, and to allow it to be studied but not exploited.

"Is that so. Well, well," Fournier said. "Thank you for taking the time to let me know. Tell me, are you based in London?"

"No, I'm here on vacation, but my editor . . ."

Fournier elicited a recitation of the ins and outs of Ms. Cowden's career as if he had nothing else on his mind. Soon other guests joined them, and the conversation shifted to a much-heralded auction of contemporary art that was coming up the following week. Fournier and Susanna stepped aside, Fournier turning his back to the crowd.

"There's no cause for concern," he said, although he appeared crestfallen. "No performing, no recording, no publishing—the Holocaust Museum would never agree to such an arrangement. The very notion is absurd. The Holocaust Museum receives government funds. I suspect this plan would be against the First Amendment. Would the museum's directors actually violate the Constitution of the United States? No, they would not. I'm guessing the buyer hasn't checked with the museum. The directors of the Holocaust Museum have always supported full transparency. I'm certain they understand that great art belongs to the world. Or at least that they will understand after I've told them. I'll fly to Washington tomorrow." At the prospect, he rubbed his hands together almost gleefully. "No worries, Susanna. I'll salvage this situation. What's important now is to pretend that this was exactly what I wanted all along. The Holocaust Museum in Washington— *brilliant*, as the British would say."

Susanna perceived that she was receiving a rather remarkable education from Frederic Augustus Fournier. Whether she'd ever be able to put these tutorials to good use, she doubted.

"Smiles on our faces, et cetera. Over forty-nine million dollars for charity, and any way you look at it, the day's been a success. We have cause for celebration."

He went to the center of the room. He took a glass of champagne from a passing server. He silenced the room and gave a toast:

"To Ian McCloud, whose perspicacity and patience has led us to this astonishing day. On behalf of the anonymous consigner . . ."

Susanna moved farther away from the group and stood alone near the windows. This was no longer her battle.

She checked her phone. Dan had sent her a text, *Thinking of you*. She looked forward to briefing him in full when she returned home.

She had more than $49 million to give to charity. That figure constituted almost five years of what the Barstow Foundation gave away. She had work to do, the type of work that filled her with energy and determination.

Although she'd had no alcohol, she felt light-headed. The continuing toasts and laughter on the other side of the room began to seem far away. She had a sense of herself outside time . . . linked to Sara Itzig Levy and her husband entertaining Beethoven in their *palais* on the Spree, to Fanny Mendelssohn Hensel directing her Sunday concerts, to Ernst and Gertrude Gensler talking on the terrace of their home in Weimar, and to her own family, in the town of Eger in the Sudetenland. One line, one history, one story, each element part of the whole.

She experienced a startling perception of freedom, as if her true self were bursting from an outdated façade. Her years of mourning were over. The rest of her life was about to begin.

## Historical Note and Sources

*And After the Fire* is a combination of fact and fiction, of characters real and imagined. The lost work of art that unites the novel's historical strands is fictional, but its content is plausible in every detail, and its quotations from the writings of Martin Luther are actual. Like other Baroque composers, Johann Sebastian Bach did in fact create cantatas with polemical religious content; this was only one aspect of his work, and by no means the totality of his endeavors.

Sara Itzig Levy and her husband, Fanny Mendelssohn Hensel and Wilhelm Hensel, Paul Mendelssohn-Bartholdy, and their family and friends, are historical figures, as is Wilhelm Friedemann Bach. I have striven to portray their lives realistically, based on what is known about them. (Their interactions with the fictional cantata are, of course, invented.) Most scholars assume that Wilhelm Friedemann Bach's *Cantilena nuptiarum* was written for the marriage of Sara Itzig to Samuel Salomon Levy. On the website of the Leo Baeck Institute in New York, one can view Sara's and Samuel's entries in the *Stammbuch* (*Album Amicorum*) of Mirjam Oppenheimer Itzig.

Dr. Joseph Werner, his daughter Dr. Gertrude Gensler, and son-in-law, Ernst Gensler, as well as Eva Reinhardt, are fictional. The description of their home is based on actual locations in and around Weimar.

In the late eighteenth and early nineteenth centuries, Jewish women were at the center of a salon culture that developed in Berlin and allowed the mingling of Christians and Jews, aristocrats and commoners, for discussions and musical performances. This was a culture fraught with contradictions, however, and anti-Jewish bias lurked beneath the surface. For example, although Wilhelm von Humboldt publicly worked for the legal emancipation of Jews, his letters reveal strong anti-Jewish prejudice. The incident involving Count Achim von Arnim at Sara Levy's home in 1811 was among the great scandals of the era.

The Mendelssohn bank was founded in 1795 by Joseph Mendelssohn, son of the philosopher Moses Mendelssohn. His brother Abraham joined the firm about a decade later. The bank prospered, joining the ranks of the most important European banking houses. Paul Mendelssohn-Barholdy expanded its work into Russia. The bank was liquidated in 1938, under pressure from the Nazi regime to "Aryanize."

Fanny Mendelssohn Hensel died just as she was beginning to publish her work, and she was essentially forgotten after her death. During the past twenty-five years, however, her compositions and her story have gradually been rediscovered. Today, thanks to many excellent recordings of her music as well as the superlative biography by R. Larry Todd, *Fanny Hensel: The Other Mendelssohn*, she is beginning to receive the high recognition she deserves. Wilhelm Hensel, her husband, was a well-known artist, especially admired for his portrait drawings.

Richard Wagner did indeed publish a screed in which he condemns the music of Felix Mendelssohn because of Mendelssohn's Jewish heritage.

The Berlin Jewish orphanage established by Baruch Auerbach and endowed by Sara Levy remained in existence until November 1942, when the last remaining children were deported on the twenty-third *Osttransport* from Berlin and murdered at Auschwitz. The Hitler Youth then requisitioned the building.

The contemporary characters in the novel, including Susanna

Kessler and her family, Daniel Erhardt, Scott Schiffman, Robertson Barstow, Dietrich Bauer, and Frederic Augustus Fournier, are fictional. Dietrich Bauer's story is very loosely based on the controversial case of the German musicologist Hans Heinrich Eggebrecht, who died in 1999.

In portraying the world of musicology, I have been inspired by the many dedicated scholars I've been lucky enough to meet over the years. Although some characters in *And After the Fire* may bear minor, superficial similarities to individuals I have met, they are creations of my imagination. Scholarly groups do exist to study the history of music from a religiously devotional perspective. For an overview of such a Bach group's activities, see *Theologische Bachforschung Heute: Dokumentation und Bibliographie der Internationalen Arbeitsgemeinschaft für theologische Bachforschung 1976–1996*, edited by Renate Steiger.

As I researched the story, I relied on letters, diaries, and memoirs as well as scholarly books and articles. I traveled to Berlin, Leipzig, and Weimar several times to do on-site research. I visited Buchenwald twice and have re-created it in the novel as carefully and truthfully as possible. The American military did, in fact, take German civilians on tours of the camp at the end of the war. More information about the camp can be found on the website: http://www.buchenwald.de/en/69/

The other materials most helpful to me in my research are listed here by topic.

### On the Jews of Germany before the Holocaust:

- *The Pity of It All: A Portrait of the German-Jewish Epoch, 1743–1933*, by Amos Elon
- *Der Berliner Salon im 19. Jahrhundert (1780–1914)*, by Petra Wilhelmy
- *Jewish High Society in Old Regime Berlin*, by Deborah Hertz
- *How Jews Became Germans: The History of Conversion and Assimilation in Berlin*, by Deborah Hertz

- *Jewish Women in Enlightenment Berlin*, by Natalie Naimark-Goldberg
- *Jewish Women and Their Salons: The Power of Conversation*, by Emily D.
  Bilski and Emily Braun
- *Profiles in Diversity: Jews in a Changing Europe, 1750–1870*, edited by
  Frances Malino and David Sorken
- *The Berlin Jewish Community: Enlightenment, Family, and Crisis, 1770–1830*,
  by Steven M. Lowenstein
- *The Warburgs*, by Ron Chernow
- *Jews in Berlin*, edited by Andreas Nachama, Julius H. Schoeps, and
  Hermann Simon; translated by Michael S. Cullen and Allison Brown
- "A Lost Paradise of a Female Culture? Some Critical Questions
  Regarding the Scholarship on Late Eighteenth- and Early
  Nineteenth-Century German Salons," by Ulrike Weckel, in *German
  History* 18 (2000)
- *The Education of Fanny Lewald: An Autobiography*, translated, edited, and
  annotated by Hanna Ballin Lewis
- *Giacomo Meyerbeer: A Life in Letters*, edited by Heinz and Gudrun Becker;
  translated by Mark Violette

## On World War II and the Holocaust:

- *The Engineers of the "Final Solution": Topf & Sons—Builders of the Auschwitz
  Ovens*, accompanying book to an exhibition of the Buchenwald and
  Mittelbau-Dora Memorials Foundation in connection with the Jewish
  Museum Berlin and the Auschwitz-Birkenau State Museum
- *Ordinary Men*, by Christopher R. Browning
- *The Eichmann Trial*, by Deborah E. Lipstadt
- *Neighbors*, by Jan T. Gross
- *The Rise and Fall of the Third Reich*, by William L. Shirer
- *Atlas of the Holocaust*, by Martin Gilbert
- *Liberating the Concentration Camps: GIs Remember*, a publication of the

National Museum of American Jewish Military History
- *Liberation 1945*, a publication of the United States Holocaust Memorial Museum
- *1945: The Year of Liberation*, a publication of the United States Holocaust Memorial Museum
- *The Rape of Europa*, by Lynn H. Nicholas

## Concerning Sara Levy:

- *"Ein förmlicher Sebastian und Philipp Emanuel Bach-Kultus": Sara Levy und ihr musikalisches Wirken*, by Peter Wollny
- "Sara Levy and the Making of Musical Taste in Berlin," by Peter Wollny, in *Musical Quarterly* 77 (1993)
- "A Bach Cult in Late-Eighteenth-Century Berlin: Sara Levy's Musical Salon," by Christoph Wolff, in *Bulletin of the American Academy of Arts and Sciences* 58 (2005)
- *"Bach-Kultus" in Berlin um 1800, Sara Levy und ihr musikalish-literarischer Salon*, Ausstellung im Gartenhaus des Mendelssohn-Hauses Leipzig, by Peter Wollny and Dagmar Paetzold
- *Paul Erman: Ein Berliner Gelehrtenleben 1764–1851*, by Wilhelm Erman

To access the *Stammbuch (Album Amicorum)* of Mirjam Oppenheimer Itzig, with its entries by Sara Levy and Samuel Salomon Levy, in the collection of the Leo Baeck Institute, New York, see: https://www.lbi.org/digibaeck/results/?term=Itzig&qtype=basic&dtype=any&filter=All&paging=25

In my research on the Mendelssohn Bartholdy family, I particularly relied on:

- *Fanny Hensel: The Other Mendelssohn*, by R. Larry Todd
- *Felix Mendelssohn: A Life in Music*, by R. Larry Todd

I also used the following:

- *Lea Mendelssohn Bartholdy: Ewig die deine; Briefe von Lea Mendelssohn Bartholdy an Henriette von Pereira-Arnstein*, edited by Wolfgang Dinglinger and Rudolf Elvers
- *Die Familie Mendelssohn: Stammbaum von Moses Mendelssohn bis zur siebenten Generation*, by Hans-Günter Klein
- *Felix Mendelssohn: A Life in Letters*, edited by Rudolf Elvers; translated by Craig Tomlinson
- *The Price of Assimilation: Felix Mendelssohn and the Nineteenth-Century Anti-Semitic Tradition*, by Jeffrey S. Sposato
- *Bach in Berlin: Nation and Culture in Mendelssohn's Revival of the St. Matthew Passion*, by Celia Applegate
- *The Mendelssohns of Jaegerstrasse*, an exhibition at the Mendelssohn-Gesellschaft, Jaegerstrasse 51, Berlin
- *The Mendelssohn Family (1729–1847): From Letters and Journals*, by Sebastian Hensel
- "Versteckt in der Geschichte—Bartholdys Meierei," by Elke von Nieding, in *Mendelssohn Studien* 15 (2007)
- *Europa im Porträt: Zeichnungen von Wilhelm Hensel 1794–1861*, by Cécile Lowenthal-Hensel and Sigrid Gräfin von Strachwitz
- *The Letters of Fanny Hensel to Felix Mendelssohn, Collected, Edited and Translated with Introductory Essays and Notes*, by Marcia J. Citron (Fanny Mendelssohn Hensel's letters in the novel are drawn from this collection.)

A fascinating examination of the architecture of Leipzigerstrasse 3 and the acoustics of the *Gartensaal* is available at: http://www.phy.duke.edu/~dtl/89S/restrict/Gartensaal/Gartensaal.html

To view the Mendelssohn family's *Gartenzeitung*, see: http://digital.staatsbibliothek-berlin.de/werkansicht/?PPN=PPN690124759&LOGID=LOG_0001

On Johann Sebastian Bach and Wilhelm Friedemann Bach:

- *Johann Sebastian Bach: The Learned Musician*, by Christoph Wolff
- *Evening in the Palace of Reason: Bach Meets Frederick the Great in the Age of Enlightenment*, by James R. Gaines
- *Katalog der Wasserzeichen in Bachs Originalhandschriften*, in two volumes, by Yoshitake Kobayashi
- *Melodic Index to the Works of Johann Sebastian Bach*, compiled by May deForest McAll
- "Wilhelm Friedemann Bach's Halle Performances of Cantatas by His Father," by Peter Wollny, in *Bach Studies* 2, edited by Daniel R. Melamed
- "Descendants of Wilhelm Friedemann Bach in the United States," by Christoph Wolff, in *Bach Perspectives* 5, edited by Stephen A. Crist

Bach Digital, http://www.bach-digital.de, is a treasure trove of information.

For detailed information about the properties of iron-gall ink, see http://irongallink.org/igi_index.html

On Martin Luther and anti-Judaism, my research was aided by the many terrific studies released in recent years by the Lutheran publisher Fortress Press. Especially helpful were:

- *Martin Luther, the Bible, and the Jewish People: A Reader*, edited by Brooks Schramm and Kirsi I. Stjerna
- *The Roots of Anti-Semitism in the Age of Renaissance and Reformation*, by Heiko A. Oberman

The collected writings of Martin Luther, including *Von den Juden und ihre Lügen* ("On the Jews and Their Lies," 1543), are available online at: http://www.lutherdansk.dk/WA/D.%20Martin%20Luthers%20Werke, %20Weimarer%20Ausgabe%20-%20WA.htm

Bach owned two massive collections of Luther's German writings, the

*Jena Edition* and the *Altenburg Edition*, both of which included Luther's 1543 treatise *On the Jews and Their Lies*. For information on Bach's personal library, I relied on *Bachs Theologische Bibliothek*, by Robin A. Leaver.

On the reception of Lutheran anti-Judaism in Bach's religious culture:

- *Lutheranism, Anti-Judaism and Bach's St. John Passion*, by Michael Marissen
- "The Character and Sources of the Anti-Judaism in Bach's Cantata 46," by Michael Marissen, in *Harvard Theological Review* 96 (2003)

In addition I relied on:

- *Complicity in the Holocaust: Churches and Universities in Nazi Germany*, by Robert P. Ericksen (which also provides an overview of the successful protests by church leaders against the Nazis' so-called euthanasia program)
- *Constantine's Sword: The Church and the Jews*, by James Carroll
- *Anti-Judaism: The Western Tradition*, by David Nirenberg
- *The Holy Reich: Nazi Conceptions of Christianity, 1919–1945*, by Richard Steigmann-Gall

On America and the Holocaust:

- *Beyond Belief: The American Press & the Coming of the Holocaust 1933–1945*, by Deborah E. Lipstadt
- *The Holocaust in American Life*, by Peter Novick
- *The Abandonment of the Jews*, by David S. Wyman

*The Lost: A Search for Six of Six Million*, by Daniel Mendelsohn, is the most moving family memoir I know. With its grace and insight, its prism of shifting perspectives, and its gradual unfolding of the past, *The Lost* is an inspiration on the craft of writing.

One of the joys of researching this novel was listening to the music of Johann Sebastian Bach. My favorite recordings (remarkably similar to those enjoyed by Daniel Erhardt in the novel) include: the oboe concertos recorded by Marcel Ponseele with Ensemble Il Gardinello; the cello suites, by Jean-Guihen Queyras; the violin concertos, by Amandine Beyer with Gli Incogniti; Jakob Lindberg playing the lute music; the 1998 (as opposed to their 2013) recording of the viola da gamba sonatas, by Vittorio and Lorenzo Ghielmi. One place I do differ from Daniel Erhardt is that I prefer the Simone Dinnerstein performance of the Goldberg Variations. For the Fifth Brandenburg Concerto, I was drawn to the performance by Frans Brüggen, Sigiswald Kuijken, and Gustav Leonhardt with the Leonhardt Consort. For the aria "Mache dich" from the *St. Matthew Passion*, the performance by Peter Kooy with the Orchestra of the Eighteenth Century, directed by Frans Brüggen. For the three (real) Bach cantatas referred to in the novel: *Was Gott tut, daß ist wohlgetan* (BWV 100), as performed by the Bach Collegium Japan, directed by Masaaki Suzuki; *Vergnügte Ruh, beliebte Seelenlust* (BWV 170), by Andreas Scholl with the Orchestre du Collegium Vocale, directed by Philippe Herreweghe; *Gottes Zeit ist die allerbeste Zeit* (BWV 106), by the Ricercar Consort, directed by Philippe Pierlot, the 2004 (as opposed to their 1990) recording. A final favorite: the concertos for two and three harpsichords, by Musica Amphion, directed by Pieter-Jan Belder.

I've also discovered the music of Felix Mendelssohn and Fanny Hensel. For the works mentioned in the novel, the recordings I like best include, for Felix Mendelssohn: *Ein Sommernachtstraum* ("A Midsummer Night's Dream"), performed by the Silver Garburg Piano Duo; the *Variations concertantes* in D major, op. 17, performed by Nancy Green and R. Larry Todd in a CD whose booklet contains detailed historical notes by Todd and also features many illustrations, including reproductions of Felix's watercolors. For Fanny Mendelssohn Hensel: Joanne Polk's recordings of the solo piano pieces; and *Das Jahr*, performed by Els Biesemans.

# Acknowledgments

I am indebted to Professor Dr. Peter Wollny, director of the Bach-Archiv in Leipzig, who discussed at length his research on Sara Itzig Levy. Dr. Michael Maul of the Bach-Archiv described the experience of discovering an unknown work by Johann Sebastian Bach—something that he has had the great good fortune to do. Dr. Daniel Melamed of Indiana University, Dr. Stephen Crist of Emory University, the Rev. Dr. Robin Leaver of the Yale Institute of Sacred Music, Dr. Joshua Rifkin of Boston University, and Dr. Barbara Milewski of Swarthmore College shared their knowledge. I'm especially grateful to Dr. Natalie Naimark-Goldberg of Bar-Ilan University for discussing her as-yet-unpublished research on Sara Levy's involvement with the Baruch Auerbach orphanage in Berlin.

Anita Nager, Carole Landman, and Marnie Imhoff spoke with me about the workings of family foundations. Jonathan Greenberg introduced me to the auction world. Margaret Holben Ellis, director of the Thaw Conservation Center at the Morgan Library, gave me a tour of the facility. (I am quick to note, however, that the MacLean Library in *And After the Fire* is very much its own, idiosyncratic institution, and any resemblance it might bear to the Morgan is purely coincidental.) Although I changed many details of her presentation,

Laurella Dotan provided the basis for Helen Krieger's bat mitzvah speech. Lucy Lang, BoHee Yoon, and Ariana Lindermayer gave cultural guidance as well as their example of professionalism and dedication. Denise Kahn guided my attempts to learn to play the piano. Theodore Feder advised me on art issues. Adam MacLean contributed his technical expertise. John Hargraves advised me to take the public bus to Buchenwald. The late Cynthia Rubin read an early draft, and her astute observations and eagle eye have enriched these pages. I miss her.

I am indebted to the staff of the Center for Jewish History, on West Sixteenth Street in New York, as well as to the librarians of the New York Public Library and the New York Society Library.

My cousin Lisa Hupf took the lead on investigating our family's history (which is not the history of Susanna Kessler's family), sparking a journey that led me, finally, to the site of a mass grave outside the town of Stryj, in Ukraine. My mother, Nancy Belfer, added her reflections and memories. Rivka Schiller did terrific work translating family letters.

Part of this novel was written in Cambridge, England, when my husband was a Visiting Fellow at the Woolf Institute. I thank Dr. Lars Fischer for the invitation and the institute's entire staff for welcoming me. I particularly thank Trisha Kessler and Dr. Edward D. Kessler, director of the institute, for their hospitality and friendship.

Any mistakes in the novel are my own.

Emma Sweeney receives my heartfelt gratitude for her wisdom, guidance, encouragement, and remarkable dedication to this project. Kira Watson assisted with kindness and grace.

Claire Wachtel, my brilliant editor, read innumerable drafts of the novel and discussed it with me for hours. At every step in the process, from first consideration to published book, she brought to the novel her astonishing discernment, acute insight, and fierce commitment. I am forever grateful.

Also at HarperCollins, the marvelous Hannah Wood soothed my nerves and answered my questions at a guilt-inducing pace. Milan Bozic designed the gorgeous jacket. Lydia Weaver, Jessica Shatan Heslin, John McGee, Heather Drucker, Amanda Ainsworth, and Renata Marchione generously contributed their many talents. I especially thank Jonathan Burnham for his faith in this novel, and Kathy Schneider for her support.

Many friends offered good cheer and companionship during the years I worked on this book, and I give them my thanks. Beth Gutcheon, Ida Nicolaisen, and the Buffalo Girls (you know who you are) helped me to navigate my way through the shoals of my chosen profession.

With their brightness and joy, Lucas and Kaleigh give me hope for the future. They and their parents, Tristan Church and Lisa Shannon Church, enhance my life.

Once again, above all I thank Michael Marissen. And once again, he knows the reasons why.

## About the Author

Lauren Belfer is the *New York Times* bestselling author of *City of Light*, a *New York Times* Notable Book, and *A Fierce Radiance*, a *Washington Post* Best Novel and an NPR Mystery of the Year. She lives in New York City.

Insights,
Interviews
& More . . .

# Meet Lauren Belfer

*Sigrid Estrada*

Lauren Belfer grew up in Buffalo, New York, and decided to become a writer when she was six years old. By the time she was in high school, her literary work was receiving rejection letters from all the best publications. After graduating from college, she worked as a file clerk at an art gallery, a paralegal at a law firm, an assistant photo editor at a newspaper, a fact checker at magazines, and as a researcher and associate producer on documentary films. Her first published short story was rejected forty-two times before it found an editor who loved it. Her second published story was rejected only twenty-seven times. Lauren's debut novel, *City of Light*, was a *New York Times* bestseller, as well as a *New York Times* Notable Book and a *Library Journal* Best Book. Her second novel, *A Fierce Radiance*, was named a *Washington Post* Best Novel, an NPR Best Mystery, and a *New York Times* Editors' Choice. *And After the Fire* received a National Jewish Book Award. She lives in New York City.

For more information about Lauren Belfer and her novels, please visit her website and follow her on Facebook:

*www.LaurenBelfer.com*
*www.facebook.com/AuthorLaurenBelfer*

☙

# Bringing Together Fact and Fiction in *And After the Fire*
## An Essay by the Author

About ten years ago, I received an announcement for an adult education class focusing on the music of Johann Sebastian Bach. Beyond what I'd learned in the piano lessons I'd been forced to take when I was growing up, I knew almost nothing about Bach's music. Nonetheless, I had a weird hunch that I should sign up for this class, that somehow it would turn out to be important to me. Acting on impulse, I sent in the registration form. And the class did turn out to be important to me, because that's where I met my husband.

What I discovered in that class surprised me. Bach's music is more transcendently beautiful than I'd ever imagined. But Bach was a committed Lutheran in eighteenth-century Germany—in fact, he was an ordained minister of music—and so some of his sacred music displays an edge of intolerance towards Catholics, Muslims, and Jews. I learned that many of his peers displayed similar attitudes, or worse, in their works. Much of my family was murdered during the Holocaust, and the religious prejudice inherent in some of Bach's sublime music was hard for me to come to terms with.

Perhaps because of my family's history,

I've always paid attention to news reports about paintings that were lost or stolen during World War II and are rediscovered decades later on the walls of museums, hidden in attics, or displayed in living rooms. The restitution of these works of art to their rightful owners had become a prominent issue by the time I was learning about Bach.

One evening as I was walking to the subway after class, I thought: What if I found a work of art that had been stolen from a Jewish family during World War II? Not a painting, but an unknown choral masterpiece, a cantata, by Johann Sebastian Bach. And what if its libretto was, by modern standards, inflammatory and, in a word, horrifying? How would I go about researching its history? What would I do with it?

For each of my novels, the moment of inspiration has come to me this way: I'm walking down the street, and all at once I feel as if a door in my mind is opening into another world.

I decided to begin *And After the Fire* with an American soldier discovering a fictional Bach manuscript in the ruins of Germany at the end of World War II. Then I set about creating a *provenance* for the unknown masterpiece, following it across the centuries from the time it was written by Johann Sebastian Bach, through the Holocaust, and into the present. I wanted all the novel's main characters, both real and imagined, to be united by their relationship to my fictional Bach manuscript. ▶

. . .

Over the years that I researched the novel, I became increasingly swept up in the magnificence of Bach's music. His compositions that might now be considered ethically troubling make up only a very small proportion of his more than 1,100 surviving works. I listened obsessively to recordings of the unproblematic majority: when I woke up in the morning, during meals, while I wrote, as I prepared for bed at night. His music offered consolation in times of stress or sadness, and accentuated joy during moments of happiness. I heard the music playing in my mind even when all was silent around me, its complex patterns spinning ever onward. I found myself especially drawn to the violin concertos, the sonatas for viola da gamba, and the Goldberg Variations. I wove my love of Bach's music into the lives of my characters, and gradually I began to think of the music itself as an integral part of the story.

As I read biographies about Johann Sebastian Bach, I learned that his eldest son, Wilhelm Friedemann Bach, was a tormented man; most likely an alcoholic, possibly someone we might nowadays diagnose as bipolar. He was extremely talented, but he quarreled with his employers continually and as a consequence had trouble holding onto jobs. Toward the end of his life, he washed up in Berlin, where he taught an adolescent girl from a prominent Jewish family to play the harpsichord.

This girl was Sara Itzig, who later married Samuel Salomon Levy. The more I read about Sara, the more I felt compelled to explore her world. She died in 1854 at the age of ninety-three, so her life spanned almost a century of tumultuous history. Her family included the composers Felix Mendelssohn and Fanny Hensel, whom she encouraged and counseled. Sara's influence continued far beyond her death, because she bequeathed her vast fortune to the Jewish orphanage of Berlin, which flourished until 1942, when its children and their teachers were sent to Auschwitz.

Historians tend to work from the perspective of the present, researching the past to determine how and why events unfolded the way they did. As a writer of historical fiction, I try to discover how people in the past felt as they lived from day to day, not knowing what the future would bring. To learn more about Sara and her family and friends, I sought out letters, diaries, newspapers, memoirs, and other documents that might capture what they were actually thinking and experiencing at the time. I examined paintings, drawings, and photographs to help me visualize the clothes they wore, the way they carried themselves and behaved, the carriages they used, the palaces and gardens where they spent their days.

On the surface, Sara Levy's milieu ▶

appeared glittering, cultured, and harmonious. The salons of Berlin were exceptional in the late eighteenth and early nineteenth centuries, I learned, because they were organized primarily by wealthy Jewish women; Christians and Jews, aristocrats and commoners, mingled freely at these gatherings. For those in a position to attend the salons, friendships had an opportunity to flourish amid discussions of art, music, and literature, as well as musical and theatrical performances.

But as I continued to read letters and diaries, I realized that the confidence Jews like Sara Levy felt regarding their place in German-speaking lands was misguided. Deep prejudice lurked beneath the surface. Sometimes hatred emerged violently, in murderous pogroms, and at other times insidiously, as with the notorious incident at Sara Levy's home in 1811, much discussed after it happened (and dramatized in *And After the Fire*). I wanted to bring Sara and her family and friends to life, to explore the compromises they made, and the assurances they gave themselves, as they tried to navigate a largely hostile society.

I visited Germany four times to research the novel. Because of my family's experiences in the war, I felt anxious planning a trip to Germany. When I arrived at my first stop, Berlin, however, I was surprised to find that I felt not only comfortable but very much at home. The Germans have done an exemplary job of confronting the Nazi era and attempting to atone for it. I walked for hours through Berlin's neighborhoods, projecting myself into the past, looking for clues to the lives of my characters, trying to conjure up their homes, the shops they might have visited, the routines they followed. I had Bach's music with me on my iPod wherever I went.

As I wove together the strands of the novel, intermingling chapters set in the past with those set in the present, I strove to make certain that each part of the story illuminated the other. My hope is that through the shifts between past and present, the reader will participate in the long sweep of history and find a new perspective on issues that are as compelling today as they were for Sara Levy and her family hundreds of years ago.

•  •  •

On my website, you'll find a link to a Spotify playlist I've created of the (ethically unproblematic) music by Johann Sebastian Bach, Felix Mendelssohn, and Fanny Mendelssohn Hensel that figures in *And After the Fire*. You will also find pictures of the real people and places that appear in the novel. I hope you'll enjoy exploring these resources.

*www.LaurenBelfer.com*

# A Conversation with Bach Scholar Michael Marissen

Lauren worked closely with her husband, the musicologist and Bach scholar Michael Marissen, to research *And After the Fire*. Michael is the Daniel Underhill Professor Emeritus of Music at Swarthmore College. Several of his books explore issues of religious polemic in classical music: *Lutheranism, Anti-Judaism, and Bach's St. John Passion*; *Tainted Glory in Handel's* Messiah; and *Bach & God*. Here, they talk about their experiences, as well as the joys and challenges of working together.

**Lauren:** *And After the Fire* was extremely difficult to write, touching as it does on fraught and often personally painful questions of art, ethics, war, and prejudice. In this interview, Michael and I would like to focus on other aspects of the book, the lighter aspects, if you will, and the joint explorations which led to the completed work.

**Michael:** First, though, we should talk about the title of the novel. Many readers ask you about it, and some find it puzzling. You were committed to it from the start. Why is the title so meaningful to you?

**Lauren**: For me, the phrase "and after the fire" brings together multiple strands of the novel. It's a quote from the Old Testament, in the Book of Kings. Felix Mendelssohn, one of the historical characters in the novel, uses the phrase in his oratorio *Elijah*. When Felix died, his brother-in-law, the artist Wilhelm Hensel, drew a death portrait of him, as was the custom in those days. Hensel inscribed the passage from *Elijah* that includes "and after the fire" on the portrait. I was deeply struck by this, especially because the words resonated with me for another reason: The word *holocaust* originally meant *a consuming fire*. Many of my family members were murdered during the Second World War. As I wrote the contemporary sections of the novel, I kept asking myself: What happens to those who remain alive after the fire, and to their children and grandchildren? How do they reconcile themselves, *can* they reconcile themselves, to what happened during the war? In the novel, all the present-day characters, whether American or German, Christian or Jewish, are attempting to come to terms with the Second World War and with the world *after the fire*.

**Michael:** For me, one of the most moving experiences of our work together was the day I arranged for us to visit the rare books room of a major research library to examine an actual Bach composing ▶

score. As a scholar, I'm accustomed to considering such artifacts with a somewhat distanced eye, but for you, as a novelist, it was much more affecting.

**Lauren:** The hours we spent poring over that original Bach manuscript were an astonishing experience for me. To touch the very paper that Bach had touched, to see the corrections he made to his work, the accidental ink blots, the small musical sketches he made at the bottom of pages to remind him of what he wanted to write at the top of the turned side of the page after the ink on the front had dried—all this was remarkable. Above all, I sensed Bach's creative drive and energy, his mind working faster sometimes than he could write. I sensed his anger and frustration when he made a mistake, which I judged from the harshness of his cross-outs. I was awestruck. I tried to give my own sense of amazement to my fictional character Susanna Kessler when she examines the manuscript her uncle bequeathed to her.

**Michael:** Among the more avid discussions we had during the years you worked on the novel were the ones concerning Fanny Mendelssohn Hensel and her hesitancy to publish her musical compositions. What drew you so strongly to Fanny?

**Lauren:** To me, Fanny is a tragic figure. Like her brother, she was considered a musical genius when she was young. She received a terrific musical education. But early on, her father told her that music would never be more than an "ornament" in her life. Even when she was an adult, her musical endeavors were primarily confined to the domestic sphere, to concerts in her home and garden. She was a gifted composer who wrote over four hundred works. Her husband and her mother supported her desire to publish at least some of these works. Her brother, the renowned Felix Mendelssohn, discouraged her ambition to publish her compositions—although he did publish six of her songs under his name.

Why did Fanny accept this injustice? The argument put forth by some scholars, that creative women of the nineteenth century were inescapably suppressed, just doesn't seem convincing to me, particularly because Fanny's husband and mother both supported her desire to publish. Fanny let her brother's opinion take priority, and in the novel I tried to figure out why. To this day, despite all the research I've done, and all the letters I've read between the siblings, I still don't feel that I've fully grasped their complex relationship.

**Michael:** On one of our research trips to Berlin, we visited the small Mendelssohn museum on Jägerstrasse, where we saw a remarkable collection of Mendelssohn portraits, documents, and memorabilia. Seeing all this was a revelation for me ▶

regarding the everyday lives of Fanny, Felix, and their family.

**Lauren:** Just as we arrived, an intimate concert was beginning, and the ushers said, *come in, come in,* so we spent an hour listening to the sublime songs of Fanny and Felix, exactly as if we were attending one of Fanny's salon gatherings.

**Michael:** Our trips to Germany together were the highlight of the years you, and by connection I, worked on the novel. I still remember the day we explored Weimar, looking for suitable settings for various scenes in the book. Suddenly we realized—there it is, the house where Henry Sachs must have come upon the lost Bach cantata. You transformed the house into fiction, of course, but we knew at the exact same moment that we'd discovered the place we'd been searching for, to be the setting of the opening scene in the book. I also very much enjoyed traipsing around old Berlin, and particularly the hours we spent on what is now Museum Island, trying to figure out just where Sara Levy's house and garden had been located.

**Lauren:** At the Jewish cemetery on Schönhauser Allee in Berlin, I came across the grave of Amalia Beer, Sara Levy's friend and a character in the novel. I was never able to find Sara's grave, but seeing the gravesite of her friend was almost as touching, and chilling, in a way, too: I was writing a novel, Amalia Beer was a character in it, and paradoxically, seeing her grave brought her into the present. In Leipzig we visited the restored home where Felix Mendelssohn had lived with his wife and children. Sitting in those rooms, studying Felix's watercolors, I felt a visceral, haunting sense of his family and their daily routine, children playing and crying, visitors arriving, concerts taking place, Felix finding the time and mental space amid the commotion to compose.

**Michael:** Let's not forget that Germany is an absolute awe-inspiring dream world for connoisseurs of beer and sausage.

**Lauren:** For me, though, pastry and cake were among our most fulfilling (and filling) discoveries in Germany. I loved that each afternoon around 4pm, we stopped our explorations, went to a café or a bakery, and chose a treat. I remember how in Berlin, in the park between the Staatsoper and the Opernpalais, as starlings flitted among the tables searching for leftovers, we indulged in two varieties of Linzer torte. In the garden of the Literaturhaus on Fasanenstrasse, I tasted an apricot tart so luscious that time stopped. At a bakery on Sophienstrasse, I selected a fresh croissant, warm, flaky, buttery, and oozing marzipan. We shared it in the ▶

leafy churchyard across the street. Doing this wasn't sacrilegious, was it?

**Michael:** There are doubtless some theologians who'd admit that marzipan croissants are among the highest goods flowing out of God's creation.

**Lauren:** In the novel, I shared my love of German cake and pastry with all my characters, real and imagined, present and past. The best cake I ever had in Germany was a dense chocolate with layers of marzipan. I ordered it at Kaffeehaus Riquet in Leipzig, at 3:35pm on a Thursday afternoon in July, while you were off somewhere meeting with a colleague. In the novel I gave it to Sara Levy and her niece, Fanny Mendelssohn Hensel, in honor of my immense respect for them. They enjoyed it, I must say.

**Michael:** Researching cake and pastry was without question the easiest part of our work together. What, for you, was the most challenging part?

**Lauren:** The way you relentlessly worked to make certain that all the musicological and religious facts in the book were correct. Not just 99.9% correct, but 100% correct. You didn't allow any shortcuts. Not one. What was the most challenging part for you?

**Michael:** The same: Trying to make certain that the sometimes complex musicological and theological matters discussed in the book were 100% correct.

**Lauren:** I'm deeply grateful to you for all you gave the novel. And for so much else. ◞

# Reading Group Guide
## Discussion Questions
## for *And After the Fire*

Dear Readers,

During the course of writing and publishing three novels, I've been lucky enough to be invited to speak to many reading groups. Experiencing the enthusiasm and insight that all of you bring to books has been inspiring.

*And After the Fire* is an ideal novel for reading groups. It raises questions about the meaning of masterpieces of art across the centuries, the effect of historical events on individuals, and recovery from trauma, among many other issues.

Here's my guide for reading groups, but spoiler alert: If you haven't yet read the novel, the guide gives away aspects of the plot.

If you'd like more information about the novel, and about the historical figures in the book—including pictures of them and their homes—please see the featured materials on the *And After the Fire* page of my website, LaurenBelfer.com.

If you'd like to listen to the music discussed in the novel, please check out the playlist I've created on Spotify. You can access the playlist directly through my website.

I hope you enjoy your discussion of *And After the Fire*. Readers like you make writing worthwhile.

Warm wishes,
Lauren

1. I was inspired to write *And After the Fire* when one day I thought, *what would I do, if I came into possession of a previously unknown, and ethically troubling, artistic masterpiece?* What would *you* do? Donate it to a library or museum? Sell it? Destroy it? Hide it under the bed?

2. The masterpiece of music at the center of *And After the Fire,* a fictional cantata by Johann Sebastian Bach, has an inflammatory libretto. This isn't a surprise, because any work of art is a product of its era, and Bach, like other composers of his day, wrote more than one piece that lashes out at different religious groups. But when we perform such pieces today, do we need to recognize and discuss the aspects which might be disturbing in our era? Or, do you believe that great works of art by definition rise above their time and place, so that their content is irrelevant and we should focus only on their beauty and magnificence? ▶

3. At the end of the novel, does Susanna make the right decision about the cantata? Has she found a way to achieve the ethical redemption she's searching for?

4. Do you think Dan will regain his religious faith? Have you struggled with issues of faith in your own life?

5. Do you think Susanna should have confronted her mother more forcefully, to learn the truth about what happened to their family during the Holocaust? Why might Evelyn and Henry have believed that they needed to conceal the truth from Susanna?

6. When Count von Arnim makes insulting, hurtful comments at Sara's salon, why does Sara react the way she does? Why doesn't she order him to leave, or argue with him, or at least challenge him in some way? If she lived today, would she handle this situation differently? What if something similar happened at a party at your home? How would you react?

7. As I was writing the novel, I began to feel more acutely the tragic story of Fanny Mendelssohn Hensel. She is among the most important women composers in the history of Western music, yet she is almost forgotten today. Her mother and her husband

both encouraged her desire to compose and to publish her music, so she did have some family support. Why do you think she had so much difficulty standing up for herself against the opposition of her father and then, after her father's death, of her brother, Felix?

And what about Felix? Was he right or wrong, to publish his sister's work under his name? Was he trying, in his own way of thinking, to help his sister? And most importantly, why did Fanny participate in the deception by preparing the materials for the publisher as if they were Felix's?

The more I learned about the relationship between Fanny and Felix, the more complex and unfathomable it seemed. They were closest companions during childhood. Have you ever known siblings who had such a highly-charged relationship?

8. Bach's music is an integral part of the story, moving the plot forward and revealing the inner lives of the characters, as it consoles their suffering and accentuates their joy—exactly as Bach's music has done in my own life. Also, however, each of the characters tries, as I myself have tried, to come to terms with the few works of Bach's that can nowadays be considered ethically problematic. ▶

What is the role of music in your life? Do you turn to music for comfort as well as for joy? Are you, on the other hand, ever disturbed by music you love?

9. What do you think about the structure of the novel, shifting back and forth in time? By designing the novel in this way, I wanted each time period to illuminate the other, step by step, letting the reader gradually resolve the mystery. Was this technique successful for you?

10. Many readers have asked me about the title. The phrase brings together multiple strands of the novel. First, the title is a quote from the Old Testament, in the Book of Kings. Felix Mendelssohn, one of the historical figures in the book, used it in his oratorio *Elijah*. When Felix died, his brother-in-law, the artist Wilhelm Hensel, made a death portrait of him, as was the custom in those days, and Hensel inscribed the passage from *Elijah* that includes "and after the fire" on the death portrait.

The title is important to me for another reason, as well: originally, the word *holocaust* meant *a consuming fire*. What happens to those who remain alive after the fire, and to their children and grandchildren? How do they reconcile themselves, *can* they reconcile themselves, to what happened? In the novel, all the present-day characters, whether American or European, Christian or Jewish, are attempting to come to terms with the Second World War and to find their way in the world *after the fire*. Do you think the title is appropriate and meaningful? ∾

# Read On:
# Author's Picks

If you'd like to learn more about the history and the issues explored in *And After the Fire*, Lauren recommends the following books, listed in alphabetical order by author:

*Jewish Women and Their Salons: The Power of Conversation*, by Emily D. Bilski and Emily Braun

*Evening in the Palace of Reason: Bach Meets Frederick the Great in the Age of Enlightenment*, by James R. Gaines

*Bach & God*, by Michael Marissen

*The Lost: A Search for Six of Six Million*, by Daniel Mendelsohn

*Jewish Women in Enlightenment Berlin*, by Natalie Naimark-Goldberg

*The Rape of Europa: The Fate of Europe's Treasures in the Third Reich and the Second World War*, by Lynn H. Nicholas

*The Holocaust in American Life*, by Peter Novick

*Fanny Hensel: The Other Mendelssohn*, by R. Larry Todd

*Mendelssohn: A Life in Music,*
by R. Larry Todd

*Johann Sebastian Bach: The Learned
Musician,* by Christoph Wolff ᔫ

# Listen On:
# Author's Picks

Lauren has created a playlist on Spotify that includes the music featured in *And After the Fire*. You can access the playlist through her website, LaurenBelfer.com.

Here is a brief list of her favorite recordings of her favorite works by Johann Sebastian Bach:

The reconstructed oboe concertos, performed by Marcel Ponseele with *Ensemble Il Gardinello*

The cello suites, performed by Jean-Guihen Queyras

The violin concertos, performed by Amandine Beyer with *Gli Incogniti*

The viola da gamba sonatas, performed by Vittorio and Lorenzo Ghielmi (their 1998, as opposed to their 2013, recording)

The Goldberg Variations, performed by Simone Dinnerstein

*Was Gott tut, daß ist wohlgetan* (BWV 100), performed by the *Bach Collegium Japan*, under the direction of Masaaki Suzuki

The concertos for two and three harpsichords, performed by *Musica Amphion*, under the direction of Pieter-Jan Belder